Praise for the novels of Susan Wiggs

"With the ease of a master,
Wiggs introduces complicated flesh-and-blood characters
[and] sets in motion a refreshingly honest romance."
—*Publishers Weekly* on *The Winter Lodge*
(starred review, on the *PW* Best Books of 2007 list)

"Emotionally intense."
—*Booklist* on *The Winter Lodge*

"Susan Wiggs paints the details of human relationships
with the finesse of a master."
—Jodi Picoult, *New York Times* bestselling author

"Wiggs is one of our best observers of stories of the heart.
Maybe that is because she knows how to capture emotion
on virtually every page of every book."
—*Salem Statesman-Journal*

"Wiggs' storytelling is heartwarming."
—*Publishers Weekly* on *Summer at Willow Lake*

"Wiggs explores many aspects of grief, from guilt to
anger to regret, imbuing her book with the classic
would've/could've/should've emotions, and presenting
realistic and sympathetic characters.... Another excellent
title [in] her already outstanding body of work."
—*Booklist* on *Table for Five*

"A human and multi-layered story exploring
duty to both country and family."
—Nora Roberts on *The Ocean Between Us*

SUSAN WIGGS

The *Winter* Lodge

MIRA®

Recycling programs
for this product may
not exist in your area.

ISBN-13: 978-0-7783-2891-9

THE WINTER LODGE

Copyright © 2007 by Susan Wiggs.

All rights reserved. Except for use in any review, the reproduction or
utilization of this work in whole or in part in any form by any electronic,
mechanical or other means, now known or hereafter invented, including
xerography, photocopying and recording, or in any information storage or
retrieval system, is forbidden without the written permission of the publisher,
MIRA Books, 225 Duncan Mill Road, Don Mills, Ontario, Canada M3B 3K9.

All characters in this book have no existence outside the imagination of the
author and have no relation whatsoever to anyone bearing the same name
or names. They are not even distantly inspired by any individual known or
unknown to the author, and all incidents are pure invention.

MIRA and the Star Colophon are trademarks used under license and registered
in Australia, New Zealand, Philippines, United States Patent and Trademark
Office and in other countries.

For questions and comments about the quality of this book please contact us at
Customer_eCare@Harlequin.ca.

www.MIRABooks.com

Printed in U.S.A.

10 9 8 7 6 5 4 3 2 1

In loving memory of my grandparents,
Anna and Nicholas Klist.

ACKNOWLEDGMENTS

The author wishes to thank the Port Orchard Brain Trust: Kate Breslin, Lois Dyer, Rose Marie Harris, P. J. Jough-Haan, Susan Plunkett, Sheila Rabe and Krysteen Seelen. Also thanks to the Bainbridge Island Test Kitchen: Anjali Banerjee, Sheila Rabe, Suzanne Selfors and Elsa Watson. As always, thanks to Meg Ruley and Annelise Robey of the Jane Rotrosen Agency, and to Margaret O'Neill Marbury of MIRA Books.

Special thanks to Joan Vassiliadis, Anna Osinski of Warsaw, Poland, Matt Haney, Bainbridge Island Chief of Police, and to Ellen and Mike Loudon of Bainbridge Bakers on Bainbridge Island, Washington.

Food for Thought

by Jenny Majesky

Kolaches for Beginners

It's funny how so many bakers are intimidated by yeast. They see it listed as an ingredient in a recipe, and quickly flip the page. There's no need to fear this version.

This particular dough is quite forgiving. It's elastic, resilient and will make you feel like a pro. As my grandmother, Helen Majesky, used to say, "In baking, as in life, you know more than you think you know."

BASIC KOLACHES

1 tablespoon sugar
2 packets active dry yeast (which is kind of a pain, since yeast is sold in packages of three)
1/2 cup warm water
2 cups milk
6 tablespoons pure unsalted butter
2 teaspoons salt
2 egg yolks, lightly beaten
1/2 cup sugar
6-1/4 cups flour
1-1/2 sticks melted butter

Put yeast in a measuring cup and sprinkle 1 tablespoon sugar over it. Add warm water. How warm? Most cookbooks say 105°-115°F. Experienced cooks can tell by sprinkling a few drops on the inside of the wrist. Beginners should use a thermometer. Too hot, and it'll kill the active ingredients.

Warm the milk in a small saucepan; add butter and stir until melted. Cool to lukewarm and pour into a big mixing bowl. Add salt and sugar, then pour in beaten egg yolks in a thin stream, whisking briskly to keep eggs from curdling. Then whisk in yeast mixture.

Roll up your sleeves and add flour a cup at a time. When the dough gets too heavy to stir, mix with your hands. You want the dough to be glossy and sticky. Keep adding flour and knead until the dough acquires a sheen. Put dough ball in an oiled mixing bowl, turning it to coat. Cover with a damp tea towel and set in a warm place where the air is very still. In about an hour, the dough should double in size. My grandmother used to push two floured fingertips into the top of the soft mound, and if the dimples made by her fingers remained, she would declare the dough risen. And then, of course, you give it a punch to deflate it. A soft sighing sound, fragrant with yeast, indicates the dough's surrender.

Pinch off egg-size portions and work these into balls. Place on oiled baking sheets, several inches apart. Let them rise again for 15 minutes and then use your thumb to make a deep dimple in each ball for the fruit filling. The exact filling to use is a source of endless debate among Polish bakers. My grandmother never entered into such a debate. "Do what tastes good" was her motto. A spoonful of raspberry jam, peach pie filling, fig preserves, prune filling or sweet cheese will do.

Create a popsika by mixing 1/2 cup melted butter with a cup of sugar, 1/2 cup flour and a teaspoon cinnamon. Sprinkle the popsika over each kolache. Now place the pans in a warm place—like above the fridge—and allow to double in bulk again, about 45 minutes to an hour. Meanwhile, preheat the oven to 375°F. Bake 20-40 minutes, until golden brown. Pay particular attention to the bottoms, which tend to burn if too close to the heat source.

Take the kolaches out of the oven, brush with melted butter and remove from pans to cool. This recipe makes about three dozen.

My grandmother used to tell me not to worry about how long this whole process takes. Baking is an act of love, and who cares how long love takes?

One

J enny Majesky pushed away from her writing desk and stretched, massaging an ache in the small of her back. Something—perhaps the profound silence of the empty house—had awakened her at three in the morning, and she hadn't been able to get back to sleep. She'd worked on her newspaper column for a while, hunched over her laptop in a ratty robe and fuzzy slippers. At the moment, though, she was no better at writing than she was at sleeping.

There was so much she wanted to say, so many stories to put down, but how could she cram the memories and kitchen wisdom of a lifetime into a weekly column?

Then again, she'd always wanted to write more than a column. Much more. The universe, she realized, was taking away all her excuses. She really ought to get started writing that book.

Like any good writer, Jenny procrastinated. Idly, she picked up her grandmother's wedding band, which had been lying in a small china dish on the desk. She hadn't quite decided what to do with it, a plain circle of gold that Helen Majesky had worn for fifty years of marriage and another decade of widowhood. When she baked, Gram always slipped the ring into the pocket of her apron. It was a wonder she never lost it. She'd made Jenny promise not to bury her with it, though.

Twirling the ring around the tip of her forefinger, Jenny could picture her grandmother's hands, strong and firm as they worked a mound of dough, or gentle and light as they caressed her granddaughter's cheek or checked her forehead for fever.

Jenny slid the ring onto her finger and closed her hand into a fist. She had a wedding ring of her own, given and received with a sense of giddy hope but never worn. It now resided in a bottom drawer she never opened.

It was hard, at this velvet-black hour, not to tally up her losses—her mother, who had walked away when Jenny was small. Then Jenny's grandfather, and finally, and perhaps most importantly, Gram.

Only a few weeks had passed since she'd laid her grandmother to rest. After the initial flurry of sympathy calls and visits, a lull had settled in, and Jenny felt it in her bones—she was truly alone. Yes, she had caring friends and coworkers who were as dear to her as family. But now the steady presence of her grandmother, who had raised her like a daughter, was gone.

Out of habit, she saved her work on the laptop. Then she wrapped her robe more snugly around her and went to the window, pressing close to the cold glass to look out at the deep winter night. Snow erased all the sharp edges and colors of the landscape. In the middle of the night, Maple Street was entirely deserted, washed in the gray-white glow of a single street lamp in the middle of the block. Jenny had lived here all her life; she'd stood countless times at this very spot, expecting…what? For something to change. To begin.

She gave a restless sigh, her breath misting the window. The snow flurries had thickened to flakes, swirling in a blur around the streetlight. Jenny loved the snow; she always had. Staring out at the blanketed landscape, she could easily picture herself as a child, hiking with her grandfather to the sledding hill. She used to literally follow in his footsteps, leaping from one hollowed-out bootprint to the next, pulling the Flexible Flyer on a rope behind her.

Her grandparents had been there for all the moments of her childhood. Now that they were gone, there was no one to hold the memories, to look at her and say, "Remember the time you…"

Her mother had left when Jenny was four, and her father was a virtual stranger she'd met only six months ago. Jenny considered this a blessing in disguise. From what she knew of her biological parents, neither had been as well-equipped to raise a child as Helen and Leo Majesky.

A noise—a thud and then a scratching sound—made her jump, startling her from her thoughts. She cocked her head, listening, then decided it had been thick snow or a row of icicles, falling from the roof. You never knew how quiet a house could be until you were totally alone in it.

Since her grandmother had died, Jenny had been waking up in the middle of the night, her mind full of memories begging to be written down. All of them seemed to emanate, like the smells of baking, from her grandmother's kitchen. Jenny had kept a diary or journal nearly all her life, and over the past few years, her habit had evolved into a regular column for the *Avalon Troubadour,* a mingling of recipes, kitchen lore and anecdotes. Since Gram's passing, Jenny could no longer check a fact with her, or pick her brain about the origin of a certain ingredient or baking technique. Jenny was on her own now, and she was afraid that if she waited too long, she'd forget things.

The thought stirred her into action. She'd been meaning to transcribe her grandmother's ancient recipes, some of them still in the original Polish, written on brittle, yellowed paper. The recipes were stored in the pantry in a latched tin box that hadn't been opened in years. Ignoring the fact that it was now three-thirty in the morning, Jenny headed downstairs. When she stepped into the pantry, she was struck by an achingly familiar smell—her grandmother's spices and the aroma of flour and grain. She stood on tiptoe to reach the old metal box. Sliding it off the shelf, she lost her balance and dropped the thing, its contents exploding at her fuzzy-slippered feet.

She uttered a word she never would have said when Gram was alive, tiptoeing gingerly as she tried not to step on any of the fragile old documents. Now she would need a flashlight, because the dark pantry didn't have a light. She found a flashlight in a utility drawer but its batteries were dead and there wasn't another fresh battery in the house. She considered lighting a candle but didn't want to have a mishap with the one-of-a-kind handwritten recipes. Leaning against the kitchen counter, she rolled her eyes heavenward. "Sorry about that, Gram," she said.

Her gaze found the smoke detector. *Aha,* she thought. She dragged a kitchen chair over to it and climbed up, opening the smoke detector, removing its two double-A batteries and fitting them in the flashlight.

She headed back into the pantry, gently picking up the papers, which rustled like dry autumn leaves. She put the loose papers in the box and brought it out to the kitchen. There were old notes and recipes in her grandmother's native Polish. On the back of a yellowed page with crumbling edges, she spotted a signature in fading, delicate strokes of ink—*Helenka Maciejewski*—practiced a dozen times in a girlish hand. That was her grandmother's married name before it had been Anglicized. She must have written it as a young bride.

There were things about her grandparents Jenny would never know. What had it been like for them, as newlyweds barely out of childhood, leaving the only home they knew to start a life half a world away? Were they frightened? Excited? Did they quarrel with each other, cling to each other?

She closed her eyes as a now-familiar onslaught of panic started in her stomach and pushed through her, pressing at her chest. These panic attacks were something brand-new for Jenny, a grim and unexpected development. The first one struck at the hospital as she was moving woodenly through the duties of the next of kin. She'd been signing some form or other when the fingers of her left hand went numb and she dropped the pen to clutch her throat.

"I can't breathe," she'd told the clerk. "I think I'm having a heart attack."

The doctor who treated her, a tired-looking resident from Tonawanda, had been calm and compassionate as he evaluated her and then explained the condition. Not uncommon, the intense attack was a physical response to emotional trauma, the symptoms as real and frightening as they would be for any illness.

Since then, Jenny had become intimately familiar with the symptoms. Practical, levelheaded Jenny Majesky was not supposed to succumb to something as uncontrollable and irrational as a panic attack. She was helpless to stop it now as a singularly unpleasant sensation rose through her, like a parade of spiders climbing up her throat. Her heart seemed to expand in her chest.

She cast a wild look around, wondering where she'd left the bottle of pills the doctor had given her. She hated the pills almost as much as she hated the panic attacks. Why couldn't she just snap out of it? Why couldn't she just suck it up and calm herself with a cup of strong coffee and a taste of her grandmother's apricot-jam kolaches?

That, at least, could be a diversion. Right now, in the middle of the night. One of the few places in Avalon where she could find someone awake at four in the morning was the Sky River Bakery, founded in 1952 by her grandparents. Helen specialized in kolaches filled with fruit or sweet cheese, and pies that became the stuff of local legend. Her baked goods were in demand from the restaurants and small specialty shops that lined the town square, catering to the well-polished tourists who came up from New York City for Avalon's cool green summers or blazing fall color.

Now Jenny was the bakery's sole owner. She dressed hurriedly, layering on fleece long underwear, checked chef pants and a thick wool sweater, tall warm boots, a ski jacket and hat. No way was she driving, not before the snowplow had made its rounds. Besides, getting the car out of the garage would entail shoveling the driveway, something she was heartily sick of doing. The bakery was just six blocks away, on the main square in the center of town. She'd be there in minutes. Maybe the exertion would stave off the panic attack, too.

Just in case, she found her bottle of pills and stuffed it in her pocket.

Grabbing her purse, she walked through frozen silence. The snow had stopped, and the clouds made way for the stars. New snow squeaked beneath her feet as she followed a route she'd walked since she was a tiny girl. She'd grown up in the bakery, surrounded by the heady fragrance of bread and spices, the busy sounds of the mixers and sheeters, timers going off, rolling racks clattering out to the transport bay.

A single light burned over the back entrance. She let herself in, stomping the snow from her boots. Outside the spotless prep area, she took them off and slipped on her baker's clogs, which were parked on a rack by the door.

"It's me," she called, her gaze tracking around the work area. It was immaculate as always, with fifty-pound sacks of freshly milled flour stacked precisely against one wall, honey in 155-gallon drums lying on their sides nearby. Specialty ingredients displayed in clear containers lined the shelves from floor to ceiling—millet, pine nuts, olives, raisins, pecans. The stainless-steel refrigerators, ovens and countertops shimmered under the pendant lights, and the rich scent of yeast and cinnamon filled the air. Three 6 Mafia was blaring from the radio, indicating that Zach was on tonight, and between the beats of the hip-hop music, she could hear the hum of the spiral mixer.

"Yo, Zach," she called out, craning her neck to find the boy.

He emerged from the mixing area, pushing a rolling cart filled with raw dough. Now a senior in high school, Zach Alger had worked at the bakery for two years. He didn't seem to mind the early-morning hours, always heading to school with a bag of fresh pastries. He had distinctly Nordic features—pale blue eyes, white-blond hair—and lanky, earnest good looks. "Is anything wrong?" he asked.

"Couldn't sleep," she said, feeling a bit sheepish. "Is Laura around?"

"Specialty loaves," he said, gesturing as he wheeled the tub of dough toward the six-foot-tall proofing cabinet.

Laura Tuttle had worked at the bakery for thirty years, as master baker for twenty-five. She knew the business even better than Jenny did. She claimed to love the early hours, that the schedule was perfectly suited to her circadian clock. "Well, look who's here," she said, yet she didn't glance up as she spoke.

"I had a craving for a kolache." Jenny swished through the rubber-rimmed swinging doors to the café, where she helped herself to a cup of coffee and a day-old pastry from the case. Then she returned to the prep area, welcoming the familiar taste but feeling no calmer. Out of habit, she grabbed an apron from a hook.

Jenny rarely did the hands-on work; as owner and general manager, she stayed busy in a supervisory and administrative capacity. She had an office upstairs with a view of the town square, and a security monitor gave her a glimpse of the café counter. She spent most days juggling the needs of employees, suppliers, customers and regulatory agencies with a phone glued to her ear and her eyes glued to the computer screen. But sometimes, she reflected, you just had to roll up your sleeves and dive in. There was no sensation quite like plunging one's hands into a warm mass of silky dough. It felt like something half-alive, squishing through her fingers.

Now she slipped the apron over her head and joined Laura at a worktable. The specialty breads were done in smaller batches and shaped by hand. Today's selections would be a traditional Polish bread made with eggs, orange peel and currants, and a savory herb loaf of Laura's invention. She and Laura worked side by side, weighing portions of dough on a one-pound scale, although both knew the size by feel alone.

Across the room, Jenny could see the refrigerated pie case, filled with her grandmother's pies. Technically speaking, these were not Helen Majesky's pies. But the original recipes for the lofty lemon meringue, the glossy three-berry tarts with the lattice tops, the creamy buttermilk chess pie and all the others came from Helen herself, decades ago. Her techniques had been passed on from one master baker to the next, and now, even after her death, she haunted the bakery as gently and sweetly as she had lived.

Jenny felt curiously detached from herself as she braided the dough into fat, rounded loaves. She looked at her white, floury hands and could see her grandmother's hands, lifting and turning the dough with a patient rhythm that seemed to come from a place Jenny didn't recognize in herself. The reality of Gram's passing settled in Jenny's bones. It had been three weeks, two days and fourteen hours. Jenny hated that she knew, practically down to the precise moment, exactly how long she had been alone.

Laura kept working, setting each oiled loaf in a pan, one by one. She bobbed her head along with the hip-hop rhythm coming from the radio. She actually liked Zach's music, though Jenny suspected Laura didn't listen too closely to the lyrics.

"You miss her a lot, don't you, doll?" Laura asked. She was the kind of person who knew things, like a mind reader.

"So much," Jenny admitted. "And here I thought I was prepared. I don't know why I feel shell-shocked. I'm not good at this. In fact, I'm terrible at it. Terrible at mourning the dead and at living alone." She squared her shoulders, tried to shake off the mingling of panic and melancholy. The scary thing was, she couldn't do it. She had somehow lost control, and even as she felt herself falling apart, she couldn't do anything to make it stop.

Somewhere outside in the dark, a siren wailed. The noise crescendoed, sounding frantic, like a scream. A couple of dogs howled in response. Automatically, Jenny turned to peer through the double doors to the window of the darkened coffee shop. The town of Avalon, New York, was small enough that the sound of whooping sirens at night attracted notice. In fact, the last time she remembered hearing a siren was when she had called the paramedics.

They had not let her ride with her grandmother. She had driven her car in the wake of the ambulance to Benedictine Hospital in

Kingston. Once there, she begged her grandmother to rescind the DNR order she'd signed after her first stroke, but Gram wouldn't hear of it. So then, with her grandmother's life force ebbing, there was nothing left for Jenny to do but say goodbye.

She felt a fresh wave of the panic attack trying to push its way to the surface. She stuck with the kneading rhythm her grandmother had taught her, working the dough with steady assuredness. Anyone watching her would see a competent baker, because she knew that on the outside, she appeared no different. The gathering steam inside was invisible.

"I'm going to step out back, grab a breath of fresh air," she told Laura.

"I just heard sirens. Maybe Loverboy will show up."

Loverboy was Laura's nickname for Rourke McKnight, Avalon's chief of police. He had a reputation that did not go unnoticed in a town this size. Jenny, of course, avoided calling him anything at all. There had been a time when she and Rourke had not been strangers. In fact, they'd known each other with searing intimacy, but that was long ago. They hadn't willingly exchanged a word in years. Rourke dropped by the bakery for his morning coffee every day, but since Jenny worked in the office upstairs, they never crossed paths. They actually both worked hard at not crossing paths.

Avoiding him required that she memorize his routine. During the week, he kept office hours like any chief of police, but, thanks to a tight municipal budget, he had to make do with substandard pay and a force that was small even by small-town standards. He often took the third watch on weekends, driving patrol like any beat cop. Sometimes he even drove a snowplow for the city. Jenny pretended she didn't know any of this, pretended to take no interest in the life of Rourke McKnight, and he returned the favor by ignoring her. He had sent flowers to her grandmother's funeral, though. The message on the card had been typically taciturn: "I'm sorry." It had accompanied a bouquet the size of a Volkswagen.

As she slipped on her parka and ducked through the back door of the bakery, Jenny felt the now-predictable pattern of the attack. There was the terrible tingling of her scalp, an army of invisible ants marching up her spine and over her head. Her chest tightened and her throat seemed to close. Despite the freezing temperatures, she broke out in a sweat. Then came the eerie pulsations of light, flickering in her peripheral vision.

Stepping into the alleyway behind the bakery, she sucked in air. Then she choked it back out immediately, tasting the acrid burn of Newport cigarettes.

"God, Zach," she said to the kid leaning against the building. "Those things will kill you."

"Naw," he said, flicking his ashes into the Dumpster, "I'll quit before that happens."

"Huh." She cleared her throat. "That's what they all say." She hated it when kids smoked. Sure, her grandfather had smoked, rolling his own cigarettes out of Velvet Tobacco. But back in his day, the dangers of the habit were unknown. Nowadays, there was simply no excuse. Grabbing a handful of snow, she tossed it at the cigarette, killing the red ash.

"Hey," he said.

"You're a smart boy, Zach. I heard you're an honor student. So how come you're so stupid about smoking?"

He shrugged and had the grace to look sheepish. "Ask my dad, I'm stupid about a lot of things. He wants me to spend next year working up at the racetrack in Saratoga to earn my own money for college."

She knew, by the chintzy tips Matthew Alger left at the bakery's coffee shop, that Alger—who worked as the city administrator—carried his stinginess into his personal life. Apparently, he applied it to his son's as well. Jenny had grown up without a father and had yearned for one more times than she could count. Matthew Alger was proof that the longed-for relationship might sometimes be overrated.

"I've heard that quitting smoking saves the average smoker five bucks a day," she said. She wondered if her voice sounded strange to him, if he could tell she had to force each word past the tightness in her throat.

"Yeah, I've heard that, too." He flicked the damp cigarette into the Dumpster. "Don't worry," he said before she could scold him, "I'll wash my hands before I go back to work."

He didn't seem to be in a hurry, though. She wondered if he wanted to talk. "Does your dad want you to work for a year before college?" she asked.

"He wants me working, period. Keeps telling me how he put himself through college with no help from his family, pulled himself up by his bootstraps and all that." He said it with no admiration.

She wondered about Zach's mother, who had remarried and moved to Seattle long ago. Zach never talked about her. "What do *you* want, Zach?" Jenny asked.

He looked startled, as though he hadn't been asked that in a while. "To go far away to college," he said. "Live somewhere different."

Jenny could relate to that. At his age, she'd been certain an exciting life awaited her somewhere far away. She'd never even made it out the door, though. "Then that's what you should do," she said emphatically.

He shrugged. "I'll give it a shot, I guess. I need to get back to work."

He headed inside. Jenny lingered outside, blowing fake smoke rings with the frozen air. Although the conversation had distracted her briefly, it had done nothing to banish the churning panic. She was alone with the feeling now; it screamed through her like the sirens in the quiet of the night. And like the sirens, the feeling intensified, closing in on her. The ceiling of stars pressed down, an insurmountable weight on her shoulders.

I surrender, she thought and plunged her hand into the pocket of her chef pants, groping for the brown plastic prescription bottle. The pill wasn't much bigger than a lead BB. She swallowed it without water, knowing it would take effect in a few minutes.

It was kind of amazing, she thought, how a tiny pill could quiet the terrified knocking of her heart in her rib cage, and cool the frantic sizzle of her brain.

"Only when you need it," the doctor had cautioned her. "This medication can be highly addictive, and it has a particularly nasty detox."

Despite the warning, she already felt calmer as she tucked the bottle away. She smoothed her hand over her pants pocket.

Still thinking about Zach, she scanned the familiar neighborhood, a downtown of vintage brick buildings that housed businesses, shops and restaurants. Years ago, if someone had told Jenny she'd still be in Avalon, working at the bakery, she would have laughed all the way to the train station. She had big plans. She was leaving the small, insular place where she'd grown up. She was headed for the big city, an education, a career.

It probably wasn't fair to let Zach in on an ugly little secret— life had a way of kicking the support out from under the best-laid plans. At the age of eighteen, Jenny had discovered the terrifying inadequacies of the health-care system, especially when it came to the self-employed. By twenty-one, she was familiar with the process of declaring personal bankruptcy, and just barely managed to hang on to the house on Maple Street. There was no question of her leaving Gram, widowed and disabled from a massive stroke.

The pill kicked in, covering the sharp edges of her nerves like a blanket of snow over a jagged landscape. She took in a deep breath and let it out slowly, watching the cloud of mist until it disappeared.

The sky to the north, in the direction of Maple Street, seemed to flicker and glow with unnatural light. She blinked. Probably just the strange aftermath of the panic attack. She should be used to this by now.

Two

$\sim$❧❧$\sim$

When the monitor in Rourke McKnight's squad car sent out an urgent tone alert and "any unit about clear" for 472 Maple Street, it flash-froze his heart.

That was Jenny's house.

He had been on the far side of town, but the moment the call came, he grabbed the handheld mike, gave his location and ETA to dispatch and fired the sedan into action. His tires spewing snow and sand, he peeled out, the back end fishtailing on the slippery road. At the same time, he put in a call to the dispatcher. "I'm en route. I'll let you know when I'm code eleven." His voice was curiously flat, considering the emotions now roaring through him.

A general page had gone out that the structure—God, Jenny's house—was on fire and "fully involved." Besides that, Jenny hadn't been spotted.

By the time he reached the house on Maple Street, the entire home was wrapped in bright ribbons of flame, with curls of fire leaping out of every window and licking along the eaves.

He parked with one headlamp buried in a snowbank and exited his vehicle, not bothering to close the door behind him, and did a visual scan of the premises. The firefighters, their trucks and equipment, were bathed in flickering orange light. Two pumper hoses attacked the blaze; men struggled to excavate a hydrant from the snow. The scene was surprisingly quiet, not chaotic at all. Yet the wall of flame was impenetrable and unsafe for the firefighters—even fully equipped and clad in bunker gear—to enter.

"Where is she?" Rourke demanded of a firefighter who was relaying messages on a shoulder-mounted radio. "Where the hell is she?"

"Haven't found the resident," the guy said, flicking a glance at another emergency vehicle parked in the road—an ambulance, its crew standing ready. "We're thinking she's away. Except…her car's in the garage."

Rourke strode toward the flaming house, bellowing Jenny's name. The place burned like a pile of tinder. A window burst, and hot glass rained down on him. Automatically his hand came up to shield his eyes. "Jenny!" he yelled again.

In one instant, all the years of silence fell away and regrets flooded in. As if he could fix anything by avoiding her. *I'm an idiot,* he thought. And then he bargained with anyone or anything that might be listening. *Let her be okay. Please just let her be okay and I'll keep her safe forever and never ask another thing.*

He had to get inside. The front steps were gone. He raced around back, slipping in the snow, righting himself. Someone was shouting at him, but he kept going. The back of the house was in flames, too, but the door was gone, having been hacked through by a firefighter's ax. More shouting, more guys in bunker gear running at him, waving their arms. *Shit,* thought Rourke. It was stupid, but it wasn't the dumbest thing he'd ever done, not by a long shot. Pulling his parka up over his nose and mouth, he went inside.

He'd been in this kitchen many times, yet it resembled a yellow vortex, all but unrecognizable. And there was nothing to breathe. He felt the fire sucking the air out of his lungs. He tried to yell for Jenny but couldn't make a sound. The linoleum floor bubbled and melted under his feet. The doorway leading to the stairs was a tall rectangle of fire, but he headed toward it anyway.

A strong hand on his shoulder hauled him back. Rourke tried to fight him off, but a second later, something—a railing from upstairs, maybe—came crashing down, raining fire and plaster. The firefighter shoved him out the back door. "What the hell are you doing?" he yelled. "Chief, you need to get back. It's not safe here."

Rourke's throat burned as he gulped in air, then coughed. "No shit. If you won't send anyone in, I'm going myself."

The firefighter—a deputy chief Rourke vaguely recognized—planted himself in the way. "I can't let you do that."

Fury flashed through him, an unreasoning sting. In one swift movement, Rourke's arm whipped out, shoving the guy out of the way. "Step aside," he barked.

The firefighter didn't say a word, just fell back with his hands raised, eyes darting behind his face shield. "Listen, we're both on the same side. You saw what it's like in there. You wouldn't last thirty seconds. We don't think the resident's at home, honest, we don't. If she was home, she would've gotten out."

Rourke unfurled his fists. Damn. He'd been about to clock the guy. What the hell was he thinking?

He wasn't thinking, that was the problem. That had always been his problem. He needed to figure out where Jenny was. Possibilities streamed through his mind. Maybe she was at her best friend Nina's house. But at this time of night? Or maybe Olivia Bellamy's? No. Though related, the two women weren't close. Shit, was she dating some guy Rourke didn't know about?

Then it hit him. Of course. "Damn," he said, and bolted for the car.

Jenny was still standing outside the bakery, waiting for the dawn, when a blue-white flash lit the sky. The sudden lightning was eerily out of place in the middle of winter. Then she heard the quick yip of a siren and realized it was emergency lights. The vehicle sounded close, as though it was in the next block. Busy night, she thought, heading back into the bakery. She passed through the kitchen, where Zach was wheeling more dough out of the proofer.

She was about to get back to work when she heard an urgent rapping on the front door. "I'll see who it is," she called to Laura and Zach, and walked through the café, which at this hour was dimly lit only by the buzzing neon sign of a coffee cup with squiggles of steam rising from it.

The electric blue of a squad car's emergency overhead lights slashed through the empty café. Hurrying now, Jenny undid the lock. The bell over the front door jangled, and Rourke McKnight strode inside, his long coat swirling on the winter wind.

Avalon's chief of police looked the part. His square jaw was clean-shaven, his shoulders broad and powerful. Though he was blond and blue-eyed, a crescent-shaped scar on his cheekbone kept him from being too pretty.

"I have a feeling you're not dropping in for a cup of coffee," said Jenny. These were probably the first words she'd spoken to him in years.

He gave her a smoldering look, one that made her wonder what it would be like to be his girlfriend, a member of the parade of bimbos who seemed to march through his life with serial regularity. Right, she thought. Why would she want to join a parade of bimbos?

Rourke grabbed her by the upper arms. "Jenny. You're here." His voice was rough, urgent.

Okay, so this was interesting. Rourke McKnight, grabbing her, pulling her into his embrace. What on earth had she done to deserve this? Maybe she should have done it long ago.

"I couldn't sleep," she said, and glanced at his hands on her. She and Rourke didn't touch, the two of them. Not since…they didn't touch.

He seemed to read her thoughts and let her go, jerking his head toward the door. "We've got a situation at your house. I'll give you a lift over there."

Despite the fuzzy edges of reality imparted by the pill she'd taken, she felt a deep, visceral disturbance. "What kind of situation?"

"Your house is on fire," Rourke said simply.

Jenny formed her mouth into an *O,* but no sound came out. What did one say, anyway, when confronted with such a statement?

"Go," Laura said, thrusting her parka and boots at her. "Call me later."

The fuzzy edges did not alter as Jenny got into the squad car Rourke drove on the weekends. Even the swirling lights sweeping the area in an ovoid circuit didn't make her flinch. Yet she was sharp with attention. The wonders of modern chemistry, she thought.

"What happened?" she asked.

"Call came in, a 911 from Mrs. Samuelson."

Irma Samuelson had lived next door to the Majeskys for years. "It's impossible," Jenny said. "I—how could my house be on fire?"

"Seat belt," he said, and the moment she clicked the buckle, he peeled away from the curb.

"Are you sure there's no mistake?" she asked. "Maybe it's someone else's house."

"There's no mistake. I checked. God, I thought—God *damn*—"

Was his voice shaking? "Oh, no," she said. "Rourke, you thought I was in the house."

"It's a safe assumption at this hour of the morning."

So that was why he'd grabbed her. It was relief, pure and simple. As they sped toward Maple Street, she became aware of a peculiar smell. "It reeks of smoke in here."

"You're welcome to roll down the window if you don't mind freezing."

"Where did the smoke smell come— Oh, God. You went into the house, didn't you?" She could just picture him, pushing past firefighters to battle his way into the burning house. "You went inside to find me."

He didn't reply. He didn't have to. Rourke McKnight was always rescuing people. It was a compulsion with him.

"Did you leave the stove on?" he asked her. "Maybe an appliance…?"

"Of course not," she snapped. The questions ticked her off because they scared her. Because it was possible she *had* been careless. She lived alone now, and maybe she was turning strange. Sometimes she couldn't shake the feeling that she was doomed to live the life of a loner, an outcast with nobody to turn off the coffeemaker if she left it on. She could end up like that old cat lady she and her friends used to make up stories about when they were kids—alone, eccentric, with nothing but a smelly house full of cats for company.

"…zoning out on me, are you?" Rourke's voice broke in on her thoughts.

"What?" she said, giving herself a mental shake.

"Are you all right?"

"You just said my house is burning down. I don't think I'm supposed to be all right about this."

"I mean—"

"I know what you mean. Do I seem anxious to you?"

He flicked a glance at her. "You're cool, under the circumstances. We're not there yet, though. Do you know what it means when the fire department says the structure is fully involved?" he asked.

"No, I—" She choked on the rest of the sentence when he turned the corner and she caught a glimpse of her street. Her heart tripped into overdrive. "My God."

The street was barricaded at both ends and jammed with emergency vehicles, workers and equipment. Amber lights on tripods blazed from the shadows. Neighbors in winter coats thrown over their pajamas were clustered in their front yards or on porches, their heads tilted skyward, their expressions openmouthed with wonder, as though they were watching a Fourth of July fireworks display. Except no one was smiling, oohing or aahing.

Firefighters in full turnout gear surrounded the house, battling flames that lit up the entire two-story height of the building.

Rourke stopped the car and they got out. A row of upper-story windows had been blown out as if someone had shot them, one after the other.

Those windows lined the upstairs hallway, which had been hung with family photos—an old-fashioned wedding portrait of her grandparents, a few of Jenny's mother, Mariska, who was eternally twenty-three and beautiful, frozen at the age she was the year she went away. There was also an abundant, fast-changing array of Jenny's school portraits through the years.

As a little girl, she used to run up and down the hall, making noise until Gram told her to simmer down. Jenny always loved that expression: simmer down. She would stand with her hands on her head, making a hissing sound, a simmering pot.

She liked to make up stories about the people in the pictures. Her grandparents, who faced the camera lens with the grave stiffness typical of immigrants freshly minted from Ellis Island, became Broadway stars. Her mother, whose large eyes seemed to hold a delicious secret, was a government spy, protecting the world while in hiding in a place so deep underground, she couldn't even tell her family where she was.

Somebody—a firefighter—was yelling at everyone to get back, to stay a safe distance away. Other firefighters ran up the driveway with a thick, heavy hose on their shoulders. On a raised ladder that unfolded from the engine truck, a guy battled the flaming roof.

"Jenny, thank the Lord," said Mrs. Samuelson, rushing to greet her. She wore a long camel-hair coat and snow boots she hadn't bothered to buckle, and she cradled Nutley, her quivering Yorkshire terrier, in her arms. "When I first noticed the fire, I was terrified you were in the house."

"I was at the bakery," Jenny explained.

"Mrs. Samuelson, did someone get a statement from you?" Rourke asked.

"Why, yes, but I—"

"Excuse us, ma'am." Rourke took Jenny's hand and led her

past the fire line to the rear of the engine. An older man was giving orders on a walkie-talkie, and another was rebroadcasting them with a bullhorn.

"Chief, this is Jenny Majesky," Rourke said. He kept hold of her hand.

"Miss, I'm sorry about your house," said the chief. "We had an eight-minute response time after the alarm came in, but this one had been going long before we got the call. These older homes—they tend to go fast. We're doing our best."

"I…um…thank you, I guess." She had no idea what to say when her house was going up in smoke.

"Your neighbors said there were no household pets."

"That's right." Just Gram's African violets and potted herbs in the garden window. Just my whole world, everything I own, Jenny thought. She was shivering in the wintry night despite the layers of warm clothes and the roar of the flames. It was amazing how hard, how uncontrollably, she shook.

Something warm and heavy settled around her shoulders. It took a moment for her to realize it was a first-aid blanket. And Rourke McKnight's arms. He stood behind her and pulled her against him, her back to his front, his arms encircling her from behind as though to shield her from harm.

With an odd sense of surrender, she leaned against him, as though her own weight was too much for her. She shut her eyes briefly, hiding from the glare and the sting of the smoke. The fire was warm against her face. But the acrid smell nauseated her, made her picture everything in the house feeding the flames. She opened her eyes and watched.

"It's ruined," she said, turning her head and looking up at Rourke. "Everything's gone."

A guy with a camera, probably someone from the paper, stood in the bed of his truck and aimed his long lens at the scene.

Rourke's arms tightened around her. "I'm sorry, Jen. I wish I could say you're wrong."

"What happens now?"

"An investigation into the cause," he said. "Insurance claims, inventory."

"I mean right now. The next twenty minutes. The next hour. Eventually they'll put the fire out, but then what? Do I go back to the bakery and sleep under my desk?"

He bent his head low. His mouth was next to her ear so she could hear him over the roaring noise, and his body curved protectively over hers. "Don't worry about that," he said. "I've got you covered."

She believed him, of course. She had good reason. She'd known Rourke McKnight for more than half her life. Despite their troubled history together, despite the guilt and heartache they'd once caused each other and the great rift that gaped between them, she'd always known she could count on him.

Three

Jenny's eyes flew open as she was startled from a heavy, exhausted sleep. Her heart was pounding, her lungs starved for air and her mental state confused, to put it mildly. Her mind was filled with a grim dream about a book editor systematically feeding the pages of Jenny's stories into the bakery's giant spiral mixer.

She lay flat on her back with her limbs splayed, as though the bed was a raft and she a shipwreck survivor. She stared without comprehension at the ceiling and unfamiliar light fixture. Then, cautiously, she pushed herself up to a sitting position.

She was wearing a gray-and-pinstripe Yankees shirt, so large that it slipped off one shoulder. And a pair of thick cotton athletic socks, also large and floppy. And—she lifted the hem of the shirt to check—plaid men's boxers.

She was sitting smack in the middle of Rourke McKnight's bed. His gigantic, California king bed that was covered in shockingly luxurious sheets. She checked the tag of a pillowcase—600 thread count. Who knew? she thought. The man was a sensualist.

There was a light tap on the door, and then he came in without waiting for an invitation. He had a mug of coffee in each hand, the morning paper folded under his arm. He was wearing faded

Levi's and a tight T-shirt stenciled with NYPD. Three scruffy-looking dogs swirled around his legs.

"We made the front page," he said, setting the coffee mugs on the bedside table. Then he opened the *Avalon Troubadour.* She didn't look, not at first. She was still bewildered and trapped in the dream, wondering what had caused her to awaken so quickly. "What time is it?"

"A little after seven. I was trying to be quiet, to let you sleep."

"I'm surprised I slept at all."

"I'm not. Hell of a long day yesterday."

Now, *there* was an understatement. She had stuck around half the day, watching the firefighters battle the flames to the very last embers. Under heavy, gray winter skies, she had seen her house transformed from a familiar two-story house into a black scar of charred wood, ruined pipes and fixtures, objects burned beyond recognition. The stone fireplace stood amid the rubble, a lone surviving monument. Someone explained to her that after the investigators determined the cause of the fire and the insurance adjustor paid a visit, a salvage company would sift through the ruins, rescuing whatever they could. Then the rubble would be removed and disposed of. She was given a packet of forms to fill out, asking her to estimate the value of the things she'd lost. She hadn't touched the forms. Didn't they know her greatest losses were treasures that had no dollar value?

She had simply stood there with Rourke, too overwhelmed to speak or plan anything. She added her shaky signature to some documents. In the late afternoon, Rourke declared that he was taking her home. She hadn't even had the strength to object. He had fixed her instant chicken soup and saltine crackers, and told her to get some sleep. That, at least, she'd accomplished with ease, collapsing in a heap of exhaustion.

Now he sat down on the side of the bed, his profile illuminated by the weak morning light struggling through translucent white curtains on the window. He hadn't shaved yet, and golden stubble softened the lines of his jaw. The T-shirt, thin and faded from years of washing, molded to the muscular structure of his chest.

The dogs flopped down in a heap on the floor. And something about this whole situation felt surreal to her. She was in Rourke's bed. In his room. He was bringing her coffee. Reading the paper with her. What was wrong with this picture?

Ah, yes, she recalled. They hadn't slept together.

The thought seemed petty in the aftermath of what had happened. Gram was dead and her house had burned. Sleeping with Rourke McKnight should not be a priority just now. Still, it didn't seem quite fair that all she had accomplished in this bed was a bad dream.

"Let's see." She reached for the paper, scooting closer to him. This was what lovers did, sat together in bed, sipping coffee and reading the morning paper. Then she spotted the picture. It was a big one, in color, above the fold. "Oh, God. We look…"

Like a couple. She couldn't escape the thought. The photographer had caught them in what appeared to be a tender embrace, with Rourke's arms encircling her from behind and his mouth next to her ear as he bent to whisper something. The fire provided dramatic backlighting. You couldn't tell from looking at the picture that she was shivering so hard her teeth rattled, and that he wasn't murmuring sweet nothings in her ear, but explaining to her that she was suddenly homeless.

She didn't say anything, hoping that the romance of the shot was only in her head. She sipped her coffee and scanned the article. "Faulty wiring?" she said. "How do they know it's faulty wiring?"

"It's just speculation. We'll know more after the investigation."

"And why is this coffee so damn good?" she demanded. "It's perfect."

"You got a problem with that?"

"I had no idea you could make coffee like this." She took another sip, savoring it.

"I'm a man of many talents. Some people just have a gift with coffee," he added in a fake-serious voice. "They're known as coffee whisperers."

"And how do you know I take mine with exactly this much cream?"

"Maybe I've made a study of everything about you, from the way you take your coffee, to the number of towels you use when you shower, to your favorite radio station." He rested his elbows on his knees, cradling the mug in his hands.

"Uh-huh. Good one, McKnight."

"I thought you'd like it." He finished his coffee.

She drew up her knees and stretched the oversize shirt down to cover them. "It's a shallow thing to say, but a good cup of coffee makes even the worst situation less awful." Closing her eyes, she drank more, savoring it and trying to be in the moment. Given all that had happened, it was the only safe place to be. Here. With Rourke. Safe in his bed.

"What's funny?" he asked.

She opened her eyes. She hadn't realized she was laughing. "I always wondered what it would be like to spend the night in your bed."

"So how was it?"

"Well—" she set her mug on the nightstand "—the sheets don't match but the thread count is amazing. And they're clean. Not just-washed clean, but clean like you change your bed more than once in a blue moon. Four pillows and a great-feeling mattress. What's not to like?"

"Thanks."

"I'm not sure that was a compliment," she cautioned him.

"You like my bed, the sheets are clean, the mattress is comfortable. How is that not a compliment?"

"Because I can't help but wonder what it says about you. Maybe it says you're a wonderful person who values a good night's sleep. But maybe it says you're so accustomed to bringing women home that you pay special attention to your bed."

"So which is it?"

"I'm not sure. I'll have to think about it." She lay back and closed her eyes. There were any number of things she could say, but she decided not to go there. Into the past. To a reminder neither of them could escape, of what they had once been to each other. "I wish I could just stay here for the rest of my life," she said, forcing lightness into her tone.

"Don't let me stop you."

She opened her eyes and propped herself on her elbows. "I just have to ask, and this is a sincere question. Who the hell did I offend? Did I upset some cosmic balance in the universe? Is that why all this shit is happening to me?"

"Probably," he said.

She threw a pillow at him. "You're a big help."

He threw it back. "You want to shower first, or me?"

"Go ahead. I'll just sit here and finish my coffee and contemplate my fabulous life." She glanced down at the floor. "What are the dogs' names?"

"Rufus, Stella and Bob." He pointed out each one. They were pets he'd rescued, he explained. "The cat's name is Clarence."

Rescued. Of course, she thought.

"They're friendly," he added.

"So am I." She scratched Rufus's ears. He was a thick-coated malamute mix with ice-blue eyes.

"Good to know," Rourke said. "Help yourself to something to eat. Even if you're not hungry, you should eat something. It's going to be another long day." He went across the hall, and a moment later she heard the radio, followed by the hiss and patter of running water.

Jenny glanced at the clock. Too early to call Nina. Then she remembered Nina was up in Albany at some mayors' convention. Jenny got up and went to the window, her legs feeling heavy, as if she'd just run a marathon, which was odd, because she hadn't done anything all day yesterday except stand around in a state of shock and watch her house burn.

Outside, the world looked remarkably unchanged. Her whole life was falling apart, yet the town of Avalon slumbered in peace. The sky was a thick, impenetrable sheet of winter white. Bare trees lined the roadway and the distant mountains wore full mantles of snow. From the window of Rourke's house, she could see the small town coming to life, a few snow-layered vehicles venturing out after last night's snowfall. Avalon was a place of old-fashioned, effortless charm. The brick streets and well-kept older buildings of its downtown area were clustered around a municipal park, the snow-covered lawns and playing fields edging up to the banks of the Schuyler River, which tumbled past in a soothing cascade over glistening, ice-coated rocks, leaving beards of icicles in its wake.

This was the sort of town where stressed-out people from the city dreamed of coming to decompress. Some even retired here, buying a rolling acre or two for their golden years. In summer and during the fall leaf season, the country roads, which once held farm trucks and even the occasional horse-drawn buggy, were crowded with German-import SUVs, obnoxious Hummers and midlife-crisis sports cars.

There were still untouched places, where the wilderness was just as deep as it had been hundreds of years before, forests and lakes and rivers hidden among the seemingly endless peaks of the mountains. From the top of Watch Hill—which now bore a cell-phone tower—you could imagine looking down on the forest where Natty Bumppo had hunted in *Last of the Mohicans*. It always struck Jenny as remarkable that they were only a few hours' travel from New York City.

Turning away from the window, she surveyed the room. No personal items, no photographs or mementos, no evidence that he had a life or a past or, God forbid, a family. Although she'd known Rourke McKnight since they were kids, a rift spanning several years yawned between them, and she'd never been in his bedroom. He'd never invited her and even if he had, she wouldn't have come, not under normal circumstances. She and Rourke simply weren't like that. He was complicated. Their history was more complicated. They were not a match. Not by a long shot.

Because the fact was, Rourke McKnight was an enigma, and

not just to Jenny. It was hard to see past the chiseled face and piercing eyes to the man beneath. He had many layers, though she suspected few were able to discover that. He intrigued people, that was for certain. Those who were familiar with state politics knew he was the son of Senator Drayton McKnight, who for the past thirty years had represented one of the wealthiest districts in the state. And people would ask why a man born to such a family, a man who could have any life he chose, had ended up in a tiny Catskills town, working for a living just like anyone else.

Jenny knew she had a part in his decision to settle here, though he would never admit it. She had once been engaged to his best friend, Joey Santini. There had been a time when each of them had dreamed of the charms of small-town life, of friendships that would last a lifetime and loyalties that were never breached. Had they really been that naive?

Neither Rourke nor Jenny talked about what had happened, of course. Each worked hard to buy into the assumption that it was best left in the past, undisturbed.

But of course, neither one of them had forgotten. The peculiar awkward tension, the studied avoidance of each other, were proof of that. Jenny was sure that if she lived to be a hundred, she would never forget. There were very few things she knew for certain, but one of them was this. She would always remember that night with Rourke, but she would never understand him.

The shower turned off, and a few minutes later, he came in with a towel slung low around his hips, his damp hair tumbling over his brow. He was unbelievably good-looking: six-foot-something tall, with broad shoulders and lean hips. He had the kind of face that made women forget their boyfriends' phone numbers. Jenny's best friend, Nina Romano, always said he was way too good-looking to be a small-town policeman. With that chiseled jaw, dimpled chin and smoldering blue eyes, and that oh-so-memorable scar high on his right cheekbone, he belonged on billboards advertising high-end liquor or the kind of cars no one could afford. Jenny felt a clutch of pure lust, so sudden and blatant that it drew a laugh from her.

"This is funny?" he asked, spreading his arms, palms out.

"Sorry," she said, but couldn't seem to sober up. Her situation was just so completely awful that she had to laugh in order to keep from crying.

"I'll have you know, this bed has been known to bring women to tears," he said.

"I could have gone all day without hearing that." She dabbed at her eyes and then studied him closely. She'd never known a man to have so many contradictions. He looked like a Greek god but seemed to be without vanity. He came from one of the wealthiest families in the state, yet he lived like a working-class man. He pretended not to care about anyone or anything, yet he spent all his time serving the community. He found homes for stray dogs and cats. He took injured birds to the wildlife shelter. If something was wounded or weak, he was there, simple as that. He'd been doing it for years. He had lived many lives, from spoiled Upper East Side preppie to penniless student, to public servant, making choices that were unorthodox for someone of his background.

He kept so much of himself hidden. She suspected it had to do with Joey and what had happened with him, with the three of them.

"…staring at me like that?" Rourke was asking.

She realized she'd been lost in thought, and she gave herself a shake. "Sorry," she said. "It's been a long time since we've talked. I was thinking about your story."

He frowned. "My story?"

"Everybody has one. A story. A series of events that brought you to the place you are now."

The frown eased into a grin. "I like law and order, and I'm good with weapons," he said. "That's my story and I'm sticking to it."

"Even the fact that you joke around to cover up the real story is interesting to me."

"If that's interesting, then you ought to be a fiction writer."

Aha. He pretended he wasn't interesting. "You're a good distraction," she said.

"How's that?"

"My whole life just went up in smoke, and I'm thinking about you."

That seemed to make him nervous. "What about me?"

"Well, I just wonder—"

"Don't," he cut her off. "Don't wonder about me or my story."

How can I not? she thought. It's *our* story. And something about the fire had changed things between them. They'd gone from avoiding each other to…this. Whatever "this" turned out to be. Was he drawn to her by his urge to protect, or was there a deeper motivation? Could the fire be a catalyst in making them face up to matters they both avoided? Maybe—at long last—they would talk about what happened.

Not now, Jenny thought. She couldn't do that now, on top of everything else. For the time being, it was easier to engage in meaningless flirtation, skirting the real issues. Over the years, she'd gotten very good at that.

"I'd better hit the shower," she said. "Where are my clothes?"

"In the wash, but they're not dry yet."

"You washed my clothes."

"What, you wanted them dry-cleaned?"

She didn't say anything. She knew that everything reeked of smoke and she ought to be grateful for the favor. Still, it was mind-numbing to realize she had exactly one set of clothes in this world.

He opened the bottom bureau drawer, revealing a fat paper parcel marked with a laundry-service label. "There's a bunch of stuff in here. You can probably find something to fit. Help yourself."

Frowning with curiosity, she tore open the parcel and inspected the contents, pulling out each piece and holding it up. There was a baby-doll top, a push-up bra, an array of impossibly tiny women's underwear. She also found designer jeans and cutoffs, knitted tops with plunging necklines.

She straightened up and faced him. "So what are these, prizes of war? Souvenirs of sex? Things left behind by women who have walked out on you?"

"What?" he asked, but the sheepish look on his face indicated that he knew precisely what. "I had them cleaned."

"And that makes it all right?"

"Look, I'm not a monk."

"Clearly not." She held a thong at arm's length, between her thumb and forefinger. "Would *you* wear something like this?"

"Now you're getting kinky on me."

"I'm keeping the boxers," she stated. As she headed to the bathroom, she paused, her face just inches from his bare chest. The damp steam that came off him smelled of Ivory soap. "I'd better get going. Like you said, it's going to be a long day."

She stepped into the bathroom. The radio, she discovered, had been set on her favorite station. On the counter were three clean, folded towels—the exact number she preferred to use, in the proper sizes—one bath sheet and two hand towels.

Sure, it was flattering to imagine he was attracted to her. But that was all in the past; he hadn't said a dozen words to her in years. He had barely noticed her until now. Until she was in her most vulnerable state—grieving, homeless, with nowhere to go and no one to turn to. He didn't notice her until she needed rescuing. Interesting.

Jenny had to lie back on the bed and suck in her gut in order to get the borrowed jeans zipped over the boxer shorts. According to the designer tag in the waistband, the pants were her size. The jeans had probably belonged to someone named Bambi or Fanny, the sort of girl who enjoyed wearing things that looked as though they had been applied by paintbrush.

The bra was a surprisingly good fit, even though the push-up style was hardly her thing. She pulled on a V-neck sweatshirt, also tight, white with crimson trim and the Harvard seal smack-dab over her left boob. *Veritas.* It was probably as close as she'd ever get to a Harvard education.

Later she came into the kitchen, her borrowed socks flopping on the linoleum. When Rourke saw her, his face registered something she had never seen before, something that was so quickly gone, she nearly missed it—a sharp, helpless lust. Gosh, she thought, and all it took was dressing like a Victoria's Secret model.

"Ho Ho?" he said.

"Hey, these clothes came out of *your* closet," she said.

He scowled. "No, I mean Ho Ho." He held out a package of iffy-looking chocolate snack cakes.

She shook her head. "You might be the coffee whisperer, but that—" she indicated the packaged Ho Hos "—is atrocious."

He was dressed for work now, looking as clean-cut as an Eagle Scout, the youngest chief of police in Ulster County. Ordinarily it took years of experience and clever department politicking to reach chief's status, but in the town of Avalon, it took no more than a willingness to accept an abnormally small salary. He treated his job seriously, though, and had earned the respect of the community.

She helped herself to a plump orange and sat at the kitchen counter. "You're working on a Sunday?"

"I always work Sundays."

She knew that. She just didn't want to admit it. "What next, Chief?" she asked.

"We go to your house, meet with the fire investigator. If you're lucky, they'll make a determination as to the cause of the fire."

"Lucky." She dug her thumbnail into the navel of the orange and ripped back the peel. "How come I don't feel so lucky?"

"Okay, poor choice of words. All I meant was, the sooner the investigation finishes up, the sooner the salvage can start."

"Salvage. This is all so surreal." She felt a sudden clutch of anxiety in her gut and remembered something. "You said you washed my clothes?"

"Uh-huh. I just heard the cycle end."

"Oh, God." She jumped up and hurried into the tiny laundry area adjacent to the kitchen and flipped open the washer.

"What's the matter?" he asked, following her.

She yanked out the checked chef pants she'd had on. Plunging her hand into the pocket, she drew out the little brown plastic bottle. The label was still attached, but the bottle was full of cloudy water. She handed it to Rourke.

He took the bottle from her, glanced at the label. "Looks like all the pills dissolved."

"You now have the most Zenlike, serene washing machine in Avalon."

"I didn't know you were on medication."

"What, you thought I was handling Gram's death without help?"

"Well, yeah."

"Why would you think I could do that?"

He set the bottle on the kitchen counter. "You are now. You have been all morning. I don't see you freaking out."

She hesitated. Braced her hands on the edge of the counter for support. Then she realized the posture accentuated her boobs in the tight sweatshirt and folded her arms. On a scale of one to ten, the doctor had asked her the night Gram passed away, how anxious did she feel? He told her to ask herself that question before taking a pill so that popping one didn't become a habit.

"I'm a five," she said softly, feeling a barely discernible buzz in her circulation, a subtle tension in her muscles. No sweating, no accelerated heartbeat, no hyperventilating.

"I know those aren't your clothes," Rourke said, "but I'd say you're at least a seven."

"Ha, ha." She helped herself to another orange. "The doctor said I'm supposed to ask myself how anxious I feel on a scale of one to ten, consciously assessing my need for medication."

Rourke lifted one eyebrow. "So if you're a five, does that mean we should make an emergency run to the drugstore?"

"Nope. Not unless I feel like an eight or higher. I'm not sure why I don't feel more panicked. After everything that's happened, it's a wonder I'm not having a nervous breakdown."

"What, do you want one?"

"Of course not, but it would be normal to fall apart, wouldn't it?"

"I don't think there's any kind of 'normal' when it comes to a loss like this. You feel relatively okay now. Let's leave it at that."

She sensed something beneath his words. A certain wisdom or knowledge, as though maybe he had some experience in this area.

The morning air felt icy and sweet on her face as she followed him outside. He made sure the dogs had food and water and that the heater in the adjacent garage was on so they could come in out of the cold if they needed to. He closed the gate and then, with a flair of chivalry, he opened the door of the Ford Explorer, marked with a round seal depicting a waterwheel in honor of Avalon's past as a milltown, and the words Avalon P.D.

Then he came around and got in the driver's side and started up the car. "Seat belt," he said. He noticed her looking at him and she wondered if he could tell she was thinking about what an enigma he was to her, the first person to distract her from her grief over Gram. He was being chivalrous because he was chief of police, she reminded herself. He would do the same for anyone.

"Are you sure you're all right?" he asked. "You're looking at me funny again."

She felt her face heat and glanced away. She was supposed to be in despair about losing her grandmother and house, yet here she was having impure thoughts about the chief of police. Please don't let me be that girl, she thought.

"Other than these clothes," she said, "I'm fine."

He took a deep breath. "Okay. Let's focus on today. On right now. We'll deal with things one by one."

"I'm all ears. See, I don't know the drill. No idea what happens after the house burns down."

"You make a new start," he said. "That's what."

His words took hold of her. For the first time since Gram died, she began to see the situation in a new light. Drowning in grief, she had focused on the fact that she was all alone now. Rourke's comment caused a paradigm shift. *Alone* became *independent*. She had never experienced that before. When her grandfather died, she'd been needed at the bakery. After her grandmother's stroke, she'd been needed at home. Following her own path had never been an option…until now. But here was something so terrible, she wished she could hide it from herself—she was afraid of independence. She might screw up and it would be all her fault.

Although she'd stood around the previous day and watched her house burn, even feeling warmth from the embers, she felt a fresh wave of shock when she got out of the car. With all the equipment gone, there was nothing but the scaly black skeleton surrounded by a moat of trampled mud, now frozen into hard chunks and ridges.

"What happened to the garage?" she asked.

"A pumper backed into it. It's a good thing we got your car out yesterday."

The loss barely registered with her. It seemed minuscule in the face of everything else. She could only shake her head.

"I'm sorry," he said, patting her shoulder a bit awkwardly. "The fire investigators will be here soon, and you can have a look around."

She felt an unpleasant chill. "Are you thinking this fire was set deliberately?"

"This is standard. If things don't add up for the fire investigator, he'll call for an arson investigation. The insurance adjuster said he'd be here soon. First thing he'll do is give you a debit card so you can get the basics."

She nodded, though a shudder went through her. A swath of black-and-yellow tape surrounded the house at the property line.

Seeing the house was like probing a fresh wound. The place was a grotesque mutation of its former self. Against the pale morning sky, it resembled a crude charcoal drawing. The porch, once a white smile of railing across the front of the house, had blackened and blistered into nothing. A couple of tenuous beams leaned crazily out over the yard. There was no front door to speak of. All the remaining windows were shattered.

The plumbing formed a strange, Terminator-like skeleton from which everything else had burned away. In the charred ruins, she could pick out the kitchen—the heart of the house. Her grandparents had been frugal people, but they had splurged on a double-door commercial fridge and a huge double oven. More than five decades ago, Gram had created her first commercial baked goods right in that kitchen.

The upstairs was down now, for the most part, and some of the downstairs was in the basement. Jenny could see straight through to the backyard fence, now a field of snow, including a rippled blanket of white over the garden bed. Throughout Gram's life, the garden had been her pride and joy. After her grandmother's stroke, Jenny had worked hard to keep it the way it was, a glorious and artful profusion of flowers and vegetables.

The high-pressure stream from the firefighters' hoses had crisscrossed the yard in clean, arching swaths. The spray had formed icicles on the back fence and gate, turning the backyard into a sculpture garden.

Heavy boots had tamped down the snow on the perimeter of the property. The entire area smelled of wet charcoal, a harsh and stinging assault on the nostrils.

"I don't even know where to begin," she said. "Interesting question, huh? When you lose everything you own in a fire, what's the first thing you buy?"

"A toothbrush," he said simply, as if the answer was obvious.

"I'll make a note of that."

"There's a method. The adjuster will hook you up with a salvage company, and they'll walk you through the process."

Cars trolled past slowly. She could feel the sting of gawking eyes. People always stared at other people's troubles and breathed a sigh of relief, grateful it wasn't them.

Jenny put on protective gear and followed the fire investigator and insurance adjuster up a plank that sloped up to the threshold of the front door in place of the ruined steps. She could pick out the layout of the rooms, could see the filthy remains of familiar furniture and possessions. The whole place had been transformed into alien territory.

She was the alien. She didn't recognize herself as she tonelessly responded to questions about her routine the night before. She answered questions until her head was about to explode. They ran through all the usual scenarios. She hadn't fallen asleep smoking in bed. The only sin she'd committed was unintentional and inadvertent. She tried to detach herself, pretend it was someone else explaining that she'd been up late working at her computer. That she'd felt as if she were about to jump out of her skin, so she went to the bakery, knowing someone would be there on the early-morning shift. She answered their questions as truthfully as possible—no, she didn't recall leaving any appliances on, not the coffeemaker, hair dryer, toaster oven. She had not left a burner on, hadn't forgotten a burning candle, couldn't even recall where she kept a supply of kitchen matches. (Under the sink, one of the investigator's techs informed her.) Her grandmother used to take votive candles to church, lighting row upon row in front of the statue of Saint Casimir, patron of both Poland and of bachelors.

"Oh, no," she whispered.

"Miss?" the fire investigator prodded her.

"I did it," she said. "The fire's my fault. My grandmother had a tin box filled with things from Poland—letters, recipes, articles she'd clipped. The night of the fire, I was…I couldn't sleep so I was doing some research for my column. I got it out, and—oh, God." She stopped, feeling sick with guilt.

"And what?" he prompted.

"I used a flashlight that night. Its batteries were dead so I took the ones out of the smoke detector in the kitchen and forgot to put them back. I disabled the smoke alarm."

Rourke seemed unconcerned. "You wouldn't be the first to do that."

"But that means the fire was my fault."

"A smoke alarm only works when there's someone to hear it," Rourke pointed out. "Even if it had been wailing all night, the house would have burned. You weren't present to hear the alarm, so it didn't matter."

Oh, she wanted him to be right. She wanted not to be responsible for destroying the house. "I've heard that alarm go off," she said. "It's loud enough to wake the neighbors, if it's working."

"It's not your fault, Jen."

She thought of the tin box filled with irreplaceable documents and writings on onionskin paper. Gone now, forever. She felt as though she'd lost her grandmother all over again. Trying to hold herself together, she studied the fireplace, picturing the Christmases they'd shared in this house. She hadn't used the fireplace since before her grandmother had died.

Gram used to get so cold, she claimed only a cheery fire in the hearth could warm her. "I used to wrap her up like a kolache," Jenny said, thinking aloud about how she and Gram had giggled as Jenny tucked layer after layer of crocheted afghan around the frail little body. "But she just kept shivering and I couldn't get her to stop." Then her face was tucked against Rourke's shoulder, and it hurt to pull in a breath of air, the effort scraping her lungs.

She felt an awkward pat on the back. Rourke probably hadn't counted on finding his arms full of female despair this morning. Rumor had it he knew exactly what to do with a woman, but she suspected the rumors applied to sexy, attractive, willing women. That was the only type he ever dated, as far as she could tell. Not that she was keeping track, but it was hard to ignore. More frequently than she cared to admit, she'd spotted him taking some stacked bimbo to the train station to get the early train to the city.

"…go outside," Rourke was saying in her ear. "We can do this another time."

"No." She straightened up, pulled herself together, even forced a brave smile. What sort of person was she, thinking like that under these circumstances? She gave him a gentle slug on the upper arm, which seemed to be made of solid rock. "Excellent shoulder to cry on, Chief."

He joined her obvious attempt to lighten things up. "To protect and serve. Says so right on my badge."

She faced the fire investigator, brushing at her cheeks. "Sorry. I guess I needed a breakdown break."

"I understand, miss. The loss of a home is a major trauma. We advise an evaluation with a counselor as soon as possible." He handed her a business card. "Dr. Barrett in Kingston comes highly recommended. Main thing is, don't make any major decisions for a while. Take it slow."

She slipped the card into her back pocket. It was amazing that she could slip anything into that pocket. The borrowed jeans were constricting her in places she didn't know she had. The tour continued and somehow she managed to hold it together despite the enormity of her loss. In less than a month, she'd lost Gram, and now the house where she had lived every day of her life.

The official determination had yet to be made, but both the investigator and even the suspicious insurance adjuster seemed to agree that the fire had started in the crawlspace of the attic. Very likely faulty wiring had been the cause. The Sniffer had detected no accelerant and there were no obvious signs of deliberate mischief.

"What next?" she asked the adjuster, exhausted after the tour of the ruins. She wondered if this was what the aftermath of battle was like, picking over the remains of something that had been whole and alive, vibrant with houseplants, family photos on the walls, mementos of milestones and gifts exchanged for birthdays and Christmases, one-of-a-kind keepsakes like handwritten recipes and old letters.

The adjuster pointed out her computer, which lay amid a pile of ugly, scorched upholstery with batting that burst out of the melted holes like entrails.

"That your laptop?" he asked.

"Yes." It was closed, the top blistered.

"We can have a technician check it out. The hard drive might have survived."

Doubtful, though. He didn't say so, but she could read it in his face. All her data was gone—WordPerfect files, financial records, photo albums, addresses, e-mail, the bakery's QuickBooks. Her book project. She kept backups, but stored them in the drawers of a desk that was now a pile of ashes.

Her shoulders slumped at the thought of trying to reconstruct everything.

"She's a writer," Rourke told the investigator.

"Really?" The man looked intrigued. "You don't say. What do you write?"

Jenny felt sheepish. She always did when people asked about her writing. Her dream was so big, so impossible, that sometimes she felt she had no right to it. She—small-town, uneducated Jenny Majesky, wanted to be a writer. It was one thing to publish a weekly recipe column, fantasizing in private about something bigger and better, yet quite another to own up to her ambitions to a stranger.

"I do a recipe column for the local paper," she mumbled.

"Come on, Jen," Rourke prodded. "You always said you'd write a book one day. A bestseller."

She couldn't believe he remembered that—or that he'd say so in front of this guy.

"I'm working on it," she said, her cheeks flushing.

"Yeah? I'll have to look for it in the bookstore," the adjuster remarked.

"You'll be looking for a long time," she told him ruefully. "I'm not published." She sent Rourke a burning look. Blabbermouth. What was he thinking, telling her dreams to a total stranger?

She figured it was because Rourke didn't take her seriously. Didn't think she had a snowball's chance. She was a bakery owner in a small mountain town. She would probably always be a bakery owner, hunched over the bookkeeping or growing old and crusty at the counter of the store, maybe even learning to call customers "doll" and "hon."

"What?" Rourke demanded after the adjuster went to his car. "What's that look?"

"You didn't have to say anything about the book."

"Why not?" His guileless expression was infuriating. "What's got your panties in a twist?" he asked.

The fact that they were men's boxers was one problem, but she didn't say anything. "Bestseller," she muttered. "How stupid would it look if I went around telling people, 'I'm writing a best-seller.' "

He looked genuinely mystified. "What's wrong with that?"

"It's totally presumptuous. I write, okay? That's all. It's up to the people who buy books to make something a bestseller."

"Now you're splitting hairs. It's giving me a headache. You once told me that publishing a book would be a dream come true for you."

He really didn't get it. "It is a dream," she told him fiercely. "It's *the* dream."

"I didn't know it was some big secret."

"It's not. It just isn't something I go around blabbing to every Tom, Dick and Harry. It's…to me, it's something sacred. I don't need to broadcast it."

"I don't see why not."

"Because if it doesn't happen, I'll look like an idiot."

He threw back his head and guffawed.

She had a clear memory of herself fresh out of school, poised to leave town, telling people, "Next time you see my face, it'll be on a book jacket." And she'd truly believed that. "This is not some joke," she said tightly.

"Let me ask you something," he said. "When was the last time you thought someone was an idiot for going for her dream?"

"I don't think that way."

He smiled at her. There was such kindness in his face that she felt her resentment fading. "Jenny. Nobody thinks that way. And the more people you tell your dream to, the more real it's going to seem to you."

She couldn't help smiling back. "You sound like a greeting card."

He chuckled. "Busted. It was on a card I got for my last birthday."

There was something about the way he was sticking so close by her. "Don't you have somewhere you need to be?" she asked. "Some police-chiefing to do here in Sin City?" She gestured at Maple Street, still pristine under its mantle of new-fallen snow.

"I need to be right here with you," he said simply.

"To pick up the pieces if I fall apart."

"You're not going to fall apart."

"How can you be so sure?"

He grinned again. "You've got a bestseller to write."

She thought about the ruined, blistered laptop. "Uh-huh. Here's the thing, Rourke. The project I've been working on…it wasn't on a hard drive. It was all there." She indicated the blackened skeleton of the house, now a smoldering ruin. She felt physically sick when she thought of the box of her grandmother's recipes and writings, which Jenny had so carelessly left on the kitchen table. Now those one-of-a-kind papers were lost forever, along with photographs and mementos of her grandparents' lives. "I might as well give up," she said.

"Nope," said Rourke. "If you quit writing because of a fire, then it probably wasn't something you wanted that bad in the first place." He took a step closer to her. He smelled of shaving soap and cold air. He was careful not to touch her here in broad daylight with people swarming everywhere. Yet the probing way he regarded her felt like an intimate caress. He was probably still mortified by the picture on the front page of the paper. She was not exactly lingerie model material.

Then he did touch her, though not to pull her into his embrace. Instead, he took her by the shoulders and turned her to look at the burned-out house. "Look, the stories you need to write aren't there," he said. "They never were. You've already got them in your head. You just need to write them down, the way you've always done."

She nodded, trying her best to believe him, but the effort exhausted her. Everything exhausted her. She had a pounding headache that felt as though her brain was about to explode. "You weren't kidding," she said to Rourke, "about this being a busy day."

"You doing all right?" he asked her. "Still a five?"

She was surprised he remembered that. "I'm too confused to feel anxious."

"The good news is, everyone's breaking for lunch."

"Thank God."

They got in the car and he said, "Where to? The bakery? Back home to rest?"

Home, she thought ruefully. "I'm homeless, remember?"

"No, you're not. You're staying with me, for as long as it takes."

"Oh, that'll look good. The chief of police shacking up with a homeless woman."

He grinned and started the car. "I've heard worse gossip than that in this town."

"I'm calling Nina. I can stay with her."

"She's out of town at that mayors' seminar, remember?"

"I'll call Laura."

"Her place is the size of a postage stamp."

He was right. Laura was content in a tiny apartment by the river, and Jenny didn't relish the thought of squeezing in there. "Then I'll use this debit card at a B&B—"

"Hey, will you cut it out? It's not like I'm Norman Bates. You're staying with me, end of story."

She shifted in her seat to stare at him, amazed by his ease with the situation.

"What?" he asked, glancing down at his crisp shirt and conservative blue tie. "Did I spill coffee on myself?"

She clicked her seat belt in place. "I was just thinking. One way or another, you've been rescuing me ever since we were kids."

"Yeah? Then you'd think I'd be better at it." He dialed the steering wheel one-handed, heading down the hill toward town. He put on a pair of G-man shades and adjusted the rearview mirror. "Either that, or your dragons are getting a lot harder to slay."

Four

⊰∽⊙∽⊙∽⊱

Daisy Bellamy stood on the freshly shoveled sidewalk in front of Avalon High School. She gazed up at the concrete edifice of her new school while her heart tried to beat its way out of her chest. *Her new school.* It was one of those brick Gothic buildings so common in old-fashioned small towns.

She couldn't believe it. Once a girl from the Upper East Side, she was now, in her last semester of school, a resident of Avalon, here in the heart of nowhere.

I really screwed up this time, she thought, feeling sick to her stomach.

Was it only two weeks ago that she'd been a senior at an exclusive prep school in New York City? That was a lifetime ago. Since then, she'd left school in disgrace and now this. Now her dad had forced her to move to Sleepy Hollow, and she had to finish her senior year here with the Archie Gang, at a public high school.

Of course, everyone said, in the most caring fashion, moving here and changing schools came about because of a bad choice Daisy made. *Bad choice.* What a riot.

So now she stood in the middle of the frozen tundra surrounding her, and she felt completely detached from the scene. It was like an out-of-body experience, where she was hovering unseen somewhere, gazing down at herself, a lone figure in the snow, with a kaleidoscope of babbling strangers circling around her, oblivious to her presence.

No. That wasn't right. Not everyone was oblivious. A pair of girls spotted her, then put their heads together and immediately started whispering. A moment later, a pack of guys tossing a football back and forth checked her out with measuring glances. Their low whistles and apelike sounds rolled right over her like a bitter wind.

Let them whisper. Let them jeer. What the hell did she care about any of this?

She brought her attitude with her into the main office of the school. A blast of damp heat filled the room, redolent of wet wool and whatever else a public high school smelled like. Daisy undid her Burberry muffler and pulled off her Portolano gloves. People on the other side of the scarred wooden counter were busy on the phone, staring at computer monitors or sliding messages into a row of mailboxes.

A tired-looking woman at a desk marked Attendance Clerk glanced up at her. "May I help you?"

Daisy unbuttoned her faux fur-trimmed suede jacket. "I'm Daisy Bellamy. Today's my first day."

The clerk sorted through the stacking trays on her desk. Then she picked up a file folder and came over to the counter, moving with a pregnant woman's waddle. Her stomach was enormous. Daisy tried not to stare.

"Oh, good," the clerk said. "We've got all your records right here. Your father stopped by on Friday and everything is in order."

Daisy nodded, suddenly feeling overheated and nauseous. Her dad would be here right now, except that she'd begged him not to come. Her brother, Max, was only in fifth grade, she'd argued. He needed their dad way more than Daisy did. Way more.

The clerk explained Daisy's schedule to her, handed over a map of the building and traced directions to her homeroom. She also told her where her locker was located and gave her the combination. There was a complicated system of bells—first bell, assembly bell, lunch bell…but Daisy barely listened. She glanced at the room number on her pink slip, left the office and headed into the tile-walled halls of her new school.

The corridor was jammed with loud kids and the smell of damp winter clothes. The sounds of slamming lockers and laughter filled the air. Daisy found the locker assigned to her, dialed the combination and swung open the metal door. The former occupant had shown a fondness for hip-hop, judging by the intricate, interlocking graffiti drawn inside.

She put away her jacket, muffler and gloves. It had been tempting, this morning, to wear something low-key, something that wouldn't attract attention, but that wasn't Daisy's style. The only possible advantage to changing schools midyear was that for the first time in her life, she would go to a school that didn't have a strict dress code. She took full advantage of that and showed up today in low-cut jeans and a cropped argyle sweater that showed off one of her many recent rebellions against her parents—a belly-button ring. She had no idea if Archie's Gang would appreciate her Rock & Republic jeans or Pringle of Scotland sweater, but at least she felt good in them.

She walked into room 247, strolled past the other students and found the teacher's desk.

Was *this* guy a teacher? He hardly looked old enough, in slightly wrinkled chinos, a more-than-slightly-wrinkled blue oxford shirt and an adorable but crooked paisley tie.

"Daisy Bellamy," she said, handing over the new-student folder the attendance clerk had given her.

"Anthony Romano," said the teacher, standing up and favoring her with a warm smile. "Welcome to Avalon High." He had a kind of puppylike charm, with those big brown eyes and that eager-to-please attitude. "You want me to introduce you to the class?"

At least he had the consideration to ask. And he seemed so chipper, she hated to burst his bubble. She nodded—might as well get this over with—and turned to face the busy, noisy classroom.

"Hey, listen up," said Mr. Romano in a surprisingly authoritative voice. He punctuated the imperative by knocking on the blackboard. "We have a new student today."

The words *new student* worked like magic. Every pair of eyes in the room turned toward Daisy. She just pretended she was in yet another school play. She'd been into drama since playing a Christmas-pageant cherub at age four, right up to playing Auntie Mame in last year's spring musical. She simply treated the home-room class like an audience, offering a hostess's smile.

"This is Daisy Bellamy. Please make her feel welcome and show her around, okay?"

"Bellamy like the Camp Kioga Bellamys?" someone asked.

Daisy was surprised that the name Bellamy actually meant something around here. Back in the city, you had to be a Rocke-feller or carry the name of a clothing label or hotel chain in order for kids to think you were anything special. She nodded. "My grandparents."

The name Kioga conjured images of the family property high in the mountains outside of town that had once been famous as the summer watering hole of well-heeled New Yorkers. The camp had closed down a long time ago, but it still belonged to the family. Daisy had only been there once, last summer. She'd worked for her cousin Olivia, renovating the place for their grandparents' fiftieth anniversary celebration.

"Daisy, why don't you take a seat right here, between Sonnet and Zach." Mr. Romano indicated a right-armed desk between a boy with light blond hair and an African-American girl who had supermodel cheekbones and a wicked manicure.

"Thank God," Sonnet said. "Now I don't have to look at him."

"Hey," Mr. Romano warned.

"Whatever," Sonnet said, leaning back in her chair and folding her arms.

Daisy expected the teacher to eject her—that would have been the procedure at her old school—but instead, he turned his back on her and went to write some reminders on the chalkboard.

"Kolache?" asked the kid named Zach.

Daisy realized he was speaking to her and holding out a golden-brown pastry on a napkin. Its fresh, sweet smell made her slightly nauseous. "Oh, that's okay," she said, taken aback. "I've already had breakfast."

"Thanks." Sonnet reached across the desk and snatched it out of Zach's hand.

"Oink, oink," said Zach.

"It speaks." Sonnet nibbled at the pastry. "Maybe it can do some other tricks."

"I'm working on making you disappear," Zach said.

Daisy felt as though she was at a Ping-Pong match, watching them trade insults back and forth. She cleared her throat.

"I work at the Sky River Bakery," Zach said conversationally. "Early shift. So every morning for fresh pastries, I'm your man."

"We've all got to be good at something," Sonnet said with a pitying glance in his direction.

"Yeah," he said. "I'm good at making them and Sonnet is good at eating them, as you can tell by the size of that ass."

"All right," Daisy said suddenly, understanding why the teacher had placed her between these two. "Do we kill him now or wait until the bell rings?"

Sonnet shrugged. "The sooner, the better, as far as I'm concerned."

Zach stretched, and folded his hands behind his head. "You need me, and you know it. You'd die of withdrawal symptoms if I didn't bring you a pastry every day. You guys hear about the fire?" he asked, changing the subject. "Jenny's house burned down."

"Bullshit," Sonnet said.

"It's not." He held his arms wide, palms out. "Swear to God, I'm not making this up. It's probably in the paper."

Daisy listened with interest. She had a sort of crazy family tie to the bakery. It was owned by Jenny Majesky—she assumed this was the "Jenny" Zach was talking about. Jenny was the daughter of Daisy's uncle Phil. So that made them cousins, though they were virtually strangers.

"Is Jenny okay?" Sonnet asked.

"Fine. I'm surprised she's not with your mom."

"Jenny and my mom are best friends," Sonnet explained to Daisy. "And my mom's out of town at a mayors' convention. She'll be back later this morning."

"Oh," Daisy said. "Does she work for the mayor?"

Sonnet took a bite of her kolache. "She *is* the mayor."

"Hey, that's awesome," Daisy said.

"Not for long," Zach interjected. "My dad's running against her in the next election."

"Yeah, well, good luck with that," Sonnet said with airy confidence.

"He's the city administrator and he's saved the city a fortune. People love that," Zach countered.

"Yeah, they love it when you cut services, like closing the municipal pool. What's he going to close next, the library?" She finished eating the kolache and wiped her hands with a napkin.

Announcements crackled over the PA system, drowning the conversation. There was a meeting of the debate club after school. Ice-hockey practice and a 4-H Club sugaring-off party, which sounded wholesome, but Sonnet whispered that it was a chance for the 4-H'ers to go out into the woods, boil maple sap into syrup and get high while doing it. Then—Daisy couldn't believe it— everyone stood up, turned to face the flag in the corner of the room and said the Pledge of Allegiance. The words came to her from some hidden well she thought she'd forgotten.

"Let's have a look at your schedule," Zach said.

Daisy spread it out on the desk and the three of them studied it.

"Whoa," said Zach. "Calculus and honors physics? And AP English? What are you, a glutton for punishment?"

"I didn't get to pick," Daisy explained. "At my old school, I had to take five AP courses." She shifted uncomfortably in her seat. "It was a really hard school."

"So you're halfway through senior year, and they made you move to the boonies," Sonnet said. "That's harsh."

"I begged my dad to let me stay in the city," Daisy said, though beg was a euphemism for screaming fit. "I even said he could homeschool me, but he wouldn't hear of it."

"Why not?"

"He claims he doesn't remember calculus. And I was, like, fine, we'll fail it together, because I don't understand it, either."

"Probably not the best way to convince him," Sonnet said. "I'm surprised they even have classes for you here."

Daisy decided not to tell her that technically, she probably had enough credits to graduate early. The only problem with that was, if she left school, then she'd have to get a life. And she was totally not ready for that.

By comparing notes, she discovered she had several classes in common with either Sonnet, or Zach, or both. Sonnet was some kind of accelerated brainiac. Though only sixteen, she would graduate with the seniors in June. And Daisy figured out that even though Zach and Sonnet teased each other, they were kind of into each other. But there was definitely a rivalry going on.

"It's a little weird," Zach agreed. "I can't wait to get the hell out of here. My college apps have been in since October. What about you?"

Daisy stared down at her pristine, empty notebook. "I applied," she admitted. The counselor at her other school had practically held her under house arrest, making her fill out applications. "I don't really want to go to college," she confessed.

Sonnet and Zach seemed to take it in stride. At Daisy's old school, saying "I don't want to go to college" had the impact of saying "I have an STD." People stared at you, hiding their disgust behind pity.

And for Daisy, the most disgusted, pitying looks had come from her own parents.

Zach and Sonnet didn't look pitying at all. Maybe at this school you weren't considered a loser and a freak just because you didn't plan on being a rocket scientist or Supreme Court justice.

So far, thought Daisy, the day didn't totally suck. That was a surprise. Of course, they hadn't even left homeroom yet.

The bell rang and everyone flurried into action, shuffling papers, stuffing backpacks and heading for the door. In the corridor, kids floated along like leaves in a stream.

Zach veered toward a classroom with French travel posters plastering the door. "Here's my stop," he said. "Find me at lunch." He disappeared into a classroom.

"So, do you have a boyfriend?" asked Sonnet.

Boyfriend? Now, if Sonnet had asked her if there were guys Daisy hooked up with, she would have a different answer. "No boyfriend," she said firmly. "Why do you ask?"

"Because Zach is totally crushing on you. He has been since the second you walked into homeroom."

"I don't even know him."

"I don't even know Orlando Bloom, but I totally know I would be his love slave until the end of time."

"Believe me, I don't want to be anyone's love slave." *Been there, done that,* she thought. "And anyway, you've got him pegged all wrong. He's into you, not me."

Sonnet shook her head, corkscrew curls bobbing. "He hates me."

"Right. He hates you so much he brings you a pastry every morning."

"If you're so smart, how come you're not going to college?"

"I'm not sure of anything." She experienced a tiny glimmer of warmth and found herself hoping this was the start of an actual friendship. "I like the name Sonnet," she said, wanting to turn the topic away from herself.

"Thanks. My mom says she picked it because she didn't want anything that sounded too ethnic. All my cousins on my mom's side of the family are Lucias and Marias and so forth. Sonnet is just…weird."

"Weird in a good way," Daisy assured her.

"She once told me she was reading a book of Shakespeare's sonnets when she went to the hospital in labor." Sonnet's velvety brown eyes softened with an expression Daisy couldn't read.

"So your last name is Romano, like the teacher," she remarked, looking at the name scrawled on Sonnet's notebook. "Coincidence?"

"He's my uncle Tony," Sonnet explained. "My mom's brother."

They didn't look related, Daisy thought, but she didn't say anything. "What's it like, being in your uncle's class?"

"I'm used to it. There are a ton of Romanos in Avalon and half of them are teachers, so it's kind of hard to avoid."

"So you have your mom's name, not your dad's," Daisy observed, hoping it wasn't a touchy subject.

Apparently, it wasn't. Sonnet answered easily, "My mom's single. She never married my dad."

"Oh." Daisy didn't know what to say to that. She was fairly certain "I'm sorry" wasn't appropriate. She scanned the crowded hallway. "Is it my imagination, or are there three teachers on this floor named Romano?"

Sonnet gave a rueful smile. "That's just the tip of the iceberg. There are Romanos everywhere. Some people say that's how my mom got elected mayor. She has eight brothers and sisters.

"So how about you?" Sonnet asked. "What are your parents like?"

Divorced was the first thing that popped into Daisy's mind. "My mom's originally from Seattle, but she got a summer job at Camp Kioga, where she met my dad. They married young and put each other through school—law and architecture. So it all seemed like it should work out, right? She got a job at a big international law firm and Dad started a commercial landscape design company. Then my mom's best friend in Seattle got cancer last year and my mom had this epiphany. She said she was just pretending to be happy or some crap like that, and in order to be really happy she needed a divorce." Daisy sighed. The whole situation just made her tired. Everything made her feel tired these days. "Which is really all right with me, since I'm practically out the door. My little brother Max—he's eleven—is taking it hard."

"So how did your dad wind up with you and your brother?"

"My mom's working on a case at the International Court of Justice in The Hague. In Holland."

Sonnet turned out to be the perfect first friend to have at this school. They had two classes together, and Sonnet introduced Daisy to a bunch of other kids. Some regarded her with suspicion, but most were friendly enough. She felt a little overwhelmed, though, trying to keep everything straight. In history class, they were studying ancient ways of burial and they talked about a cairn, which was a pile of stones used to mark a burial site, and to keep scavengers from picking at the bones of the dead.

Lunchtime rolled around and Zach joined them. The cafeteria was vast, with tall windows that were fogged by steam from the big iron radiators. There were long Formica tables crammed with kids sitting in distinctive groups.

"Okay," said Zach, "so here's the deal. Over there are the jocks, and they're fine, so long as you don't mind talking sports until you want to puke. The big sports in this school are hockey and baseball. The table on the end—theater crowd. Dancers, actors, singers. The skater table kind of speaks for itself. Around here, skaters and snowboarders are the same. Do you ride?"

"I ski," Daisy said.

"You don't rate with them, then." He moved on, giving her a quick tour—Goths, nerds, Eurotrash, headbangers, gangbangers.

The oniony smell of cafeteria food made her feel queasy. She followed Sonnet through the line, picking only a fruit bowl and a bottle of seltzer water.

"Oh, man." Sonnet looked at Daisy's tray in dismay. "You don't have an eating disorder, do you?"

Daisy laughed. "Believe me, that's not a factor. I'm just not feeling too hungry at the moment."

They sat at a table with an interesting, eclectic mix of people.

Zach went to get a refill and Sonnet propped her chin in her hand, studying Daisy intently. "There's something you're not telling me."

Daisy nibbled idly at a bit of pineapple. *No shit.*

"I can't quite put my finger on what it is. I mean, why would a girl, taking all college prep classes at the best school in the country, suddenly drop out her senior year and decide she doesn't want to go to college?"

Still Daisy didn't reply. There was nothing to say. Sonnet was like a buzzard, circling overhead, spiraling lower and tighter as she approached the truth.

Daisy told herself she'd better get used to being scrutinized and questioned. She was hoping she'd have at least a little more time to settle in at school, to let people get to know her and, she hoped, form a decent opinion of her before the truth came out, before everyone found out the secret she'd been holding under her heart.

Five

It was a Monday like no other, Jenny realized as she headed once again to the ruin at 472 Maple Street. She was back again, along with the fire investigator. Later in the week, the salvage operation would begin. She couldn't imagine that there was anything to salvage, but Rourke swore she might be surprised.

As they got out of his car at the curb, she glanced up at him and caught her breath. She wasn't used to being around a guy this good-looking. Staring at him had a strange effect on her. It was destroying her brain cells.

He noticed her look. "Something the matter?"

"I really don't think I should be staying with you. At your house, I mean."

"You're staying. It's the best idea for the time being, at least."

"It's embarrassing. People will talk."

"That's always been your problem, Jenny. Worrying about what people will say."

An interesting observation, coming from him. "You mean you don't care?"

"Do I act like I care?"

She thought about the women he dated. "I guess not. But I do."

"Look, nobody's going to think anything about this. You're a disaster victim, I'm the chief of police. It's a match made in heaven."

"Cute." She brushed past him and headed up the walkway to the ruins of the house. She used her booted toe to nudge at what had once been a wooden file cabinet. This was where she had stored her notebooks. As soon as she learned how to write, she had written all her secrets, all her girlish dreams, all her thoughts in spiral-bound notebooks, and she had stored them in the file. There was almost nothing left, just blackened pages that disintegrated at the slightest touch or sodden papers destroyed by water.

How will I remember? she wondered. How will I remember the girl I used to be?

Surrounded by the devastation of the only home she had ever known, she told herself it was silly, fretting over each little loss. If she let herself do that, she would be grieving from now until Judgment Day. She plunged her hand in her pocket and felt the cylindrical shape of the pill bottle; she'd refilled the prescription this morning. Hold on, she told herself. And then she looked up at Rourke McKnight and the strangest, most irrational feeling came over her. Safety. Security. Even a small glimmer of hope. And she hadn't even taken a pill.

She wasn't sure why. He was just standing there, watching her as though he'd throw himself in front of a train if that was what it took to keep her safe. And she believed him. Trusted him. Felt safe with him. Which made her either the dumbest woman in town, or the most insightful.

The sound of a car engine caught her attention. She turned to see Olivia Bellamy exiting a silver Lexus SUV and hurrying across the street toward her. Blond and adorable, in designer boots and an embroidered Scandinavian jacket, she resembled the kind of woman Rourke usually dated, but with one key difference— Olivia Bellamy had a brain.

"Jenny," she said, pulling her into a hug and then stepping back. "I just heard. Thank God you're safe." She gaped at the smoldering ruin of the house. "I'm so sorry," she added.

"Thanks," Jenny said, feeling awkward. She and Olivia were sisters—half sisters—though they didn't know each other very well. They'd met for the first time last summer, almost by accident, when Olivia had moved up from the city to renovate the Bellamy family summer camp, high in the mountains on the shores of Willow Lake.

Discovering that they were both the daughters of Philip Bellamy had been…at first startling, and then bittersweet. Jenny was the result of a youthful affair; Olivia was born to the woman Philip had married and later divorced. Now Jenny and Olivia were still getting used to the idea that they were sisters. Far from the happy-go-lucky twins in *The Parent Trap,* they were just finding their way toward each other.

"You should've called me right away," Olivia said. She sent Rourke a swift glance. "Hi, Rourke." Then she turned back to Jenny. "Why didn't you call me?"

"I, uh, I was at the bakery when it started and then…" Jenny didn't know why she felt apologetic. She just wasn't sure how to act around her newfound sister. "Things went crazy, as you can imagine."

"Excuse me," Rourke said as the fire captain motioned him over.

"I can't imagine." Olivia touched her arm. "Oh, Jenny. I want to help. What can I do?" Olivia seemed almost desperate and utterly sincere. "I want to help, in any way I can."

Jenny summoned a smile, grateful beyond words that even after losing Gram, she still had her sister. If not for Olivia, Jenny would be alone right now, the last of her family gone. Yet at the same time, she felt a pinch of melancholy, regretting the years they'd lost. She had grown up with Bellamys all around her, never knowing of the connection they shared. She and Olivia were so different. Olivia had spent her life surrounded by the wealth and privilege of the Bellamy family. The adored—and, according to Olivia, overindulged—only daughter, she had attended the best schools, graduated with honors from Columbia, and by the age of twenty-four had launched her own business. She was gorgeous, successful…and she was in love with the perfect guy—a local contractor named Connor Davis. It would be easy to envy her to the point of dislike.

Except Jenny truly liked Olivia. She honestly did. Her half sister was kind and funny, and she genuinely wanted to have a relationship. Jenny had read somewhere that the true test of the strength of a relationship is whether or not it held up in a crisis.

I guess I'm about to find out, she thought.

Taking a deep breath, she said, "At the moment, I'm kind of disoriented. I hope you'll forgive me."

"Forgive? My lord, Jenny, you must be devastated."

"Well, when you put it that way…"

"God, listen to me. I'm awful."

"It's all right. There's really no etiquette in this situation." An awkward silence stretched between them. Jenny studied her sister's face, as she sometimes did, seeking something—any-thing—they shared in common. A certain tilt of the eyes? The shape of jaw, chin, cheekbone? Their father swore they looked like sisters, but Jenny believed it was wishful thinking. "Listen, there is something you can help with. I'm going to need some clothes."

"You're going to need everything," Olivia added. "I'll drive."

Finally, Jenny felt it—the relief and gratitude of knowing someone wanted to look after her. She went over to Rourke. "Are we done here?"

"For now. The fire investigator is going to be working most of the day."

"All right. I'm going with Oliv—my sister—to pick up a few things." She felt a curious satisfaction at saying it aloud. *My sister.*

"Call me," he said.

There was no excuse not to. Her cell phone had been in her purse, safe from the fire, and Rourke had already replaced the charger. She got in the car with Olivia, the heated leather seat sighing luxuriously beneath her. Further proof that the rich were different. Even their cars felt special.

"Where are you staying?" Olivia asked.

Jenny didn't say anything, but her glance in Rourke's direction gave her away.

"You're staying at his place?"

"It's just temporary."

"I'm not saying anything is wrong with it," Olivia clarified. "But…Rourke McKnight? I mean, if you put that together with the picture of the two of you on the front page of the paper, then, I don't know—it starts to look…"

"Like what?"

"Like something. Like you two are—"

"Me and Rourke?" Jenny shook her head, wondering how much Olivia knew about their history. "Not in this life."

"Never say never. That's what I said about Connor, and look at us now. Next summer, I'll be married."

"I think you're the only one who's surprised by that."

"How do you mean?"

"You and Connor are made for each other. Anyone can see that."

Olivia beamed at her. "You know, you're welcome to stay with us."

No offense, thought Jenny, but I'd rather have a root canal. Olivia and Connor lived on the most gorgeous parcel of riverfront land in the area. They were building a house of stone and timber and romantic dreams, and Jenny had no doubt that a blissful future awaited them. However, the house was only half finished, so Olivia and Connor were living on the property in a vintage Airstream trailer. Not exactly made for overnight guests. "That's really nice of you. But I'll pass, thanks."

"I don't blame you. I wouldn't stay there, either, if I didn't know it was only temporary. Connor promises to be done by April," Olivia said. "I keep reminding myself that he's a contractor. Isn't it true that they always underestimate?"

"Not to their fiancées, I hope."

Before Olivia pulled away from the curb, Nina Romano arrived in a battered pickup and motioned for them to lower the window. Jenny's best friend was as unpretentious as she was loyal. She often dressed in clothes that might have come from a rummage sale in Woodstock, causing her opponents to label her the "happy hippie." Yet her earnest dedication to the community, coupled with a no-nonsense way of getting things done, made her popular enough to be elected mayor.

"I heard you've moved in with Rourke," she said without preamble. She peered into the SUV. "Hi, Olivia."

Olivia smiled in greeting. "I just love small-town life. You never run out of things to talk about."

"I haven't 'moved in' with Rourke," Jenny said. A blush crept up her face.

"That's not what I heard," Nina said.

"Listen, he found me at the bakery in the middle of the night and told me my house was toast. I went back to his place because I was dog tired and it was too early to bother anyone else. I'm still there because…" She stopped short of telling them about his coffee-making skills, the thread count of his sheets and the undeniable feeling of security she got from being with him.

Nina sniffled and blew her nose. "Sorry. I caught a bug at the hotel in Albany. You could have gone to my place," she said. "I was out of town, but Sonnet wouldn't have minded."

Jenny knew that Nina didn't have room for company any more than Olivia did. Nina and her teenage daughter lived in a tiny bungalow. The office of mayor was practically a volunteer position, the salary was so low. "Thanks," Jenny said, "but like I said, it's only until I figure out what to do next."

Nina, as usual, was a whirlwind of business. Her cell phone went off and she had to race for an appointment. "Call me," she mouthed, and then put her truck in gear.

Jenny and Olivia drove to the town's main square, where the bakery stood shoulder to shoulder with a jewelry store, a bookstore and various other boutiques and tourist shops. They headed for a boutique called Zuzu's Petals, a favorite for women's clothing.

It was unexpectedly pleasant, shopping with her sister. And undeniably liberating to start from scratch with a whole new wardrobe. She insisted on keeping purchases to a minimum. "I have a feeling I'm going to be traveling light for a while," she said. "I still can't quite believe everything's gone."

Olivia's eyes misted. "Oh, Jenny." She pulled out her cell phone. "We need to tell Dad, right away."

"No, we don't." Jenny didn't think of her father as "Dad." Perhaps she never would. Until last summer, the only information she had about him was the cryptic notation on her birth certificate: "Father Unknown." Once they had discovered each other, they both made an effort to get to know one another. Still, in her mind, he wasn't Dad but Philip. A nice enough gentleman who, many years ago, had the poor judgment to fall for Jenny's mother, Mariska.

"All right," Olivia conceded. "But you should tell him what happened."

"I will. I'll call him later."

"And…" Olivia hesitated, her cheeks coloring with a blush. "I should also warn you, my mother and *her* parents—the Lightsey side of the family—are planning to come up soon to help me with the wedding."

"Of course," Jenny said. "I appreciate the heads-up, though."

"Is it going to be awkward for you, seeing them?"

Seeing the woman their father had married after being dumped by Mariska? How could that not be awkward? "We're all grown-ups. We'll deal."

"Thanks. My mom's parents and Nana and Grandpa Bellamy have been friends forever. I think between the four of them, they decided my mom and dad would marry long before my parents even met. That might be why they ultimately got divorced. Maybe the marriage wasn't their idea in the first place."

To Jenny's discomfiture, she could too easily imagine marrying someone because it was the right thing to do, the practical thing. She had almost done exactly that, long ago. She skirted the thought and accepted the bra. Olivia had excellent taste. Jenny picked out seven pairs of underwear. Though the sexy wisps of lace caught her eye, she selected plain beige hip-huggers. She needed to be practical.

Olivia moved on to a display of pajamas, holding up and then discarding a frumpy high-necked nightgown. She held a pink baby-doll top up to Jenny and nodded her approval.

"Maybe it was meant to be, you staying with Rourke."

"Believe me, it wasn't."

"You never know. Look at me. If anyone had told me I'd wind up living in a trailer with an ex-con, I would have thought they were joking. My mother practically went into therapy when I gave her the news. It was a jolt, you know. Last May I was dating an heir to the Whitney fortune, a guy who was once featured in *Vanity Fair.* By the end of summer, I'd fallen in love with Connor Davis. So it just goes to show you."

"Show you what?"

"You don't always get to pick who you fall in love with. Sometimes love picks you."

"Why do I get the sense that you're trying to tell me something?"

"I'm not," Olivia said, tossing her the pink baby dolls. "Not yet, anyway."

By the end of the day, Jenny had discovered a new level of fatigue. Until now, she had taken the concept of "home" for granted, as most people did. The simple knowledge that your home—your favorite chair, your stereo, your bed, the stack of books on your nightstand—was waiting at the end of the day was a true source of comfort, something she hadn't thought about until it was gone. Now weariness dragged at her, and she thought wistfully of her own home, her own bed. The moment she stepped inside Rourke's house with her shopping bags, the fatigue hit her like a giant wave.

"You look like you're ready to drop," he said. The dogs came galloping in from their run in the yard, shaking snow from their fur, tails waving in greeting. Clarence, the one-eyed cat, followed, slipping into the fray.

"Good guess," she said.

He fed the animals, talking to them as though they were people, which Jenny found unexpectedly charming. "Move aside, boys," he instructed. "And don't gulp your food. You'll get the hiccups."

Despite her fatigue, she caught herself smiling as the dogs lined themselves up, watching with adoring eyes while he fixed their dinner. Why hadn't she ever adopted a pet? That unconditional love was incredibly nice to come home to.

"How about you?" Rourke asked her. "What do you want for dinner?"

Oh, boy. "Anything. At this point, I'm not picky."

"Good, because I'm not much of a cook."

"You want some help?" she offered.

"Nope. I want you to take a good long shower, because you're going straight to bed afterward."

She thought about his cushy bed and felt a wave of yearning as she headed into the bathroom. The shower, like everything else in his house, was meticulously clean yet oddly generic. She resisted the temptation to snoop in his medicine cabinet. There was, she knew for a fact, such a thing as learning too much information about a person. Besides, the more she learned about Rourke, the deeper his mystery seemed.

After her shower, she put on the soft yoga pants and hoodie she'd bought earlier, combed her hair and went to the kitchen, where Rourke was putting dinner on the table.

"So this is the 'serve' part of 'to protect and serve,'" she commented.

"I take my mission very seriously, even if it's just canned soup and ham on rye. Made with the best rye bread in the known world," he added.

"You have excellent taste in bread," she said, recognizing a loaf of Sky River Bakery's traditional Polish rye. "Did you know the starter for this bread is more than seventy years old?"

He looked blank. Most people did when asked to consider bread starter.

"It's a live culture. You use a bit to make the dough, and cultivate more so it never runs out. My grandmother got it from her mother when she was a new bride in Poland. A traditional wedding gift is the pine box the size of a shoebox for the pottery container. Gram brought the culture in its carved pine box to America in 1945, and she kept it alive all her life."

Rourke slowed down his chewing. "No kidding."

"Like I would make this up?"

"So some part of my sandwich dates back to Poland before World War II." He frowned. "Wait a minute. You didn't lose it in the fire, did you?"

"No. We keep all the bread cultures at the bakery."

"Good. That's something, at least. So if you ever lose it or run out or whatever, can you make a new starter?"

"Sure. But it'll never be exactly the same. Like wine from different vintage years, the aging process adds character. And it's tradition for a mother to pass it on to her daughter in a chain that's never broken." She picked at her sandwich. "Although I guess my own mother took care of that."

"The stuff's safe and sound at the bakery," he said, clearly shying away from the topic of her mother. "That's what matters."

"What, a rye bread starter matters more than my mother?"

"That's not what I said. I didn't mean to bring up a sore subject."

"Believe me, she's not a sore subject, not after all this time. I have bigger worries at the moment."

"You do," he agreed. "And I'm sorry if I said anything to upset you."

How careful he was being with her, Jenny observed. "Listen, I'm going to be okay," she said.

"I never said you weren't."

"That look says otherwise. The way you've been treating me says otherwise."

"What look? What way I've been treating you?"

"You're watching me like I'm a bomb about to go off. And you're treating me with too much care."

"I can honestly say that's the first time a woman has ever accused me of being too caring. So I'm supposed to…what? Apologize?"

She wondered if she should bring up the pact of silence that had governed them for so long. At some point, they were going to have to discuss it. Not now, though. Right now, she was too tired to get into it. "Just cut it out," she said. "It feels strange."

"Fine. I won't be nice anymore. Help me with the dishes." He got up from the table. "Better yet, you do the dishes and I'll see what's on ESPN."

"Not funny, McKnight," she said.

They ended up loading the dishwasher together. She noticed a small, framed photograph on the windowsill over the sink. It was one of the few personal items in the house, and she wasn't in the least surprised to discover it was a picture of Joey Santini, Rourke's boyhood best friend—and also the man to whom Jenny had been engaged. The shot showed Joey, a soldier in the 75th Ranger Regiment, serving in the Komar Province of Afghanistan. Against a desolate airstrip with a Chinook cargo helicopter in the background, he looked completely happy, because that was Joey—happy to be alive, no matter what. In his sand-colored BDUs, his elbow propped on a jeep, he was laughing into the camera, in love with the world, with life itself, even in the midst of the scorched earth of battle.

"I have that same picture," Jenny said. "Or, *had.* It was in the fire."

"I'll make you a copy."

It was on the tip of her tongue to ask him if he ever thought of Joey, but she didn't have to ask. She knew the answer: *Every day.*

"I have dessert," Rourke said, shutting the dishwasher and cranking the dial. Apparently, he considered the subject closed.

"I'm not eating a Ho Ho."

"Ice-cream cones," he said.

"The perfect winter dessert."

He fixed her three fist-size scoops, ignoring her when she protested the size. Then they sat down on the sofa, and both dived for the remote control. He beat her to it, and even though she whined, he refused to watch *Project Runway,* insisting instead on a classic rerun of *American Chopper.* Tucking the remote between his hip and a sofa cushion, he said, "Now you can't accuse me of being too nice."

She licked her ice cream and watched the careful, intricate assembly of something called—in tones of reverence—a master cylinder. Her eyes started to glaze over. "Can't we compromise?" she asked. "Maybe watch one of those crime investigation shows?"

"You mean the ones that make police work look noble and sexy?"

"What, it's not noble and sexy?" she asked.

"Honestly, it's detail work. I spent half the day inventorying cruisers, which was completely depressing, since the budget doesn't allow for equipment upgrades for another two years. Either the city administrator is an idiot, or he's Scrooge."

"Matthew Alger, you mean."

He nodded.

"Then why do police work if it's all boring details?" she asked.

"Because it's my job," he said simply, staring at the TV screen.

"But why is it your job? You could have picked anything you wanted, gone anywhere. Instead, you picked this little mountain town where nothing ever happens."

A commercial came on, and he turned to face her. "Maybe I'm waiting for something to happen," he said.

She was dying to ask him to elaborate but didn't want to seem too interested. "And here I thought being a cop was one adventure after another."

"Hate to burst your bubble, but it's not noble and sexy. Now, making buttermilk pie and raspberry kolaches—that's sexy."

"Well, then, I hate to burst *your* bubble, but I don't do the baking."

"So? You're still sexy."

In spite of herself, Jenny grew flushed. It was stupid, at her age, getting flustered over something some guy said. Especially a guy like Rourke McKnight. She tried to pretend she wasn't affected, even though she felt a sting of heat in her cheeks. Good lord, were they flirting? This was getting complicated but…irresistible. "Now, what part of protect and serve is that?" she asked, trying for a light tone.

"It's got nothing to do with the job. And you're blushing."

"I'm not."

"Sure you are. I like it. I like that I can make you blush."

And with such pathetic ease, she thought. They had a rhythm still. They always had. She'd spent years trying to forget but it all came back. "I'll keep that in mind. You're really easy to please, Chief McKnight."

"I always have been," he said. "You of all people should know that."

Food for Thought

by Jenny Majesky

Pine Box Traditions

It's a Polish wedding tradition to give a new bride a supply of starter for sourdough rye bread. I suspect it's a combination of tradition and desperation on the part of the bride. It just doesn't seem fair to add the pressure of making a good bread right out of the gate to everything else the poor girl is juggling.

My grandmother told me that the day before her wedding, when she was just a scared girl of eighteen, her mother gave her a carved pine box, just like the one that had sat on a shelf above the kitchen stove all her life. It's kind of nice, really, thinking of that chain of women, spanning the decades and centuries.

Now, the reality of today's world is that new brides don't give a hoot about making bread. However, if the breadmaking mood strikes you, here's a recipe with a starter that only takes one night to set up. The process begins somewhat mysteriously. Flour, buttermilk and onion meld together in the beginnings of a hearty bread.

POLISH SOURDOUGH RYE BREAD

2 (.25-ounce) packages active dry yeast
1 teaspoon white sugar
2 cups water
1 thick slice onion
4 cups rye flour

1 cup buttermilk, room temperature
1 teaspoon baking soda
1 tablespoon salt
8 cups bread flour
1 tablespoon caraway seeds (optional)

The night before making the bread, in a medium-size mixing bowl, dissolve one packet of yeast and the sugar in the water. Let stand until creamy, about 10 minutes. Stir in rye flour until mixture is smooth. Slip onion slice in. Cover and let stand overnight then remove onion.

The next day, dissolve remaining package of yeast in buttermilk. Add rye flour mixture, baking soda, salt, 4 cups of the bread flour and stir to combine. Add the remaining 4 cups of bread flour, 1/2 cup at a time, stirring well after each addition (you may not need to add all the flour). When dough has become a smooth and coherent mass, turn it out onto a lightly floured surface and knead until smooth and supple, about 8 minutes. Sprinkle caraway seeds on dough and knead them in until evenly distributed throughout.

Lightly oil a large mixing bowl. Place dough in the bowl and turn to coat with the oil. Cover with damp cloth and let rise in a warm place for about 1 hour or until volume has doubled.

Preheat oven to 350°F.

Turn dough onto a lightly floured surface and divide into three pieces. Form each piece into a loaf and place in 3 lightly greased 9 x 5-inch bread pans. Cover and let rise until nearly doubled, about 1 hour.

Bake at 350°F for about 35 minutes or until the loaves sound hollow when tapped.

Six

Summer 1988

Rourke McKnight tried not to act too excited about going to summer camp. He was afraid that if he showed even the smallest amount of pleasurable anticipation, his father would forbid him to go. During the limo ride down Avenue of the Americas to Grand Central Station, Rourke sat quietly, watching the traffic through tinted, bulletproof windows. It was raining, the hard, summer kind of rain that caused geysers of steam to rise from the asphalt.

His best friend, Joey Santini, was riding in the front seat with Joey's dad. Mr. Santini had been the McKnight family driver since the beginning of time, as far as Rourke knew. It was just a total stroke of luck that Joey was Rourke's age and that father and son—there was no Mrs. Santini, not anymore—lived in the service quarters of the McKnights' building. This was a good thing, since otherwise Rourke would have grown up with no one to play with except Mrs. Grummond's Dandie Dinmont terriers. Although the sliding glass privacy window was shut, Rourke could see Joey and Mr. Santini laughing and talking the whole way, in contrast to the quiet, tense occupants of the luxurious back of the limo.

Even though he was twelve years old, Rourke had never been to camp before. His father was against it, of course, and when his father said no, that was that. Period. End of story.

But everything changed when two things happened the same week—the Bellamy family made a big contribution to the senator's campaign, and Drayton McKnight was given a rare appointment to a committee that was going on a lengthy junket to the Far East to discuss trade agreements that would benefit his district.

Now it made perfect sense to send Rourke away for the summer, to the Bellamys' Camp Kioga in the Catskills wilderness. When Rourke's mother was young, she had gone to Camp Kioga, and she thought Rourke should, too.

Rourke had to act all bummed out that he'd be away from his parents all summer. He had to pretend he was just as worried about his own well-being as his father was. He even had to pretend that he wasn't excited about the fact that Joey would be going to camp, too, so the boys could look out for each other. Rourke knew for a fact that this camp cost an arm and a leg, which his family could easily afford. Not Joey's, though. He was going to camp on scholarship, which meant Rourke's father was secretly picking up the tab.

Not out of the goodness of his heart, though. Rourke's father was completely paranoid. That was what Rourke figured, anyway. The guy was freaked. He was sending Joey to camp so Rourke wouldn't be alone among strangers. In a way, worrying about attacks on his family probably made the senator feel important. And that was what Drayton McKnight was all about—feeling important.

That, and being perfect. No, thought Rourke. *Looking* perfect. Looking like you had the perfect family and the perfect life. "Make me proud" was the phrase Rourke heard most often from his father. It was a sort of code. By now, Rourke had figured that out. It meant he had to win at every sport he played. Get straight A's in school. Learn to use his looks and confident smile to win people over so they would vote for his father each election year.

All that stuff, it was so easy. He was big and strong and had no problem conquering any sport he tackled. And getting good grades? All you really had to do was listen to what the teacher said and figure out what he wanted you to say back to him. Rourke was a politician's son. He knew how to do that.

He couldn't wait to get to Camp Kioga, where nobody cared what his grades were. He pinched the inside of his lip between his teeth to keep from smiling.

"Your hair is too long," his father said suddenly. "Julia, why didn't he get a haircut before we let him run wild all summer?"

Rourke didn't move. This was a crucial moment. On a whim, his father might decide they needed to head right back uptown, to the ancient barbershop where electric clippers were used to buzz white sidewalls around the ears of hapless boys.

He kept staring out the window. Raindrops raced backward across the glass, the silver tracks like streams of mercury. He spotted two of them that were neck and neck, and picked one as the winner, tensing as it pulled ahead and then fell back. Finally, the raindrop merged with the others and he lost track.

"He did have a haircut," Rourke's mother said. She was using her soothing, reassuring voice. The one she used when she didn't want Rourke's dad to get upset. "It's the same cut he always gets."

"He looks like a girl," the senator remarked. He leaned forward, closer to Rourke. "You want to spend the summer looking like a girl?"

"No, sir." Rourke kept staring at the rain-smeared window. He held his breath, praying his dad wouldn't order the driver to turn uptown.

"It's fine, really," Rourke's mother said.

Way to tell him, Mom, Rourke thought cynically. Way to stand up to the bastard.

"Mildred Van Deusen told me all three of her boys will be on the same train," his mother continued. "Rourke, you ought to see if you can find them. Maybe you can sit with them."

Bingo, Rourke thought, watching his father's interest shift.

Rourke had to hand it to his mom. She might not be any good at standing up to his dad, but she sure as heck knew about diversionary tactics. The Van Deusens were one of the richest, most important families in the district, and anytime Rourke's dad saw a chance to connect with them, he jumped on it.

"I'll be sure to look for them," Rourke said.

"You do that, son," his dad said, apparently forgetting about the haircut.

"Yes, sir."

And then, thank God, they arrived at Grand Central. There was a mad shuffle as they got his backpack and duffel bag out of the trunk and made sure he had his ticket and travel documents. The honking of taxi horns and whistles and shouts of porters filled the air. The marble archway opened to a salon that swarmed with travelers and panhandlers, vendors and performers. Mr. Santini came around with an umbrella, sheltering the three McKnights from the rain. Joey didn't bother trying to fit under the umbrella; he yanked up the hood of his windbreaker, leaped across a puddle and was the first to reach the awning of the station.

Rourke walked between his parents through the entryway. After parking the car, Mr. Santini slipped away to join Joey. The McKnights stopped below the big lighted display board, where they verified the track number and the fact that the train was on time. Some of the people they passed gave them admiring looks. This happened a lot when Rourke was out with his parents. Together, the three of them looked like the all-American family—blond and healthy, well-dressed, prosperous. Sometimes Rourke even sensed envy from people, as if they wanted what the McKnights had.

If only they knew.

Rourke sidled away from his parents. He and Joey exchanged a glance. Sheer delight danced in Joey's eyes. Some of the girls in their soccer league said Joey looked like one of the New Kids on the Block. Rourke didn't know about that, but Joey's grin was infectious. *Camp,* Rourke exulted, and he knew Joey understood his silent glee. *We're going away to camp.*

Rourke wondered if Joey understood how big this was, and how much he owed Joey himself. If not for Joey, Rourke wouldn't be going anywhere. When the subject of Camp Kioga first came up, the senator had immediately dismissed the idea. It had been Joey who had—in that casual way of his—named off all the kids from school who were going to summer camp. He'd pretended he was talking to Rourke, but he was careful to mention all the most important families, the kind of people Rourke's father admired and whose support he cultivated. Rourke had convinced his parents that it was a good idea to send Joey, too, and that had tipped the decision in his favor.

When they reached the track, Rourke said his goodbyes. He and the senator shook hands, his father's grip crushing hard for a few seconds, as if to leave some sort of imprint. "Never forget who you are," his father advised. "Make this family proud."

Rourke looked him in the eye. "Yes, sir."

Then his father's attention wandered as he scanned the platform. Here he was, saying goodbye to his kid for ten whole weeks, and he was working the room, looking for constituents.

At least it gave Rourke's mother a few extra seconds for her own goodbyes. She held him close. He was a little bit taller than her now, so it was easy for her to whisper in his ear while hugging him.

"You are going to have an amazing time," she said. "Camp Kioga is just…magical."

"Julia." The senator's voice cut through the moment. "We have to go."

She gave Rourke one final squeeze. "Don't forget to write."

"I won't."

He stood on the platform and watched them walk away, slender and fashionable in their raincoats. His mother tucked her hand into the crook of her husband's arm. Rourke blurred his eyes, and his parents melted together so they weren't two separate people anymore, but one single being. SenatorandMrs.McKnight.

All around him, he could hear kids and parents saying goodbye. Some of the girls and mothers were shedding real tears, professing that they'd miss each other horribly and write every day. Mr. Santini, a big bear of a man, yanked Joey in for a hug, kissing the top of the boy's head with a loud *smack.* "I'm gonna miss you like ice-cream sundaes, sonny-boy," said Mr. Santini, unabashedly crying.

Rourke wondered what it would be like to have the kind of family you'd actually miss when you left them.

Camp Kioga was as magical as Rourke's mother had promised. He and Joey shared quarters with ten other guys in a long wooden bunkhouse called Ticonderoga Cabin. Every single day was packed with activities—sports and crafts, nature hikes, rock climbing, sailing and canoeing on Willow Lake, stories around the campfire at night. They had to sing and dance some nights, which Rourke could definitely do without, but since everyone had to participate, there was no getting around it.

One thing Rourke was good at was putting up with something he didn't feel like doing. And he sure as hell had endured worse than leading some giggling, sweaty-handed girl around the dance floor, muttering *quick-quick, slooow, quick-quick, slooow* under his breath in time to the music.

At camp, he met several Bellamys. Mr. and Mrs. Charles Bellamy, the owners and directors, seemed kind enough. "Your father's wilderness-conservation bill means the world to us. Thanks to that bit of legislation, we don't have to worry about industry closing in on us," Mrs. Bellamy had said on opening day. "You must be quite proud of him."

"Yes, ma'am." Rourke didn't know what else to say. *Yes, he's a good public servant but a complete bastard in private*—that would go over like a fart in church.

"We're very glad you're here," Mrs. Bellamy went on. "I remember your mother. Julia—Delaney, wasn't that her maiden name?"

"Yes, ma'am."

"She was a favorite. So full of fun. She used to play practical jokes all the time, and on talent night, she did a stand-up-comic routine that had us all in stitches."

Rourke didn't believe her, but then, one rainy day when outdoor activities were canceled and Joey was gone on a solo expedition, she showed him some of the camp's treasured photo albums housed in the library. The collection was in the main pavilion, a gigantic timber building from the 1930s. It was the heart of Camp Kioga, housing the dining hall, library, infirmary, the kitchen and camp offices.

And sure enough, there were several snapshots of his mom in the 1970s, hamming it up. She wore a smile Rourke had never seen before. She looked so completely happy that he almost didn't recognize her.

He thanked Mrs. Bellamy for showing him some of the camp's history. He lingered in the library until the rain let up, perusing the books, from Hardy Boys mysteries to birding manuals, classics by Thoreau and Washington Irving, and the inevitable collections of ghost stories. Long after the rain stopped, he sat looking through books, trying to imagine a different life for himself. When they were little, he and Joey always talked about joining the army together and traveling the world, but as they grew older, the fantasy dimmed. By the seventh grade, Rourke was already feeling the crushing weight of his father's expectations, and Joey was now aware of the realities of working-class life.

Rourke wondered what Joey was doing, out on his solo expedition. It was something each boy was expected to do at least once over the summer. You had to gear up and spend an entire night alone on Spruce Island, a small island in the middle of Willow Lake. The head counselor, Greg Bellamy—the younger son of the directors—said, "It's supposed to build character. And if it scares the shit out of you, at least it'll keep your bowels open." You were supposed to make a fire and contemplate deep things, although Rourke suspected Joey was just whacking off, which was pretty much the favorite thing of any guy their age.

The beeping sound of a truck backing up distracted him. He went to the window and saw a boxy white panel van. The sides of the truck were painted with a rushing river and "Sky River Bakery—Established 1952" in fancy lettering.

Rourke was already a fan of the camp's kitchen, and the baked goods in particular. The bread and rolls, Danishes, donuts and desserts were incredible.

He was about to turn back to the book collection when he noticed three guys sneaking up on the truck. They were guys from his cabin—Jacobs, Trent and Robson—and he didn't know them very well, but he knew they were jerks. They tended to pick on weaker kids, which meant they didn't bother Rourke. In fact, they seemed to think he was one of them, even though he never joined in when they decided to pick on somebody.

At the moment, they weren't bullying anybody but they were stealing. They had sneaked into the back of the truck and were helping themselves to all the cookies they could stuff in their mouths and pockets from the tall, rolling racks.

Jerks. This was somebody's livelihood. Although Rourke had no experience at earning a living, he knew what it was like because of Joey and his father. Rourke knew that somebody driving a bakery delivery truck probably couldn't afford to give away cookies by the dozen to rich kids at camp.

This put him in an uncomfortable position. If he told the guys to cut it out, he'd be labeled a snitch by his bunkmates for the rest of the summer. If he ignored what was going on, he'd hate himself for a coward.

When Trent picked up what appeared to be a whole blueberry pie, Rourke made up his mind. He was about to head outside when someone got out of the truck—a dark-haired girl who had apparently been sitting in the passenger seat. She was about Rourke's age, maybe a little younger. Her hair was in two braids and she wore cutoffs, a red T-shirt and unlaced sneakers. She was just some girl.

Except, when he looked at her, Rourke felt funny, although he couldn't put his finger on the reason why. She had a kind of old-fashioned, big-eyed prettiness and a quizzical expression on her face.

And right now, she was being robbed.

Maybe. He couldn't hear what she was saying but the three guys sure as heck weren't listening. They kept helping themselves to pastries and rolls. They were probably stuffed by now, but kept grabbing things anyway.

The girl was still talking. Maybe she was in on the prank with the guys. Maybe it was fine for her to stand by and watch them steal.

Or maybe Rourke was reading the situation all wrong.

He bolted for the exit and ran down the stairs and around the kitchen from the outside. Through a window he could see the truck driver—an older guy—sitting down and having a chat with Mrs. Romano, who ran the kitchen. They seemed oblivious to the go-ings-on outside. The tinny sound of a radio drifted to his ears.

He came around the side of the building in time to see…well, now. He wasn't sure what he was seeing. Trent had the girl pressed against the side of the truck and they were…gross, were they making out? He was about to turn away in disgust when he noticed one small, telling detail. Trent wasn't holding her hand, but her wrist, pinned against the side of the truck. Her hand was raised in fear like the hand of a drowning person about to go under for the last time.

Something happened to Rourke. He could have sworn he heard a popping sound go off in his ears. And he went all hot as though suddenly surrounded by a forest fire. "Get the hell away from her," he said, a low-voiced command that caused all three of them to turn toward him.

Trent grinned. "Hey, McKnight. Have a donut and wait your turn."

Rourke was close enough now to see a sheen of sweat on the girl's upper lip and the stark look of fear on her face. He grabbed Trent and yanked him away from the girl in a swift, violent motion. Trent was a big, solid guy, already a member of the eighth-grade wrestling squad at his school, but he felt like nothing as Rourke slammed him to the ground.

The other two recovered from their surprise and leaped on Rourke. He barely even slowed down. Jerking his head up, he smashed Jacobs in the face with the back of his skull. He slammed an elbow into Robson, who staggered, the wind knocked out of him. Trent threw a few punches but Rourke barely felt them. He didn't punch in return but pounded with both fists, methodically and mindlessly, ignoring Trent's bleating pleas for mercy.

Finally, something broke through the rage. Rourke wasn't sure how he was even able to sense the light, fluttery touch at his shoulder.

"Stop," said a quiet, trembling voice. "That's enough."

Rourke's inner fire glimmered and went out. Trent scrambled to his feet, his bloody, swollen face a mask of fear. "Jesus Christ," he said, catching a drop of blood with the back of his hand. "You could have killed me. You're crazy, man. You're fucking insane."

His friends led him off, probably to the infirmary. Rourke watched them go. His insides felt absolutely empty, scoured by rage.

"Hey," said the girl.

His attention snapped to her and she jumped back, hands raised in self-protection. All of a sudden he felt sheepish, as though she'd seen him naked or something. "Hey," he said, and forced himself to relax, to show her he meant no harm.

"There's a first-aid kit in the truck. Come on." She went around the side of the panel truck and took out a well-stocked first-aid kit. "Hold out your hands," she said.

He was amazed to see that the skin of his knuckles was red and broken in several places. She dabbed at the raw spots with an antiseptic wipe, then used some sort of liquid from a bottle to brush a stinging film over the broken skin and then cover the cuts with Band-Aids.

Though surprised by the violence of his response to Trent,

Rourke had to admit to himself that this was not the first time he'd gone all defensive on behalf of somebody else. There was something that happened to him. He hated, absolutely freaking hated, seeing a person—anyone, even a dog—being bullied by someone else. It made him—how had Trent put it?—fucking insane. Last year, when he'd seen some guys from Joey's school teasing Joey about his long hair and baby face, Rourke had run the guys off with little more than a threat delivered with low-voiced menace. If it had come to blows, he might have done something permanent to them.

"Now I need to do your cheek," the girl said.

"My cheek?" Rourke angled the truck's side mirror and was amazed to see a livid cut high on his cheekbone. "I didn't even feel that happen," he said.

She used a fresh antiseptic wipe to clean the cut. "It's not bleeding very much but you might need stitches."

"No way. Then they'd have to report it to my parents and I'd get sent home." He didn't think he could stand it if he had to leave camp now. And if they called his parents, his mother would probably have him airlifted to Mount Sinai for plastic surgery, to save his face.

Up close, the girl was even prettier than she seemed from far away. He could see the gold and brown facets of her eyes. He could see a constellation of freckles scattered across her nose. And he could smell her scent, something like Kool-Aid. Some completely alien part of him suddenly understood why Trent had been so determined to steal a kiss.

Cut it out, Rourke told himself. Don't even think about it. Yet he was surprised to see that she was staring at him, too, at his mouth and at his chest where his torn shirt gaped open.

Then she blushed and got busy. She peeled open two Band-Aids and covered the cut on his cheekbone. "It's gonna scar."

"I don't care."

She snapped the first-aid kit shut. "So you don't think you'll get in trouble?" she repeated.

He narrowed his eyes. "That's kind of up to you."

She narrowed her eyes right back at him, as if calling his bluff. "What do you mean, up to me?"

"Depends on how bad you want those guys to pay for stealing and for—" He didn't even want to say it. "For messing with you."

"Why does it depend on me? Suppose that boy with the bleeding mouth squeals on you."

"Trent? No way. If he says I hit him, he knows I'll say why— that they were stealing, and that he—" Rourke paused again, studied her. "Did he hurt you?"

She absently rubbed her wrist. "I'm okay."

He wasn't sure whether or not to believe her. She seemed a little embarrassed, so he didn't push for an answer. "Anyway," he continued, "they don't want to get in trouble any more than I do, so they'll keep their mouths shut."

"I see."

"I could make them pay for the stuff they stole—"

"No," she said quickly. "I think you already made them pay. It wasn't that much stuff, anyway."

He looked at the blueberry pie, now spreading a purple stain in the mud. "You're not going to get in trouble either?" he asked.

For the first time, she smiled. And when she did, something crazy happened to Rourke. It was completely random, but suddenly the world seemed different just because she was smiling. He half expected some kind of theme song to start playing.

"The driver's my grandfather," she said. "I never get in trouble with him."

"That's good." He found an old newspaper and cleaned up the worst of the pie. "I'm Rourke," he added, realizing they didn't know each other's names. "Rourke McKnight."

"I'm Jenny Majesky," she said. "My grandparents have the Sky River Bakery in town. I'm working for them this summer. Saving up to get my own computer."

"Your own computer," he echoed like an idiot. Being around this girl pretty much sucked all the brains out of his head.

"Yes. A notebook computer that runs on batteries so you can take it anywhere with you."

"Oh. So you must really like computer games."

The smile flashed again. "I want it for writing. I like to write."

God. That was like doing homework without even being told. "What do you write?"

"Stories, poems, things that happen to me." She reached under the passenger seat of the truck and pulled out a thick spiral-bound notebook. Flipping through it, she showed him page after page covered with writing in bright turquoise ink.

"You wrote all that?" he asked.

"Yes."

"How long did it take you?"

She shrugged. "I don't keep track."

"Are you going to write about—about today?" he couldn't help asking.

"Are you kidding? Of course I am."

He found himself wondering what she would write about him. To his surprise, he realized that it mattered. He liked this girl as much has he'd ever liked any girl.

They heard a clatter from the kitchen, the sound of a rack being rolled toward the door.

"My grandfather," Jenny said. "I'll be leaving soon."

Don't go, he thought. "Listen, you shouldn't be afraid to come back here. I'll make sure those guys don't mess with you again."

"I'm not scared of them." She paused, took a step back, folding her arms protectively across her chest. "The scariest thing about today was you."

What the heck…? He sure hadn't expected that.

"Rourke," someone called. *Joey.* Back from his solo expedition. "There you are. I've been looking all over camp for you." He arrived from the lakefront, still wearing his backpack and clanking with gear.

Sure, they were best friends, but just this once, Rourke wasn't all that glad to see Joey. Rourke was having a real actual conversation with a real actual girl, and he wanted her all to himself. There wasn't anything he could do about it, though. He introduced them, feeling formal and awkward as he did so.

Joey wasn't awkward at all. He grinned from ear to ear, shook back his long black hair, turned on his boy-band charm, then launched into an animated account of his solo adventure in the wilderness. He'd only been gone two days, yet he seemed…different. More sure of himself, maybe.

"What's up with the Band-Aids?" he asked Rourke.

"Trent," was all Rourke said. It was all he had to say. Joey got it.

Jenny Majesky didn't even seem to mind that Joey was filthy and sweating. "Are you hungry?" she asked.

"Does a bear crap in the woods?" Joey replied.

"I guess you'd know," she said, and headed to the racks in the back of the truck. "Maple bars," she said. "They're my favorites." She handed one to him and then one to Rourke.

"Thanks," he said, but Joey was already gabbing away, some story about seeing the red eyes of wild animals at night.

And Rourke's heart sank. Because it was already too late. Now Joey was checking her out, too. And Rourke knew that when two best friends wanted the same thing, it could only mean trouble.

Seven

July 3, 1988

Dear Mom,
   This morning I was working behind the counter so Laura could get caught up on the books. When I was little, I used to feel really important, standing on a step stool behind the curved glass cases while people agonized over their choices. Kolache or cruller? Napoleon or cream puff? I suppose you could say it gave me a sense of power, having what they want so bad. Badly. I always get the -ly words mixed up, sorry.
   And then this morning the Alger family came in, Mr. and Mrs. Alger and their little boy, Zach, who is about as cute as a kid on a Cheerios commercial. They have a big house up on the River Road and a new car every year.
   They make me uncomfortable for several reasons. The top three are:

1. They are just a totally normal family, so traditional, it makes me feel like a freak, because our own family is so totally *not* traditional.
2. Mr. Alger is always asking me if I remember stuff about

you, even though everybody in town knows I was really little when you took off. I would probably be carted off to the tee-hee farm if people knew all these diary entries are letters to you. But then again, maybe not. Anne Frank called her diary "Dear Kitty" so maybe it's not that weird for me to call mine "Dear Mom."

3. Mrs. Alger feels sorry for me, and she doesn't even try to hide it. I hate that. I hate it anytime somebody thinks I'm this pathetic orphan and starts feeling sorry for me.

As soon as they left, I told Gram and Laura I wanted to do deliveries with Grandpa on the afternoon run. I had to get out. Because sometimes the bakery smells like safety—warm and sweet. But other times, like today, that same smell presses down on me and it's hard to breathe.

"Such a glorious summer day," Laura said. "You should be out in the fresh air."

Laura always understands me. She says she's like a second mom to me but that's not quite right. In order to have a second mom, I'd need a first, and I don't have that. I tell people you are doing undercover work for the government. When I was little, I thought they believed me but now I can see it in their faces—people think you took off and never came back because you didn't want the trouble of raising a kid by yourself.

Well, you know what? I'm really not that much trouble. Ask anybody.

Like today, Grandpa was happy to let me ride along in the truck. He just retired from the glassworks down in Kingston. He's hard of hearing on account of the noise at the plant. Now he helps out at the bakery and, every chance he gets, he goes fishing at Willow Lake. He's friends with Mr. Bellamy, who owns the lake and Camp Kioga.

Fishing is Grandpa's passion, and he does it year round, even in the dead of winter, when he has to walk out on the frozen lake and make a hole in the ice that's a foot thick. Sometimes he has to borrow a snowmobile to get up to Willow Lake because the roads aren't plowed. He says he likes being all by himself in the middle of nowhere.

Sometimes I go with him, but to me fishing is Boring with a capital B. I mean, you sit and wait for some random fish to take the bait, and then you yank it out of the water, take it home, fillet and eat it. What a lot of trouble when you can just open a can of tuna from the pantry anytime you want.

When I say this to Grandpa, he chuckles and says *mój misiaczku,* which as you probably know means *my little bear* in Polish. He tells me fishing is not about what you take from the water. It's about what you give to the silence. Or something like that. It sounds better in Polish. Here's the funny thing about Grandpa. When he talks in English, he sounds like Yoda. He really does. And with his bald head that only has, like, nine hairs sprouting from it, he kind of looks like Yoda.

So I try not to squirm too much when he takes me fishing. Mostly, I daydream the usual daydream (I've told you about this before) of moving to the city and being a famous writer, and one day I'm having a book signing and my fans are lined up out the door, like I'm Judy Blume or R.L. Stine. And that's when I look up from signing books and there you are, Mom, looking just like you do in the pictures, and you smile and tell me how proud you are of me.

And I don't even ask you where you've been all these years and why you went away, because it's my daydream and I know there's no good explanation or excuse, so the subject doesn't even come up. We just go for a Cherry Coke or egg cream, and we go shoe shopping and everything is perfect.

When he's fishing, Grandpa thinks about you, too, but not the way I do. He thinks about the past, when you used to be his daughter. He tells me how you loved fishing as much as he did and even when you grew up and had me, you would still go fishing with him.

He said you made your own sinkers at night in the kitchen, melting the solder—which has a low boiling point, which I know because we studied chemistry in school—over the stove and pouring it into the molds shaped like upside-down pyramids while the radio played.

And that's when I start to remember, just a little. Okay, maybe it's not an actual memory, maybe I just think I remember because Grandpa has told me the story so many times. I'm in the kitchen, sitting at the scrubbed pine table that smells like kitchen Lysol. And you're standing at the stove and singing to the radio. I even know what song you're singing because it's the Jenny song. It really is: "867-5309/Jenny," by Tommy Tutone.

Jenny is an okay name, I guess. Even though the guy singing the song got it off a bathroom wall.

But really, it's kind of a happy, bouncy tune and I have a perfect memory of you with your hair held back in a butterfly clip, wearing one of Gram's aprons, singing along while you make fishing sinkers.

At some point in the memory, Gram comes in and she scolds you for using her good gravy pan and now it's contaminated and she'll have to go out and get a new pan.

I remember your laugh and the sparkle in your eyes when you say, "Ma, I'll buy you a hundred gravy pans! And a servant to make the gravy, and another to pour it on your potatoes. I'll buy you anything you want!" And then you pick me up and we dance around the room with the Jenny song playing on the radio.

I think that might be my last memory of you. I don't know how much of it is real and how much of it I made up. But I do know all the sinkers you made are still in the bottom of Grandpa's tackle box. He never uses them. He uses shot pellets instead. He says the ones you made are too heavy and besides, he doesn't want to lose them.

Like hanging on to something you made is going to bring you back.

Today Grandpa had a delivery to make to Camp Kioga. In the summer, they're our best customer because they have like a few hundred kids at their summer camp. It was one of those blue-sky-perfect days, and I was glad to be out on deliveries with Grandpa instead of cooped up at the bakery. At the camp, he went inside and I was just sitting, listening to the radio, WKRW, which plays oldies. And you'll never guess which song came on: "867-5309/ Jenny."

I took it as a sign.

It turned out to be a bad sign because three boys from the camp started stealing from the back of the truck. When I first saw them, I got confused. I mean, I've never been stolen from before. It felt really…icky. Like someone was doing something directly to me. I'm feeling icky just remembering.

I'm also very sorry to tell you that I got scared. I almost chickened out and slid down to the floor of the truck to hide until they stole everything they wanted and went away.

There, I admit it. I was scared. What a baby.

In social studies, I once wrote a report on Eleanor Roosevelt and she said a lot of famous quotes. One of them I memorized is this: "We gain strength, and courage, and confidence by each experience in which we really stop to look fear in the face."

(I get straight A's in school, did I tell you?)

And when I was sitting there frozen while those kids were stealing from the back of the truck, I remembered those words exactly. And I was like, *Okay, Eleanor, whatever you say, but I'll probably get my ass kicked.*

I almost did, too. Well, not really. The bullies—they were your typical rich boys, with shiny hair and straight white teeth—they did something else, something I didn't expect. They made fun of me for working on a bakery truck. And then they started shoving me around, saying, "How about a kiss?" And "I bet you can do more than kiss."

The main boy—the one who was calling the shots—pushed me back against the truck and kept trying to kiss me. And here's the thing: I think about kissing boys all the time. Me and all my friends. We even practice making out with our pillows. So it's not like this was a big mystery to me.

Except it wasn't nice or romantic or fun or anything like I imagined.

I would rather get my ass kicked.

I like to think I fought him off but that's not exactly what happened. What happened was, I was rescued.

Can I just say, I hate being rescued?

It's simply another form of being helpless. One minute I was helpless while El Creepo was trying to kiss me and feel me up. And then the next minute I was helpless while another kid swooped in and took on all three creeps. In about a half a minute, he had them all howling. And, me, I stood by during the fight like the stupidest girl in the stupidest movie ever made. Just stood there biting my knuckles. A total dork.

If I'd seen me in a movie I would have screamed, "Don't just stand there, help him, already!"

I mean, how lame is that, standing there while the kid went berserk? It's hard to describe but it was kind of mesmerizing, the way he fought. He pounded the biggest kid like the kid was a hunk of meat. I looked down and saw that dots of blood had spattered my feet and legs.

And finally, I unfroze enough to say something, one word: *Stop.* Then I said two more words: *That's enough.*

It shouldn't have worked, but it did. The wild kid raised his hands and got up and stepped away from the guy who tried to kiss me.

And all three boys ran away like a pack of scalded dogs.

I was still staring at the boy who had rescued me. I say *rescued* but did he really? I stood back, eyeing him like something that explodes when you touch it. He was sweating and his face was red but then, almost like magic, a kind of calm came over him. The blue of his eyes changed from hot to cool. The color of his red-flushed face subsided.

I just stared with my mouth moving like a trout out of water. Because now that he was standing completely still, I could see that this kid was not just your garden-variety camper. This kid was, like, incredibly cute. Like movie-star, magazine-cover cute. He seemed totally different from the maniac who had chased off the others.

He was staring right back at me. Into my eyes and I think maybe at my mouth. We both got embarrassed at the same time and shuffled our feet. And then I finally found my brains again and gave him the first-aid kit.

I learned his name is Rourke McKnight. He probably thinks I'll never go back to Camp Kioga again on deliveries with Grandpa. He's totally wrong. I'll go back there every chance I get. Because here's the thing. I wish you were here, Mom, because this is not the kind of thing I can discuss with Gram. I had a funny feeling, talking to this kid, like butterflies in my stomach—except that it was a good feeling. Maybe I would have talked to him some more and figured out why he made me feel that way, but then this other kid showed up. I was worried at first that he was another bully, but he turned out to be Joey Santini, Rourke's best friend.

Okay, so now I'm looking at both of them and thinking, this can't be happening. They're both being really really nice but especially Joey, who has the biggest, brownest, softest eyes I ever saw. If he was a girl, those would be cover girl eyes. He kept trying to tell stories to impress me, which was kind of sweet. Now Rourke didn't seem sweet at all, but for some reason, he's the one who gave me the butterflies.

Anyway, I can't wait to tell Nina. She will have a cow when she hears I just met the two cutest boys at Camp Kioga. Correction: the two cutest boys *on the planet*.

Jenny's best friend was Nina Romano. They had met when they were in grade school. Nina was more than a year older than Jenny but they were in the same grade. Nina claimed her mom forgot to enroll her in kindergarten for a whole year on account of there being nine kids in Nina's family. The fact was, Nina struggled in school, and being from a family that big meant she didn't get a lot of help with her homework. Mrs. Romano used to show up at the bakery nearly every day, fifteen minutes before closing time. She knew exactly when the day-old bread went on sale for half price.

Jenny had looked into Nina's friendly, inquisitive eyes and had seen a kindred spirit. They became the best of friends, migrating seamlessly from Jenny's house on Maple Street to Nina's on Elm. Nina loved the peace and quiet of Jenny's house. She would stop right in the middle of playing Barbies to say "I can hear a clock ticking!" with a reverent sense of wonder.

Jenny, in turn, loved the noise and chaos of the Romano household. The older the kids got, the louder and more boisterous they became. Somebody was always yelling at somebody else. Tempers flared and subsided like kitchen matches being struck. Jenny adored the life and passion she found there. She was fascinated by the ability of siblings to argue over absolutely nothing.

"I'd give anything to have a sister," she said.

"Count your blessings," Nina would say, rubbing her head where her big sister Loretta had just pulled her hair. "You do *not* want a sister. Or a brother." One time, her brother Carmine had stolen her diary and read it aloud over the school's PA system when he was supposed to be reading the morning announcements. The prospect of her writing being broadcast like that secretly thrilled Jenny, but she didn't say so.

On a summer day the grown-ups had declared a "scorcher," Jenny and Nina found themselves with nothing to do. They went to the bakery then, which was something Nina loved so much that her pleasure made it seem special to Jenny, too, even though it was as ordinary to her as her own backyard. To Jenny's surprise, they found about a dozen little girls in the bakery kitchen, all lined up in the prep area. Laura Tuttle explained that it was Parents' Weekend at Camp Kioga. The parents of all the campers came from far and wide for a visit, and the camp hosted special outings, like tours of an actual working bakery. It seemed people had an endless fascination with how a simple loaf of bread came into being.

The girls were wearing red shorts and gray T-shirts with the Camp Kioga logo. Their parents—the mothers in crisp, sleeveless blouses and the fathers in golf shirts and Bermuda shorts—stood back, looking on. On each girl's chest was a sticker that said "Hi! My name is…" followed by what Jenny considered rich-girl names—Ondine and Jacqueline, Brooke and Blythe and Garamond. Dare and Lolly.

"We're the Fledglings," the perky counselor "—Hi! My name is Buffy—" was telling Laura. "That means we're in the eight-to-eleven age group. And it also means we get to do the best field trips, don't we, Fledglings?"

The girls chirped in reply.

Jenny and Nina clapped their hands over their mouths to keep from laughing aloud. A chubby blond girl at the end of the line lingered near Jenny. While the rest of the group checked out the prep area, she said, "I'm Olivia Bellamy."

"Hi, Olivia," Jenny said, though she observed that the name tag read "Lolly."

She glanced over at a tall, serious-looking man who stood with the other visiting parents. He had sandy hair and light eyes, and he seemed to be wishing he could be anywhere but crammed into a bakery prep area. The girl glanced at him and whispered, "My parents are getting a divorce."

"I'm sorry," Jenny said awkwardly. Sometimes kids were funny, telling their secrets to strangers the way Jenny told them to her diary. "Have a donut, Olivia."

Laura clapped her hands to get everyone's attention. "My name is Miss Tuttle," she said. "Let me show you around, and then we'll have a cookie tasting."

Bored, Jenny and Nina helped themselves to fountain lemonade from behind the counter and headed outside. They could easily pick out the Camp Kioga parents. They didn't wear uniforms like the campers, but they were all creased and expensive-looking, as though they'd spent hours trying to achieve that casual air. The kids in camp colors swarmed the town in packs, showing off the town to their parents.

Jenny immediately spotted Rourke McKnight, off by himself. And he was looking right at her.

Okay, she thought. Now what? Decision time. She could pretend she hadn't seen him. Or she could act like his friend.

"Come on," she said to Nina. "There's someone I want you to meet." Maybe she would go with Rourke, and Nina would go with Joey, and the four of them would be friends forever. How cool would that be? Except Nina wouldn't be interested. She had a secret boyfriend who went to the prep school in the next town. She had to keep him a secret because she said her brothers would rearrange his face if they found out, because they considered her way too young for a boyfriend.

Jenny tried to figure out which set of parents belonged to Rourke. Unlike most of the other campers, he wasn't playing tour guide to anyone. Maybe his folks hadn't shown up. Maybe he'd be glad to see a friendly face. Towing Nina behind her, she went right up to him and said hi. She was amazingly not tongue-tied. He looked even better than he had the first time she'd met him. He had a golden suntan and even blonder hair, and the scar on his cheek had nearly healed, though it was still visible, a small crescent moon.

"Hi," he said. "I was just—"

"Rourke, hey, Rourke!" Joey joined them, grinning with exuberance. Unlike Rourke's cautious smile, he wore an exuberant grin. "Hey, Jenny," he said without a shadow of bashfulness. "This is my father, Bruno Santini."

Jenny greeted him and introduced Nina.

Mr. Santini didn't look a bit like the other parents. He was squat and strong, with dark, wavy hair and a way of gazing at Joey that just glowed with love. Watching them, Jenny felt a pinch of envy.

"So you made some friends," Mr. Santini said, giving Joey a gentle slug on the shoulder. "Good job, sonny-boy."

"That's Jenny's bakery over there." Joey pointed it out. "And Nina's mom runs the kitchen up at the camp."

"I can tell they been feeding you well," Mr. Santini said, beaming. "My mama used to say good food is more important than a long life."

Rourke was very quiet, politely so, standing off to the side a little. He was eyeing Joey not with the envy Jenny felt, but with genuine affection. She knew he was best friends with Joey the way she was with Nina. Then, as Jenny watched, Rourke's face changed, his blue eyes turning hard and cold. She followed the direction of his gaze and spied a handsome couple coming toward them. His parents, for sure. The father was tall and slender, with light hair going slightly gray at the temples. The mother wore a slim khaki dress and expensive-looking shoes. Rourke got his blond hair and blue eyes from her.

The round of introductions was much more formal this time. Jenny found herself tongue-tied, though Nina bombarded the McKnights with nosy questions, because that was what Nina did. She was nosy and fearless, demanding to know where they lived, what Mr. Santini's and Mr. McKnight's jobs were. When Rourke's father said he was in the state assembly, Nina slapped her forehead. "Senator Drayton McKnight," she exclaimed. "Get *out*."

Jenny had never heard of Drayton McKnight. Who, besides Nina, would know such a thing? Of course, Nina was obsessed with politics and planned to run for office someday. She had studied every level of government from dogcatcher to state assemblyman to the president of the United States.

Rourke was clearly not enthralled by the prospect of being a senator's son. "We'd better get going," he said.

Jenny and Joey shared a look, and they didn't really have to speak. They were the same, the two of them, quiet, raised by immigrants. Joey's too-pretty eyes shone at her. After being bullied by those boys at the camp, Jenny had been ready to swear off kissing. Looking at Joey and Rourke, she was willing to reconsider.

A counselor's whistle sounded, and Rourke nudged Joey. "Let's go."

"See you around," Joey told them.

As the parents herded them away, Nina reeled and clutched at her heart. "Omigod, you weren't kidding. He is *so* cute."

"Which one?"

"Good point, they're both cute. But Joey looks too much like my brothers."

It was true. Joey would fit right in with the Romanos. By contrast, Rourke McKnight looked as blond and patrician as Prince Charming.

"Anyway," Nina said, "it doesn't matter, because he likes you, not me."

Jenny's face instantly caught fire. "You're crazy."

"Don't deny it and don't be all, like, he's practically a stranger. I know what I know. Including the fact that Joey has a crush on you, too."

A feeling of giddiness whirled through Jenny, but she was embarrassed. This whole boy business was both wonderful and terrible at the same time. "First of all," she said, "you're wrong, and second of all, if you say anything to either of them, I'll tell everyone at the bakery you're a diabetic, and to never, ever give you anything to eat again."

Nina sniffed. "You wouldn't dare."

Jenny set her hands on her hips. "Try me."

"He totally wants you," Nina insisted.

Jenny's face burned with a blush. She liked both of these boys. Joey because he was funny and easy and a lot like her, and Rourke because he was handsome and mysterious and kind of troubled. When she looked at him, she felt a funny tug at her heart. This business of liking boys was complicated, she decided. Maybe it was a good thing they both lived in the city. At summer's end, they'd both be gone, and she wouldn't have to like either of them.

Every summer after that, Jenny would anxiously watch the campers getting off the train at the station to see if Rourke McKnight would be coming to camp that year. And there he was again, taller and more golden than the previous year. Joey didn't change much. He was always laughing at something, and studying Jenny in a way that didn't embarrass her but made her feel special. Rourke was quieter, and when *he* looked at her, she didn't feel special but...unsettled.

The third summer, he told her it would be the last for him and Joey as campers. It was the day before the Fourth of July. She was on a bakery run to the camp and slipped away when she spied Rourke. When he told her, she had the strangest reaction. On the one hand, she was disappointed, because it meant she'd never see him again. On the other hand, her heart gave a leap, because the first thing that occurred to her was that if she wanted to get him to kiss her, she'd better work fast because time was running out.

She'd waited two whole summers for this.

She glanced around. They were alone because it was pouring, and most of the campers were in their cabins or in the main pavilion, doing crafts or playing board games. They ducked under the deck of the pavilion for shelter.

"I can't believe it's your last summer as a camper," she said, taking a step toward him. She stared at his mouth, just like it said in *Seventeen* magazine, a nonverbal cue.

He shifted uncomfortably from foot to foot. Yes, she thought, yes, he knows. Jenny took another step, closing the gap between them. She tried something else—putting out her tongue to moisten her lips—another tip from *Seventeen*.

"Uh, yeah," he said, adorably flustered. "About that. We'll be back. I mean, as counselors. Mr. Bellamy invited us both to work here next summer if we want."

Oh. Maybe that was her cue to step back. She didn't, though. But he was being so danged clueless, she didn't know how to proceed, so she just grabbed him and hugged him. "I'm so glad, Rourke. I'm glad you're coming back."

For one magical moment, maybe the span of a heartbeat, he hugged her back, and it felt like in that split second she went to heaven. Then he turned all stiff and set her aside.

"So anyway," he said, acting as if the moment never happened, "I'm pretty sure my dad will go ballistic and forbid me to do it. He'll want me to spend my time more productively, as he puts it."

"Does that mean you're *not* coming back?"

"Nope. Just means I'll have to fight to get my way. I always do." He glared out at the curtain of rain sprinkling the lake.

"Do you and your dad fight a lot?" she asked.

He shrugged. "I try to pick my battles. He's a mean son of a bitch."

"What do you mean, 'mean'?"

"How many kinds of mean are there?"

She figured it was a rhetorical question. She tried to adjust her thinking about the McKnight family. Like everyone else, she considered them picture-perfect, living the American dream. "You're just lucky to have a dad," she told him.

"Right." He snorted.

"Sometimes I want a father so much, I'd even take a mean one," she stated.

"Then you're crazy."

"Am not. I was once bitten by a dog," she said, "and it turns out the reason the dog was mean was that it was abused."

"A dog doesn't know any better."

"I'm just saying, there might be a reason. When people get hurt, they turn mean." Or they just turn and run. She thought that might have happened to her mother.

He glared at her, and she saw that scary flash of temper he sometimes exhibited. Too bad, she thought. She wasn't backing down. "How did we get on this topic?" she asked him. "All I wanted was—" She hesitated. Could she say it? Could she tell him? "I wanted you to kiss me. I still do."

A soft sound came from him, a sort of groan. "No," he said, "you don't." Then he stalked away, striding right out into the rain, not even hunching his shoulders in the downpour.

Jenny felt stupid. Tears smarted in her eyes. She hated Rourke McKnight. She would hate him forever. With that thought firm in her mind, she waited for the rain to stop, and then went to help her grandfather. As they finished the delivery, the sun came out again, and a rainbow arched over Willow Lake.

She walked around the side of the panel van and there was Joey Santini, waiting for her, a smile on his face. They spent a few minutes talking and laughing about nothing at all, and she reintroduced him to her grandfather.

Grandpa beamed approvingly as Joey shook his hand and said all the right things, like how much he liked Gram's maple bars.

Thank God for Joey. He made her feel content and valued, and he was never on the verge of exploding. She was so comfortable with him. He never made her feel awkward or stupid. He never made her feel like crying.

The next night, she and Nina went up to Camp Kioga for the Fourth of July fireworks display at Willow Lake. And Joey made his move. A group of kids was sitting together on a blanket at the lakeshore, and he pressed his shoulder close to hers, leaning over to whisper in her ear. "I want you to be my girlfriend," he said.

Jenny didn't know what to say. She didn't know if she wanted that or not. And even as Joey was scooting closer to her, she glanced over at Rourke. He stood nearby with his thumbs hooked into the waistband of his shorts. He was staring at her with the oddest expression on his face. She tried to ask him with her eyes if there was a chance for them, but either he didn't get the message, or he didn't care. Then he easily slipped his arm around some girl's waist and leaned down to whisper in her ear until she giggled.

Rourke hoped it had worked. He'd spent half the evening with the Giggler. He couldn't really remember her name, but he needed her. He didn't know what else to do. Jenny was starting to fall for him; he'd fallen for her long past, but he couldn't let that matter. Joey liked her, he had from day one and there was no way Rourke would take that away from Joey. Rourke just needed to make Jenny believe he was a son of a bitch, which according to his father, he was. Then she'd stop liking him and start liking Joey, which was the way things were supposed to be. Joey deserved her in a way Rourke never would. Joey knew just how to treat a girl like Jenny. He didn't feel as though someone had set him on fire, the way Rourke did, burning with feelings so intense they would consume them both.

For the rest of the summer, he made sure she saw him with any number of girls. Just to remind her—he was a son of a bitch, and she was better off with Joey.

Food for Thought

by Jenny Majesky

Happy Cake

Here's something I bet you never noticed. But once I point it out, you'll never fail to notice it again. A small, family-owned bakery is a happy place. Think about it. When was the last time you walked into a bakery and found a cranky person? It just doesn't happen. The people behind the counter are cheerful. The customers are cheerful. Even the sounds and the smells of the place—totally cheerful.

I bet if a study was done on the air quality of a bakery, pheromones would be found. One of the happiest recipes in my grandmother's arsenal is this one. It's actually a pound cake, but Gram created a neologism for it: *Szcześsliwe ciastko.* Roughly translated into English, that means—you already guessed it, didn't you? "Happy Cake." This is distinguished by its sunny yellow color and by the fact that it's impossible to eat a slice and not feel happy.

HAPPY CAKE

- 1 pound cake flour (3 cups)
- 1 pound eggs (about six)
- 1 pound (4 sticks) unsalted butter, softened (don't substitute)
- 1 pound (about 2-1/4 cups) sugar
- 2 teaspoons vanilla

1/2 teaspoon salt
1/2 cup buttermilk
1/2 teaspoon baking soda
1 teaspoon baking powder

Preheat oven to 325°F. Grease and flour Bundt or tube pan. Beat butter until light and gradually add sugar, vanilla and then eggs, one at a time. With mixer on low, add buttermilk. Sift together all the dry ingredients and add slowly. Pour batter into pan and bake for about 1 hour and 20 minutes, until a thin blade or toothpick comes out clean. Allow cake to cool 15 or 20 minutes in pan. Then gently remove it, and serve at room temperature with fresh fruit or lemon curd. Makes 12 generous servings.

Eight

All of Jenny's earthly possessions fit in the back of a rented panel truck. And actually, she was mildly surprised that the salvage operation had managed to recover so much. Everything had been cleaned up and placed in marked containers, then loaded onto the truck. She was supposed to go through the salvage and determine what to keep and what to discard, but she had no perspective on that, none at all. For the time being, she would store the items. She stood back and crossed her arms, shivering and stamping her feet. She had lost her favorite gloves in the fire, the leather ones with the cashmere lining.

Rourke pulled up in the driveway behind the truck. Today, as part of his crime prevention initiative, he had visited the local junior high, and he was dressed accordingly. He believed the police uniform, or even a suit, was a barrier to communicating with kids, so he was wearing loose cargo pants and boots unlaced to the ankles, an oversize jacket and knit cap, and he looked more like a snowboarder than the chief of police. "'S'up?" he said.

"Everything's up," she said, gesturing at the loaded truck. "How was your school visit?"

"I think they like me. About a dozen kids signed up for community service projects."

She couldn't imagine how anyone, kid or adult, could resist

him. Kids could spot a phony a mile off, and Rourke seemed to know that. He was completely at ease in the casual getup. It wasn't just to patronize the students. "How'd you get so good with kids, Chief?" she asked.

"You listen to them and show respect, and after that, it gets easier. And you're looking at me funny. Is it the clothes?"

"It's not the clothes." She hesitated. What the heck, she thought. "Do you ever wish you had kids of your own?"

He stared at her in astonishment, then burst out laughing.

"I'm not trying to be funny," she said. "I can't help but wonder what sort of father you'd make, what sort of family man."

"No kind of father, and no kind of family man, thank you very much."

"Oh, come on, McKnight. You're not the first kid to have a lousy childhood. That's no excuse."

"There's also the small matter of how to acquire those kids you're so convinced I want. It's not so easy for a guy."

The way he was looking at her was way too intimate. "Listen, we really need to have another talk about this…living arrangement. It's crazy, me staying with you."

"Why is it crazy?"

"We have no current relationship."

"Maybe we should," he said. "Roommates." He turned away abruptly, going around the back of the truck to check out the work the salvage company had done.

Roommates, thought Jenny. What the heck did he mean by that? She couldn't figure out a way to ask him, so she changed the subject. "One truckload. Kind of pathetic, huh?" she asked.

"No," he said. "It's not pathetic. It's just something that happens."

"Pathetic," she repeated. "How about you let me wallow a little?"

"All right. If it'll make you feel better."

"It won't. But it'll make you feel worse and that will make me feel better. I'm a taxpayer. It's the least you can do."

"Fine." He folded his arms across his chest. "Seeing this stuff, seeing that it's all that's left of your house—makes me feel like shit. Okay?"

A massive four-wheel-drive pickup truck with a snowplow blade pulled up. Out jumped Connor Davis, and then Greg Bellamy. Greg was Philip Bellamy's youngest brother, which made him Jenny's uncle, though he was only a few years older than she was. Recently divorced, Greg had moved to Avalon with his two kids, Daisy and Max. Daisy was going to be working at the bakery, Max was in the fifth grade. Like all the Bellamys Jenny had met, Greg had that affable, effortless charm, coupled with the natural good looks of the well-bred. She didn't feel at all like a Bellamy, and those sunny, upper-crust looks had definitely passed her by. Everyone who had known her mother swore she looked just like Mariska—who of course was beautiful, but in a totally different, dark and earthy way.

"Hey, guys, thanks for coming," Jenny said.

"No problem at all," Greg assured her.

As she introduced him to Rourke, she reflected that the three men together—Rourke, Connor and Greg—looked like the kind of fantasy a woman didn't want to wake up from. Each was tall, strong, sexy. And there was something about the presence of heavy equipment and work to be done outdoors that seemed to cause the testosterone level to rise.

"I really appreciate this," she said. "Are you sure it's all right to take all this stuff up to Camp Kioga?"

"Sure," said Connor. "There's nothing but space up there, and no one around all winter."

"Well, I'm grateful. I was going to move everything into the garage, but it was damaged, too, and it's got to be torn down along with everything else." She was still a little dazed by the concept of not having a home, no place to park her things, or what was left of them. It was agreed that Connor would drive the pickup to the camp, with Rourke and Jenny following in the panel van. They had to drive the private road to the camp at a crawl, with the plow blades producing founts of snow on either side as it cleared the way.

"I can't believe how nice everyone's being," Jenny said.

"You're not that hard to be nice to."

"Is that why you're helping me? To be nice?"

"I'm not nice," he said. "You of all people should know that."

Both of them had made mistakes in the past. Jenny was haunted by regrets, while Rourke still suffered from an old guilt that ran bone deep. That was the reason they'd grown so distant, but since they'd been spending so much time together lately, she felt entitled to bring up old business. "You've never forgiven yourself for Joey," she said, bringing up the sorest of subjects. "What's it going to take, Rourke?"

He kept his eyes straight ahead, on the road. "Interesting question, coming from you."

"That's not an answer."

"All right, how about this. Maybe I haven't forgiven myself for Joey because some things…they aren't forgivable. You just try to move on and live with it."

And spend the rest of your life doing penance, she reflected. For some reason, she thought about *Beauty and the Beast*—the raging, violent French version, not the squeaky-clean Disney version. In the original, the beast's fury was calmed by the unquestioning love of the heroine, yet the redemption came with so much pain and sacrifice from both of them that it made her wonder if it was worth the struggle.

She stayed silent during the rest of the drive. The south end of the lake was close to town, where cozy cottages, most of them closed for the winter, huddled shoulder to shoulder along the shore. The frozen docks, piled high with snow, projected out onto the field of white. They passed the Inn at Willow Lake, a 19th century mansion rumored to be haunted. When they were young, Jenny and Nina used to ride their bikes past the place, speculating about who might be haunting it. Nina always said she wanted to own the inn one day, but after she got pregnant with Sonnet, her life shot off in a different direction.

The lake wound through a deep valley that quickly turned to wilderness, and soon there was nothing to do but watch the winter woods slip by. The otherworldly perfection and quietness mesmerized her. The thin trees were inked upon a background of snow, which was marked by the crisscrossings of animal tracks. Chickadees and cardinals flitted in and out of the branches. The streambeds resembled small ice floes and glaciers. By the time they reached the grounds of Camp Kioga, she felt as though she were worlds away, rather than mere miles.

An historic seasonal resort, the camp reflected the style of the "great camps" of the Gilded Age. Marked by a rustic timber-and-wrought-iron archway, the entrance to the camp was a smooth drift of snow leading to the main pavilion. There were sports courts now buried in snow, equipment sheds, a boathouse situated out over the lake, which was now frozen into a vast, flat field of white.

Everything was in a slumberous state of hibernation. The timber bunkhouses and cottages had drifts of snow sloping up each stairway. In the lake stood an island with a gazebo hung with icicles. Jenny found herself caught by the impenetrable quiet and the spun-sugar scenery. She had never seen the remote camp in winter, and it looked magical to her.

Connor's truck lumbered to a halt at a storage shed. Greg unlocked it, and within just a short time, they had everything stowed in the big wooden building.

"It's beautiful here," she said. "I'm glad you and Olivia have decided to reopen the place."

"It'll be open year-round one day," Connor said.

She noticed that Rourke was standing apart, looking out across the lake, maybe lost in memories. He'd spent many a summer here, he and Joey. There, ankle deep in the frigid lake water, they had stood together skipping stones, keeping score of every skip. And there at the dock, they had started their swim races. There had been a rope swing suspended from a huge tree with its branches arching out over the lake, and they had challenged each other to swing higher or farther, to dive deeper. Everything had always been a contest with them.

She tried to remember the moment it had started, the rivalry that had torn an unspoken rift in their friendship. Was it the moment the three of them had met? Had it been invisible, like magma in an underground conduit, seeking a way to burst forth?

Greg stood back and regarded the stacked and labeled boxes. "All set."

"Thanks again." Jenny refused to think about the fact that everything she owned was in those boxes. That one day in the near future—perhaps at the spring thaw—she would have to go over every single item and decide its fate. Should she keep her grandmother's bent eggbeater, her grandfather's box of fishing tackle, a clay ashtray made by her mother in Campfire Girls?

It started snowing lightly, and Jenny lifted her face to the sky, feeling the flakes touch her forehead and cheeks. Everything was going to be all right, she told herself. The world was beautiful, and she had all kinds of options open to her.

"We'd better get back." Connor headed for his truck.

"Meet me at the bakery," Jenny suggested. "I need to get some work done in the office. I'll give you a cup of coffee and any pastry you want."

"I'll take a rain check," Connor said. "I need to get back to work."

"Same here," said Greg. "But I'll see you Saturday, right? For dinner?"

"Of course." Her father, Philip, was coming up from the city to see her. She'd told him she didn't need anything, that she would be okay, but he'd been insistent.

After Connor and Greg left, Jenny and Rourke followed more slowly, lingering for one last look at the lake. "It's beautiful here," she said. "I feel…nostalgic. Don't you?"

"Maybe," he said. "A little." He quickened his pace, and she felt him shutting down. It was probably just as well, she decided. They had never been good at talking about the things that really mattered.

Nine

Jenny was finishing up at town hall after spending a seemingly interminable afternoon filling out forms to replace lost records. The process was less tedious because Nina Romano took time out to visit with her. "So be honest," Jenny said. "How many tongues are wagging because I've been staying at Rourke's?"

"Would you believe none at all?"

"In this town? Hardly." Jenny signed her name to the tenth page of a title-to-deed request.

"Trust me, people have bigger worries than that." Nina held out her hand for the forms. "I'll file these with the city clerk for you." They walked together through a hallway lined with municipal offices.

"What kind of worries?"

Nina waved a hand. "City-finance stuff. I won't bore you with the details. I'd rather hear about you living with Rourke."

"See?" Jenny snapped. "I shouldn't be there. It's crazy."

"I'm teasing. Listen, we still don't know what happened at your house," Nina pointed out. "You should stay with him at least until they figure that out."

"Oh, God. A conspiracy theory?"

"No. I'm just being practical. And if it's that big a deal, move into my place."

"I might take you up on that." Jenny knew she wouldn't, though. Nina and Sonnet didn't have room. "What I really need to do is figure out a permanent arrangement."

"Don't rush into anything. Remember what the adjuster said— don't make any major decisions right away. And the most major of all is where you're going to live, spend the rest of your life."

Just hearing the words caused Jenny's heart to kick into high gear, warning her that a panic attack was always lurking just beneath the surface. It was the strangest feeling to wake up in the morning and not know what your life was going to be.

Nina must have read the worry in her face. She gave Jenny a reassuring pat on the arm. "The last thing you need to be worrying about is what people think. Just take your time, okay?"

Jenny nodded and bundled up for the cold, and headed back to Rourke's house. Three grateful dogs burst from the mudroom into the yard, and Jenny headed inside with a sack of groceries and a stack of books from the library. Eventually, of course, she would need to buy new copies of all those precious volumes she'd lost in the fire. There were childhood favorites, mercifully still in print—*Charlotte's Web, Harriet the Spy, The Borrowers.* Others, the town librarian had warned, might be out of print, but she promised to track down a copy of *You Were Princess Last Time,* a tale of two sisters Jenny had wept over countless times when she was little. Then there were books she returned to again and again—a collection of essays on writing by Ray Bradbury. Tales of escape and reinvention, like *Under the Tuscan Sun,* and stories about food by Ruth Reichl. But those were the books Jenny remembered. One of her greatest regrets was that she had no record of the many books she *wouldn't* remember.

Slowly peeling off her gloves and parka, she wandered to the living room and looked at the bookshelves there. She caught herself doing this often—searching Rourke's house for evidence of who he was. Maybe, she admitted to herself, she was looking for who he used to be. People's books said a lot of about them, but Rourke's choices were as impenetrable as he was—police procedure, old textbooks, repair manuals. There was a big collection of well-thumbed action-adventure paperbacks with titles like *Assault on Precinct 17* and *Murder Street,* which probably depicted a very different style of police work than Rourke did in Avalon. Some books, probably gifts from frustrated ex-girlfriends, appeared to be pristine and unread—relationship manuals doubtless intended to show him the error of his ways. She counted at least three separate editions of *Relationship Rescue.* The *Relationship Rescue Workbook* was still in its shrink-wrap.

Dream on, she silently told the women who had given him those books. She seriously doubted it was in any man's nature to read a book like that and think it applied to him.

She went back into the kitchen to put away the groceries. She had never lived with a man before, so she didn't know if Rourke was typical or not. She had been so used to taking care of her grandmother, rising early, getting her ready for the visiting nurse. It was a revelation to simply wake up on her own, to go through her day without planning it around Gram's needs. After just a few days at Rourke's house, a rhythm established itself. He got up early and fixed his amazing coffee. She would drink a cup while he showered, and then they switched. They had breakfast together—she quickly broke his habit of eating second-rate grocery-store pastries—and went off to work.

And at the end of the day, sounding hopelessly domestic, she found herself fixing tuna sandwiches and asking, "How was your day?" *How was your day, dear?*

She couldn't help it. It felt perfectly natural. As did the subtle lift of her heart when she heard him come through the back door, stamping the snow from his boots and whistling to the dogs before stepping into the warm kitchen.

"Hey," she said, "how was—" oh, God, she was doing it again "—your day?"

"Busy." He didn't seem bothered by the familiar tone of the question. "We had thirteen traffic incidents, seven involving alcohol, all of them involving slippery road conditions. A domestic disturbance, a check-forging scam, kids defacing school property and a woman who left her small child home alone while she went to work."

"How do you stand it?" Jenny asked. "You see people at their worst, every day. It must get depressing."

"I suppose what makes it okay for me is that I try to make things better. Doesn't always work, though."

"You mean sometimes you have to let the bad guys go?"

"Yeah. Sometimes. If there isn't enough evidence or somebody screwed up, or because we have bigger fish to fry and can't spare the manpower. Lots of reasons." Before she could ask another question, he waved a hand. "Some of the stuff I do during the day, it's not good dinner conversation."

Like everyone, he brought home an invisible burden from work every day. But for most people, the burden didn't consist of the petty crimes and cruelties of small-town police work. "Our lives are so different," she said. "You go to work every day and see people behaving badly."

He laughed. "No one's ever put it quite that way."

"And at the bakery, I see people who only need a cup of coffee and a fresh cruller, and they're happy."

"I should retire from the force and buy a hairnet," he said. He gratefully ate half his sandwich, and she could see him visibly relaxing. Was it her, she wondered, or simply getting to the end of another day?

She suspected she had her answer when she glanced across the table and caught him staring at her with the most unsettling, smoldering look.

"What?" she asked.

"Nothing," he said. "I didn't say a word."

"You're staring."

"I like looking at women. So shoot me."

She ducked her head to hide a smile. They were taking tentative steps toward each other, yet proceeding with caution. By the time dinner ended—and bless him, he cleared the table and did the dishes—Jenny was ready to admit it. She was a goner.

Fortunately, he didn't seem to notice this troubling new development. "I need to go out tonight," he said.

And—fortunately again—he didn't seem to hear the thud her heart made when it fell. "Oh. Um, okay," she said. What else was she supposed to say? She was a visitor here, someone passing through. He didn't owe her any explanations.

He grabbed his cell phone and slipped on his shoulder holster. Jenny pretended not to watch, but she couldn't help herself. It was intriguing—maybe even sexy—to contemplate the idea that he wore a concealed weapon.

He caught her staring and grinned. "Want to come?"

"Come where?"

"To the indoor range," he said. "Shooting practice." He was a stickler for training in his department, and he practiced what he preached, explaining that he went to the indoor range at least once a week.

Shooting practice? "Maybe I will," she said. "I've never thought about what it would be like to shoot a gun."

"I'll teach you," he said easily.

She hesitated a moment longer. Did she want to learn, or was it just something she'd said so he wouldn't think she was as boring as she actually was? And did he want to teach her because he liked her, or because he thought she should learn self-defense? She told herself to quit looking for reasons to turn him down. "I'll get my things."

It was a short drive to the indoor shooting range. The facility had two buildings, one with the range and the other with a classroom. In the classroom, he helped her gear up and showed her the gun she would be firing.

"This is a .40-caliber Glock," he explained, and guided her through the way it worked. "Stance is the key to hitting what you aim at." He lifted the gun two-handed in a movement that looked perfectly natural. "Now you try."

All right, thought Jenny, feeling the powerful heft of the black, angular gun in her hands.

"Watch out for the slide when you hold it. How does this feel to you?"

"You're going to think I'm one sick puppy—but it feels…sexy to me."

He grinned. "That's a good sign. It's good for your confidence."

In her Avalon P.D. sweatshirt, earmuffs and goggles, she didn't look nearly as sexy as she felt.

"Close your eyes and raise the gun."

"What?"

"Don't worry, it's not loaded. You need to raise the gun with your eyes shut so you'll learn what your natural arm position points to."

She lifted the gun, opened her eyes and found herself looking at a big X on the classroom wall. He was incredibly fussy about her posture and position, adjusting the level of her extended arms, the angle of her chin, the placement of her feet, her grip, until she nearly burst with frustration.

"I feel like a poseable Barbie doll."

He chuckled as he adjusted her stance again. "Firing Range Barbie. The all-American doll. I like it."

He fussed some more, going over the trigger squeeze and the natural respiratory pause, which he said was the ideal time to squeeze the trigger, because she would be at her most relaxed. She tried to remember everything he was telling her. It seemed that shooting a gun required doing at least a dozen things simultaneously and well. "I've never had to work this hard to satisfy a man," she said.

"It's nice to know you're willing to work at it. Now, quit flirting with me and concentrate."

"I'm not flirting with you," she objected.

"I feel flirted with."

"Then it's your imagination. I know better than to flirt with you. Now, show me how to shoot something."

"Fine. Rule number one, you want to be a little more specific about what you're going to shoot. 'Something' is too vague."

"Whatever. I want to shoot one of those cutouts of a bad guy."

"Then let's go into the range."

The place was divided into shooting stalls where people who didn't need close supervision could practice. At the moment, only a couple of stalls were occupied. Other cops, Rourke told her, waving at them, and a few locals. She was surprised to see Zach Alger there with his father. Matthew was a big, barrel-chested man whose Nordic features made him look younger than he actually was. Father and son were in adjacent lanes, oblivious to anything but the shooting. Each shot went off with a popping sound that made Jenny wince. Rourke explained that the walls could stop any handgun round at point-blank range. "A .40-caliber bullet can penetrate a dozen layers of regular Sheetrock," he said.

"Good to know. I won't hide behind a wall if someone's shooting at me."

"The best defense in almost any situation is to fight. To fight, and never give up. But you need to know what you're doing." He gestured at the silhouette at the end of the range. He used something called a smart pad to cause it to move, and positioned it at the end of the alley. She prepared herself exactly as he'd shown her—arms extended, feet planted to align the arm with the target, grip, sight alignment, target alignment, breathing, then trigger squeeze. *Don't pull,* he'd said. *Squeeze.*

She squeezed.

The gun recoiled violently in her hand, causing a reverberation down her arm.

"Follow through," he reminded her, mouthing the words. "Don't forget to follow through."

After firing, you were supposed to align with the target again to improve the steadiness of your hand. She realigned, smelling the burnt cordite. But the target hung mockingly at the end of the range, unscathed.

"Hey," she said, pushing aside one of her earmuffs. "That should have been a perfect shot."

"Nah." He waved his arm. "I knew you'd miss."

"What?"

"You were excellent with your stance and grip. But you'll never hit anything until you see it first." He touched his temple.

"What?"

"See it. Then shoot it."

Jenny didn't quite get that, but she was determined. She took several more shots, each time amazed by the kick of the recoil. Finally she grazed the edge of the target. *See it, then shoot it* became her mantra.

After too many rounds to count, she improved somewhat. There was so much to remember—the mechanics of the weapon and the stance. The fine adjustment of breathing and trigger squeeze. And Rourke was absolutely right. She learned to visualize where to put the bullet, and then she put it there. See it, then shoot it.

Once the target was riddled with holes in all its vital areas, she lowered the Glock and turned to Rourke, smiling more than she had since losing her grandmother.

He mouthed "good job" and gave her a thumbs-up.

Afterward, he showed her how to clean the gun "—a clean gun is a safe gun—" and stow the protective gear. "I'm proud of you," he said.

It was a simple statement, yet it drew an unexpectedly emotional response from her. She glanced away, fluffing her hair where it had been mashed by the earmuffs.

"That was meant as a compliment," he pointed out.

"I know and I…I'm grateful." She took in a deep breath. How could she explain it? "I was thinking I'd outgrown the need for approval."

"Everybody's born with that," he said. "God knows, I spent my whole childhood looking for it."

Interesting, she thought. These glimpses into his past were rare. "And then you gave up trying to get along with your father and walked away," she recalled.

"What makes you think I walked away from anything?" he asked. "Maybe I was walking *toward* something."

"Like what?"

"Like the kind of life I wanted, not the one my family wanted for me," he said simply.

"And did you succeed?" she asked him. "Is this the life you wanted?"

"It's the one I've got," he said. "Same as anyone else." He turned away then, closing the conversation. Jenny was just as glad to drop the subject. It was getting too personal. She wasn't sure she wanted to go there.

They stowed their protective gear. Then she cleaned the gun, step by step the way he'd shown her while he looked on appreciatively. "So are you going to write about what happened today?" he asked as she finished up.

Caught off guard, all she could think about was the feel of his arms around her as he helped her with her stance. She wouldn't be writing about that anytime soon. "It might be a stretch to fit a shooting lesson into a food column."

"It might fit into your memoir."

She slipped her muffler around her neck. "I wish I'd never said anything about a memoir."

"Why not? I want to read it."

Like he'd read all those books in his house with the unbroken spines? she wondered. "Why would you want to read a memoir about a family bakery?"

"Maybe I want to know the ending."

"I don't get to plan the ending."

"But if you could, what would it be?" he asked.

"I can't answer that."

"Why not?"

"I'd need days to think about it. Maybe weeks or months." That was the problem with too much freedom, she thought. Now that she had it, she wasn't sure what to do.

"Bull. Everybody has a vision of how they want to end up."

"They do? Do you?" She zipped up her parka.

"Yep."

"And...?"

"And maybe I'll tell you someday."

At some point, without Jenny noticing it, they'd stopped walking and were standing very close, bathed in the yellowish glow of the sodium-vapor lights of the parking lot. She could feel his body heat. When she tilted her head back, she saw that he was studying her mouth with unmistakable interest. The thought that he was going to kiss her nearly caused her bones to melt. She wanted it. She dreaded it. She wanted it.

The indecision—and then the desire—must have shown on her face, because he took her arm and spoke in a rough whisper. "Jenny..."

She studied him in the pale, shadowy light and a terrible notion took hold of her. Falling. She was falling for him. She could almost hear the wind rushing through her hair as she fell, and this was bad. It was bad because it wouldn't work out for them. She already knew that. They'd end up hurting each other and he'd withdraw and she'd get stuck here in this town forever.

She couldn't think with him standing so close and looking at her like this. "I think, before we..." She didn't want to put this into words. "We need to talk, Rourke."

His smile held a hint of bitterness. "We've been talking plenty."

He really thought so. He actually seemed to believe nothing more needed to be said.

"I'm not going to fall into your bed like one of your bimbos," she said.

"I didn't ask you to," he pointed out. "And you did fall into my bed."

"Alone," she said.

"Your call." With that, he turned, walked to his car and held the door for her.

Glaring at him, Jenny got in and fastened her seat belt before he could remind her. She shivered against the cold seat. The night was bitterly cold, and they'd reached the stage of winter when the days were so dark and the snow so deep, it was hard to imagine the season would ever change, or that the sun was shining some-where in the world.

"I'm going to remember that promise," she said as he slid into the driver's seat and turned on the ignition.

"What promise?"

She nearly laughed at the raw panic on his face. "Rourke McKnight" and "promise" were a bad combination. "You said you'd tell me how you want to end up one day," she said. "Per-sonally, I think it's a bad idea to plan things." She paused, then went for it. The issue had been lying between them, unspoken, since he'd taken her home after the fire. She might as well put it out there. "Look at me and Joey—the best-laid plans can be de-railed in a single instant."

She waited for his reaction. Waited for him to point out that maybe what had happened was merely proof that lying and betrayal did destructive things to the innocent. She knew they'd both thought it.

Rourke's only reaction was to crank up the heater, blasting her with warm air.

Ten

On Saturday morning, Jenny and Rourke went to the Sky River Bakery. She had some work to do in the office, and he was going to take a duty shift for an officer who was out sick. When they stepped inside, a bell jangled over the door, and the warm, fragrant embrace of the bakery surrounded them.

Mariel Elena Gale, the counter girl, greeted them with a smile. She was the bakery's youngest employee, with a zany sense of humor and a decided streak of independence. She was responsible for such delightful innovations as moose-head sugar cookies and chocolate cupcakes sprouting sugar-dough crocuses. Beside the cake-of-the-day, she'd placed a sign that read, "You want a piece of me."

"Hello, Jenny, Chief McKnight." Mariel didn't seem at all surprised to see them together. "The usual for you?"

"Sure."

Jenny poured coffee into a pair of thick china mugs. "I'm a little suspicious," she admitted, "now that I know about your coffee-making skills."

"I never came here for the coffee," he said. "I figured that was obvious."

She didn't know what to say to that, so she sidled away and concentrated on making sure everything on the condiment counter was precisely aligned. Being with Rourke so much was affecting her in unexpected ways. Things she hadn't let herself think about in years came bubbling to the surface, and to her surprise, the memories had not lost their sharpness. And she was worried, too, that she was teetering on the edge of something that was, at best, foolhardy. At worst, dangerous. She needed to do something different, but she felt frozen by inertia and indecision.

As she stood at the counter, Jenny saw a woman drop a napkin beside Rourke's table and then bend to pick it up. Which of course, was no big deal, except that the woman was zipped into a tight magenta ski bib and an even tighter white angora sweater, and she was making no secret of her interest. Jenny couldn't hear what they were saying, but the woman clearly found him vastly amusing. Rourke had always had that effect on women, even as a kid. He didn't even have to say anything. There was just something about him, and it wasn't only the matinee-idol looks. Whether on purpose or not, he exuded a brooding sexiness that seemed to promise endless nights of pleasure. Or so it seemed to Jenny, as she reluctantly admitted that she and the ski bimbo shared the same taste.

Fortunately, the moment was broken by Mariel, who brought two plates to the table. The skier's gaze lingered a moment longer and then she moved on to join her friends, who were getting ready to leave.

His "usual" was a sweet-cheese Danish with a honey-orange glaze, served warm, and he was already eating it when Jenny returned to the table.

"Sorry," he said around a mouthful. "I couldn't wait. This is almost as good as sex."

She glanced in the direction of the magenta ski bunny. "I'd say that depends on the sex. And I'm changing the subject immediately. Nobody wants their chief of police talking like that."

"Yeah, I've always been so concerned about my image."

The place was hopping. Shoppers stopped in for loaves of rye or a special pie for Sunday dinner. A few intrepid tourists—downhill and Nordic skiers and snowmobilers—were having coffee and planning their day on the cross-country trails that wound through the area or at Saddle Mountain, the local ski hill. Three old men gathered at their regular corner table, their thick overcoats, mufflers and flat wool caps hanging on a nearby hat tree.

Despite the chaos her life was in, Jenny felt a strong sense of connection to the community at moments like this. The chatty customers, the smells, the smiling counter girl, the busy sounds from the kitchen, all combined to create an atmosphere that was safe, familiar and timeless. Although looking after the place had consumed her entire adult life, she was grateful for the old-fashioned, changeless building on the town square. When everything else had been taken from her, the bakery still stood, solid and real and secure.

At the same time, the weight of responsibility pressed on her. The emotional one-two punch of losing her grandmother and then her home had left her reeling, but she had a business and employees to look after. She told herself she should be grateful to have the family bakery, but the fact was, sometimes she wondered what her life would be like if she'd been allowed to choose. The bakery was her grandparents' dream, not hers. She felt disloyal even thinking such a thing, but she couldn't help herself.

Rourke leaned back in his chair and looked at her. "I would love to know what's on your mind."

"Maybe I don't have anything on my mind."

He chuckled. "Right."

"Just feeling ambivalent about this place. The bakery, I mean."

"Ambivalent? Come on, this is the happiest place on earth. Forget Disneyland. Look at these people."

She scanned the faces of the customers, seeing easy smiles and unhurried pleasure in their faces. "I just took it for granted, I suppose. And I'm ambivalent because I watched my friends all leave after high school. That's what people do in a town like this—they leave."

"Some of us come here to stay," he pointed out. "Me. Olivia

Bellamy and now Greg. I always envied the way you grew up, here in this place."

Oh, my, she thought. And didn't that open a private door? "You did?" she asked. "You envied this?"

"Is that so strange?"

"My mom took off when I was small, and I never knew my dad. My grandparents worked all the time—"

"And you were always one of the happiest, most well-adjusted kids I'd ever met."

She nodded, understanding that even though her upbringing had been unorthodox, she'd enjoyed a childhood full of love and safety, one rich in ways that had nothing to do with money. Rourke had grown up in luxury with servants, private schools, summer camp, trips to Europe. Yet she knew what he had endured. Joey had told her once, their second summer together. She had gone up to the camp to watch the annual boxing matches, and Rourke seemed to win every bout. Although the crowd cheered wildly, he seemed to take no joy in winning. In fact, when he was declared the champion, he got out of the ring, puked in a bucket and stalked away, unable to savor his victory.

Joey had touched her shoulder and leaned over to whisper in her ear, "His father beats him."

Jenny had been stunned. "Are you sure?"

He nodded solemnly. "I'm the only one who knows. And now you."

So now, when Rourke looked at her across the table and said he envied her childhood, she understood. "I'm sorry," she said. "I wish things had been different for you."

"They're different now."

Maybe, she thought. But he still held things in. A part of him was still a prisoner of the past, held hostage by his father's cruelty and his mother's indifference.

Matthew Alger came in for his usual morning coffee, and Jenny noticed that he left his usual stingy tip of leftover pennies. He wasn't Jenny's favorite person and he sure wasn't Rourke's. She knew that. In charge of the town's purse strings, Alger tended to make it difficult for Rourke to do his job. Too often, Rourke had to go to Alger, hat in hand, when he needed any sort of special funding. Zach came through the doors from the back and went over to his father's table. Although she couldn't hear them talking, Jenny could see the tension in both father and son. She wondered what the dispute was about, but Zach tended to keep things to himself.

Zach was a dedicated member of Rourke's youth group. He'd formed it when he first became chief of police. There had been several incidents of violence at the high school, and Rourke was determined to do something about it. His first step had been to take down the barriers between the generations by visiting their schools, listening to them, finding out what was going on in their lives.

That was another reason he was such an anomaly. His personal life seemed to take a distant backseat to the community. He had kids in the youth group going to the old folks' home at Indian Wells and making oral-history videos with the residents there. He'd formed a group charged with picking up day-old bread from the bakery and delivering it to the church pantry. Some of his work teams had done a mural on the side of a derelict building at the edge of town. This year, a team of them was going to create an ice sculpture for Valentine's Day.

And the kids. They told him things. Maybe that was the reason Matthew Alger didn't like Rourke—because he was worried about what Zach might say about him. Zach's face was pale and grim as he left his father, shoving through the swinging doors as he went back to work. The older man picked a secondhand newspaper out of the discard pile, folded it back to the crossword puzzle and got to work at the window counter.

She shifted her attention back to Rourke and gazed across the table at him. "I wonder what that was all about," she said.

"What?"

"Zach and Matthew."

He shrugged. "I didn't notice. Too busy with this pastry." He took a bite and sent her a beatific smile.

Jenny's heart sped up. This was starting to feel too good. Too comfortable. Too romantic.

"What?" he asked, noticing her stare.

"I need to find a place to live," she said.

"You have a place to live."

"Listen, you've been really nice to let me stay with you, but I'm wearing out my welcome."

"Who says?"

"I say. At the very least, I'm cramping your social life."

"Maybe *you're* my social life."

"Yeah, I'm a barrel of laughs," she said. "I was referring to the women you date."

"That's not a social life," he said. "That's…" He couldn't seem to find the word for it.

She refrained from suggesting "sleeping around."

He shook his head and said, "You're not cramping my style."

"You haven't had a date since the fire."

"It's only been a week," he pointed out.

"When was the last time you went a whole week without dating?"

"I don't keep score, but obviously, you do. Why, Miss Majesky, I didn't know you cared."

Yes, he did know, and he was reveling in it. "I can't stay with you forever," she said.

He studied her for a long moment, his expression unreadable. How did he manage to shave like that? she found herself wondering. It was flawless, and now that she knew his routine, she knew he did it in about two minutes flat.

"Nope," he agreed. "Of course not."

She sensed that she had hurt him. Which simply did not compute, since he was the one who had been teasing her. "You know," she said, "I could simply walk away from everything." Saying the words aloud both frightened and exhilarated her. It was scary, because the town and bakery had been her whole world. Even scarier was the fact that she was finally making some sort of connection to this man. Yes, she thought, that was scarier than running away. If she stayed, she might have to deal with this uncomfortable collision of their past and present.

He leaned forward across the table. "You can't walk away. You need the bakery so you'll have something to write about."

Here's what she hated—the fact that he could read her. "Nice, Rourke."

He threw back his head and laughed. Every female in the room turned to watch him, and Jenny didn't blame them. What was sexier than a big, handsome, laughing man?

Okay, a big, handsome, laughing, *naked* man.

The smile lingered on his lips and in his pale blue eyes. "Seriously, Jen," he said, leaning toward her again as though this was an intimate restaurant rather than a busy café. "I do want to talk to you about something. See, I was thinking we could—"

"Jenny?" said a deep, masculine voice.

We could what? she thought in frustration. But she arranged her face in a welcoming smile and stood up. "Philip," she said warmly. "You must have caught the early train."

He nodded. "I know you said you didn't need anything, but I had to come."

And with such perfect timing, she thought. "Well, I'm glad. Philip, this is Rourke McKnight. Maybe you remember meeting him last summer at the Bellamys' fiftieth anniversary celebration… And Rourke, this is Philip Bellamy. My…" *Father.* It was still impossible to get that word out. *Father* implied many things that Philip Bellamy was not. It implied a connection between a man and his daughter that simply didn't exist for them.

"Sure, I remember." Rourke stood and offered a firm handshake. "Please, sit down."

"You really didn't have to come," Jenny said, feeling both giddy and self-conscious, as she always did around Philip. "I'm glad you did, though."

She had first met him one day last August, when he'd simply shown up on her doorstep and said he believed he was her father.

Just like that. In one moment, he'd solved the biggest mystery of her life. Since then, the two of them had been in a sort of awkward dance, bumbling toward each other and then backing off, trying to figure out what their relationship would be.

Part of her wanted the situation to be as simple as a Hallmark card, in which she opened her heart to him and brought him into her life. But another part was filled with doubt. She had only his word that he'd loved her mother and planned to marry her. Only his word that he had no idea Jenny had ever been born. And since she didn't know him, she didn't know how good his word was.

"Rourke's been kind enough to give me a roof over my head," she told Philip. "Temporarily, of course. We were just talking about my options."

Philip beamed at her. "Then I came just in time," he said. "I wanted to talk to you about that."

Jenny was about to ask him to clarify, when Laura came down from the upstairs business office.

"I heard you were down here," Laura said to her. "Hi, Rourke." Then she turned to Philip Bellamy. "Hello."

Philip stood and politely took her hand as he greeted her. "Laura. It's been a long time."

Rourke pushed back from the table. "I should go. I've got some things to take care of."

Maybe he did, maybe he didn't. Jenny couldn't tell if it was true or if this was just a polite cop-out. Cop-out. Ha, ha.

He held a chair out for Laura, who looked pleased as she had a seat.

Don't go, Jenny thought. Finish what you were saying. You wanted to talk to me about…?

"See you later," Rourke said. "Good seeing you," he added with a nod in Philip's direction.

"Was it something I said?" asked Philip, watching him go.

"He works hard," Jenny answered.

"Has he figured out what caused the fire?" Philip asked.

"An investigation team is working on it," she said. "It was an old house. I expect the cause will be faulty wiring." She busied herself busing the table. "So, is this your first visit to the bakery?"

He and Laura exchanged a glance.

"The first in a long time," he said.

"You were here before," she said. A chill slid over her skin.

"Anyone who comes to the town of Avalon visits the Sky River Bakery."

Then Jenny noticed the expression on Laura's face. "You two knew each other…back then."

Laura simply nodded. "I've been here all my life. I knew the Bellamys, Philip included."

Philip looked around the café. The skiers were layering on their gear, preparing to head out. Matthew Alger had finished his coffee and crossword puzzle, and was getting ready to leave, too.

"My God," Philip said. "Is that who I think it is?"

"You know him, too?" Jenny asked.

"I did a long time ago." Philip got up and approached Alger. "I recognized you right away."

They shook hands, but it was clearly not a warm handshake. Alger had a sort of boyishness that made him look younger than his age. His hair was blond, impeccably styled in a cropped, Rutger Hauer-like fashion. He was shorter than Philip and not so well built, but he had a certain presence. He greeted Philip with a peculiar cordial distance, then walked over to Jenny's table.

"What's the progress on the fire investigation?" he asked her.

"The salvage crew just finished up," she said, a little startled by his interest.

"So quickly?"

"There wasn't much to salvage," Jenny said.

"Zachary tells me you're taking some time off."

"I am," she said. "I'm trying, at least. I seem to find myself torn between managing the bakery and dealing with the fire."

"Well. I hope you're able to save some of those irreplaceable family treasures."

The comment startled her. Sentiment, from Matthew Alger? "I hope so, too. Thanks."

After he left, she and Laura gave Philip a quick tour around the bakery. "It all started with my grandmother's rye bread," she said. "Maybe you knew that."

He shook his head. "Mariska didn't tell me much about the family business."

What did she tell you? Jenny wondered. That she hated it here, that she wanted to run away? That having a child wasn't enough to hold her?

"Gram started out baking bread in her kitchen," she said in a neutral tone, reminding herself that her mother's choices were not Philip's fault. "My grandfather would deliver the loaves door to door. Eventually, they moved into this building. The coffee shop opened about thirty years ago. I basically grew up here."

"She was adorable," Laura said. "Everyone's favorite."

"That doesn't surprise me." There was a world of sorrow in his expression.

Jenny ached with it, too, thinking of all the times, growing up, that she'd wondered about her father.

"Did you know," Philip asked, "that my dad's best fishing buddy was your grandfather?"

"Yes, my grandfather told me." Jenny felt a pang of regret. Charles Bellamy's son and Leo Majesky's daughter had fallen in love. They'd made a baby. But neither man had ever known it. Regrets pierced her sharply, and she quickly changed the subject.

"Daisy's working here now, did you know that?" she said.

"I didn't. Moving here is bound to be a big adjustment for her. It's good of you to include Daisy at the bakery." He hesitated. "She's, uh, having a hard time with my brother's divorce."

Jenny suspected there was more he could say about his troubled niece, but he wouldn't, of course. Jenny was still more stranger than daughter to him. She hoped Daisy would like working here. Zach had brought her by during the week, and she'd seemed eager to start training. Jenny scarcely knew her cousin, but she felt sorry for Daisy. Something had happened at her school in New York, though Jenny wasn't privy to exactly what. And Daisy's mother was working overseas, and Greg Bellamy had returned with his kids to the small town where he'd grown up. In the middle of her senior year in high school, Daisy had transferred to Avalon High. There was something wistful about the girl. Perhaps when Jenny got to know her better, she'd understand more.

She led the way back to the café. "Check this out." There was a wall covered with permits, certificates and memorabilia. Jenny pointed out the first dollar ever earned by the bakery and her grandparents' first permit from the health department.

And then there were the photographs, most of which had hung there so long that she hadn't really looked at them in ages. Showing her father around the bakery, Jenny was struck by how drab the place looked. It could definitely use some sprucing up. A fresh coat of paint, perhaps some artwork on the walls.

"The *Avalon Troubadour* gave the place a rave review the first summer they opened. Over the years, the bakery's been mentioned five times in the 'Escapes' section of the *New York Times*." She showed him the framed clippings.

Philip checked out the most recent. "Catskills Hideaway— 100 Miles to Paradise."

"There's always a surge in business after a mention like that," Jenny said. She noticed Philip studying a shot of her standing on a step stool behind the counter, helping her grandmother with a display of cookies. Jenny was about eight years old, her hair in two fat pigtails, a crooked, gap-toothed grin on her face. "Before the fire, I had a lot more pictures to show you," she said. "The usual stuff, candid shots of Christmas and Easter, the first day of school, first communion…"

Philip cleared his throat. "Jenny, it would've been great to see all those photos of you growing up, but that's not what I regret. In all of this, what I really regret is that I missed those years."

She had no idea how to respond. His yearning seemed to reach for her, touching tender, lonely places inside. "It's not your fault," she said, her voice husky. She swallowed hard and forced a smile. "Why do you think she never told you about me?"

"I don't know. Your mother was…" He shook his head. "I thought I knew her. I thought we wanted the same things. And I did love her, Jenny, but something changed for her. I don't know why she kept you from me."

Jenny felt Laura watching her. "I'm sure she had her reasons," Laura said.

"There's nothing we can do about it now," Jenny said. She showed him a picture of her mother at eighteen, laughing into the camera. "This is the picture Olivia noticed last summer, the one that made her realize there was a connection between our families."

Jenny had never realized that the photograph of her mother was actually only half a photograph. It had been cropped by someone, years ago. And that someone who had been cropped out of the picture was Philip Bellamy. It was only when Olivia had found a copy of the intact photo of Mariska and Philip together that they realized there was a huge story behind the picture. Olivia had come across the picture while going through Philip's old camp memorabilia, and the discovery had opened up a Pandora's box of the past, punctuating the way people had of coming and going in each other's lives.

"I wonder who cut me out of the picture?" Philip asked. "I assume it was your grandmother."

"I suppose we'll never know," Jenny said, "unless my mother magically reappears someday." She regarded the yellowing photograph of the beautiful young woman who would never get any older than she was in that instant. Was that the girl Philip remembered when he thought about Mariska?

"Listen, you two," Laura said with sudden briskness. "I need to get back to work." She hurried through the double doors.

Food for Thought
by Jenny Majesky

Chess Pie

Nobody knows the origin of the name "Chess Pie." It surely doesn't have anything to do with the game of chess. My grandmother got her recipe decades ago from a tourist visiting from Texas to see the turning leaves. I don't know anything else about the woman except that her recipe is called "Miss Ida's Buttermilk Chess Pie."

Don't be put off by the buttermilk. This pie is so sweet and intense, you need a large cup of coffee to go with it.

MISS IDA'S BUTTERMILK CHESS PIE

4 eggs
3/4 cup sugar
2 tablespoons flour
1-1/2 cups buttermilk
1/4 cup butter, melted
grated peel of 1 lemon
3 tablespoons lemon juice
1 teaspoon vanilla
1 9-inch graham cracker pie shell
fresh berries for garnish

In large bowl beat eggs and sugar until light and lemon colored. Beat in flour, then buttermilk, melted butter, lemon peel, lemon juice and vanilla. Pour mixture into pie shell. Bake in a 375°F oven for 35-40 minutes, or until knife inserted near center comes out clean. Garnish with fresh berries.

Eleven

1977

"Oh, Laura, look at this one. I like this shot, don't you?" Mariska Majesky handed her a photograph from the envelope of prints she'd picked up from the one-hour photo. "I really like this new haircut on me."

Laura Tuttle studied the photo with an enthusiasm that was, she admitted to herself, forced. While Laura worked the early shift at the bakery all summer, her best friend, Mariska, had been having a storybook romance, complete with Prince Charming. Laura had fallen into a secondary role, and now at summer's end, she was weary of it. But she put on her game face and admired the picture, which showed a laughing Mariska and a tanned and gorgeous Philip Bellamy holding a tennis trophy cup. The green hills and placid lake of Camp Kioga rolled out in the background.

"I like this shot, too." Still hiding her discontent, Laura handed back the photo. A pleasant breeze rippled through the alleyway behind the bakery, where she and Mariska were supposed to be rolling empty racks out of the truck after a delivery. They had paused to take a break before heading back to the yeasty-scented heat of the bakery.

"Tell you what," Mariska said, shaking out her attractive, layer-cut hair. "I had double prints made. I'm going to find a frame for this. Philip's heading back to Yale in a few days and this is the only picture of us together."

"That's because you're not supposed to be together," Laura pointed out.

"Don't start." A warning flashed in Mariska's eyes.

Laura could handle her friend's temper. "He's engaged to someone else," she reminded her.

"Yeah, to Pamela Lightsey, who ditched him for an entire summer so she could go to Italy. She deserves to lose him."

"You don't even know her, so how do you know what she deserves?"

"I know what she's like," Mariska insisted. "A spoiled rich girl. When Philip breaks up with her, she'll probably buy a new BMW to console herself."

"That doesn't mean she doesn't bleed, same as you and me," Laura said. She didn't know why she was defending Pamela Lightsey, a stranger.

"Aw, Laura." Mariska rolled the last rack out of the truck. "Be happy for me and Philip. He's so, so…everything."

"Listen to yourself." Laura felt like the adult in this friendship. She always had. Mariska was the free spirit, the adventurous one, who worked hard and played harder. Laura was the practical one, who worked hard and then worked harder. So *everything*. "Is it Philip you love, or the Bellamy money?"

"Don't be silly. You can't separate the two. Philip is Philip because he's a Bellamy."

"So if the family went bankrupt tomorrow and you'd have to live like a pauper, that wouldn't matter?" Laura couldn't help asking the question because, deep down, she knew the answer. And if Philip knew, maybe he wouldn't be so gaga over Mariska.

Mariska laughed, that shimmering, sexy laugh that had made her the most popular girl at Avalon High. At graduation last June, she'd been voted the girl most likely to get by on her looks. She'd taken it all in stride, because she knew darn well there was a lot more to her than looks. She had an incredible work ethic, for example. She worked two jobs—one here at her parents' bakery and another as a part-time salesclerk at the jewelry shop next door.

"What are you going to do with yourself after you get rich?" Laura asked. "Seriously, you're going to be so bored."

"Nonsense. I'm going to see the world and shop my whole life away."

"And what about Philip?" Did Mariska even know him? Laura wondered. Did she know he saved the middle of his pain au chocolat for last, that he'd seen the Allman Brothers at the Fillmore East before Duane Allman got killed, that his eyes crinkled at the corners when he laughed?

"What about Philip?" She sighed. "He's—Laura, you have to promise not to say anything…"

"About what?" Laura frowned. "Where does he fit in with all the traveling and shopping?"

"That's just it. Sometimes I'm afraid I'll get bored with him."

Laura wanted to shake her. "If you're afraid of that, then why are you planning a future with this man?"

"God, I swear, you're like an old, wet blanket," Mariska said with a frown. She bent to check her reflection in the side-view mirror of the truck, feathering her hair out at the temples. "I never should have told you about us." She fixed her lipstick and leaned back against the white panel truck. "That's not so. I had to tell somebody. This secret is just too good to keep to myself all summer long, and you're the only one I can trust."

Despite her yearning for Philip, Laura felt privileged that Mariska had entrusted her with the details of her clandestine love affair, because that was probably as close as Laura would ever get to a love affair of her own. She had the dullest life on the planet. Her best source for drama and romance was Mariska, who lived her life as though she was a character in a soap opera.

Unfortunately, characters in soap operas usually ended up heartbroken and alone, or at least with a bad case of amnesia.

"Listen," she said to Mariska. "I really hope everything works out."

"But what?"

"I didn't say but."

"You didn't have to. I heard it, anyway. But what?"

Laura took a deep breath. "I'm just worried about what's going to happen with you now that summer is over and Philip's going back to Yale. He might…well, you know what can happen. It's where the term *summer romance* comes from. When summer ends, so does the romance."

"Not for Philip and me," Mariska insisted.

Laura bit her tongue. Mariska and Philip were from two completely different worlds, and they were fooling themselves if they thought it would be easy to fit their lives together. Laura had seen this kind of thing before. People with such different backgrounds simply didn't have enough in common to stay together. Cinderella and Prince Charming was a fairy tale. In real life, princes married their own kind, not household servants.

"Besides," Mariska added, "I have an insurance policy."

"I don't get it."

Mariska smiled mysteriously. Her hand strayed down to her stomach and rested there. "I haven't told him, so don't say anything."

Laura felt as though someone had punched her.

Mariska's smile blossomed into laughter. "You should see your face. You're more surprised than I was, that's for sure."

Because you planned this, thought Laura with a sudden clarity of understanding. Although Mariska claimed love was all she and Philip needed, she'd hedged her bets by getting pregnant. And while Laura didn't know much about Philip, she did know that not only was he the handsomest guy on the planet, he was also extremely decent. He brought Fresh Air kids from the city, and he was getting a special leadership award from President Carter for working with New Haven's poor. And now that Mariska was pregnant, he would never leave her.

"I, um, don't know what to say. I mean, I'm happy for you." Her heart sank, because she couldn't fathom a way to see this working out. Mariska hadn't even finished growing up. Having a kid this young was a mistake.

Laura felt a little sorry for the Majeskys. They had wanted a big family, but according to Laura's mom, Helen had so much trouble having Mariska that she almost died, and she was unable to bear any more children. Maybe that was why Mariska was so spoiled. They lavished all they had on her. And here was the trouble with spoiled people. No matter what you gave them, they were never content. They always wanted more.

"So when are you going to tell Philip?" she asked.

"I haven't thought about that yet."

"Mariska, you have to—"

"I will, I swear, I will. I just found out myself. You're the first person I've told…well, almost."

"Almost?" Laura did not like the sound of that.

"I was kind of in shock when the clinic called with the results. I sort of blurted it out to some of the customers in the bakery."

"Uh-oh."

"Uh-oh is right." Then Mariska laughed again. "You won't believe who they were—Mr. and Mrs. Lightsey."

Laura could only shake her head. Clearly, blurting out the news had been no accident. "Pamela's parents."

"Philip says they're best friends with his parents. They came up for the closing ceremonies of the camp. He told me they do every year."

"And they know you're pregnant." Laura felt a chill despite the summer heat. This was the way Mariska operated. She was going to manipulate the situation, Laura just knew it. Making sure Pamela's parents learned the score was all part of some plan Mariska had up her sleeve. "Do they know it's Philip's?"

"It doesn't matter. As soon as he sees Pamela, which will be next week at Yale, he's going to tell her the engagement is off. He'll marry me before the baby comes, and everything will be just fine."

"Except for Pamela Lightsey."

"She'll be all right after the BMW," Mariska said airily.

Two days later, Laura was trimming the asters in the planter boxes in front of the bakery when she heard the train whistle, and remembered that Mariska had gone to the station to say goodbye to Philip. Minutes later, Mariska returned to the bakery, looking pale and defeated, a stranger Laura had never seen before.

Sweat beaded Mariska's upper lip. She swayed a little and clutched her stomach as if she was about to throw up.

"What happened?" Laura demanded, setting aside her gardening shears. "You look awful."

Mariska lowered herself to a chair at one of the bistro tables on the sidewalk in front of the bakery. "I broke up with him."

"I don't understand." Laura's mind swirled with confusion. "Did he take it badly? Did he not want anything to do with the baby?"

"I didn't tell him about the baby." Desperation shadowed Mariska's eyes. "He can't ever know, do you understand? Ever."

"Don't be crazy. He has a right to know."

"Stop it, Laura. I swear, if you say a word…" She rubbed her temples. "I need to think."

"Listen, a couple of days ago, you were planning a future with him. Did he change his mind?"

"No. He begged me not to break up with him."

"Then why did you?" Laura demanded, trying to figure out what had really happened.

Mariska took a deep breath. She looked at her reflection in the big window of the bakery. "I got a better offer."

"What do you mean, a better offer? From whom?"

Mariska didn't answer. She gave a bitter laugh, got up from the table and strode away. Although Laura called after her, she didn't respond as she walked along the sidewalk with her head held high. She took something out of her purse, ripped it down the middle, threw it in the green enamel trash bin and kept walking.

Laura couldn't resist. She pulled out the paper her friend had ripped. It was an enlargement of the beautiful shot of Mariska and Philip, torn neatly down the middle. Without hesitation, Laura rescued it from the trash. Mariska was surely being too hasty.

Food for Thought

by Jenny Majesky

Friendship Bread

At the Sky River Bakery, a lot of our breads begin with a sour-dough starter, and Friendship Bread is one of the favorites. It's called that because the starter can easily be shared among friends, who are invited to create breads of their own. It seems a little counterintuitive to let a vat of ingredients ferment for days on end, but ultimately, it gives the bread a special depth of flavor. This makes enough starter to share with your friends, along with a copy of the recipe.

This particular recipe is very flexible. You can add dried fruit, nuts, almond extract or sweet spices.

FRIENDSHIP BREAD STARTER

3 cups sugar
3 cups flour
3 cups milk

Day 1: In a nonmetal bowl, combine 1 cup sugar, 1 cup flour and 1 cup milk. Stir with wooden or plastic spoon (don't use metal spoon or electric mixer). Cover bowl loosely with a tea towel. Keep at room temperature, not in fridge.

Stir mixture once each day on days 2, 3 and 4.

Day 5: Add 1 cup sugar, 1 cup flour and 1 cup milk, and stir.

Stir mixture once each day on days 6, 7 and 8.

Day 10: Add 1 cup sugar, 1 cup flour and 1 cup milk. Remove 3 cups of mixture and give 1 cup each to three friends, with instructions. Save remaining starter for yourself.

FRIENDSHIP BREAD

1 cup starter
1 cup oil
1 cup sugar
1/2 cup milk
2 teaspoons cinnamon
1/2 teaspoon baking soda
2 cups flour
1-1/2 teaspoons baking powder
1/2 teaspoon salt
1 teaspoon vanilla extract
3 eggs
1 large box instant vanilla pudding mix

Combine starter with all the other ingredients, mixing thoroughly. Grease 2 large loaf pans and dust with mixture of cinnamon and sugar. Spoon batter into pans. Coat top of batter with butter and sprinkle with remaining cinnamon/sugar mixture. Bake at 325°F for 50-75 minutes, or until done.

Twelve

~~~◦<>◦~~~

There was something melancholy about Greg Bellamy's new home. Jenny sensed a curious press of sadness immediately as she stepped inside the boxy Victorian house on Spring Street. From the outside, it was fairly typical of the homes in Avalon, a tall, gabled house surrounded by white snow and bare trees, like a blank canvas waiting to be painted.

Inside was a different story. Items were placed haphazardly here and there—moving boxes, the odd article of furniture, a stack of mail on a windowsill. It reminded her of a hotel. Except she knew it was not. Greg and his two children, Max and Daisy, were here to stay.

"Let me take your coat," Greg offered, greeting her in the vestibule.

Philip was already there, seated on a stool at the counter, nursing a glass of wine. Rourke had been invited tonight but he'd declined, saying he was working late. And he probably was, but she had the impression that family gatherings weren't his thing. Offering Philip a tentative smile, she wasn't sure they were her thing, either, but at least she wasn't afraid to give it a shot. The whole idea of having relatives blew Jenny's mind. She'd grown up believing herself to be the only child of an only child. Now there was this whole undiscovered family of strangers.

"This is for you." She handed Greg the parcel she'd brought. "Friendship bread. It's said to bring good luck to a new home."

"Hey, thanks." Greg flashed her a boyish grin. "I need all the luck I can get."

Daisy and Max came thumping down the stairs, Max swinging around the newel post with a flourish. "Hey, Jenny," he said. "Hey, Uncle Phil."

Jenny was looking forward to getting to know her uncle and cousins. They had the trademark Bellamy looks—straight hair and straight teeth, good posture and natural charm.

A senior in high school, Daisy was understandably complicated. She was blond, beautiful and quiet, and her manners as she greeted Jenny and Philip were more than adequate. Max was in fifth grade. He was tall and lanky and filled with a marked exuberance, evident in his ready smile and restless enthusiasm.

Jenny gave them a container of bread starter and explained how to cultivate it and share with friends. "So in theory, you can send it on in an endless chain," she concluded.

"What if you don't feel like making bread every ten days?" Max asked. "Is there, like, a curse if you break the chain?"

"Yes, how did you know?" Jenny asked. "The youngest member of the household gets a rash on his scalp and has to shave his head."

Max's hand went to his thick, sandy-brown hair. "Very funny."

"I suppose you could ignore it and find out," Daisy said.

"Honestly," Jenny said, "you can put the starter in the freezer and leave it there indefinitely."

Connor and Olivia arrived in a swirl of snow blowing on an icy wind. As they greeted everyone, Jenny stood back and quietly observed the family dynamics. She was such a novice at this. Olivia effortlessly exuded affection for her uncle and cousins, and particularly for her father. The two of them shared an easy bond that could only have come from a lifetime of intimacy. Jenny felt a pang, not of envy or resentment, but of regret that she had missed out on this part of her family.

She felt someone watching her and looked up to see that it was Connor. He was a big, ruggedly handsome man who, Jenny knew, had endured a difficult childhood of his own, yet he seemed supremely content with Olivia, and comfortable in his own skin. "Don't worry," he said as if he'd read her thoughts, "you'll get used to it."

"Housewarming gift," Olivia said to Greg, handing him a voluminous shopping bag.

"This is the third one since we moved here," Greg protested. "You have to stop."

"Not until this house is warm," Olivia said with a teasing laugh. "It still looks like a transit station."

Jenny could easily pick out Olivia's other contributions around the house. There was a fringed blanket of warm, moss-colored cashmere, flung over the back of a chair. Next to it was a pillow covered in a rich brocade. Both items bore the stamp of Olivia's exquisite taste. Her current gift was a small reading lamp with a shade of leaded glass, clearly intended to turn the plain brown armchair and end table into a reading nook.

"I have to admit," Greg said, "you're good at this. You ought to do it for a living."

"Good plan." Olivia surrendered her coat and muffler to Max.

It was more teasing, of course. Olivia did do this for a living. She was a real estate expert, or what was known in the business as a house fluffer, specializing in preparing property for sale. She was so adept at decluttering, repurposing and remixing that she had founded her own firm in Manhattan, called Transformations.

The current decor of Greg's house, if it could even be called a decor, was early frat house. In place of a dining table, there was a massive pub-style pool table in the middle of the room, with a piece of plywood over its surface. The light fixture featured a colored plastic shade with Enjoy Budweiser spelled out in the faux-leaded glass. On the wall was a dart board and in the fireplace was an electric barbecue grill.

"For fixing hot dogs," Greg explained.

"And marshmallows," Max chimed in. "We call it indoor camping."

Jenny couldn't decide which was stronger—the frat house theme or the camping theme. Instead of regular bedding, they had down-filled sleeping bags. On bare mattresses.

"I am *so* taking you sheet shopping," Olivia murmured to Daisy as they checked out the upstairs. Jenny lost count of the bedrooms, closets and bathrooms. Most were empty and unheated, the doors shut.

"Thank God," Daisy said. "My dad forgot a few things. It's kind of okay, though, starting over from scratch."

"There's plenty of room for you to come and stay with us, Jenny," Greg said. "For as long as you need."

She felt a surge of warmth and gratitude. This was what a family did. They pulled together, helped each other out. Still, she couldn't quite put her faith in the process. Without a shared history, it was hard to buy into the idea of family.

"That's incredibly nice of you," she said. "Everything is crazy right now." She suspected there could be problems with such an arrangement, however. Greg was her uncle by birth, but they were still virtual strangers. He was newly divorced and his ex was a lawyer. Too many complications, she thought. "I'm all right for the time being," she said.

"True," Olivia agreed. "Who wouldn't be all right with the chief of police?"

Jenny's cheeks instantly stung with color. "It's only temporary. Very temporary."

"We know," Olivia said.

Jenny was surprised when Laura Tuttle showed up. Apparently, Philip had invited her. "I brought a pie," Laura said, moving easily into the kitchen. And just like that, everyone pitched in to get dinner on the table. It was strange and wonderful for Jenny to feel the rhythm of a family once again. Dinner was spaghetti, bag salad and bread from the bakery, nothing fancy but served with great generosity. The camping theme continued with paper plates and plastic flatware, though Greg had actual wineglasses for the adults.

Afterward, there was more wine, along with coffee and dessert—a chess pie from Sky River. The kids were excused to go watch TV, and the others discussed Jenny's situation again. Everyone wanted to help out, and none more sincerely than her father.

"I don't want to rush you or push, but I know this is a crucial time for you," he said.

Understatement, she thought.

"Maybe you'd like to give more time to your writing," Philip said. "You're an excellent writer."

"You've been reading my column?" she asked.

He nodded. "I ordered a subscription to the *Avalon Troubadour* to be mailed to me in New York so I could read 'Food for Thought' every Wednesday." He smiled at her stunned expression and helped himself to another slice of pie. "Anyway, in the city, you could meet people in publishing, determine whether or not you want to pursue writing as a career."

Lost in wonder, Jenny wasn't sure she'd heard correctly. "It's a weekly column, not a full-time job."

"At the moment," Philip pointed out. "I always wanted to be a writer. Didn't seem practical for me, though."

"And it seems practical for me?"

"You're still young enough to take a risk," he said.

She felt flustered as she looked at her sister and father. "Thank you. I'm flattered that you've been reading my column." She smiled, determined to conquer the panic knocking in her chest. "I've often wondered what it would be like to be a full-time writer, maybe gather my recipes and essays into a book." There. She'd said it. She'd told these people her dream. The idea of being a writer had always seemed so fragile and unlikely, a secret best kept to herself. Yet maybe Rourke was right. When she shared her dream, it took on shape and substance, grew sturdier.

And she would need to work full-time if she was going to rebuild all the writing that had been lost in the fire. Although the paper had archived her columns, everything else—the things she hadn't published because they were too raw or too personal or too new—were gone now, and she didn't know if she could ever get them back.

"Then you should go for it," Olivia said.

"Your writing is delightful to read," Philip added. "I love the glimpses into the life of the bakery. I feel as if I know your grandparents, the regular customers and the people who worked there over the years. And I'm proud of you. I've never read a food column before, but lately I've been bragging to everyone about my daughter's writing."

It felt shockingly good to hear those words. Never in her life had she thought she would experience this—a father's pride in something she had done. Sure, her grandparents had recognized her accomplishments, but neither had been a big reader of English. Now here was this intellectual man—Philip Bellamy—proud enough to tell his friends about her.

"How do you feel about spending some time in the city?" he asked in all sincerity.

"I…" Jenny took a gulp of wine. The city? New York City? Was he kidding? All right, she thought. Be cool. "I'm not quite sure… I haven't considered it."

"Maybe you should."

"But the bakery—"

"You could take a sabbatical from the bakery."

The Bellamys, Jenny had realized some time ago, did not always understand the way the real world worked. "It isn't that simple. You don't just take a sabbatical from the bakery. It's open seven days a week."

"It could be done," said Laura. "I can look after the place while you take some time for yourself."

There had never been a time in her life when Jenny wasn't involved in the bakery. Even as a child, she had spent a portion of every day there, sweeping floors, stacking trays or sometimes just keeping her grandmother company. They used to sing old songs together in Polish.

As if it were yesterday, she could feel the caress of her grandmother's hand, smoothing over her head. "You have the most important job of all," Gram used to say to her when she was tiny. "You make me remember why I bake."

A lovely memory, yes. And Jenny admitted that she was blessed with an abundance of them. She reminded herself that she had a lot of blessings—including the entire town of Avalon. She loved this town and she loved the bakery, yet there was something, some unfulfilled yearning that haunted her. She had gone from school to the bakery to sole ownership and, all right, it wasn't a bad life, but maybe, just maybe she should grab this chance to walk away, to live a different life.

Now? The question nagged at her. Since the fire, she was finally feeling a connection with Rourke. Maybe that was the biggest reason of all to turn tail and run. She took another sip of wine, hoping the others wouldn't notice the emotion that seemed to emanate from her. And then she felt it—a familiar panic, chugging toward her like a locomotive gathering steam. God, not now, she thought. Please, not now.

Okay, she told herself. Okay. She could simply excuse herself, go to the restroom and take a pill. No problem. As she sat there, expressionless, struggling to hide her distress, a curious thought pushed up through the quagmire of anxiety. She had not suffered a panic attack while staying with Rourke.

Coincidence? Would this have happened anyway, or did it have something to do with the way she felt when she was with Rourke McKnight?

Greg, Olivia and Connor cleared the table and went to do the dishes, leaving Jenny with Philip and Laura.

"Talk to me about Mariska," Philip said suddenly to Laura. "I want to understand."

Jenny leaned forward, intrigued. He seemed to be making a point of asking with Jenny present. Laura seemed to take the blunt question in stride. "She spent a lot of time away," she said, glancing from Philip to Jenny. "And then after she moved back here with Jenny, she still went out a lot. Her parents were more than happy to look after the baby." Laura beamed at Jenny. "You were everybody's angel."

Jenny tried to read between the lines. Going out a lot meant partying, probably. She knew from things her grandparents had said that her mother didn't always come home at night. A weekend trip was likely to stretch out to a week, sometimes two. That was why no one raised an alarm when she failed to come home one night. Of course, no one could know that first night was the start of forever.

"The Majeskys were wonderful," Laura said. "They gave Jenny all the love in the world. A happy child is a powerful thing. It's impossible to be sad when you have a laughing little girl in your lap."

Jenny tried to hold a smile in place. Yes, she'd been a happy child, but she was also a girl who, by the age of four, was accustomed to the fact that her mother had a habit of taking off.

"When did people realize she wasn't coming back?" Philip asked.

"I couldn't say exactly. Might have been a month, six weeks. I remember Leo telling a sheriff's deputy who stopped in for coffee and pastry every morning that she usually called but that the calls had stopped. Eventually, the concern became a formal report, which in turn grew into an investigation. However, we were told from the very start that when a grown woman with a history of lengthy, unexplained absences took off, chances were she wanted it that way."

Clearly, Jenny's mother hadn't wanted to be found and brought back to the small town where she'd never been happy.

The anxiety thrummed in her chest, and she excused herself to go to the bathroom. She swallowed half a pill, dry. When she returned to the dining room, she paused in the hallway outside the door. Laura and Philip were leaning across the table, talking intently and unaware of her. She sensed an intensity in their voices that made her pause, loath to intrude.

"...didn't know if I'd see you again after that summer," Laura was saying. "You visited Camp Kioga with your new wife and, a few years after that, your little daughter."

"But you knew, Laura." He drained his wineglass. "My God, you knew."

"There were things we didn't talk about, ever. You were one of them."

"Why didn't you say anything?"

"It wasn't my place to say anything."

"You were the only one who could have spoken up for Jenny, and you didn't say a word."

"I was protecting that child," she snapped.

"What the hell is that supposed to mean?"

"Think about it, Philip. She was a supremely happy little girl who was being raised in a world of love and security. I couldn't imagine what might happen if some strange man suddenly came into her life and started calling himself daddy. For all I knew, you had enough Bellamy money and power to take her away from us."

"From us?"

"Her grandparents," Laura amended, and then she grew fierce. "And yes—me. I loved Jenny but I had no claim on her. I was terrified of losing her."

"Did we seem like such monsters to you?"

"You seemed like a normal family. And I simply could not picture Jenny with you. Why would your wife accept her? Another woman's child. And your daughter, Olivia—I had no idea if giving her a sister would be a good thing or not. Either way, I would be playing God with a little girl's life, and I wasn't willing to do that."

That little girl didn't exist anymore, Jenny thought as a decision firmed in her mind. She was a grown woman now, and she was through being ruled by secrets and fear.

* * *

After dinner, Jenny drove home and automatically turned down Maple Street before she realized her house was no longer there. She was supposed to go back to the vast, too-comfortable-to-be-good-for-her bed at Rourke's house. But now that she was so close, something compelled her, even at this hour, to drive past the place.

The tires of the car crackled over the salted roadway, and she parked at the curb rather than turning into the driveway, now covered in deep drifts of snow. The empty spot where the house had been looked incongruous. There was a pair of tall maples in the front yard. In the fall, when Jenny was little, her grandfather used to rake the leaves into a pile so high, she could jump into it and disappear. Now the trees looked out of place, bare skeletons randomly standing in the middle of nowhere. She could see clear through to the backyard. A demolition company had followed in the wake of the salvage workers, leveling the place to rubble. Freshly cleared, it had resembled a war zone of black, scorched earth.

But it had snowed the previous night and most of the day, and thick drifts had virtually erased all traces of a house that had stood on the site for seventy-five years. Now all she could see was a lumpy expanse of white, cordoned off by safety tape. In the light of the street lamp, she could make out every contour. A set of rabbit tracks bisected the area where, she guessed, the living room had been, where her grandmother used to sit in the evenings and talk with Jenny.

Before her stroke, Gram had been a great talker. She loved to discuss things in endless detail, and loved to answer questions. This made them a good match, because Jenny had always been full of questions.

"What was it like when you were a little girl in Poland?" she would ask.

That was one of Gram's favorites. Her eyes would soften and shift focus as she went away somewhere, to a far-off place. Then she would tell Jenny about the old days in a village called Brzeźny, surrounded by wheat fields and sycamore woods, the air filled with birdsong, the rush of a fast-moving river and the sound of tolling bells.

When she was sixteen, Helenka's father put her in charge of driving the wagon loaded with wheat or corn to the miller for grinding. There, she met the miller's son, a young ox of a man who was strong enough to operate the mill single-handedly, and who had eyes the color of a robin's egg and a laugh so loud and merry that people who heard it tended to stop what they were doing and smile.

And of course, she fell in love with him. What else could she do? He was the strongest, kindest man in the village, and he told her she was brighter than the sun.

To Jenny, it sounded like an idyllic fairy tale. But she knew that unlike a fairy tale, there was no happily-ever-after for the newlyweds. Just two weeks after they married, the Germans initiated their September Campaign and invaded Poland. Soldiers overran the village, burning homes and shops, murdering or conscripting able-bodied men and boys, terrorizing women and children. When Jenny grew old enough to research the massacre of Brzeźny, she realized her grandmother had protected her from the ugliest of details.

The only reason Helenka and Leopold had escaped the carnage was that they had been sent that day to the district capital to register their marriage. When they returned, the village was in chaos, and their families gone—murdered or fled.

"The next day," Gram would tell Jenny, "we started to walk." It took several tellings and much questioning before Jenny learned that they had walked away from their village with only the clothes on their backs, a sack of withered apples and a few supplies, including the coffer of rye starter Gram's mother had given her on her wedding day.

The Germans attacked the Poles in the west and the Russians in the east. For the people of Poland, every river and roadway became a battleground, and not one square inch was safe for the people who lived there, tilled the soil, raised their children and buried their dead. About six million Poles died in World War II. Jenny's grandparents were lucky to escape with their lives.

"Where did you walk?" she used to ask.

"To the Baltic Sea."

When Jenny was little, she thought it was like walking to the corner store to buy a quart of milk. Later she learned that her grandparents, who were little more than children themselves and had never before left their tiny rural district, traveled hundreds of miles on foot and, once they reached the port of Gdansk, paid for their passage by the labor of their backs.

Sometimes, Jenny would think about the people Gram had never seen again—her parents, six brothers and sisters, everyone she'd ever known. "You must miss them so much," Jenny would say.

"That is true," Gram told her. "But they are here." She pressed her hand gently to her chest. "They are here in my heart, forever."

Leaning against the idling car, Jenny closed her eyes and pressed her fists to her chest, praying that Gram was right, that you could never really lose someone, so long as you held their memory in your heart and tended to it, nurturing it with love.

She let out a long, unsteady breath, opened her eyes and blinked at the cold night. It wasn't working. There was nothing in her heart. She felt hollow, with unreasoning panic ricocheting back and forth inside her.

A car rounded the corner and washed the area in white light. Across the way, a curtain stirred in the window of Mrs. Samuelson's house. As the visitor drew closer, Jenny recognized Rourke McKnight. He pulled over to the curb and got out of his car and walked toward her. Jenny's heart skipped a beat.

He was still dressed for work, his long overcoat billowing out behind him as he came closer.

She shivered and stuffed her hands into her pockets. "Hey," she said.

"Hey, yourself." He looked around the empty lot. "Everything all right?"

"Sure," she said, knowing that the real question was, What are you doing here? "I, um, I drove here by mistake. You know, driving home on autopilot." She offered an ironic smile. "It takes some adjustment, this homeless business." She couldn't bear to look at his expression—a mixture of compassion and kindness—so she leaned back and studied the spot where the second-story bedroom window used to be.

"Do you know," she asked, "that when I was a kid I used to climb out the window and onto that branch?" She pointed at the maple tree. "I never once got caught."

"What were you doing, sneaking out?"

She tried to figure out the source of the sharp note in his voice. "Depends," she said. "It was usually to meet my friends down by the river and hang out. Sometimes we went to the drive-in movie at Coxsackie. I wouldn't say we were juvenile delinquents or anything. I really tried to stay out of trouble for my grandparents' sake."

"I wish all kids tried to do that," Rourke said. "It would make my job a hell of a lot easier."

"I always felt sorry for my grandparents, because of my mother," Jenny explained. With each breath she took, the panic in her chest was subsiding. "She broke their hearts. There was always a sadness in them—my grandfather, especially. When the doctors told him he wasn't going to make it, he said maybe she would come back for his funeral." Jenny stabbed the toe of her boot into the snow. She'd always felt she should somehow atone for her mother's abandonment. "Since my mom would never come back to see them, I promised I would never leave them." At a very young age, Jenny came to realize that her job was to keep her grandparents' sadness away, and she had played that role for years. It felt strange, not having to do it anymore.

He was quiet for a few minutes. She did the self-check the doctor suggested. Moments ago, she'd been an eight out of ten. Now she'd subsided to a six, perhaps even a five or four, a huge relief. Maybe it was that half a pill she'd taken. Or maybe she was finally moving past this phase.

"There were several boxes of reports about my mother's disappearance," she said. "They were lost in the fire."

"The department has everything archived," Rourke assured her. "If you want, I can check and see what they've got in the records."

"Thanks. I've been thinking about her more than I usually do, these past few days." A sprinkle of snow flurries started. "It's funny, but some part of me thought she might come back after my grandmother died."

"Why is that funny?"

"Poor choice of words. Strange is more like it. It was strange for me to think of that. I mean, if she didn't come back when her father got sick and died, and she didn't come back after her mother had a stroke and we filed for bankruptcy…if those things didn't bring her back, then it was silly to think Gram's death would."

He didn't say anything, and she was glad. Because one conclusion was that her mother had never come back because she was dead. Jenny refused to think that. If Mariska had died, they would have heard.

"What's ironic," she said, "is that Philip showed up, out of nowhere, practically. Just when I think I'm completely alone in the world, this whole other group of relatives shows up."

"You don't ever have to be alone," he said.

His words and the tone of his voice startled her. "Rourke?" she asked softly.

He seemed to catch himself, and then the Officer Friendly mask dropped back in place. "What I mean is, you're part of this town," he explained. "Everybody here loves you. Your best friend is the mayor."

"You're right. I'm incredibly lucky." She took in a long, slow breath that chilled her lungs. "There's very little I'd call good about what happened," she said. "Finding myself homeless, with my family gone, is something I wouldn't wish on my worst enemy."

"You don't have any enemies," he pointed out.

"Unless they find out someone torched my house."

"No one torched your house."

"Well, one good thing came of this. Being homeless has opened up a world of possibilities for me."

"Meaning?"

"I can start over with a clean slate, anywhere I want." She watched his face but couldn't tell what he was thinking. "That's why leaving here is going to be so hard."

He didn't move or make a sound. In fact, it was so quiet that she could hear snowflakes landing on the fabric of her parka. She waited, breath held, anticipating his next question.

It never came. He simply stood there, stone-faced.

Maybe he hadn't heard. "I said, I'm leaving Avalon."

"I heard you."

"And you don't have anything to say about that?"

"Nope."

"Rourke—"

"It's your life. Your decision. I don't get a say in it."

Tell me you want me to stay, she thought. Just say the word, and I won't go. Then she felt pathetic. If he did tell her that, would she stay? "Say something."

"What do you want to hear?"

"I want to hear what you think of my plan."

"Does it matter what I think?"

"Yes."

"Why?"

"Because you matter to me," she blurted out. Then, in horror, she backpedaled. "It's just that you've been so generous. Too generous. I feel bad about the way I've inconvenienced you. I've imposed on you for too long. I can't just move into your life, Rourke."

"Why not?"

"Because it's wrong. We've each got our own lives to live, and we can't keep cramping each other's style."

"So now I'm cramping your style."

"No. My God, you are frustrating to talk to."

He didn't say anything.

"I've decided to go to New York," she said. The impact of the decision reverberated through her. This was the first time she'd said it aloud. "I'm going to be staying in Olivia's old apartment. Philip Bellamy suggested it. He wants me to get to know him better, meet his sisters and spend some time with his parents—my grandparents—and…I don't know. Once all my business is settled here, I'm going to take him up on it. Laura will handle the bakery and I'll finally have a chance to get serious about my writing."

She felt oddly breathless when she finished telling him the plan. Talking about it felt strange. This was going to happen. She was actually going to leave the place where she'd been born and raised, where she had lived her whole life. Unless Rourke gave her a reason to stay. And why on earth would he do that? "I'm taking advantage of the freedom the fire has given me."

"Sounds to me like you're running away." He opened her car door. "I'll meet you back at my place," he said.

Feeling unsettled, she got behind the wheel.

"See you later," he added, leaning slightly into the car. "Seat belt," he reminded her, then slammed the door shut.

Thirteen

So far at Avalon High School, Daisy had made two actual friends, and she hadn't even had to lie to get them to like her. Of course, she'd held back certain information. She wasn't sure whether or not that was considered lying. No, she decided. It wasn't. However, she was keeping a few cards close to the vest. For the time being, anyway.

She was good at keeping secrets. Like when her parents started sleeping in separate rooms a year before the divorce, she hadn't told anyone, not even her little brother. Or when Logan O'Donnell said he didn't want anybody to know they were having sex, she'd totally kept it to herself, even though Logan was considered the hottest boy in the school.

Of course, hottest never meant the smartest, as she had soon found out. Just because a boy was sexy didn't mean he knew how to practice safe sex.

Although, now that she looked back from her current perspective, she could clearly see that the truly stupid one in the relationship had been her. Even though it was dark, even though she'd wanted to do it so bad she nearly came out of her skin, she should have taken two seconds to check and make sure Logan actually knew how to put on a condom.

But who would have figured? she wondered. Who on earth

would have actually thought Logan O'Donnell, who was going to Harvard, could be so clueless?

"You want to go skiing on Saturday?" asked Sonnet. The three of them were going to Sonnet's house after school to study for a global-history exam. Daisy didn't much care for school, but she genuinely liked Zach and Sonnet, and even though they'd be studying, it was a chance to hang out with them.

"I can't go anywhere on Saturday," Daisy reminded her. "I'm working, remember?"

"You didn't waste time getting a job," Sonnet said.

"Yes, well, I figure if I'm gainfully employed, maybe my folks won't pressure me so much about college. I haven't told my mom yet, though." She could just hear her mother now. *A Bellamy? Working as counter help in a bakery?* Like that was some big stigma.

"What's your mom got against working?" Zach asked.

"Nothing," Daisy said. "That's, like, the main reason she and my dad split up, because she's a workaholic. She spent more hours at her law firm than she did at home, that's for sure. Last year, she worked on a case in Seattle, meaning she only came home every other weekend. And now she's in The Hague, and she almost never comes back to New York anymore. We e-mail, though," Daisy admitted. "E-mail and phone calls. I think we actually talk more now that she's in Europe than we did when she was home." Daisy actually liked—no, loved—those talks. It was the one time she had her mother's undivided attention.

"She'll probably respect you for getting a job," Sonnet pointed out.

"She would want me to have a job that, according to her, *matters.* And to my mom, that means a job that leads somewhere, like being a page for a politician, or an intern at a brokerage firm or something. Working for somebody who can write me a good reference for college."

"Jenny will write you a reference," Zach pointed out.

"Yeah, right— 'My cousin did a really good job selling muffins and pull-aparts.'" She looked at Zach. "Not that there's anything wrong with it, but my mom wouldn't think it's anything special."

"It's not," he said. "But I like working for Jenny. I think it's cool that she's your cousin."

"Here we are," Sonnet said, stopping at a mailbox that was nearly buried in a bank of snow. "Home, sweet home." She collected the mail and led them up the walkway to her house.

In the dimness of the falling light, the snow rippled with purple shadows and the boxy white house looked like something from a distant time. It was incredibly plain, an unadorned white saltbox in the middle of a flat white yard. Daisy hoped there were flower beds or shrubs under the thick blanket of snow, because if not, the place would probably qualify for one of those makeover shows. She knew, though, that it didn't matter what someone's house looked like. Her parents used to have not one but two beautiful houses—a town house in Manhattan and a weekend place on Long Island—but it hadn't managed to make them happy.

"My mom's sick today," Sonnet said as they trooped into the side door. "She came home from the conference with a cold."

Daisy heard the sound of a radio somewhere in the house. Nina Romano turned out to be a fan of Air America. Sonnet led the way into what appeared to be the family room.

Nina was on the sofa with an afghan covering her, the radio on and a laptop computer in front of her. On an end table, there was an array of mugs and cold remedies, a box of Kleenex, a regular phone and a BlackBerry. She looked up and a smile lit her face. "Hey, you guys. How was school?"

Daisy had to pause for a moment to cover her surprise. She expected the town mayor to be a brisk, efficient, Marian-the-Librarian type, with thick ankles and sensible shoes. Instead, Nina Romano looked way too young to have a daughter who was a senior in high school. And she was white, though that wasn't a surprise, since Daisy had met two of Sonnet's uncles at school. Another thing that didn't surprise Daisy—Nina was drop-dead gorgeous. Judging by Sonnet's looks, that was to be expected. However, mother and daughter appeared as though they came from different continents.

Sonnet made the introductions, and Nina beamed at Daisy. "Don't come any closer," she said. "I've got the mother of all colds and I don't want to get you guys sick. I've been hoping to meet you, Daisy. My brother Tony says you're in his homeroom."

"That's right."

"And you're already working at the bakery, I hear. That's great."

"Word travels fast," Daisy said.

"You have no idea. Did you know Jenny Majesky is my best friend? We grew up together." Nina turned to Zach. "How are you?" she asked. "I haven't seen much of you lately."

"I increased my hours at the bakery." Zach appeared slightly uncomfortable, standing in the doorway as though poised to flee. Daisy knew that there was tension between his father and Sonnet's mother, undoubtedly because his dad, the current city administrator, was after Nina Romano's job. Zach didn't say much about his dad, but she had the impression that Matthew Alger was strict and very focused on money. And he probably didn't think much of his son coming here, fraternizing with the enemy, so to speak.

The three of them went into the kitchen to find something to eat and get to work.

"Your mom looks like a college girl," Daisy said to Sonnet.

"She was just fifteen when she had me."

Daisy didn't know what else to say. *I'm sorry* didn't seem right. "So what happened?" she asked, blurting out the question before she could decide whether or not she should ask it. "I mean, besides the obvious."

"She met a guy from West Point. He had no idea she was underage. My mom looked way older than fifteen. Now she looks way younger than thirty-one. I'm really proud of her."

"I don't blame you. She must be something, to go from teenage mom to town mayor. You're something, too," Daisy added. "You'll only be sixteen when you graduate. Why the rush?"

Sonnet shrugged. "There wasn't much to it. I doubled up on English classes and that gave me enough credits to finish, so it didn't feel like a rush. I guess I'm kind of in a hurry to move away, start college. My mom would never say anything, but I just get this feeling she's waiting for a shot at her own life."

"What about your dad?"

"I don't really call him my father or my dad. That implies a relationship that isn't there. He is…the guy whose DNA I have. The guy who made me biracial."

"So where is he now?"

She shrugged, the casual gesture probably masking a world of hurt. "He works in Washington, D.C. At the Pentagon."

"What is he, like some military VIP?"

"That's what they say. And he has this incredible trophy wife who's a Rhodes scholar and the granddaughter of a famous civil rights leader, and they have two perfect kids who look like movie stars."

Again, Daisy didn't know what to say.

"I'm okay with all that," Sonnet quickly explained. "Except…"

"Except what?"

"Except sometimes I have no idea who I am. I see my dad maybe once a year. My mom's like, the town hippie. A throwback to Woodstock."

"She must be more than that, to be elected mayor."

They opened their backpacks and took out their notes. Daisy also took out her camera, a digital with Carl Zeiss optics. She'd gotten it for her birthday last summer and had discovered a new obsession. At her former school, photography had been the only class she enjoyed. She absolutely loved taking pictures, capturing a particular moment or image or slant of light.

There was something compelling and oddly intimate in the way Sonnet and Zach sat at the table, studying together, occasionally teasing. The angle of their heads formed a curious symmetry.

"Don't mind me," Daisy said, powering up her camera. "I just want to take a few shots."

The space between them formed a heart shape, but it wasn't too cutesy because their expressions were so intense. Daisy took a few pictures and then put the camera aside. Sonnet offered her a Coke but she declined. Daisy was starving. Lately she got the munchies in a way that was, like, ten times more intense than when she smoked pot. At odd hours, too, sometimes in the middle of the night. So when Sonnet put out a bag of chips and a tub of sour-cream dip, Daisy dug in as though she hadn't eaten in days.

She asked for a glass of water. The moment she finished drinking it, all the cold liquid seemed to head straight for her bladder.

"Where's the restroom?" she asked, suddenly about to burst.

Sonnet pointed down the hallway.

Daisy hurried. She passed the study where Nina was now talking on the phone, something about city finance.

The chips and dip had been a mistake. A huge mistake. She felt them heading northward, until she felt like a volcano about to erupt.

Bathroom. Where the hell was the bathroom?

She wrenched open one of the hallway doors. Damn. Coat closet. Tried the next one. Damn. Cellar stairs. Almost panicking now, she tried door number three. It wasn't a bathroom, either. She was about to explode when she heard Nina say, "End of the hall, honey."

Daisy ran. She didn't know which was more urgent—the need to pee or the need to puke. But she had to get to that bathroom.

Ten minutes later, pale and completely empty, having sponged herself off and rinsed her mouth, she staggered out of the bathroom. *Get a grip,* she told herself. *Go to the kitchen and act normal.*

Shoulders back, chin up, she walked down the hall. As she passed the study where Nina was working, Daisy pretended not to see her. She almost made it past, when Nina spoke up.

"Have you seen a doctor yet, honey?"

Food for Thought

by Jenny Majesky

Heaven in a Bottle

A nursing mother should drink something alcoholic every day, as long as she doesn't have a drinking problem. A doctor wouldn't tell you this, but my grandmother and her friends all believed it. Give a nursing mother a glass of beer to drink every evening, and it's good for her milk production. A very moderate amount doesn't affect the baby at all.

My grandmother was never much of a drinker, but we always had liquor in the house to use in her baking—sherry for Fanny Farmer cakes, Triple Sec for the fruitcake, Kahlúa with its variety of uses, rum and, of course, Irish Cream. Decades ago, Gram found a recipe for a cake on an Irish Cream label, and Grandpa liked it so much that he finished off the rest of the bottle. Afterward, they could be seen snuggling on the porch swing.

She made the cake so many times, she never really had to refer to the recipe again. This cake freezes well, and makes a nice gift.

IRISH CREAM CAKE

1/2 cup finely chopped pecans
1/2 cup finely shredded coconut
1 (18.25 ounce) package yellow cake mix
1 (3.4-ounce) package instant vanilla pudding mix
4 eggs
1/4 cup water

1/2 cup vegetable oil
3/4 cup Irish Cream liqueur
1/2 cup butter
1/4 cup water
1 cup white sugar
1/4 cup Irish Cream liqueur

Preheat oven to 325°F. Grease and flour a 10-inch Bundt pan. Sprinkle chopped nuts and coconut evenly over bottom of pan.

In a large bowl, combine cake mix and pudding mix. Mix in eggs, 1/4 cup water, 1/2 cup oil and 3/4 cup Irish Cream liqueur. Beat for 5 minutes at high speed. Pour batter over nuts in pan.

Bake for 60 minutes, or until a toothpick inserted into the cake comes out clean. Cool for 10 minutes in the pan while you prepare the glaze. To make the glaze, combine butter, 1/4 cup water and 1 sugar in a small saucepan. Bring to a boil and continue boiling for 5 minutes, stirring constantly with a whisk. Remove from heat and whisk in 1/4 cup Irish Cream.

Invert the cooled cake onto a serving platter. Prick top and sides of cake. Spoon glaze over top and brush onto sides of cake, until the glaze is absorbed.

Fourteen

"**I**'ve made up my mind," Nina said to her friends, who were waiting for her outside the clinic where she'd gone for a counseling session. "I'm keeping it."

Jenny, Joey and Rourke sat silently in Rourke's Volvo. As a camp counselor this year, he was entitled to bring a car. He and Joey had permission to be off-premises for the afternoon. A breeze from the river blew through the open windows. "Alive" by Pearl Jam was playing on the radio. The three of them had been waiting for Nina for over an hour. Jenny imagined she could feel the guys squirming, although she couldn't actually see them move. Pregnant girls and family-planning clinics were not exactly favorite topics with boys, that was for sure. As for Jenny, she greeted the news with mixed emotions, but for Nina's sake, she smiled as she scooted across the backseat and motioned for Nina to get in. "All right," she said. "Then…congratulations."

Rourke adjusted the rearview mirror. "Seat belt," he said, and both girls complied.

Jenny kept looking over at Nina and trying to imagine what she was feeling. Nina just looked down at her lap. A moment later, she took some colorful brochures out of her purse and started looking through them. She was just fifteen. *Fifteen.* She didn't even have her license yet, but before long she'd have a baby to look after twenty-four/seven, and no husband to help her with it. And actually *having* it—Jenny had seen the standard film in health class, and wanted no part of giving birth. The very idea that a whole baby came out down there was… Jenny resisted the urge to squirm right along with the guys. She still went to a pediatrician, for cripe's sake, and as far as she knew, so did Nina. There was a kind of doctor called a "gynecologist," but Jenny didn't even know whether that was pronounced with a hard or soft "g" and was too embarrassed to ask. Not having a mother meant not having someone to ask stuff like that. At least Nina had a mom. A mom who was probably going to ground her for life when Nina told her she was pregnant.

The guys were quiet. Joey was staring out the window. Rourke was scowling at the road; she could see his frown of concentration in the rearview mirror. As always, Joey and Rourke were a study in contrasts, earning them the nickname Bill & Ted, after the goofy movie about likable boneheads who were best friends. Rourke was the blond, suntanned surfer, while Joey's black hair, dark eyes and full mouth reminded her of Keanu Reeves. Privately, Jenny thought they were more like Jay Gatsby and Nick Carraway, but that reference was lost on most people.

Rourke glanced into the rearview mirror and caught her looking at him. Flustered, she shifted in her seat and turned to the window with a fake-interested look. She had to be careful around Rourke, because even though he swore Joey wanted her to be his girlfriend, she was suffering from the most unbelievable crush on Rourke. She had from the first day she'd met him, when he'd gotten into a fight to protect her.

She wondered if she would ever get used to the way he looked. Doubtful. Each summer it was the same. Kioga would open for business and she would help her grandfather with the bakery deliveries. Going up to the camp was like stepping into a different world, an idyllic place from the past. She always marveled at the people who attended the camp. She was reminded of something she'd read by F. Scott Fitzgerald—who was required reading for school but actually a pretty good writer—"The rich are different." Much as she wanted it not to be true, it was. These people had a certain air of self-confidence and style. They knew who they were and where they belonged in the world—at the top.

And each year, she thought, this is the year Rourke will change. He'll be geeky or have pimples or B.O. or he'll turn into a jerk. But each year, he proved her wrong. He just got better looking and more self-confident. And nice enough that, when she told him she and Nina needed a favor today, he hadn't batted an eye.

The truth was, she kept looking for reasons not to like him, because there were so many reasons she shouldn't, including the fact that he would never like her back. She always failed, though. Although Rourke acted all serious and gruff, he was as kind as he was good-looking.

Enough, she told herself. Her obsessive thoughts about Rourke McKnight were getting downright scary. He was Prince Charming, too good to be true, and as unreachable as the moon. Now, Joey was the real thing: funny and down-to-earth, the son of the McKnights' driver who dared to dream of a bigger life for himself. Joey was the kind of guy a girl could introduce to her family and it wouldn't be awkward. If Rourke was the type a girl dreamed about marrying, Joey was the type she actually married.

She reached across the seat and patted Nina's leg. "You okay?" she asked.

Nina looked up, pale and flustered. "I'm totally freaked out, that's how I am," she said. "I can hear everybody now—'She was *such* a smart girl from *such* a wonderful family. She had *so much* going for her…'"

"And now you've got even more going for you," Jenny said, scrambling to find something positive to say. "You're smart, you've got a great family and you're going to have a baby. My grandmother says babies are proof that God exists."

"Listen, that's really sweet, but I'm not kidding myself. This is not going to be a picnic."

Jenny couldn't agree more, but didn't let herself say so. She also didn't bring up the plans she and Nina had been making for years. They were supposed to see the world after high school. Then Jenny planned to get a fabulous job and a loft in the city and hang out like the *Mad About You* people. Nina planned to return to Avalon and buy the Inn at Willow Lake, a once-grand hotel she'd always dreamed of owning. Jenny would take all her vacations at the inn, where she would work on her novel. Now, of course, none of that was going to happen, and Jenny felt an unbidden sting of anger at Nina for messing up their plans. Then she felt disloyal and forced a smile. "Just because it's hard doesn't mean you shouldn't do it."

"I have to tell Laurence," Nina said. "He's going to hate this."

Joey turned around, hooking his elbow over the back of the seat. "Want us to kick his ass for you?"

"No. God, Joey. You'd never be able to kick his ass anyway. He knows self-defense. He goes to West Point."

Jenny had met Laurence once—a tall, broad-shouldered African-American, he was intimidating with his shaved head and military bearing.

"Then what the hell is he doing dating a high-school girl?" Rourke asked.

"He's only seventeen, same age as you guys."

"Yeah, and you don't see us knocking you up," Joey said, cluelessly trying to be helpful and earning a slug on the arm from Rourke.

"It's his first year at the Academy. And besides, I told him I was eighteen," Nina said.

Jenny could easily see how Laurence Jeffries had been duped. Nina, with her dark-eyed beauty and killer figure, had a knack for making herself look older than her age. To his credit, Laurence had immediately dropped her when he found out how young she was.

"If I tell him about this," Nina said, "and he abides by the honor code, he'll have to tell his superiors and then he'll be expelled. So maybe I won't say anything at all."

The suggestion sent a chill through Jenny. "All my life, I've wished my father knew about me. I keep thinking everything would be different if my mother had told him." If, in fact, that was the case. She didn't know for certain. Maybe she had a father somewhere who *did* know about her but didn't care enough to step forward.

"Why would you want anything different?" Rourke asked.

Good question. It was funny, how he looked at her and thought she had the perfect life. "I'd just like to know, is all," she said.

"So am I driving up to West Point now?" he asked Nina.

"No," Nina said. "I need to go home. I've got some thinking to do." She was quiet the rest of the way, idly paging through the information they'd given her at the clinic. Amy Grant's "Baby Baby" drifted from the radio now.

Before long, they reached a sign marking Avalon city limits near the covered bridge.

"You'd better pull over," Nina said. "I'm going to puke."

She staggered out of the car but she didn't puke. She took a deep breath and made a visible effort to conquer the nausea.

"Are you all right?" asked Jenny, getting out of the car.

"Yes." Nina collected her bag and a packet from the clinic. "I want to walk the rest of the way home."

"I'll drive you," said Rourke.

"It's just a few blocks," Nina pointed out. "I need to clear my head before I drop the bomb on my parents."

"Fair enough."

Nina looked pale but resolute. "You guys are the best friends ever. I don't know what I'd do without you."

After she left, Jenny, Joey and Rourke lingered by the river. It was one of the prettiest spots in Avalon, an old-fashioned covered bridge with weathered siding spanning the Schuyler River.

"It's peaceful here," Joey said. "You're lucky to live in a place like this."

"Huh. I can't wait to get out of here," Jenny said.

"Why would you want to leave?" asked Rourke.

"Because it's all I've ever known. I've always wanted a chance to go someplace else. Live a different life. Find out who I am besides Jenny the bakery girl."

Though Joey seemed to understand, Rourke stared at her oddly. "What's with being Jenny the bakery girl? People like her."

"Yeah, well, maybe I don't like her." She sighed and stared down at the clear water rushing over rocks. "Nina and I had big plans. We were going to move to the city after high school. Get jobs. Go to college. Now she's going to have a baby, so it looks like I'll be on my own."

She regarded Joey and Rourke, both so handsome, so comfortable with who they were. She wasn't sure why, but she felt compelled to tell them things. All kinds of things. "If I tell you something, do you promise never to say a word?"

Rourke and Joey exchanged a glance. "Promise."

"When Nina came out of the clinic today and said she was keeping the baby, I had a moment when I felt—this is crazy—I felt jealous. I mean, I know having a baby is a scary thing, especially when you're a kid, but all the same, I couldn't help what I felt, and it was ugly."

Rourke shrugged. "People think ugly thoughts all the time. It's only a problem when they act on them." He spoke with a casual air, yet she suspected there was some sort of powerful knowledge behind his words.

"So what did you think?" she asked him.

"About her having a kid?" He pressed his lips together, shook his head. "Like she said, it's her choice. Man, I'll never have kids."

"All guys say that," she pointed out. "I bet in ten or fifteen years, you'll be pushing a stroller, or maybe you'll be walking around with one of those baby carriers—"

"Not Rourke," Joey said.

"Right," he agreed. "Some people shouldn't ever be parents."

She stared at him. "You mean your father."

"I didn't say that."

"You didn't have to." Jenny found it quite startling, the contrast between Senator Drayton McKnight's public persona and his private. Sometimes even she didn't believe it, although Joey assured her the guy was a bastard of the first order. When the senator made a public appearance with his family, they looked wonderful together—the sincere public servant, his lovely wife, his handsome, well-groomed son. But over the years, Rourke had given her glimpses of the turmoil behind the polished facade.

"I've made a decision, too," he said.

Both she and Joey leaned forward, listening.

"I'm going to break with my father."

"What do you mean, 'break with him'?" Joey asked.

"I'm going to be on my own."

His father had big plans for him. He was supposed to go to Columbia or Cornell. Graduate with honors. Carry on the family tradition. It all sounded great to Jenny, but clearly Rourke had other ideas.

"This is all about what you don't want," she pointed out. "You don't want kids, don't want to go to Columbia, don't want to follow in your dad's footsteps. So what do you want?"

"I've got some ideas, none of which will thrill the old man. And that's all I'm going to say about it for now."

"What about you, Joey?" she asked, noticing that he had gotten very quiet.

"I got a plan," he said. "I'm going to enlist in the army."

She frowned. "The army? Like boot camp and all that?"

"Sure," he said. "Starting next fall."

She knew nothing about the military except through the "be all you can be" TV commercials that promised you'd get an education and see the world. She was pretty sure there was a catch somewhere. Like you had to go to dangerous places where hostile people were trying to kill you. She turned to Rourke. "What do you think of his plan?"

"I think Joe should do whatever he wants."

"So do you want it?" Jenny asked him.

Joey looked at her for a long time. They weren't touching or even standing that close, but she felt that look coasting over her like a warm breeze. "Yeah," he said. "Yeah, I want it. I want a lot of things."

His infatuation—or whatever it was—felt palpable, as though he'd caressed her. Jenny couldn't help smiling. He always made her smile. "Like what?" she said, and hoped he knew she wasn't teasing or flirting. "I really want to know."

"I want to go to college, so serving in the army'll earn me that."

"Why college? I thought you hated school."

"I do, but it's the best way to make something of myself. I want to be able to get married, support a family. You know, the whole happily-ever-after thing." He elbowed Rourke and mimicked his friend. "And that's all I'm going to say about it for now."

Food for Thought
by Jenny Majesky

Starting from Scratch

Lots of people use this phrase and understand perfectly what it means, although few know its origin. To start from scratch is to begin from the beginning, from square one. It's to start with nothing, no odds in your favor, no head start or advantage. It is ground zero, which is another phrase that needs explaining, but maybe not here.

In the middle of the eighteenth century, "starting from scratch" was a sporting term. It referred to a starting line, usually scratched into the dirt with a sharp stick. In cricket, "scratch" is the line in front of each stump where the batsman stands. And finally, in bare-knuckle boxing, a line was drawn across the ring, and the boxers would come "up to scratch" to begin their bout.

Nowadays, starting from scratch is synonymous with starting from nothing, and in baking, something made from scratch is generally presumed to be excellent. You can add flavor with a pinch of herbs, and don't forget—lavender is an herb. Make a batch of lavender sugar and keep it on hand.

SCRATCH BISCUITS WITH LAVENDER SUGAR

2 cups all-purpose flour
2 teaspoons baking powder
1/4 teaspoon baking soda
1/4 teaspoon salt

　　1/2 cup unsalted butter, cold and sliced into about a
　　　　dozen pieces
　　3/4 cup buttermilk
　　1 tablespoon melted butter
　　sprinkle of lavender sugar

Heat oven to 450°F. Combine dry ingredients and cut in butter
with two knives or pastry blender until crumbly. Stir in buttermilk
just until moistened. Turn dough onto lightly floured surface;
knead about 10 times or until smooth. Roll out dough to 3/4-inch
thickness. Cut with a 2-1/2-inch biscuit cutter, or use a juice glass.
This makes about a dozen biscuits. Place 1 inch apart on un-
greased baking sheet. Brush biscuits with melted butter and sprinkle with lavender sugar. Bake for 10-14 minutes or until lightly
browned. Serve warm with butter.

LAVENDER SUGAR

　　1 cup sugar
　　1 vanilla bean, halved and snipped into pieces
　　1 tablespoon dried lavender buds

In a spice or coffee grinder, pulse 2 tablespoons sugar with vanilla beans. Transfer to a jar. Then pulse the lavender with 1 tablespoon of the remaining sugar until finely ground. Combine
everything in the jar, cover tightly and let stand for about 5 days.

Fifteen

Jenny's plan to move to New York still didn't seem quite real to her. One reason, she conceded, might be that she was having a hard time actually leaving. There were a thousand details to take care of, matters that had to do with her grandmother's property, and the house and bakery. It was amazing how long it took to figure out how to go about replacing all the items she never thought about, like her birth certificate and social security card, all her banking and finance information. She felt as though she had a permanent crick in her neck from being on hold with people who were not terribly eager to help her.

In her office above the bakery, she had separated things into neat stacks. For some reason, the neatness of the stacks pleased her and made her feel less anxious. And definitely caused her to worry that she was turning eccentric.

And of course, Jenny knew she wasn't turning eccentric at all. She was stalling. She was putting off everything—even her dreamed-about trip to New York—because she'd been avoiding something.

No more, she thought, grabbing her jacket and purse. There was something she needed to do, and putting it off was not going to make it any easier. Fifteen minutes later, she was knocking on the front door of the Alger house. It was a big ranch-style home with a view of the river. From a distance, it appeared grand and imposing, pretentious, even. Up close, she noticed peeling paint on the trim and crumbling brickwork—an air of neglect. Perhaps it had started when Matthew's wife had left, suddenly and without explanation, years ago. This was one of the reasons Jenny felt a connection to Zach. Both of their mothers had walked away.

When no one came to the door, Jenny felt both frustrated and relieved. This was a reprieve. She didn't have to do it today. She gave one last knock and leaned on the bell. Nothing. There was no one home, and here it was dusk, the windows all dark. As she was turning to go back to her car, the front door cracked open.

"Jenny?" Zach Alger looked as though he'd just rolled out of bed, with rumpled hair and flushed cheeks. He was wearing an oversize plaid hunting jacket. "Is something the matter?"

All right, she thought. *Let's get this over with.* "I need to talk to you, Zach."

"Sure. I can come by the bakery—"

"Now."

"Okay. Let me grab my boots."

"You don't need boots. I drove all the way out here. We can talk inside."

"But—"

"It's important." Due to her insistence on going to the city, Rourke had been giving her lessons in self-defense. One of the basic tenets was self-assurance. Walk into situations as though you're in charge, and you won't be challenged. She put the concept to the test, gave the door a shove and strode into the house.

The place was freezing cold, and her footfalls echoed on bare floors. She paused, momentarily forgetting her self-assurance. "Uh, is there somewhere we can sit down and talk? Actually, where do you keep your computer? I need to show you something."

Zach looked as though he wanted to throw up. It was quite possible he already knew why she'd come. He said, "The, um, my computer's not working."

She could probably make her point without it. "Fine, then let's just have a seat."

His shoulders slumped as he turned and led the way down a dark hallway to the kitchen, where weak gray light streamed in through unadorned windows. A small stack of white cardboard bakery boxes littered the counter. Catching her look, Zach said, "It was discard stuff, I swear it. That's all I ever bring home."

Not quite, Jenny thought. She grew increasingly confused, though. She had never been to the Algers' home before, yet the condition of the place shocked her. It was frigid here, and there was barely a stick of furniture. Maybe it was the lack of a feminine touch, she rationalized.

But that wasn't it. Even Greg Bellamy kept his house warm. Even Rourke, the Ho Ho-eating bachelor, had *furniture*.

"Zach, is everything all right?"

He indicated a pair of three-legged stools at the counter. "We can sit over here."

"You didn't answer me. Is everything all right?"

"Sure," he said. "Everything's great."

She took a video-storage disk out of her purse and showed it to him in its plastic holder. "This was what I wanted to show you on the computer." She didn't see a computer. She suspected there wasn't one in the house. "We don't need to look at it, though. It's the security video from the bakery. I suspect you know what's on it."

Wild alarm flashed in his eyes. Then he made a visible effort to compose himself. "I don't know what you're talking about."

"Sure you do, Zach." Jenny found it hard to speak. She felt absolutely terrible. "I'm the only one who's seen this. I don't review it every day, so I don't know how many times this scene has been repeated, but the camera doesn't lie. When I saw this, it was like a punch in the gut."

She had watched it over and over again, certain she was making a mistake. But no, Zach was very deliberate. He moved a tall rack in front of the camera eye. What he didn't know—what no one but Jenny knew—was that there were two other camera lenses aimed at the counter.

"Help me out here, Zach," she said. "Please. I want to understand."

His face was as pale as the snow, his eyes milk-glass blue. He looked like a statue, unmoving, unfeeling.

Then, finally, he hung his head and began to talk. "We're broke," he admitted. "My dad and me. No one's supposed to know."

Of course not, she thought bitterly. Matthew Alger was a proud man and an aspiring mayoral candidate, to boot. She could easily see how a man like that would sacrifice his own son's safety for the sake of appearances. "If it's any consolation, I don't think anyone knows," she said.

"Please don't say anything." His voice was low, urgent. "He'd kill me if he knew I told anyone." He gestured at the evidence in her hand. "I meant to put back what I took as soon as I was able." He flinched. "Are you going to tell Rourke?"

The question surprised Jenny. It had never occurred to her to hand this over to Rourke. "I would never do that. I can't imagine what you were thinking, Zach, but I know there's got to be some explanation, and I'm here to listen."

Zach kept his eyes on the floor. A sense of shame seemed to roll off him in waves. He wasn't a bad kid, Jenny knew. But he was in big trouble.

"Zach?" she whispered.

"He—my dad—keeps saying he's got some scheme going, that I should just be patient and it'll all work out. That's all I know, swear to God."

She tried to imagine how Matthew had managed to dig himself into such a deep hole. He didn't seem the type to be on drugs or alcohol, but some people were good at hiding it.

"Online gambling," Zach muttered as though sensing her speculation. "He's addicted to it, or something. It's crazy, you know, but he can't stay away. He wins a little and he's all, like, we're on easy street now. And then he loses that and more. It started last fall and just got worse and worse. So really, the computer's working. It's the only thing he won't hock or sell."

"I'm sorry," Jenny said. She had only a vague understanding of the phenomenon; she did know that people could get into big trouble with it. "I don't know what to say, except that you need to convince him to get help for his problem. You can't compromise yourself just to get him out of a bind, do you understand, Zach?"

"He doesn't know I took money from the bakery. I just needed it to pay the gas bill."

"Tell you what. Let's take a look at the utility bills. I'm going to take care of them so you don't freeze to death."

"I shouldn't let you—"

"But you're going to, so let's not waste time arguing."

He took a deep breath, and the tension seemed to drain out of him. The expression on his face brought tears to her eyes. All this boy needed was someone to understand him, to show him a little compassion. "Zach, when was the last time you were in touch with your mother?"

"We don't talk," he said hurriedly. "She's got, like, this whole new life in California, and she's expecting a baby and all. I'm not telling her about this."

Jenny gritted her teeth in frustration. "I want to help," she said, "but I need a little cooperation from you. For starters, you need to promise you'll talk to your dad, make him get help."

"What, you think I haven't done that?"

"Keep doing it. Don't give up on him, Zach."

"Fine," he said, sounding tired and far older than his years. "I know what he'll say, though. He just needs a little more time. There's a big jackpot with his name on it, and once he gets his hands on that, we won't have to worry about a thing." At last, Zach lifted his gaze to hers. His eyes, those extraordinary pale eyes, held a world of pain. "Yeah, right," he said.

Sixteen

❧〜❧〜❧

Daisy had been raised to expect much of herself, yet she always fell short and managed to disappoint herself time and time again. So working at the bakery was a surprise. She liked it and was good at it, a new concept for her. This made her realize that maybe the problem wasn't her. Maybe the problem was buying into other people's expectations.

"You look happy," said Zach, who was moving racks out to the loading dock.

"I am," she said, stepping out into the cold winter day with him. "I mean, it's totally crazy, but I like everything about working here—the smells, the other employees, the customers. It's fantastic."

He grinned at her. "You're right—crazy."

"If so, then it's a good kind of crazy. You know, what's funny is I've had a lot of jobs, and I hated them all. See, at my school in the city, we had to do these rotations to explore different careers. But they were all the 'right' kind of careers. Wall Street, PR, law, the legislature. No way would they have sent someone to work in a bakery."

He drew down the back door of the truck and locked it. They had decided to spend their break taking a walk because Daisy wanted to shoot some pictures. As they started walking, Zach pulled out a cigarette. She plucked it from his hand before he could light it. "Oh, no you don't," she warned.

"Great, so you're some kind of antismoking radical."

"Ex-smoker," she admitted.

"You?"

Daisy knew what he was thinking. She looked like the all-American girl, the kind who could do no wrong. That was why she used to get away with so many things.

"So here's the stupid part," she said. "Not only did I know smoking would kill me, I knew it would drive my parents nuts."

"Did it work?" he asked her. "Did you drive them nuts?"

"No," she said with a bitter laugh. "They drove each other nuts. Me, they just kind of ignored." Divorce did that to kids, no matter how hard people worked to make it bearable. The truth was, when a married couple was doing all the emotional work of breaking up, the kids got pushed aside.

They stopped in the city park, which was a study in black and white—the wrought-iron fence, benches and tables against the snow. The steel tubes of the swing set. The black granite of the statue of Avalon's founder. Daisy took out her camera. Zach took back the cigarette and lit it.

She acted unimpressed, although she couldn't help it—he looked sexy in a kind of bad-boy way. "Lean against that tree," she said. "I'll take your picture."

He shrugged, and then complied. He was getting used to her habit of taking pictures, and by now was relaxed in front of the camera.

She took a few more shots. Zach had an interesting face—bony angles counterbalanced with full lips, and that shock of straight, white-blond hair. Wreathed by a thread of cigarette smoke, he looked intense and for some reason, sad.

"Very *Rebel Without a Cause*," she said, capturing him in profile, his gaze looking into some distance she couldn't see, a helix of smoke rising from the tip of the cigarette.

"What's that?"

All right, this was something she needed to get used to. Kids at her old school got all references to classic films and books. Here in Avalon, she found herself explaining things. "It's an old movie about a middle-class teenager pointlessly rebelling." Which, on reflection, sounded far too familiar for comfort. "A chain-smoking teenager," she added.

"So what got you to quit?" he asked.

"Someone I met last summer." She ducked her head, suddenly filled with an urge to smile. "Julian Gastineaux."

"Boyfriend?"

"Nothing like that." She gave in to the urge. Julian was certainly good-looking enough to be boyfriend material. But like Daisy, he wasn't looking for that when they met.

"We had jobs together at Camp Kioga," she explained to Zach. "He went back to California, though." Like Sonnet, Julian was biracial. He was absolutely gorgeous, too, but he had an incredibly sad life. He and Daisy kept in touch by e-mail every day. Sometimes twice a day. Sometimes six times a day. But…boyfriend?

"And all he wanted," she told Zach, "was to go to college and learn to be a pilot. Anyway, he's the one who made me see how stupid it was, the smoking. We had this ritual burning of my last pack of cigarettes. Because I realized the only one I was hurting was myself."

"If you're expecting me to be all, 'Okay, I'm motivated, I'm going to quit,' you're wrong."

"I don't expect you to do anything." It would be nice, Daisy thought, if getting rid of the cigarettes and pot had been the pivotal moment for her. Nice and neat. Her teenage rebellion concluded with a positive act. It didn't work that way, because the things that made her crazy didn't end. She knew it was no coincidence that she started having careless sex with Logan O'Donnell the same day her mom announced she'd be working overseas for a year.

"My dad used to work up at Camp Kioga," Zach said.

"I didn't know that."

"Yep. Back in the day."

Daisy put away her camera and shivered. When Sonnet's mother, Nina Romano, had asked her if she'd seen a doctor, she had been like a deer in headlights. And of course, her stunned reaction had totally given her away.

Oh, she had tried to cover. She'd said, "I don't know what you're talking about."

Nina—God, Mayor Romano—had not pressed the issue. Instead, she had scribbled a name and number on a Post-It note and said, "I figure, being new in town, you'd want to find a good doctor."

So far, Daisy had dialed the number so many times, she had it memorized. But then, as soon as a voice said, "Dr. Benson's office," she hung up. She was being totally stupid about it. Every day she put off making a decision, her options were narrowing.

"You all right?" Zach asked. "You look all pale."

"Do I?"

"Is anything wrong?"

For some reason, that did it. For far too long, Daisy had been keeping a tight rein on herself. Anyone looking at her would see a regular high-school girl, but just beneath her clean-cut, all-American surface was a hysterical girl barely hanging on to sanity. She felt herself unraveling, and she laughed as it happened, and the more Zach stared at her, the funnier it seemed.

Food for Thought

by Jenny Majesky

The Scent of Ginger

Baking cookies is good for the soul on so many levels. The most basic virtue is simply the smell of a batch of cookies in the oven. The scent of ginger and butter floats through the house, lingering for a few hours afterward. The addition of a pinch of cayenne in gingerbread might seem unorthodox, but it's subtle and gives it a little extra bite.

GINGERBREAD BARS WITH ORANGE CREAM CHEESE FILLING

3/4 cup butter, softened
3/4 cup sugar
1 egg
1 tablespoon ground ginger
1 teaspoon cinnamon
1/4 teaspoon cayenne pepper
1 1/4 cups flour
1/4 teaspoon baking soda
1/4 teaspoon salt
1/3 cup molasses + 3 tablespoons hot water

ORANGE CREAM CHEESE FILLING

1/2 package (4 ounces) cream cheese, softened
1/3 cup powdered sugar
2 tablespoons orange juice
1 tablespoon Cointreau, Grand Marnier or Triple Sec
(optional)

Preheat oven to 350°F. Line a 13 x 9 x 2-inch baking pan with wax paper. Spray with no-stick cooking spray and dust with flour. Beat butter until smooth. Beat in sugar and egg. Gradually mix in dry ingredients, alternating with the molasses/water mixture. Spread in prepared pan.

Beat cream cheese until smooth. Stir in sugar, orange juice and Cointreau. Spoon by teaspoons over batter in pan. With a knife, swirl through batter with long strokes in each direction to create marbled effect.

Bake for 30 minutes or until gingerbread begins to pull away from edges. Lift out of pan using edges of wax paper. Cool on wire rack. Cut into bars. Store in refrigerator.

Seventeen

June 19, 1995

Dear Mom,

If you ever show up in my life again, you're going to have a lot of reading to catch up on. Since I was old enough to write, I've been telling you about my life, just in case you're interested, and I've saved everything in boxes at the back of my closet. Actually, it's pretty clear to me now that you're *not* interested, but writing stuff down has become a habit. In high school, my teachers all told me I was a good writer. I always thought I would study journalism in college. More about that later.

Looking back through these pages, I realize so much has changed since I last put my thoughts down for you. I figured after high-school graduation I'd have all kinds of time to devote to my writing, but things have a way of throwing me off track. Like losing Grandpa. It hurts to see those words in my own handwriting. To put them down in ink on this page.

Do you even know he died, Mom? That near the end, he sometimes called me by your name? And at the very end, I didn't even bother to correct him? I think you'd know why.

Gram is a totally different person now. Everyone's been so

good to her, the whole town, really. For weeks after Grandpa died, it was raining tuna casseroles. People visited, they brought food, they sat with us. She did real well at first, but once all the formalities were over, she just seemed empty. Even when she went to church, she would come home lonely and lost. They were married so young, and they survived so much together.

We're broke now, did I tell you that? Grandpa's insurance and Medicare didn't cover everything, not even close. When Grandpa was first diagnosed and we saw the way things were going, we filed for bankruptcy in order to keep from being sued to kingdom come for nonpayment of debts. If I had to pick the top three humiliating moments of my life, going through bankruptcy with Gram would definitely be in one of them. It wasn't that we did a bad job or anything like that. We just had to do it as a way to keep from having to let all our employees go and close the bakery.

So you'll understand if I've been too busy to fill these pages with sweetness and light.

Gram says you were never one to worry about money, even though you liked having nice things. You never seemed concerned about finances and, in fact, you always acted as though the land of milk and honey was right around the corner. According to Gram, anyway. She still talks about you sometimes. Still misses you. To be honest, I don't. I'm sure, at the age of four, I adored you. But for me, missing you is like missing a shadow or a dream. I can't quite grasp it. When Nina's little girl, Sonnet, lost a helium balloon at a parade, she cried more about that than she did when her great-grandmother Giulietta died the next day. It's the way kids are, I guess.

I'm in love with two different boys, did I tell you? Oh, it gets worse. They're best friends—Joey Santini and Rourke McKnight. They're summer people. Rourke is working at Camp Kioga, same as he has every year. Joey's been in the army to earn money for school, but he's got a compassionate leave this summer because his dad was in a car wreck and has a long recovery. Joey comes up to work on weekends and holidays at the camp. When his dad gets better, Joey's going to reenlist for another tour of duty, because now he wants to go to medical school and will need all the education money he can get. He plans to be a ranger now, which I understand is one of the most secret and dangerous things you can do in the military.

I like Joey because he loves the world and makes me laugh, and I'm not going to lie to you. Being in the army has turned him into a total hunk. Of course, Rourke was already a hunk, and he's so strong and smart, and sometimes just looking at him makes me dizzy. It's as if my heart doesn't want me to choose one over the other.

Okay, I lied. It's Rourke. I've been crazy about him since I was in pigtails. He's really intense, and he has this awful father he hasn't spoken to since he got out of high school and refused to go to the "right" school, choosing instead the state school at Stony Brook, where he studies law enforcement. He fascinates me, and he's the sexiest boy I've ever known. We've never done anything, though. We have this unspoken agreement that we're just friends. It's the only possible way I can see any kind of relationship with either guy working—I keep my feelings for Rourke in check and go along with the charade.

Gram likes to remind me that people like the McKnights and the Majeskys don't mix. Besides, Rourke claims it's not cool to like the same girl your best friend wants and he goes out of his way to hang out with other girls. Not that either of them consulted me about any of this. And sometimes, I wish I *could* have deeper feelings for Joey. I mean, I do, but more as a friend than a boyfriend. It probably doesn't matter, because Rourke's in college now and Joey's leaving again at summer's end. As for me…well, I need to stay with Gram so she doesn't start feeling as if *everyone* has left her.

After the traditional Fourth of July parade, there was an enormous picnic at the county park by the river. At dusk, people made their way up the mountain to Camp Kioga for a display of fireworks over Willow Lake. The camp directors invited the whole town. Jenny and Nina went up together, with Sonnet strapped in her car seat in the back. "Her first fireworks display," Nina said. "Think she'll be afraid?"

"She's not afraid of anything." Jenny half turned to gaze at the little girl, cute as a Cabbage Patch doll in red, white and blue overalls, clapped her hands in delight. She was potty trained, although Nina toted along a diaper bag just in case.

Nina pulled into the gravel parking lot. "Where did Rourke and Joey say they'd meet us?" she asked.

"Main pavilion," Jenny said, gesturing at the large, timber lodge. She spotted the guys in their gray athletic sweatshirts with the Camp Kioga logo. As always, the sight of Rourke caught at her heart and as always, she ignored the feeling. It was, she knew, yet another facet of being an adult. After losing her grandfather and going through bankruptcy, keeping herself from falling for a boy should be a cakewalk.

Except that it wasn't. When she looked at him, she felt a searing pain that left her breathless.

"I'll carry her," Jenny offered, holding out her arms for Sonnet. In addition to being a welcome armful, the little girl was a shield Jenny could hold up to keep her distance.

Unlike Jenny, Sonnet didn't hold in her feelings by any measure. She took one look at Joey Santini and shrieked with joy. The first time she'd seen him, she had decided that he was the love of her life. While it was sad that she was growing up without a father, it had its advantages. There were so many people in the little girl's life who adored her. Surrounding a child with love was the key, not whose DNA she carried.

Like most young men, both Joey and Rourke regarded small children with the same horrified caution as a cottonmouth snake. And like most toddlers, Sonnet didn't care. She squealed and bucked in Jenny's arms until Jenny surrendered her to Joey. He gazed into the small, nut-brown face. "One peep outta you, and I'm giving you back," he said.

"Peep," said Sonnet, gazing back at him.

As they headed down to the beach with their guests to enjoy the fireworks, Rourke kept his distance, as though Joey was holding a volatile substance. It was dusk, and people gathered around the campfires strung along the lakeshore. They toasted marshmallows and lit sparklers, which the kids whirled tirelessly in circles and figure eights. When darkness fell, the fireworks began shooting from the island in the middle of the lake. Colorful starbursts were reflected in the still water, greeted by the *oohs* and *aahs* of the onlookers. Sonnet adored the fireworks, clapping her hands and chortling with each explosion. But, like most toddlers, she soon grew bored with the display and wanted to go swimming in the lake.

"Not a good idea," Nina said. "We don't have our swimsuits and it's dark."

"Mom," said Sonnet, her Minnie Mouse voice edged by the threat of a tantrum.

"Let's go for a walk," Nina suggested, jumping up.

The four of them slipped away. Rourke shone his flashlight along the lakeshore trail. They passed the boathouse and then the staff pavilion, informally known as the party shack, where camp workers and counselors were already gathering now that the campers were down for the night. "Where you going, Rourke?" called a flirty female voice. He walked faster, the only indication that he'd heard.

"What's that?" Nina asked, pointing to a large, bulky structure off by itself, well past the staff cottages.

"It's where the caretaker lives in winter," Joey said. "It's empty now. Let's go check it out."

"It's probably locked," said Rourke.

"It's definitely locked," Joey agreed. "Good thing I have a key."

It was a beautiful old lodge, musty with disuse and filled with peeled log furniture and camp memorabilia. Originally the camp owners' residence, it was now used by the Bellamys as an off-season retreat or guest cottage. Joey opened the fridge but found nothing. Sonnet scurried around, exploring everywhere, helping herself to games and toys stashed in a bench. She stopped in front of the moose-head trophy over the river-rock fireplace and went very still.

"Don't worry, it won't hurt you," Joey said, lifting her up. Then he set her down as though she was on fire. "God, what's that smell?"

"I pooped," Sonnet explained.

"God," he said again. "It's making my eyes water. I thought you said she was housebroken."

"Potty trained. And the bad news is," Nina said, "the diaper bag is in the car."

Sonnet started to sob as though her heart was breaking. It was decided that Joey would show Nina back to the car while Rourke and Jenny put away the toys and games Sonnet had taken out. Jenny opened a window to air the place out. She tried not to laugh at Rourke's horrified expression, but couldn't help herself.

"You think that's funny?" he asked.

"No, I think your reaction is funny. It's not toxic waste, Rourke."

"They should use kids like her in high-school parenting classes. The birth rate would go way down."

She rounded up the cribbage pieces Sonnet had spilled. "It's not that big a deal."

"Maybe not to you."

"Honestly, changing a diaper is far from my favorite thing in the world, too." She thought how amazing Nina had been, right from the start. Changing a diaper was only one tiny facet of an awesome responsibility. Despite being so young, she treated Sonnet with endless patience and love.

"My grandfather used to come up here in the winter," Jenny said, paging through a photo album with old pictures glued to black pages. She stopped at a shot of him standing on the dock, smiling sweetly. "He and Mr. Bellamy would go ice fishing." She touched the face in the photo and grief crashed over her in a wave that felt almost physical.

"I'm sorry," Rourke said. Like so many people, he seemed to be at a loss for what to say.

"It's okay." Her voice sounded thready and uncertain as she gently closed the album. "It's just…I miss him so much."

And then—she never quite worked out how it happened—she was in Rourke's arms, and she felt such an overwhelming sense of comfort that she hugged him back, and then they were kissing.

Finally, miraculously, they were kissing. It was the kiss she had imagined a thousand times—long and deep, the kind that made the world stand still, the kind she never thought she'd experience, even though it had been building between them, summer after summer, for years. She was lit with fire, and for the first time in her life she felt swept away. Oh, she wanted this, she had been wanting it forever, and it was even better than all her fevered imaginings. It was a perfect moment, and she didn't want it to end. Finally, when they came up for air, she made a bold move, slipping her hands beneath his sweatshirt. He caught his breath as though she'd hurt him. The moonlight streaming through the window glinted off the pale scar on his cheek. And Jenny faced a cold truth—from this moment onward, every other kiss would forever be ruined for her.

"Rourke—"

"Sorry," he said, moving away from her. "I shouldn't have— that won't happen again."

But I want it to, she thought. She wanted to kiss him again, and she wanted whatever came next with him.

"We should go," he said. "They'll be waiting for us." He headed for the door without looking to see if she followed. He stood there, holding it open. She glared at him, torn between feeling turned on and rejected. He glared right back, and didn't budge from the door. She took one more look around and then marched outside and down the steps, and she kept going while he closed the place.

He caught up and walked fast, as if in a hurry to get away from her. The fireworks were over and the moon was high as they made their way back to the path along the lake.

"You're mad at me," she said. No point in pretending it hadn't happened.

"I'm not mad at you."

"You are. I can tell. You're giving me the silent treatment and your eyes are all squinched up."

He stopped walking and sighed heavily. "My eyes are not squinched up, and I'm not mad."

"Liar."

"Okay, now I'm mad," he said.

"I knew it. See, I was right. So now you have to tell me why."

"Because you called me a liar."

"I mean before that."

"Before that, I...this is stupid. I'm done talking about it." He shoved his hands in his pockets and glared at her. Shadows cut deep across his face.

"You're not mad because you kissed me," she said. "You're mad because you liked it."

"I like girls, so sue me. And anyway, if you already know everything, why do you keep talking about it?"

"Because I'm trying to understand, Rourke."

"It's not hard," he said.

She lowered her gaze. "It's Joey, isn't it?" she said softly.

"He's been trying to figure out a way to ask you out since the beginning of summer."

She knew that. On some level, she was aware of it. "I might not want him to ask me out."

"Why wouldn't you? He's great."

"Maybe I like somebody else." The words slipped out, whispered like a scandal.

He gave her a hard look. Outlined by the moonlight, he appeared large and menacing. "Well, you shouldn't."

"Great. Thanks for the advice." She covered her pain with sarcasm. It was, from every possible angle, an impossible situation. There was no way she could be with either boy without hurting the other. No, that wasn't quite right. Nothing could hurt Rourke. He wore a hard shell of emotional armor, galvanized over the years by his father's cruelty. He knew how to protect himself. But Joey didn't, even after two years in the army. Sweet, sensitive Joey didn't try to protect himself at all.

"What took you guys so long?" Joey called. He was waiting out by the staff pavilion, where the party was in full swing.

"Nothing," Jenny said, and realized she was on the verge of tears. She ducked her head, hiding her face. If Joey got a good look, he might guess she had just been kissed to kingdom come. "Where's Nina?"

"She took Sonnet home. I told her Rourke and I would give you a ride later."

Great. Ditched by Nina, and forced to spend the rest of the evening here.

"Let's go inside," Rourke muttered. He, too, seemed to be avoiding Joey's eyes.

Jenny had only been to a few parties at Camp Kioga. Mostly, they were one big mosh pit with loud music thumping from blown speakers. The lights were dim, but somehow, three girls noticed Rourke right away and drifted over, swarming him like groupies around a rock star. As she watched, he seemed to turn into a different person, with a smooth, consciously sexy smile and an easy manner as he slid his arm around one of the girls and moved onto the dance floor. The girl he chose was wearing a short skirt and tank top so tight the hardware on her bra was visible.

Jenny must have let all her hurt and confusion show on her face, because Joey came over and touched her arm. "Let's go outside."

As she left the party, she threw a glance over her shoulder— just in time to see Rourke watching her, as if to make certain she'd seen what he was doing. And what was he doing, anyway? Trying to convince her she was wrong to like him? If so, it was working. That ought to make him happy.

"Don't worry about Rourke," Joey said. "Sometimes he acts like a jerk for no reason."

Oh, I gave him a reason, she thought.

"It's hard on him, you know? The way he grew up."

She couldn't help smiling. Joey always seemed to believe the best of everyone. Things would be so much simpler if she and Joey… Could you talk yourself into loving someone because he seemed so right?

Jenny did her best. When Joey called to ask her to a movie, she readily accepted. She invited him to the house, and watched with a softening heart the way he and Gram got on. A series of TIA strokes had impaired Gram, but Joey didn't focus on that. He didn't shout at her as if she was deaf (she wasn't) or talk to her as though she was a moron (she wasn't that, either). Instead, he treated her with dignity and respect, and when he was around, Gram took on a happy glow. Jenny loved the way he treated Gram, as if she was his own grandmother.

Bruno Santini came to visit one weekend. Spending time with him, she understood exactly where Joey came from—a place of love and acceptance. He treated his grown son with unabashed affection and pride, and didn't hesitate to open his heart to Jenny and her grandmother. "You're the prettiest girl Joey's ever introduced me to," he said.

"Pop, she's the only girl I've ever introduced you to," Joey pointed out.

In August when the weather grew so hot that even the crickets fell still, Joey hung a two-seater swing on the front porch and he and Jenny would sit there late at night, gently swaying, hoping for a breeze. Jenny was beginning to think she'd never move away from this house. After Grandpa died, she still held on to the dream, but when Gram had her first stroke, that was it for Jenny. She was staying. Gram needed her. They were companionable roommates and made the best of the situation. Since Gram couldn't do stairs anymore, they converted the downstairs den to her bedroom and

Jenny had the entire upstairs to herself. Sometimes she pretended it was a loft in SoHo, but then the crickets would start up or a coyote would howl, and she'd remember: she was in Avalon.

"It's so nice here," Joey said, his arm slipping around her.

Jenny smiled at the irony of it. "My thoughts exactly."

"I'm going to miss you so much," he said softly.

"Are you afraid?" she asked.

"Nervous, I guess. But scared?" He smiled. "I know this next tour of duty's going to be more intense because I'll be a ranger, but it doesn't scare me." His smile faded. "But…leaving you. Now, that scares me."

"Why would it scare you?"

"Because everything feels so good right now, I don't want it to change."

She paused, took in a breath of the heat-heavy air. "Everything changes. We both know that."

"But if we were together, we'd change and grow together." He gave a self-deprecating laugh. "I know, I'm crazy. You might go chasing off to the city and turn into a stranger."

She laughed, too, even though his comment bothered her. "I'm not going anywhere. Gram needs me here. You have to understand, Joey, I'll never leave her."

He leaned over and touched his lips to her forehead. "She's lucky to have you. And so am I."

In that moment, Jenny felt like the lucky one. There was a nearly full moon riding high in the sky that night, and its silvery light slipped over him, illuminating a face that had become precious to her. What a gift it was to have someone like this in her life, someone who loved her without question, whose chief worry was being separated from her.

For the rest of the month of August, Rourke watched Joey and Jenny growing closer. He tried to be happy for them but, failing that, settled for acting as though he didn't care. He ran around with girls from the camp, drank too much, slept too little and avoided his best friend. And somehow, finally, summer was winding down. He was starting to count the days until he, Joey and Jenny would go their separate ways.

The week before Labor Day, the traditional staff field day was held. Counselors and workers at the camp would compete in various events, egged on by the campers. Rourke's event was tennis, and he easily won the preliminary rounds. In the final round, his opponent was Joey. Great, he thought. Just great. He'd be fighting his best friend for the title. Even worse, Jenny had come to watch. He could see her sitting with Nina in the bleachers. Jenny was wearing a wide-brimmed hat and drinking a glass of lemonade, and even from a distance, he could hear her laughter.

With his opening serve, he knew what this was going to be—a punishment. Every shot was designed to punish Joey, which was so stupid because Joey was his best friend. Joey was also a good player, having shared lessons and practice sessions with Rourke as they were growing up. But Joey had the girl, and Rourke had nothing but his temper and his powerful tennis game, which he used without mercy. This was an all-out battle. He drove Joey around the court until he could see the sweat pouring down his friend's face and body, saturating his clothes. He creamed him two sets in a row, lured him up to the net and then lobbed him. In the end they shook hands over the net, but Rourke didn't even look at Joey.

Rourke took possession of the trophy—a silver-plated cup— but as he stood there holding it, Joey walked away with the girl. To Rourke's surprise, Philip Bellamy came over to congratulate him. He was the eldest son of the camp owners and a friend of Rourke's parents, which made Rourke immediately suspicious.

"I held the title myself one year," Mr. Bellamy said, "back in 1977."

"It's, uh, quite an honor, sir," Rourke said.

Mr. Bellamy looked over at Joey, who was standing in the shade with Jenny. She had taken off her sun hat. Joey had a towel slung around his neck, and he was earnestly talking to her. "Who's that?" Mr. Bellamy asked. "The girl, with your opponent?"

Rourke shrugged, as if he didn't care. "Some girl. Name's Jenny, I think. Why do you ask?"

"She reminds me of someone, is all. Someone I used to know." Philip glanced over at him. "Someone I used to look at the way you're looking at her."

"I'm not—"

"Of course not," Mr. Bellamy said. "I once made the mistake of letting a girl go without a fight. To this day, I wish I hadn't."

Although he didn't want to admit it, even to himself, the suggestion haunted Rourke. *Tell her,* said a voice in his head. *Just tell her the truth, because the truth never hurt anything. Tell her, before the chance slips away.*

At summer's end, Joey left for Phase 1 of Ranger School in Fort Benning, Georgia. He wasn't even able to stay for the closing ceremonies at Camp Kioga. Jenny knew it would be eight weeks or more before she would see him again. He'd called from the pay phone up at Camp Kioga to let her know he had something to ask her, and something to tell her. She suspected she knew what it was, and didn't quite know how she felt about it. When he came to tell her goodbye, she was inexplicably nervous.

"I'll walk over to the train station with you," she said, meeting him at the back door of the bakery.

He shouldered his duffel bag and slipped his free arm around her. Over the summer, Joey had let his thick, wavy black hair grow out, but he still had a soldier's physique, fit and muscular.

"I still can't imagine you as a rifle ranger," she said.

"That's what my dad says."

"You're too…peaceful, I guess. Too nice."

"That's why my first tour was in protocol in D.C., I guess. I'm ready for something else this time," he said. "Some action."

"I can't believe they're going to train you to kill people."

"They're going to train me to do a lot of things," he said. "To survive and serve my country, among other things."

She immediately felt contrite. He was doing this for his education, for his future. She had no right to question him. "I know. I'm sorry. You're going to do great and they're lucky to get you."

"Nice to know somebody thinks so. I'll try to remember that when I'm screaming for mercy during training exercises." He stopped at a bench outside the entrance to the station. "Hold up a minute, will you?"

The area was beautifully manicured, designed to welcome visitors to Avalon. Tall elm trees and sugar maples formed an archway over the main walk, which was flanked by flower beds. By August, the dahlias and delphiniums looked spent and exhausted. A few drying leaves swirled on the breeze, a reminder that autumn would soon be here. A small flock of crows circled overhead, then alighted noisily in one of the trees.

"I need to ask you something." Joey set down his bag.

She stopped walking and glanced around, not sure what she was looking for. All she saw was the town where she'd lived her entire life, the shop fronts and groups of tourists milling around the main square. Then she faced Joey. There was an intensity in the way he was looking at her, and something else, something she couldn't escape, even if she'd wanted to—love. Joey loved her. She could see it in the way his eyes lit when he gazed at her, and in the tender turn of his smile, a special smile just for her.

"I want to marry you, Jenny," he said without preamble.

Marry? Her mouth went dry and her throat closed, and she couldn't speak. Probably not the reaction he was looking for. There was so much going on inside her—elation that here was somebody unafraid to declare that he wanted to spend his life with her. But there was fear, too. He trusted her with his heart.

He didn't seem bothered by her silence. He reached into the pocket of his jeans and pulled out a small box she recognized from Palmquist's. "I know we can't do anything right away, but I got you this." He wore an adorable, bashful smile as he opened the box to show her a slender gold ring with a single, tiny diamond solitaire in the middle. "It's the best I could afford. I hope you like it."

"I do, Joey. I—"

He bent and kissed her then, and she felt safe in his embrace, as though nothing could ever hurt her. She could hear the arrival of the train from the north. It hissed to a halt and a whistle sounded. The startled crows exploded into the sky on a burst of black wings.

"I know we're young," he whispered. "But I know what I want, and I know we can make it work. In twenty-four months, I'll be done with this enlistment. We'll live right here in Avalon and I can commute to the state college. You'll never have to leave your grandmother."

At that, Jenny couldn't help smiling. "Gram loves you. When she hears that, she'll declare you a candidate for sainthood."

"I'm no saint. If she was the Wicked Witch of the West, I'd still love her because she's your grandmother." With that, he slipped the ring on her finger. "Look at that," he said. "It's a perfect fit."

She gazed down at her hand, at the glint of the diamond. "It is," she agreed. "Perfect. But two years is a long time—"

"I've loved you for longer than that," he said. "Two years is nothing. This decision is not something that came out of the blue. I've thought about being with you forever."

"I haven't," she confessed.

"I know." He pulled her close, his chest expanding as he inhaled deeply. "I'm asking you to take a leap of faith. I'm asking you to trust that I love you, that this will work."

"First boarding call," came a tinny-sounding voice through the speakers mounted outside the station. "This is your first boarding call for the southbound express."

Jenny shut her eyes, picturing herself on the brink of a dark chasm, teetering, about to make that leap of faith. Against her will, she thought of Rourke. Well, of course she thought of Rourke, because he was the one person who could have made a difference in this moment. If he'd just said something, given her any kind of sign that he had feelings for her, that would have changed everything. But ever since the night of the fireworks, he'd kept his distance. He'd even seemed to go out of his way to make sure she saw how many girls he dated. That, she knew, was the sign she was looking for. It wasn't the one she wanted to see, but he was telling her, loud and clear, her place in the pecking order.

Joey held her face between his hands and must have spotted the gleam of tears in her eyes. "It'll be all right," he said, misreading the tears. "I'll be back before you know it. We'll live here and take care of your gram for as long as she needs us, I swear it."

She didn't know how to answer him. He had such gentle eyes, such a sweet nature. And most important of all, he would never, ever break her heart. He was perfect for her—loyal and affectionate and dedicated.

"Final boarding call," came the canned voice. "This is your final boarding call for the southbound express."

"I need to go," Joey said. He took her left hand and placed a kiss on her palm, then closed her fingers around it. "I'll call you every chance I get. I'll write you every day."

"Good luck," she said, fighting tears. "Keep yourself safe."

"I will."

"Promise me. I swear, Joey, be safe, no matter what."

"Of course."

A whistle sounded. He bent and kissed her, then grabbed his bag and ran along the walkway and through the waiting room. She could see him emerge on the other side of the wrought-iron bars of the platform. He stepped up to a passenger car, turned to give her a last wave. A cloud of dust from the tracks swept across the platform, shrouding him in translucence as the train pulled away.

Jenny simply stood there in the park in front of the station, staring at the empty space where the train had been. The air smelled hot and cindery, and sounds were oddly muted—the traffic, the voices of people passing by. At some point, she sat down on the park bench. With her left thumb, she touched the hard circle of Joey's ring. *What have I done?* she asked herself again and again. *What have I done?*

She lost all track of time. It might have been minutes or even hours later. Afternoon shadows slipped over her. In the clock tower of the town hall, a bell sounded. Finally she got up and wiped her hands on her skirt. She'd best get home. Gram would worry.

But Gram didn't seem worried. She was waiting, her soft white hair freshly done by the visiting nurse who looked after her each day. She was watching *Oprah,* but when Jenny came through the door, she turned off the TV.

Jenny sat down across from her, still feeling a bit stunned. She held out her hand with the ring on it. "Joey gave me this. He wants to get married."

"Yes," Gram said. "I know. He asked me." Gram's smile was crooked, a side effect of the stroke, but her eyes shone with happiness. "It is such a blessing. I have always wanted you to find someone who looks at you and sees what I see. He will make you happy."

"I'm afraid," Jenny said. "I'm not sure I love him in a marrying way." She had dreams. Aspirations. She didn't know if any of them were enhanced by this engagement. "I didn't say yes."

"You took the ring."

"Oh, Gram."

"Joey is a good man. He is like us, not like a rich boy who is careless with your heart."

"I want to make sure I'm not being careless with him," Jenny said. She felt weighed down by the awesome responsibility of making another person happy, sharing her life with him. She had no idea if she could do that. Joey thought she could, though. He believed in her.

When Rourke pulled up in front of Jenny's house, he saw her on the front porch, writing longhand in a spiral-bound notebook. She worked with such deep concentration that she didn't seem to notice him as he parked at a bad angle along the curb and jumped out, leaving the door ajar.

She looked up and saw him and for a split second he was sure he saw unguarded pleasure in her eyes. Then she slapped her writing book shut and stood up. "Rourke, is something wrong?" she asked.

He stood at the bottom of the porch steps and looked at her, and the tightness in his chest finally unfurled. Her question was ironic because something had been wrong all summer, and he'd finally figured out how to make it right. It was so simple, really. He was in love with this beautiful brown-eyed girl, whom he'd known since they were kids. Sure, it was complicated, since she'd been going out with Joey, but that was over now. Joey had left on the morning train.

Rourke had put himself through hell, trying to convince himself that what he felt for her wasn't love. He was done with all that. He joined her on the front porch and took her hand. "I came to talk to you about something," he said. He voice sounded too low and rough. He cleared his throat. "It's kind of important." And God, he hoped it was to her, too. "I wanted to tell you that I'm—"

A train whistle sounded, drowning out his next words. At the end of the street, red lights flashed as the gates started to close. A car heading toward town sped up, clearly attempting to get across the tracks before the train arrived. Rourke tensed as the gates lowered, nearly crashing onto the hood of the car. Idiot, thought Rourke. His hurry could have gotten him killed.

The moment passed and he looked back at Jenny. "Sorry. What I meant to say was—"

"There's something I need to tell you, too," she said, very gently extracting her hand from his.

Only when she took back her hand did Rourke realize that her fingers had been icy cold—on one of the hottest days of the year. She swallowed, wincing as though the effort pained her. Her eyes shone brightly with tears. "Joey left a while ago."

Rourke nodded. He'd said his goodbyes the previous night. Things had been strained between him and Joey this summer, but they'd been best friends all their lives. Rourke had to believe that meant something. He hoped like hell it meant Joey would forgive him for making a play for his girl.

"Maybe he already told you…" Jenny was saying.

"Told me what?"

"He and I…he asked me to marry him."

Right, Rourke thought. Just perfect. This had to be some cosmic joke.

She twisted the slender band of the ring around and around her finger. "Anyway, I thought…" Her voice trailed off into a wisp of uncertainty.

She really wasn't joking. Rourke forced himself to focus on what she was saying. She was going to marry Joey. She was going to be his best friend's wife. He turned himself to stone because he didn't want to feel anything—not hurt, not disappointment, not rage. "That's good," he said evenly. "Congratulations."

She nodded, her eyes still swimming. "Thanks. Um, you said you needed to talk about something?"

He gave a little laugh then, thinking, thank God. Thank God he hadn't said what he'd come here to say. It was the only thing he could think of that would make this moment worse.

Food for Thought

by Jenny Majesky

Bittersweet Dreams

Eileen has been a bakery regular for years, and she loves chocolate more than any other customer we know. Chocolate has magical properties when prepared correctly. It's an appropriate ingredient for days when it feels as though the whole world is against you, or on the anniversary of a sad event, because it tends to enhance one's mood. The addition of a hint of liqueur brings out some of chocolate's finest nuances. Frangelico is a good choice. Made in Italy with roasted hazelnuts and bottled in a container that will remind you of Mrs. Butterworth's, it won't overwhelm the other flavors.

The cocoa content of chocolate matters; don't let anyone tell you otherwise. The very best taste comes from chocolate with a cocoa content of 70 percent or more. Also, avoid anything with an ingredient called "vanillin," a chemical substitute for real vanilla. Possibly most important of all, choose chocolate that uses cocoa butter. Interestingly, it melts at 93°F, which is close to body temperature. This, I think, is no coincidence.

EILEEN'S BITTER CHOCOLATE CAKE

Sugar for dusting pan
2 sticks unsalted butter
6 ounces semisweet chocolate, chopped
3 ounces unsweetened, strong, dark chocolate, chopped

1-1/4 cups sugar
4 extra-large eggs
1 tablespoon all-purpose flour
Lightly sweetened whipped cream
1 tablespoon Frangelico liqueur
toasted chopped hazelnuts

Preheat oven to 325°F. Butter a 9 inch-diameter springform pan. Sprinkle bottom and sides with sugar. Wrap foil around bottom and 2 inches up outside of pan.

Combine butter and both chocolates in a glass bowl and melt in microwave, stirring until smooth.

Whisk sugar and eggs together. Mix in flour. Stir in warm chocolate mixture. Pour batter into prepared pan. Place cake in large baking pan. Pour enough boiling water into baking pan to come 1/2 inch up sides of cake. Bake cake until top is firm and toothpick inserted into center comes out with some moist crumbs attached, about 1 hour.

Remove cake from water and cool completely on rack. Transfer cake to platter, release pan sides. Add Frangelico to the whipped cream. Garnish each slice with whipped cream and a sprinkle of hazelnuts.

Eighteen

"You're making a big mistake," Rourke said. "You're running away instead of sticking around and figuring things out."

Jenny didn't let herself look at him as she moved around the bedroom, packing her only bag. "Figuring what out?" she asked, discomfited by the way he was watching her. "Us?"

He didn't answer; she didn't expect him to. Nor did she want to pursue the issue. It was one thing to fantasize about Rourke—that wasn't a stretch. But when she'd begun to imagine that this was her life, she realized that the time had come for her to move on from this place. There wasn't much to pack, of course, which she found strangely satisfying. "I've been here long enough, anyway."

"Long enough for what?" He leaned back against the wall, crossing his ankles and folding his arms.

She wondered if he missed sleeping in his own bed, but she would never ask him. "For me to get over the initial upheaval, to tie up loose ends." She picked up a shirt and tossed it haphazardly into the suitcase. "At least it's nice to know I was never that attached to my clothes. I hardly miss anything." She shook out her new flannel pajama bottoms and then wadded them up.

"What do you miss?"

"Exactly what you'd expect—my journals, the stuff on my

hard drive. One-of-a-kind photographs and mementos. Little things that belonged to my grandparents. This is not a mistake, Rourke. I have to move on with my life."

He picked up the suitcase. "In that case, don't let me stop you."

He could, she realized with a lurch of her heart. There were things he could say that would keep her here, or at least make her listen. Now, if he'd said, "I need you," or "There's this thing between us," maybe she would already be unpacking her bags. It was unsettling to admit to herself that he could tempt her to stay with just two words—*don't go.*

He didn't say anything of the sort. He wouldn't. They couldn't talk about Joey. Rourke was mired in guilt over what had happened, and Jenny knew they both had the sense that it would never be resolved. It was just as well. If he asked her to stay, she might say yes, and they'd end up having some sort of drama that would end badly and ruin their newly recaptured friendship.

They walked outside together into the cold, crisp morning. She said goodbye to the animals, feeling an unexpected tug as she petted them and rumpled their ears one last time. Rourke already had the car warming up. As they drove the short distance to the train station, she looked out at the old-fashioned, snow-topped houses and stately bare trees, the covered bridge over the river and all the quaint churches and shops. Everything was so familiar. She took a mental snapshot, replacing some of the photos lost in the fire.

Rourke parked at the drop-off lot at the train station. They got out and he set her suitcase upright and pulled it to the entrance to the station. They stood facing each other, snowflakes flurrying around them.

"So I'm off," she said.

"Good luck in the big city," he said.

"Thanks, Rourke. Thanks for everything."

"Can I say something?" he asked.

"Sure. Anything."

"I'm going to miss you like hell."

She laughed to cover her reaction. "At least you'll get your own bed back."

"Hey. I'm very attached to my sofa."

"Well, now you can get back to your love life."

"I have no love life."

"So what do you call all the gorgeous women you date?"

He laughed. "Not love."

"Then why do you do it?"

He laughed even harder. "I'm not even going to answer that."

"You have to. You once said you'd tell me anything." Which was such a lie, since he hid so much of himself. "What's up with the supermodels, Chief?"

"Nothing's up. They come, they go, end of story. They'll never be more than something to do on my night off."

"How can you know that? Have you ever really given some girl a chance?"

"How can I know that?" he echoed. He stepped close to her. Very gently, with his leather-gloved hand, he touched her under the chin and tilted her face up to his. "I think we both know," he said simply, and placed a chaste—yet devastating—kiss on her lips. "Have a safe trip to the city," he added, and then he walked away.

Nineteen

Jenny had brought a book to read on the train. She had downloaded three episodes of *This American Life* to her iPod. And she'd brought her new laptop, which had so many bells and whistles she would take years to discover them all.

Yet throughout the trip, all she did was sit and stare out the window. Rourke's unexpected parting words and the way he'd looked at her and kissed her haunted Jenny as the train steamed southward, toward Grand Central Station. What was she supposed to do now? Dismiss the things he had said? The more she thought about it, the madder she got. He'd finally decided to show his hand when she was heading out of town. How convenient for him to choose a time when it was safe for him to do so, when she couldn't stick around and force him to make a commitment.

Then again, she was the one leaving. Fleeing, if she wanted to be accurate, fleeing a past they couldn't resolve and Rourke's conviction that he'd failed Joey—that they'd both failed him. The patchwork snowscape rolled by, as rural and timeless as a Currier & Ives etching. Gradually the scenery shifted. She saw less snow and more traffic. The sky felt heavier and the world appeared more dingy. Strip malls and suburbs gave way to urban high-rises.

As she watched the changing scenery, a familiar and most unwelcome throb of panic thrummed in her chest.

No, she thought. This can't be happening.

In the space of just a few minutes, the palms of her hands grew slick with sweat. Her heart rate accelerated. She shut her eyes and did the exercises Dr. Barrett had shown her. She breathed in through the nose, out through the mouth. She visualized a safe place filled with golden light, where nothing and no one could harm her. She imagined a world in which there was only kindness and love.

It didn't work. She hadn't really expected it to. She felt miserable and trapped, and not a little foolish. She was a practical, down-to-earth person. She didn't go into a panic for no reason.

Nearly jumping out of her skin, she swayed and lurched her way to the washroom. There, she blotted her hands and face with a damp paper towel. Then she swallowed half a Xanax and went back to her seat.

The pill kicked in, wrapping a gauzy cushion around the sharp edges of the panic, and imparting the dull surrender of sleep. This, Jenny knew, was an artificial reprieve, but she would take any and all she could get at this point.

She leaned back in her seat and stared out at the great nothingness of the world outside. She tried to concentrate on the people she saw scurrying here and there, and imagining what their lives were like. Did they have families? Laugh together? Hurt each other? Struggle with regrets?

But no matter how she tried to distract herself, her mind kept returning to one crazy thought. She had believed the panic attacks were over, because she hadn't experienced one since the night at Greg's house. Like a fool, she had believed the days of assessing her freak-o-meter on a scale of one to ten were over.

Yet the panic had returned with a vengeance, and she had to reassess her thinking.

Maybe the attacks had not stopped because she was finally adjusting to all the changes in her life. Maybe the attacks had stopped because she was with Rourke.

Which was insane, because she wasn't actually *with* him. Even when he kissed her goodbye at the station—oh, God, he'd kissed her and she'd nearly melted—she wasn't *with* him.

Because that would make her even more insane than the panic screaming through her. She took out her cell phone. Scrolled to Rourke's number. Her thumb hovered over the Send button. She could call him. She needed to ask him about that kiss. Ask him what, though?

Enough, she told herself, flipping the phone shut. Philip was waiting, a man who seemed desperate to be a father to her. To be in her life. That was something to focus on.

She couldn't let her irrational attachment to Rourke McKnight hold her back from this opportunity to start a new life. This was her shot. Her chance to prove herself. She wanted to stand on her own, to discover who she was away from Avalon, and the bakery, and the people who had known her as the dutiful granddaughter, the responsible business owner, the girl who had overcome a tragic past. Maybe she was running away, like Rourke said, but since when was that a crime?

Twenty

Greg Bellamy was mildly shocked when Daisy agreed to go cross-country skiing with him. She and her brother were diehard downhill skiers who teased their dad about his passion for Nordic skiing.

"Too healthy," they scoffed. "Too much work."

So when he invited her and she agreed to get up at 6:00 a.m., he thought he was hearing things. And then he felt a rush of gladness. *Yes.* He'd hoped moving to Avalon would bring him closer to his kids. Maybe this was the first step. Max had spent the night with a friend and wouldn't be back until afternoon. He and Daisy would have some quality time together.

Dawn was a thin thread of light on the horizon as they layered on clothing and put their gear in the back of the truck. "I'm starving," she blurted out a minute after they got on the road.

"You said you weren't hungry for breakfast," Greg objected, still full from a big bowl of oatmeal.

"I am now."

He reminded himself to be patient. "How about we stop at the bakery and grab something."

She smiled over at him. "Perfect."

The bakery was busy even at this hour. He spotted a group of downhill skiers and some early risers reading the paper. And… Greg did a double take at the woman in line ahead of him.

"Nina," he said, and reminded her, "Greg Bellamy."

She gave him a Sofia Loren smile. "I remember. How are you?" He tried not to stare, but damn. This Nina was different from the one he'd met when he'd first moved to town, the mayor in executive-dominatrix mode. This Nina wore soft blue jeans and snowmobile boots and a knitted cap that made her look no older than her teenage daughter, Sonnet. "You're up early," she commented.

"I'm taking my daughter skiing," he said. "Cross-country, over at Avalon Meadows."

"Sounds fun. How is Daisy, anyway?"

He tried to read between the lines of her question. No clue. Maybe she was just being a politician. "She's doing all right. I'm looking forward to hanging out with her today. Do you ski?"

"Of course," she said. "Cross-country and downhill. Both badly."

Good to know.

At the counter, she ordered a single-shot espresso from the boy…Zach, recalled Greg, just in time to call him by name and place his own order—two hot chocolates and two sweet-cheese kolaches to go.

So this is bad, he thought, unable to stop eyeing Nina. His marriage had only been over for a few months, and he was already having impure thoughts about another woman.

He paid and turned toward the door, nearly dousing Nina with hot chocolate. "Sorry," he said, steadying the cardboard tray. "I didn't see you standing there."

"Actually, I was waiting for you."

Uh-oh.

She smiled as though she'd heard his uh-oh, and handed him a business card. "No need to panic. I was just wondering…if you'd like to have coffee or…something."

Yes. Yes. Yes.

His mouth went dry. "That's nice of you, Nina. Really. But, uh, probably not." He paused and took a deep breath, trying to figure out how to explain.

She didn't give him a chance. "That's okay," she said brightly. "Just thought I'd ask."

"But I—"

"See you, Greg." She went over to a table crowded with locals and took a seat.

"I'm an idiot," he muttered under his breath. He put the card in his wallet and headed out the door.

"Was that Nina Romano you were talking to?" asked Daisy.

"Uh, yeah." He put the cups in the drink holder and handed her the bag of kolaches.

"So what did she want?"

"Who, Nina?"

"Yes, Nina. Geez, Dad."

"She just wanted to say hi," he said.

"What a liar."

"I'm not—" Yes, he was. And he was so damn bad at it. "She asked me out. There. Are you glad you asked?"

"Oh," said Daisy. "Ew."

He headed for the river road. "My thoughts exactly." Another lie, but he wasn't about to admit to his daughter that he had the hots for the town mayor. "Anyway, I said no, thanks."

Daisy nibbled on her pastry. "Was she mad?"

"No. She was really nice about it."

"She's really nice, period. That's probably how she got to be mayor."

"So you think she's nice but I shouldn't go out with her."

"Honestly, Dad, it's your choice. But I think it would be bizarre. Completely and totally bizarre."

"I told her no. End of story." It wasn't, of course. It felt more like a beginning.

The parking lot at Avalon Meadows Golf and Country Club was nearly empty, though recently plowed. The course had an agreement with the city that during the winter it would be groomed for cross-country skiing. He parked and went around to get the gear out of the back of the truck—skis and poles, backpacks with bottles of water, a bag of trail mix and Daisy's camera. Greg looked out over the snow—the smooth knolls and slopes of the golf course, and a wave of nostalgia engulfed him. The sensation was as sharp and sweet as the cold winter air. This was a place where time stood still, where the passing of the years left no mark. It looked exactly the same as it had when he was a boy, the colonial-style brick clubhouse, the beautifully sculpted landscape of tree-lined fairways, ponds fringed by cattails, dramatic rolling slopes and preternaturally flat greens, which were now white disks crowning each hole.

As a kid, Greg had always been as taken with the landscape itself as with the sport of golf. It didn't matter to him whether he was driving a golf ball or simply standing in the hush of the forest where it was so quiet he could hear the falling leaves as they hit the forest floor.

Just for a few seconds, it was possible to stand here and be that kid again, filled with wonder and at ease in the world. Just for a few seconds, he wasn't a confused thirty-eight-year-old guy trying to start all over again, juggling family and work and life and a new town.

"Let's go this way," he said to Daisy, and they glided along a marked path, their narrow skis entrenched in the tracks formed by the early-morning groomer.

It felt good here in the quiet outdoors, alone with Daisy. The only sound was the rhythmic swish of their skis on the trail and the accompanying cadence of their breathing. Gliding along, he disappeared into himself and didn't think. After a while, they were both sweating with exertion.

Daisy said, "I feel like taking some pictures. Do you mind if we stop for a break?"

"Not at all."

She had chosen a spot where a grove of birch trees bordered a small stream, which in turn emptied into a pond, now a field of snow-covered ice. A man-made footbridge arched over the stream. In warmer weather, there would be parties of golfers everywhere. Now the whole place was empty of everything but chickadees and snowshoe rabbits.

"How are you doing?" Greg asked her.

She leaned back against a fence rail. "I'm okay." Her cheeks were rosy red, and yet there was something in her eyes, a flicker of trouble.

"You sure?" He handed her a bottle of water from the backpack.

She twisted off the top and took a long drink. "Sure."

The old Greg, the one who hadn't spent enough time with his kids, would have taken her reply at face value. One thing that came of the divorce was that Greg had become friends with his own kids. What a concept. Now he knew "Sure" didn't necessarily mean she was fine. Judging by the look in her eyes, it meant, "Dig a little deeper, Dad. It won't take long to figure out what's going on if you just ask the right questions."

"How are things at school?" he asked.

She smiled briefly as if he'd said something ironic. Maybe he had. In the past, he'd asked the same question, accepting her reply that all was well. Then one day she came home and said, "I'm failing four classes."

"All right," he said, "moving right along. How's work? You like working at the bakery?"

"The bakery is fine. I've made two friends—Zach and Sonnet, and they're fine, too. And it's fine to be working for my long-lost cousin. See? It's all good."

Another thing Greg had learned in his crash course in fatherhood was the power of silence. Sometimes if you kept your mouth shut and waited, a kid would come out with things. He was amazed more adults hadn't figured that out. So many people he knew who were parents tended to fill every silence with talk, talk and more talk. Greg's kids had taught him that sometimes the important things came out in the middle of a long silence, after sitting in a boat for an hour or two, trying to catch a fish. Or standing in the middle of a quiet snowscape.

It took some discipline, but he simply waited. Shook the snow off one of his skis and took a Chap Stick from his pocket and smeared it on his lips. Squinted at the sun. There was a peculiar quality to the blue sky, a hardness that contrasted sharply with the white of the snow and the bark of a grove of birch trees. And for the time being it was easy to stay quiet. He could hear sounds undetectable in the city—the burble of a creek choked by ice except for a single trickle down the middle. The rustle of the wind through dried cattails fringing the pond. The trill of a chickadee in the bushes.

It was, he decided, a perfect moment, standing here in the middle of this empty, gorgeous spot with his adored daughter who had suffered through such a miserable time during the divorce. And now, at last, things seemed to be looking up for her.

She got out her camera, the new one he'd bought for her last September. Daisy had always had a quirky, creative eye for a photograph. Now, with a camera that actually matched her skills, her talent shone through. The images she came up with never failed to surprise him.

Greg watched her with appreciation. She worked with self-assurance and a natural instinct to find the best angle for each shot. Her facility with the camera had emerged…when he thought about it, her passion for photography coincided with his and Sophie's decision to separate.

When he'd first given her the camera, she'd been obsessed with photographing him and Sophie and Max, preferably together. He figured it was because a picture froze a moment in time: *here is my family now, before it gets shattered apart.* Then in her photography class, she had branched out, taking pictures of architecture, nature, any color or shape or motion that caught her eye. In a way, he was reminded of himself at her age, discovering his passion for design. In time, his success had actually been his downfall.

Creating his own firm had consumed him, leaving little time for family—and his marriage. Ultimately, he'd lost the latter and was hanging on to the kids by a thread, by reorganizing his life. He wished he could tell Daisy to balance her passion for her art with other elements, so she wouldn't be consumed and neglect the things that really mattered. But you couldn't tell her anything, just as his own elders couldn't tell him anything when he was a kid.

For a while, Daisy seemed to forget he was there. He suspected the shots she was getting today would be outstanding. It was one of those perfect winter days that arrived like a gift of gold.

"Keep looking off to the side," she said, surprising him by aiming the barrel-like lens at him. "Okay, now take a drink from the water bottle."

He humored her, taking a drink, then propping himself on the split-rail fence, arms crossed, then leaning on his ski poles, then grinning.

"I didn't say to smile," she scolded.

"I can't help it. You're so serious about your work."

"And this is funny?"

"Nope. I just like watching you. Now, put the shutter on timer and come get in a picture with me."

"Dad—"

"Humor me. I don't have enough shots of us together."

Understatement. Of course he and Sophie had many photographs of the kids growing up. And for him, one of the saddest, most wrenching moments of the divorce had occurred, not when they were divvying up wedding gifts of expensive crystal and silver, but when they went through photo albums, marking the pictures they wanted duplicated. Halfway into the first album, Greg had paused at a shot of blond, laughing Sophie holding the toddler Daisy aloft like a trophy she'd won. They looked so beautiful it made his eyes smart, like staring too long into the sun. At that point he had shut the book with a thud and said, "I'm sending everything off for copying."

Sophie had not argued, he suspected, because it was as pain-

ful for her as it was for him to page through album after album
crammed with all the moments they'd shared. Because that was
the thing about photographs. There was a reason they were called
Kodak moments. When the camera came out, people put on a
happy smile every time. You didn't get shots of screaming tan-
trums, of couples giving each other the cold shoulder after a long
day, of teenagers coming home from school to announce they
didn't want to go back.

When Daisy set the camera on its retractable tripod, trig-
gered the shutter and then stood next to Greg for the shot, he
couldn't tell whether or not it would be a Kodak moment. She
just kind of leaned against his arm while they both looked
straight ahead.

They did a few more shots together, and then he got the camera
and pointed it at Daisy.

Predictably, she protested. "Hey. I don't need any more pictures of me."

"I do." He fired the shutter several times. One nice thing about
digital was that you never worried about wasting a shot. "Humor
me, okay? I like taking pictures of my kid."

"Sure, whatever," she said, and gamely smiled for the camera.
After a few shots, however, something changed. An angle of the
light. A shift in the breeze. The shadows on the snow.

It took Greg a moment to realize that the change was in his
daughter. It was subtle but unmistakable, something he'd seen earlier in the day—a flicker of trouble in her eyes, a softening of her
mouth, which, he suspected, was a prelude to tears.

"Daisy?" He lowered the camera.

Something about her melted, as though her bones had gone
slack and she had to lean back against the split-rail fence for support. "Daddy." Her voice was faint, pleading.

"What is it?" His mind raced through the possibilities. Daisy
had dished out a lot in her adolescence. She had admitted to drinking, smoking cigarettes and pot. To skipping school, flunking
tests on purpose, getting failing grades until they had to withdraw

her from school. But none of those had caused her to look at him the way she was now.

"Honey?" he prompted.

"There's no easy way to say this, so I'll just say it." She took a deep breath, looked at the sky and then back at him. She released the breath with a cloud of mist formed by her next words: "I'm pregnant."

The words didn't even register. It was as if she had spoken in a foreign language he didn't understand. He could see her mouth moving, forming the syllables, could hear the sound coming out, but it made no sense. The announcement simply hung there, suspended and meaningless between them. Then something happened—another shift in the breeze, maybe—and the full impact of her words slammed into him like a bullet shot from point-blank range.

I'm pregnant.

All the air rushed out of him. Daisy was pregnant. His daughter—his little girl—was standing here telling him she was pregnant.

Only one thought streamed through his mind. Oh, holy shit. Oh, holy fucking shit shit shit. The words raced through his head until they lost their meaning.

He saw a line of tracks in the snow between them. A dividing line. Ten seconds ago, he was struggling to be a father. Now he was—oh, sweet Jesus, Mary and Joseph—on the verge of becoming a thirty-eight-year-old grandfather. Shit. Shit. Shit.

All the usual questions crowded up into his throat—*How did this happen? Are you sure? How could you be so careless?* But as the words spun through his mind, he realized they were merely recriminations cloaked as questions.

Questions to which he already knew the answers.

How it happened was simple biology.

Was she sure? Good God, only absolute certainty could induce her to say this to her father. There was no way she would drop this bomb if she wasn't absolutely a hundred percent certain.

And how could she be so careless? She was seventeen. It was what teenagers did—careless, stupid things. He'd done them himself. He had been wild, maybe even wilder than Daisy. And like her, he'd been trapped by his own wildness. He and Sophie had met when they were both counselors at Camp Kioga, just having finished their first year of college. It was no great secret that they'd "had" to get married. Anyone who did the math from Daisy's birthday could figure it out. And now Daisy was in the same damn place. Ah, dammit. Shit, shit, shit.

"Daddy," she prompted, her voice a rough whisper. "Say something."

"I'm standing here thinking, 'Oh, shit,'" he admitted. "That's about as far as I've gotten." He stabbed a ski pole deep into the snow. "Damn it, Daisy. How the hell could you—" He stopped himself. The words echoed across the empty golf course and died away. He knew exactly how she could, the same way kids had since the beginning of time. Honest, he thought. Be honest. Tell her how much this sucks. No, not that. She would already be aware of that. "What, um, so now what?" he asked.

"I'm seeing a doctor on Monday," she said.

"You haven't been yet?"

"No. I did, you know, the home pregnancy test, like, four times. I kept hoping maybe it was wrong but…" She shrugged her shoulders. "Then I was so freaked out, I didn't say anything."

"To anyone?"

"No. I'm not sure, but I think Nina Romano might have guessed."

God. Nina, of all people. He felt a surge of anger to know a stranger was in on the secret before he was. *How is Daisy, anyway?* That was what Nina had wanted to know this morning in the bakery. *How's your pregnant teenage daughter?*

"I didn't tell her," Daisy reiterated. "I didn't say a word, though. I couldn't lie. I've never been much of a liar."

That sure as hell was true. One reason she got in so much trouble was that she tended to own up to things.

"Have you talked to your mother about this?"

"No."

So this was a surprise. She'd told Greg but not Sophie. "You're going to have to."

"I know."

"And the, uh, boy." Greg felt something akin to murderous rage. If the little fucker was here right this moment, Greg would kill him slowly and deliberately, with no qualms. "You need to tell me about the boy," he prompted.

"Logan O'Donnell," she said.

O'Donnell, O'Donnell, O'Donnell. Oh, God. "Al O'Donnell's boy."

She nodded her head.

Great. They were one of New York's big-money, shipping-fortune Irish families. The O'Donnells were rich, powerful and ferociously Catholic.

Again, Greg schooled himself to say nothing. He needed to figure out how Daisy felt about the boy first. The little turd who had knocked her up.

She began to talk, her voice insulated by the snow all around them and carrying clearly through the stillness. She told him about the parties she and her friends had had in Manhattan apartments and Long Island weekend homes. Greg felt queasy, not because he was shocked but because it all sounded so damn familiar. He and his friends used to do the same thing and for all he knew he'd knocked up some girl and she'd never told him.

There was no denying the separation and divorce had been rough on the kids. And Daisy's reaction had been classic—a full-on rebellion complete with substance abuse and unprotected sex. The precise date of conception, she confessed, seemed to coincide with the weekend Sophie had flown overseas.

That weekend, Daisy had come to him with a forlorn expression on her face. "Can I go with some friends to Sag Harbor on Friday? Bonnie Mackenzie invited me."

"Are her parents there?"

"Of course. You can call them if you want."

"No need. I trust you, honey."

And—God help him—he had. He had stupidly trusted her to go where she said she was going. He'd probably figured maybe there was going to be some drinking and fooling around. It was what kids did in high school. Telling her she couldn't go would not stop her.

She studied him, and apparently was reading him like a book. "Don't blame yourself, Dad. Or Mom or Logan. It was me. My stupid decision."

"So what do you want to do about Logan?" he asked her. Greg knew what he wanted to do to the kid, but it was illegal and probably wouldn't help Daisy.

"I'm not telling him anything until I decide what I'm doing," she said. "If I decide not to have it, then there's no reason to say anything." She stabbed the toe of her ski boot into the snow. "Is it horrible, that I might want to have an abortion?"

He studied her, and could clearly see his towheaded little daughter, so proud of her first lost tooth, or crawling into his lap for a story, coming down the stairs all dressed up for a school dance…. She was gone now. Gone forever, as if she had died. In her place was this shamefaced stranger, and just for a second, the sight of her brought on a flash of dislike—maybe disgust?—and the feeling was so powerful that it scared him.

No, he thought. No. He was not going to let this thing cause him to waver. *No.*

"Dad?" she said, looking up at him. "You didn't answer my question."

"There's something I forgot to say," he told her. "I love you, and that will never change."

A little shudder rippled through her. "I know, Dad. Thanks for saying so. But…you still didn't answer my question," she reminded him.

He didn't know. He honestly didn't know. "My days of making your decisions for you are over." He studied the camera, which she held carefully cradled in her hands throughout the conversation. Later, he knew, he would look at the pictures she had taken today and remember that this was him and his daughter *before*.

Twenty-One

After Jenny went to the city, Rourke returned to a life that felt strangely hollow. He told himself he ought to be happy to get his routine back. He was used to living alone, on his own terms. Bringing Jenny to stay with him, even temporarily, was a huge disruption.

Really, she was a pain in the ass. She took long showers and cluttered the bathroom with a mind-boggling array of soaps and shampoos and beauty products. She insisted on eating a nutritious breakfast and she watched the most god-awful TV shows he'd ever seen—*Project Runway* and *America's Next Top Model*. Who thought up these things?

So it was a relief to get back to his uncluttered bathroom, uncluttered life. Hostess Ho Hos for breakfast and boxing on TV. Definitely a relief.

Yet for some reason, he was restless and irritable. He snapped at his coworkers, snarled at his assistant and yelled at both deputies. Memos and paperwork pressed down on him like a great weight. During a budget meeting with Matthew Alger at his city hall office, he discovered he was on his last nerve.

Alger made no bones about the fact that Rourke wasn't his favorite person on the city's payroll; the city administrator tended to object to Rourke's spending habits. From the look on his face now, he was about to object to something else. "I've been going over these numbers," Matthew said, handing Rourke a well-thumbed spreadsheet. "There's no room in the budget for the four squad cars you put in for."

"Then make room," Rourke said simply. "I'm not withdrawing them."

"Fine. I'll withdraw them myself."

Rourke reminded himself not to get riled up. Alger tended to argue over every item, line by line, and to make much of this habit to the taxpayers. "Don't," Rourke said simply, a note of warning in his voice.

"The money's not there." Alger had a deceptively mild delivery, behind which was a steely resolve. "We're not going into reserve spending."

"Did you read the requisition?" Rourke asked, his delivery anything but mild. "We're driving cars that should have been replaced five years ago. One sedan was just judged unsafe at any speed. I'm not backing down on this, Matthew."

"You don't have a choice." Alger took another document down from a shelf behind the desk—the city code manual. "Capital expenditures are subject to the final approval of the city administrator. And I don't approve."

"Then you're an ass, and I'll make sure people know you don't give a shit about public safety."

"Sure, send your bleeding-heart friend Nina to whine about it in her next speech. People drive old cars all the time, Chief—"

"And someone's life could depend on a cruiser being in perfect condition."

"That's a long shot and you know it."

Rourke felt the fire of his temper crackling just beneath the surface, ready to burst forth. Without taking his eyes off Alger, he opened a desk drawer and took out a document of his own. "I did the math," he stated. "The budget can cover it."

"Doing the math is my job, and the revenue isn't there."

"Tell you what," Rourke said. "There's an independent audit coming up next month—"

"That has to be rescheduled," Alger said.

"Look it up in your damn city code. It can't be changed." As he strode out of the office, Rourke reminded himself that there was no point in getting pissed. They simply needed to fix the problem. This wasn't supposed to be his issue, but since a hefty percentage of the city's budget went to public safety, he had to justify every penny his department spent. City revenues were down and no one could understand why. Something didn't add up, and Nina was scared, because she was up for reelection this year. With city finances in such bad shape, she was a sitting duck for her opponent. Matthew Alger would ride in like a white knight, promising to take control.

Rourke headed into Nina's office, his annoyance unabated. Even the decor of her office irritated him. Everything was just so damn friendly, from the sunny-yellow walls to the cheerful pictures of special Avalon citizens and Nina's personal heroes—Gloria Steinem and Madonna—to the framed photos of Nina's daughter, Sonnet. Not for the first time, Rourke felt a twinge of envy. Nina had a kid who was pure joy, a huge extended family she adored. Rourke had none of those things, and it didn't usually bother him, but today it did.

If she noticed, she didn't let on as she opened a file of spreadsheets. "We need to go through your departmental budget again," she said. "We're going to have another shortfall this quarter."

"Oh, no," he said, holding up his hand, palm out. "You're not revising the budget again. Jesus, Nina, our cars are ten years old. I'm not cutting another dime, so don't even bother asking."

"I'm not asking for cuts," she assured him. "I know there's nothing left in your department to trim away."

"Thank you." He was still suspicious of her. She wouldn't have asked for a meeting if she didn't have something up her sleeve.

"What I'd like is to apply for a state grant for the digital video cameras you requested for the cars."

Okay, now he saw where this is going. "My father is chairman of the state law enforcement division."

"That's right. Rourke—"

"We're not doing it. Find another way to fund the project."

"Like what?"

"Like how about you figure out why the budget's in such trouble, Madam Mayor?"

"Quit being a wise guy. I've been trying to figure this out for months." She swallowed hard, pressed her palms on the blotter on her desk. Something was making her nervous. "I think it's time we had a forensic accountant go over our books. And yes, I know how paranoid that makes me look."

"And it costs money."

"If we find the bleeding artery, then maybe we can stop the flow."

"Have you talked to Matthew Alger? Seems to me you'd start with the city administrator."

"He was no help at all. His books are in perfect, squeaky-clean order." She scowled. "Of course they are."

"Why do you say that?"

"He wants to look perfect because he's going to run against me in the next election."

She looked so completely stressed out that Rourke nearly forgot his own troubles. "Listen, what about ordering an independent audit instead of the forensics at this point? Then you don't look paranoid and maybe you'll figure out what's going on."

"And the funding for an independent audit comes from, what, your department?" she asked.

He slapped his hand down on the desk. "I'm trying to be helpful."

Unlike most people he worked with, Nina ignored his temper. "What is with you, McKnight?"

He glared at her. "Nothing's with me, unless you want to count trying to run this department on a budget the size of an egg roll."

"Liar. You've never let yourself get rattled over a budget shortfall." She folded her arms on her desk and studied him.

He refused to let her scrutiny affect him. Nina Romano was beautiful. She was single and everyone loved her. For years, people in town had wanted them to fall in love and live happily ever after. The city mayor and the chief of police. It was just too cute to resist.

The only problem was, they weren't a match. They both knew it. Yet they respected each other. When she demanded to know what was eating him, he wasn't going to pull any punches.

"I've been all pissed off lately," he said.

"Oh." She gave a sage nod. "PJSD."

"What's that?"

"Post-Jenny Stress Disorder."

Very funny, he thought. "She drove me nuts when she was staying with me. I figured I'd be glad to see the back of her."

Nina laughed. "McKnight, you are one hell of a piece of work."

"What do you mean?"

"You've carried a torch for that girl ever since we were kids."

"I, um, kind of told her so before she left."

"And she still left?" Nina looked amazed.

"Yes."

"Then you must not have told her."

"I just said I did."

"All right, how did you tell her?"

He thought for a moment. "I told her the reason I date so many girls is that none of them is her."

It took Nina several minutes to stop laughing and pull herself together. Then she flipped a pencil at him, hitting him in the chest. "Good job, genius."

"What?"

"If I have to explain why that was so completely inappropriate, then you'll never get it."

"Listen, can we move on? It's pretty clear she's better off heading to the city—"

"God, McKnight, you always do this," Nina said.

"Do what?"

"You always try to find all the reasons you shouldn't be with Jenny, or with anyone decent. Why is that?"

"I don't need you to analyze my personal life, Nina," he said.

"Right. You're doing so well on your own." She showed him a banker's box overflowing with photographs and papers. "This might cheer her up."

"What is it?"

"The call I put out in the paper? Things have been flooding in."

Shortly after the fire, Nina had written an open letter to the citizens of Avalon, explaining Jenny's loss and asking for copies of any photos or memorabilia people might have of the Majesky family or bakery. To no one's surprise, items came flooding in—old photos, Sky River Bakery calendars dating back to the '60s, cards with heartfelt memories handwritten on them, a startling number of pictures of Mariska Majesky. The school district had donated copies of the high-school yearbook from each year Jenny had been a student there. He shuffled through a few items and was struck anew by the feelings she roused in him. She was so damn beautiful in picture after picture, smiling out at the camera. He tried to imagine what it was like to lose everything. At one point in his life, he had walked away from everything with only the clothes on his back, but that wasn't quite the same. He had been glad to leave his old life and all its trappings behind.

He came across a clipping from the paper, dated August 30, 1995. There was a photo of Jenny and Joey, their faces filled with happiness. "Mrs. Helen Majesky announces the engagement of her granddaughter, Jennifer Anne Majesky, to Corporal Joseph Santini…a summer wedding is planned."

Memories burned inside him, still painful even now. He replaced the lid on the box. "Does she know about this stuff?" he asked Nina.

"No, things are still coming in. I thought maybe you could be in charge of it."

"Nope. No way." One thing was clear to Rourke. He was still haunted by the emotions that had engulfed him during the fire.

There was a moment when he thought he'd lost her, and the one searing thought that wouldn't leave him alone was that he'd never told Jenny how he felt about her.

Twenty-Two

Jenny felt like an impostor as she emerged from the subway station at Rockefeller Center. She tried to join the flow of hurrying, sharply dressed professionals heading off for appointments, but she felt like a phony. She was a stranger here. Sure, she'd visited the city before, but she'd been a tourist. Her grandparents had brought her to visit museums or to see a ballet, and on two blessed, cherished occasions, they had taken her to see a Broadway play. *Beauty and the Beast* had made Gram weep with joy while Grandpa had struggled to stay awake. Another time, they'd seen a drama called *Da* about an Irish family, which was terribly sad but beautiful to watch.

Other times, they had gone to the Frick, the Met, Wall Street. By far the most memorable visit had been to Ellis Island. There was something haunting about the place where so many millions had taken their first breath of air in America. Gram and Grandpa had said little as they regarded the pictures of crowded waiting rooms and dormitories, a rooftop where children used to play. They had spent a long time studying the display cases of random objects—a cracked leather satchel, a child's stray shoe, a printed ticket, a stamped certificate of immigration. With a feeling of hushed awe, they had found their names among the engraved brass lists that marked the perimeter of the park. They'd traced the letters of their names with their fingertips, and Jenny would never forget the way they embraced each other, standing before the plaque with the wind blowing their hair and the Statue of Liberty in the background. It was such a mingling of sadness, regret and gratitude that she could finally see, in that moment, a glimpse of what it had been like for them, teenagers and newlyweds, fleeing to a new land, knowing full well that they would never see their families again.

Jenny had been thirteen years old. She was full of love for her grandparents and, she discovered, full of anger at her mother. That year, they'd also gone to the Cloisters, a medieval museum clear at the other end of Manhattan. To get there, they'd ridden a bus, and when it went through the Upper East Side, she'd known she was in Rourke McKnight's neighborhood because he and Joey had once explained where it was. She'd looked out in wonder at the beautiful Gilded Age buildings and parks, nannies in their crisp aprons pushing prams, manicured parks and shiny limos transporting their precious cargos here and there.

She remembered thinking, This is his world. She'd felt like an alien then, and she did now.

Everyone in the city seemed intense and full of purpose—the food vendors on the street corners, the black-clad young execs chattering into cell phones as they rushed along the crowded sidewalk. Even the smokers clustered around their sand-filled ashtrays seemed busy and important.

Maybe in time she would feel a part of this rushing scene, but for now, she was simply going through the motions. She turned down Forty-Seventh Street, bustling with shoppers, diamond merchants and brokers, many of them Hasidic Jews in traditional long black coats and brimmed hats, earlocks and beards framing their faces. Diamond jewelry glittered in the windows of shop after shop. On one corner, she noticed a peculiar smell—the hot reek of exhaust and the smoky-sweet aroma of roasting nuts. She spotted a little girl with a woman, hailing a taxi. The woman was hurrying; the child stumbled as the mother half dragged along.

Watching them, Jenny had the most extraordinary sensation of déjà vu. She could hear, as clearly as a voice spoken in her ear, a clipped command: "Come along, Jenny. You have to keep up. We have a flight to catch."

"I don't want to fly away."

"Fine, I'll leave you at home."

Jenny felt, for a moment, as though she'd become detached from her own life. Though the memory was dim, like a half-remembered dream, she had the eeriest notion that she had been here before.

In the next block, she watched the numbers on the buildings decrease, and found the address where she was to meet Philip Bellamy and Martin Greer, a man Philip had known since college, who was now a successful literary agent with his own firm.

As Jenny surrendered her coat, hat and gloves to the cloakroom of the restaurant, she felt the unpleasant tickle of panic. Oh, come on, she thought. Not now. Talk about your lousy timing. She contemplated taking a pill for it but dismissed the idea. For the next hour, she would simply ignore the symptoms.

She wiped her sweaty palms on her skirt, pasted a smile on her face and approached the podium. "Has Mr. Bellamy arrived yet?" she asked.

"I've just seated him." The Eastern European hostess, as slender as a pencil in a sleek skirt and blouse, led Jenny to the table where Philip and Martin awaited.

Both men stood to greet her, Philip with a brief kiss on her cheek and Martin with a handshake. She prayed he didn't notice the sweat.

"Thank you for seeing me," she said, taking a seat.

"It's my pleasure," Martin said. He had the pleasant and resonant voice of a radio announcer.

Jenny looked around the beautiful restaurant. It was airy and light with a view of the building's atrium, lush with tree-size tropical plants. They had been given prime seating—Martin and Philip were persons of consequence.

"How do you like New York so far?" Martin asked.

"It's fascinating. Olivia's apartment is great." So much in New York was over the top and larger than life, but Olivia's place was a comfortable oasis in an adorable brownstone filled with chintz-covered furniture, homey houseplants, bright Fiestaware in the china cupboard. Olivia had combined her good taste with the natural warmth of her personality, reflected in the cozy, sunny apartment.

"I've had the pleasure of reading some of your columns and essays," Martin said, turning businesslike.

Jenny held her breath. She felt Philip doing the same.

"And here's the thing," Martin continued, leaning toward her a little. "I'm a fan. I like the material. And I'm not just saying that because Philip would strangle me if I didn't. I'm saying that because there's something special in your writing."

"I don't know what to say," she told him. "I'm flattered, really."

Martin held up his hand. "I'm just getting started. Like I said, I'm a fan. I could feel the atmosphere of this little family bakery as if I was right there. You brought your grandparents to life for me. I could hear their voices and picture them in my mind's eye. I'm no baker but the recipes make sense to me. Your writing is lively, authentic and unpretentious."

Jenny was still in the clutches of the panic attack. She could feel her face burning. Perhaps he would think it was just excitement. "Thank you," she said a bit breathlessly. She took a quick sip of her Voss water. "But at the end of everything you said, I hear a great big 'however' coming."

Martin and Philip exchanged a glance. "You have good hearing," Martin said. "Very perceptive."

"So what's the however?" she asked.

The waiter came for their orders. She barely glanced at the menu, and opted for one of the specials, which contained at least three things she'd never heard of.

"The however is this," Martin said. "You've given us the bakery. The recipes, the characters involved—your grandparents and co-workers, the quirky customers. It's all there. What's missing is one key ingredient."

"What's that?"

"You."

Jenny hadn't expected this. "I'm not sure what you mean."

"You need to be more present. Not just a narrator but a character yourself. Sure, people are going to like these vignettes, the recipes and character sketches. But in order for this book to be extraordinary, we need to see you in it. We need to see the things that define you, your dreams and emotions, and what this place represents for you. Show us your heart."

"I don't really consider myself interesting enough to write about."

"Then you're not thinking hard enough." Martin was clearly unmoved by the fact that the whole notion distressed her completely. "You've given us little tantalizing glimpses of key things that happened in your life. The bitter-chocolate cake your grandmother made every year on your mother's birthday. How could the reader not want to hear more? And the fiftieth-anniversary cake you yourself made for Philip's parents. I'm thinking there's much more to the story. I mean, come on—somebody orders a cake, and it leads to discovering the father you never knew. *That's* what people want to read."

Now Jenny got it. She glanced at Philip and knew he got it, too.

"You want me to write about my mother," she said.

Martin steepled his fingers together. "What was it like to have her walk away? And to have your father come into your life last summer? And here's a question—who's Joey?"

Oh, God. "You read the archives." It was not a question.

"Sure," Martin said. "I'm taking this project very seriously."

She didn't know what to say. The raw nerves of the past were suddenly exposed. Neither of these men wished her ill, but their scrutiny was painful. Years ago, when she had first started her column, Joey had been a part of her life. Naturally, allusions to him and his Italian heritage had made their way into the column.

His father, Bruno, a lovable bear of a man, had even convinced
Gram to add fiadone to the menu at the bakery.

"He, um…Joey and I were engaged," she finally said, studying the crisp white tablecloth. Even now, it hurt to say the words.
And even now, she could picture Joey, laughing and innocent,
so in love with her that his fellow rangers used to rib him for
spontaneously bursting into song every time he thought of her.
There was so much more Jenny could say about Joey, but she
wasn't used to talking about him, especially not to a man she
was just coming to know. And in front of—good lord—a literary agent.

"Honey, I'm sorry," Philip said, touching her hand in a gesture
both awkward and comforting. "I hate that certain things happened
to you, and I wasn't there to…I don't know. Help or just listen.
Just be there."

His painful honesty touched her, yet she felt a faint shadow of
bitterness, too. She wished he'd found her sooner, wished he'd
been there when she desperately needed someone. Of course, that
was impossible, and it wasn't his fault. "I'm all right now. It was
a long time ago," she told him. Then she turned to Mr. Greer. "I
never put anything too personal in my writing. I'm not sure I'd
know how to do it."

"Little anecdotes work fine for a newspaper column." He
paused. "But you've got some thinking to do—about the personal
stuff. Because here's the thing about a food memoir. It's never
about the food."

"In other words," Jenny said to Nina on the phone that night,
"he wants me to bleed on the page."

"Can you do it?"

"Of course I can. The question is whether or not I'm willing
to," Jenny said. "And does anybody really care? I'm just a girl who
grew up in a small town, helping out with the family business. Nobody special. I thought that was what people liked about my writing. They could relate to my story, make it their own. Why do I

have to write about my mom and admit I never knew my dad? Why in God's name do I have to bring up Joey?"

"People like that stuff. An ordinary person facing the out-of-the-ordinary."

Jenny tried to imagine herself putting certain things on the page. "All I've ever wanted since I was a girl was to be heard. I wanted people to know my story, even though there was nothing particularly unique about it. People tell about their lives and they want them to be happy stories. When you have to go somewhere not so happy…" She looked out the window at the apartment buildings across the way, standing shoulder to shoulder in an impenetrable blockade. "It's going to change what this book is."

"And that's a bad thing?" Nina asked.

"I'm not sure. I had a pleasant collection of recipes and anecdotes about the bakery—that's what I thought it was. Now I'm about to change it into a story of abandonment and anger, and a failed love affair, and I'm supposed to pull out some sort of epiphany in the end." She shook her head. "I have no idea how to end it."

"Could be when you met Philip Bellamy or made the fiftieth-anniversary wedding cake for people you didn't even know were your grandparents, take your pick," Nina said. "How bad do you want this?"

Bad enough to hurt and bleed for it. Jenny took a breath, got up and paced restlessly. "I want it."

"Then I guess you'd better get busy finding that epiphany."

She smiled and poured a glass of water on a houseplant. "It doesn't work that way."

"You know what I think? I think it's Rourke McKnight."

Jenny held the receiver away from her and scowled at it. "Come again?"

"You and Rourke. Maybe that's the ending."

"There is no me and Rourke. God, Nina."

"And you know what else?" Nina said, unrepentant. "You sound miserable. I don't think heading to the city was the best idea for you."

"I've always wanted to do this, always. You of all people know that."

"I think you liked the *idea* of it more than the reality," Nina pointed out. "You know, the cute little apartment, the bustling crowds, the excitement. But the reality is, your life is in Avalon. It's where the people who care most about you are."

"I'm supposed to be meeting my new family," Jenny pointed out. "My father's sisters, my paternal grandparents, cousins I never knew existed until half a year ago."

"Fine, get to know them, but I still think you belong back here."

Jenny winced. Was she that girl? The shop owner destined to spend her life in a small town while dreaming of a different life like a latter-day female George Bailey? She paced back and forth in front of the window. Outside, people hurried along on their errands, lines of traffic crushed and expanded like a giant accordion. In a doorway across the street, a woman in a gray cloth coat leaned against the jamb, brooding as though the scene was a personal affront to her.

"I like it here," Jenny insisted, though the impersonal snapshot out the window made her wonder if she was fooling herself.

"Come home. You know you want to."

"I don't have a home, remember? I refuse to stay at Rourke's any longer, and I love you dearly, but there's no way I'm moving in with you and Sonnet."

"You can find a rental. No big deal." Nina, whose heart and soul belonged to Avalon, who loved it so much she worked fourteen-hour days as mayor, simply couldn't seem to understand why someone would want to live anywhere else.

"I'll think about it," Jenny said, mainly because the whole issue was giving her a headache. A confusion-induced headache. In all honesty, she didn't know her own mind—her own heart—anymore. "I've got some things I need to do here besides meeting my father's family."

"Like what?"

Jenny took a deep breath. "I need to go see Joey."

"Aw, Jen." Nina's voice wavered. "Don't do that to yourself."

"I'll be all right," she said. "It's just…something I need to do."

She took a taxi because the day was so cold. There wasn't much snow around, just grainy gray heaps along the curbs here and there. The sky was heavy and colorless over the Manhattan Bridge as the taxi crossed to Brooklyn and made its way along Flatbush Avenue. She'd been here once before, but her memory of that day was faulty, a blur of pain. Yet since the meeting with Martin Greer, she'd been thinking a lot about the stories inside her, and she was beginning to realize she'd been hiding from the past rather than facing up to it.

The taxi passed through the arched iron gate and trolled along the gray paved driveway. She silently counted the rows, and then spoke up. "I think it's here," she said faintly. "Can you wait?"

The driver nodded and she got out. She seemed to be the only one here. The cold was etched into the very ground beneath her feet, the grass flattened and drained of color. She walked along, counting as she went, and then she stopped and turned, suddenly glad no one else was around. Her stomach fluttered with nervousness.

"Hey, Joey," she said. "It's me." She took a deep breath, blew it halfway out and started talking. "There's something I'm thinking about doing, and I wanted to tell you about it. You know how I've always wanted to write a book? You used to tease me about writing everything down, remember? I still do that, and now it looks as though I've been given that chance. It's not easy, though. Some of the things I'll be writing are going to take me back to…difficult times. I don't know, maybe it's masochistic, but I want to write about those times. It's something I probably should have done a long time ago. I think you know why. Anyway, that's the plan."

The cold wind caused her eyes to water. She stood for a few moments longer, thinking, remembering. The headstone was situated next to an older marker for Joey's mother. Joey's still looked brand new, rounded at the top and gleaming, the carved letters crisp at the edges:

Joseph Anthony Santini, 1976-1998. Beloved son.
Step softly—a dream lies buried here.

The buzzer sounded from the street. Jenny hurried to answer, opening the door for Jane Bellamy. Her grandmother—Philip's mother—stood beaming at her. A wave of silver hair winged out from beneath her soft angora hat, and she wore a handsomely tailored burgundy wool coat. There was nothing the least bit unkind about her, but Jenny simply didn't know how to act around her.

"Hello, dear," Jane said. "I'm so pleased you agreed to come."

"I really appreciate the invitation." Jenny wondered if she looked as rattled as she felt. She'd been trying all day to get some writing done, but had managed nothing more than organizing her e-mail files and playing a dozen games of Minesweeper. She gave her grandmother a hug. Her *grandmother*. They had not known each other long, but there was nothing to dislike about Jane Gordon Bellamy. Jane's grandfather had founded Camp Kioga and she had grown up there.

In 1956, she had married Charles Bellamy in a ceremony at Camp Kioga. Helen Majesky had created their wedding cake, a splendid confection covered in sugar-dough flowers. Fifty years later, Jenny had made an exact replica of that cake for their golden anniversary, also celebrated at the camp. Jane was sixty-nine years old, beautiful, with bright eyes, her silver hair fashionable, her cashmere winter coat draping nicely over her slender figure. There was an unpretentious air about her, even though she was married to a Bellamy and lived in one of the venerable old buildings on the Upper East Side.

Jane looked around the room, a bright spot even in the dead of winter. "How are you liking Olivia's apartment?"

"I absolutely love this place. It's just perfect." Even so, Jenny was haunted by the things Nina had said on the phone the other day. Was it perfect, or was she forcing herself to feel that way because this was what she thought she wanted?

"I'm not surprised the two of you have similar taste," Jane said. "After all, you're sisters."

Half sisters, Jenny thought. The other half of Olivia was her mother, Pamela Lightsey—divorced, well off, socially connected, intimidating. Yet another thing she had in common with Olivia. They both had difficult mothers. The difference was, Pamela was made difficult by her presence and Mariska by her absence.

"So, are you ready for our outing?" asked Jane.

"Absolutely. I've always wanted to see the St. Regis." Jenny went and got her coat. Going to a legendary hotel for tea might be a common occurrence in Jane Bellamy's life, but it was a first for Jenny.

"I usually have tea there once a month," Jane explained. She had her own driver, a low-key man in a good suit, who murmured in a foreign language into his Bluetooth as he expertly navigated the car through traffic. "In the past, I nearly always took Olivia along. It was quite the tradition with us."

Jenny and Gram had traditions, too, but they were much more humble. Jenny would go to the bakery after school each day. She would sit at one of the worktables with a glass of cold milk and a warm cookie, spinning around on a stool as she exuberantly told Gram about her day.

"Olivia and I started this when she was ten or eleven," Jane went on. "I'm sure she wouldn't mind my telling you that she took her parents' divorce very hard."

"She told me," Jenny said.

"I can't say taking her to high tea did much good, but I'm sure the extra attention didn't hurt." Jane reached over and patted Jenny's hand. "Listen to me, rambling on and on."

"I don't mind."

The car pulled alongside the curb in front of the hotel, a Beaux Arts landmark in midtown. A doorman in formal livery hastened to open the car door for them, offering Jane a hand to help her out. "Good afternoon, Mrs. Bellamy," he said.

We're not in Kansas anymore, Jenny thought, stepping into the opulent lobby.

The hostess also knew Jane Bellamy by name. She led them through an indoor palm court to their table in a bright, elegant tea-room. Murmured conversation and soothing harp music filled the air. Jane beamed at Jenny. "Are you impressed? I wanted to impress you."

Jenny laughed. "Are you kidding? Definitely impressed. They treat you like a VIP."

"It's a privilege of old age." Jane grew serious. "When Charles and I first moved to the city after we were married, I felt the same way you probably do—lost and confused. The only thing that saved me was knowing my summers would all be spent at Camp Kioga. I want you to know, Jenny, there's no shame in feeling homesick."

"I don't feel homesick. I'd better not." At Jane's confused look, Jenny said, "I'd be disappointed in myself if I was homesick."

"Dear, although we haven't known each other long, I am your grandmother and I can smell a lie a mile off."

"But—" Jenny stared down into her cup of tea, warm amber Earl Grey, redolent of bergamot. "All my life, I thought I wanted this. I'd feel like a failure if I didn't think this was a dream come true."

"Nonsense," Jane said. "You can't force your feelings to do your will." She smiled wistfully. "I've been away from Avalon for fifty years and I still miss it."

Jenny was stunned. "Why not move back?"

"My life is here because Charles is here. When you're with the person you love, you're home. Have you ever been in love, Jenny?"

She thought about Joey, the plans they'd made, and the way everything had shattered apart. "Not that way," she admitted. "Not in a follow-you-to-the-ends-of-the-earth way." She took a sip of her tea, faced Jane's steady gaze. "I was engaged," she said. "His name was Joey, and he was a soldier in the army."

"I take it things didn't work out."

"He died." Jane probably deserved a fuller explanation, but Jenny didn't trust herself to say more without coming apart. She thought about Joey constantly, but all the memories and all her plans didn't clarify anything for her. God, she thought, and she was supposed to write about this? She couldn't even say it.

Jane's eyes softened with shock and concern. "I'm sorry. He must have been so young. It must have been terrible for you."

Jenny nodded. "I'm all right now. It's been several years. Eventually, I dated a little." She was embarrassed to admit how little. "My last boyfriend—Don—was a nice guy. We had fun together. He was an awful driver, though. He got more traffic tickets than anyone I've ever known. In fact, I think he eventually skipped town because he didn't want to pay them. Come to think of it, another guy I dated used to get a lot of tickets, too." She'd nearly forgotten about Tyler. He hadn't left much of an impression.

"Oh, dear. Does this mean you're attracted to reckless men?"

"I don't think so. They were just unlucky. In the wrong place at the wrong time. Failing to signal, a taillight out… One of Don's tickets was for not having mud flaps on his truck, can you imagine? Who even knew that was a rule?"

"Avalon's finest," Jane said. "Good to know they're so vigilant. Olivia tells me the chief of police has been especially good to you since the fire. I'm pleased to hear that."

Uh-huh. And what else had Olivia said? The snitch. Maybe there was a downside to having a sister. "Rourke and I have known each other for a long time," she said. "He was Joey's best friend."

"I see. And how did he come to settle in Avalon?"

The question startled Jenny. "He studied law enforcement in college and then he just…settled there."

Jane lifted one delicate eyebrow. "And you and Rourke are… close?"

No one was close to Rourke. "Like I said, the two of us go way back, but it's…complicated."

"Well. I won't pry, much as I'd like to," Jane said, beaming at her.

Jenny laughed, liking this woman more and more. "I don't mind the prying," she said, "but there's nothing to find out. Rourke McKnight and I are... We found out a long time ago that we're better off staying out of each other's range. Much better off. I have been conspicuously single for a while."

Jane carefully blotted her lips with a linen napkin. "I lied," she said. "I *am* going to pry. I can't pretend I know anything at all about the situation, but you don't get to be my age without learning a thing or two about love. Now, this Joey—I'll bet he loved you very much."

Jenny gave a cautious nod.

"He would have wanted you to move on. To fall in love again."

Jenny stared at her lap. "We talked about it—about the possibility of him not coming back—each time he was deployed. All soldiers do that. They have to. I hated those conversations. And...yes. He always said if he was gone, I should fall in love again."

"And yet, you haven't."

Jenny looked up. She wanted to be angry at her grandmother, to accuse her of meddling, but she saw only wisdom and compassion in Jane's eyes. "I haven't," she admitted. "Taking care of Gram and running the bakery kept me busy."

"Helen was lucky to have you," Jane said. Mercifully, she seemed to sense Jenny's desperation to change the subject.

"I was lucky to have her."

Jane nodded. "I went to the Sky River Bakery on its opening day back in 1952."

"You're kidding." She tried to picture Jane as a young woman in Avalon.

"Not at all. And I have to tell you, the minute I set foot in that place, I had a good feeling. It was everything you want a family bakery to be." She studied the tiered tray of petits fours and truffle butter canapés, but didn't take one. "I had a jam kolache. And within a week, my parents had made a contract with your grandparents to supply Camp Kioga with baked goods in the summer."

The memory filled Jenny with both warmth and sadness. She felt so distant from that world. She pictured Helen and Jane together, younger than Jenny herself was now. How strange that they had met, that Helen had created Jane's wedding cake, and then unknowingly, they had both become grandmothers at the moment Jenny was born.

"Did you know my mother?" Jenny asked.

"Mariska? Oh, my, yes." Her hands fluttered down into her lap.

"I don't mean to make you uncomfortable—"

"I'm not at all. I dearly wish I had known her better. I understand you haven't seen her since you were very young."

To this day, Jenny could still smell a whiff of perfume—Jean Naté—and hear her mother's voice: *I'll see you when I come back around again.* It was what she always said, never explaining where she was going or when she'd be back.

"Helen and Leo were extremely proud of her," Jane said. "She was a beautiful girl—you look very much like her. She was smart and hardworking. And she liked going fishing with her father, which seemed curious to me. They used to come up to Willow Lake, year-round."

"Why was that curious?"

"She just didn't seem the type. She was lovely, and very feminine, and she was utterly determined to see the world. I believe she was what's known as larger than life," said Jane. "Prettier, more fun-loving, more daring. No wonder Philip fell in love with her. I'm quite surprised they were able to keep it secret all summer long."

The summer Jenny had been conceived.

"And all this time," Jane said gently, "there's been no word? Nothing?"

Jenny shook her head. "It's as if she dropped off the face of the earth." She helped herself to more tea. "If I decide to pursue this book, I'll be writing about it."

"Is that what you want to do?"

"Yes." Even knowing the memories she'd have to explore, she wanted to do it.

"That's very brave of you. When I was young, I used to dream about publishing my poems."

"And did you?"

Jane smiled and shook her head. "They were extremely bad poems. Your father always wanted to write," she added.

Jenny felt a jolt at the words *your father.* Discovering a whole new world of relatives was like finding a hidden door in a house she'd lived in her entire life, and learning that it led to new places she never knew existed. "I haven't made any progress, though. Here in the city, I feel…distracted," Jenny said, unable to be anything but honest. "Philip introduced me to Martin Greer, a literary agent who thinks I might actually have a book in me. Unless he was just saying so out of respect for his friend."

Jane shook her head. "I know Martin. He would never be so disingenuous. He understands a book has to stand on its own merits."

"That's good to know." Jenny hesitated, then confided, "The truth is, I'm having trouble with the project."

"What sort of trouble? Perhaps I can be of some help."

Jenny took a deep breath. "Being here in the city is not quite…what I'd expected. I mean, I knew it would be noisy and full of life, but I'm letting myself get distracted."

"Perhaps you're a peace-and-quiet sort of writer."

Jenny recalled the endless silent hours in Avalon. She would become so absorbed in what she was doing that hours would pass, unnoticed. She used to work late into the night, when the only sound was the wind sighing in the leaves, or in springtime, the chirping of frogs. Here, there was no silent time of the night. She acknowledged, though, that it wasn't just the noise distracting her.

"I'd like to offer a suggestion," Jane said. "It's one of the reasons I wanted to see you today. The winter lodge, up at Camp Kioga, is vacant. I'd like to offer it to you, for as long as you like."

Jenny set down her teacup with a clatter. Camp Kioga? That would mean leaving the city, going back to Avalon. Was she ready to call it quits after just a few weeks in the city? "I don't know what to say. It's very generous of you. In fact, it's too much."

"Nonsense. The lodge is perfect for a winter guest. It's simple but quite lovely and comfortable."

Jenny was aware of this. She hadn't seen the place in years, but she remembered sneaking in one Fourth of July. It was the place where Rourke had kissed her for the first time. She remembered the kiss far better than she did the lodge, though.

"Last fall, we lent the place to a woman recovering from cancer and her family," Jane went on. "They needed some time away to get over the ordeal of her illness. It's been vacant since then. The road up the mountain is impassable after a big snow unless it's plowed. Both your grandfathers used to go up there by snowmobile, for ice fishing on Willow Lake." Jane pushed a copper key across the table to Jenny. "Think about it. You could get a lot of writing done, without distraction."

Twenty-Three

By the time she went for her appointment at the clinic in Kingston, Daisy felt as if her head was going to explode from all the counseling she'd sat through, hours and hours of it. The doctor had pronounced her healthy in every respect, nine weeks into her pregnancy. She'd gone over every option and urged Daisy to explore each one deeply, to live with the decision, imagining her life seven months from now, and in a year, and five years and beyond.

That was a scary exercise, pregnant or not. Daisy didn't know what the future held for her. She didn't know what she wanted or who she wanted to be.

She glanced over at her mother, who was driving. Within twelve hours of Daisy's call, her mom had dropped everything, walking out of the international court with its white-wigged justices. Because of Daisy, Sophie Bellamy had turned her back on the case she had been working on half of her professional life.

"I'm really sorry, Mom," Daisy said. Boy, understatement of the year.

"Sweetie, don't be sorry."

The words were kind enough, but Daisy couldn't escape the thought that her mother was struggling with disappointment and fear. And really, Daisy didn't blame her. She'd probably feel the same way if their roles were reversed. "You had to walk out of the World Court."

"And I can walk back in. People have family emergencies. It happens."

Daisy lapsed into silence and thought back over the options. She had seriously considered adoption, had even watched videotapes of prospective couples who all seemed so needy and earnest. But try as she might, she could not picture herself handing over her newborn baby forever. As to having the baby, she had already done that reality check. The counselor had given her a virtual baby, which was a little device like a pager that forced her to live through twenty-four hours with a real newborn that cried at all hours, wet and pooped and spit up and, according to national statistics, cost an average of $240 a week for eighteen years. And finally, there was abortion—a safe and legal procedure.

Daisy gazed out the window at the gray winter world floating by. Having a baby was the kind of thing she'd dreamed about doing someday. Not seven months from now. In seven months, she would be a high-school graduate. In a year, maybe she'd figure out what she wanted to do with her life. Five years from now, she probably wouldn't even remember this day.

"Thanks for doing this," she told her mother.

"Of course."

"I wish you'd say how you really feel."

"I…Daisy, I can't, because I just don't know what I'm feeling. There's no easy resolution for your situation."

"You got pregnant at nineteen, and you married Dad and had me. Do you wish you hadn't? Was it a mistake? Was Max? Or the past eighteen years?"

"Of course not. Having you was the best and the hardest thing I ever did. Going to law school, trying cases, all that was nothing compared to getting you to sleep at night and keeping you safe. And the only thing that made it bearable was having your dad— my partner, my husband, by my side to help me."

"But now you're divorced and we're all miserable."

"Our lives are different. Not miserable."

Speak for yourself, thought Daisy. I'm *miserable.*

Mom rubbed the back of her hand. "I don't regret anything about the past eighteen years," she said. "We were a happy family, but your dad and I stopped…being happy together. It happens." She paused. "Maybe you should think a bit more about talking to Logan—"

"No way." That decision had been an easy one to make. She had pictured herself going to Logan O'Donnell, telling him about the baby. That scenario was almost laughable—she and Logan together, raising a baby. Logan had a big ego and a dangerous affinity for beer and worse. Living with him would be like raising two kids, one of them badly behaved.

She had also thought long and hard about raising the baby by herself. For a young, single mom with no college education and few job skills, it was bound to be a challenge. The counselor she'd seen drummed it into her—the commitment was unrelenting. Raising a child alone meant being without that second pair of hands to help out, that second income to make ends meet, that shoulder to lean on in hard times. A single mom, even one with a loving, supportive family like she had, ultimately had no one but herself to rely on. To Daisy, this was the scariest option of all— that she would somehow fail the child, inadvertently harming it with her ineptitude or inadequacy, making a blameless child the victim of her own stupidity. And, okay, she was selfish. She knew if she decided to go through with the pregnancy, her youth would end. She wasn't ready to give up being free and adventurous, going to concerts and staying out all night, seeing the world, maybe becoming a famous photographer.

At the clinic, a surprisingly homey place in an older building a few blocks from the hospital, she went through more counseling. She was told exactly what to expect, the exact progression of events. At the end of twenty-four hours, she would no longer be pregnant. She would be…empty. It was agony, wondering if she was doing the right thing. She thought of Sonnet, whose mom had faced the same dilemma. And her cousin Jenny, who would never have been born if her accidentally pregnant mother had gotten rid of her. Once this was over, it was something Daisy could never undo, and the permanence of it made her shudder.

The waiting room was half-full. One woman stared at the floor, as though dog-tired, or ashamed. Another leaned back, looking ill and desperate. Another looked absolutely furious. Two girls younger than Daisy, alike enough to be sisters, sat together whispering and giggling, probably giddy with nerves. Daisy couldn't imagine saying a word to anyone. As far as she was concerned, you didn't make idle chitchat about something like this.

There was a checklist to be gone over and filled out and signed, acknowledging the risks and agreeing to hold the clinic blameless in the event of a mishap. The language looked scary to Daisy. Her mom reached over and rubbed her back, the way she used to when Daisy was small. "It'll be all right. I've studied the statistics. The risks are far lower than the risk of carrying a pregnancy to term."

Daisy nodded, wishing some sign would come down from above, telling her once and for all the right thing to do. Instead, the minutes crawled by. Her mom waited with her until her name was called. They stood up together and embraced.

"I love you, baby," her mom whispered.

"I'll see you soon," Daisy said.

"I'll be right here in the waiting room."

"Okay." Then she stepped back, took a deep breath and walked through the open door.

Greg paced. He was surprised there wasn't a path worn in the floor, he'd been pacing so long. Where the hell were they?

He could hear the TV droning in the next room, ripples of dialogue interspersed with studio laughter. Max was at that indiscriminate age; he would watch anything on TV.

For no reason he could put his finger on, Greg felt like crying. He ought to be relieved right about now. Daisy would come home and she'd no longer be pregnant and everything would get back to normal.

Not that normal was any great state of affairs, he thought, hearing a commercial for toenail fungus from the other room. Here he was, in the middle of his life, starting all over again. And he didn't have his youthful foolishness and drive and naïveté to spur him on. Just the daily grind of worries about his kids and his business. And the God-awful loneliness howling through him as he lay awake each night.

One thing Greg knew about himself—he wasn't meant to be alone. It wasn't in his makeup. Sophie used to make this observation about him, postulating that as the youngest sibling, he wasn't accustomed to being content in his own company.

Sophie, Sophie, Sophie. She postulated about a lot of things. She was a lawyer. She was good at it.

He dug his wallet out of his back pocket and found the business card Nina Romano had given him. It had a water wheel on it—the seal of the city—and Nina Romano, Mayor, with three phone numbers and an e-mail address. He turned the card over to see that she'd written, "Welcome!" on the back. Did she do this for all newcomers or was he somehow special?

The sound of a car engine startled him and he slipped the card away. Then he ripped open the side door and burst outside. "Is everything all right?" he demanded as Sophie emerged from the driver's side of her rental car.

Thin-lipped, her expression grave, Sophie nodded. "She's fine."

His hands shaking as relief coursed through him, Greg opened the passenger-side door and Daisy got out. She looked unexpectedly well, her cheeks flushed with color and her eyes bright.

"Let me help you inside," he said.

"In a minute," she said. "I need to tell you something."

He glanced at Sophie. Her cool expression told him nothing.

"Dad, I didn't do it." There was a giddy, almost hysterical note in her voice.

"You didn't what?"

"I changed my mind. I'm having this baby."

Twenty-Four

Jenny's stomach was in knots as the train's brakes gnashed to a halt in Avalon. She told herself not to feel bad. Not to be nervous. This was a homecoming. She should be happy about it. About coming home.

Instead, it felt like a defeat. A month ago she had gone to New York City expecting…what? For her life to suddenly turn into an episode of *Sex and the City?* To fling her hat in the air while the world discovered how fabulous she was? To find herself instantly surrounded by interested, fascinating friends? She should have thought things through. If she had, she would have realized that it was impossible to run away from herself. Being in the city, meeting a literary agent who pointed out exactly how much work she needed to do, only magnified the truth. She was like her unfinished book—a work-in-progress. And city life wasn't what she wanted after all.

With a heaviness in her limbs, she collected her belongings from the overhead rack and headed for the exit. She stepped down onto the platform and was immediately lashed by a blast of cold air, scented with the burning-cinder odor of the engine's fuel. When the cloud of blowing snow and dust cleared she saw Rourke there, shimmering like a figure in a dream. Very *Casablanca*, right down to his scowl.

She found herself remembering the day she got engaged to Joey. Rourke had been on the verge of telling her something and if she'd let him, maybe everything would have turned out differently. If she lived to be a hundred, Jenny would never forget the look in Rourke's eyes that day. They'd turned flinty and hard, flash-frozen by her words. *Joey asked me to marry him.* One moment, she thought. One moment, she'd let her true feelings waver. One moment of doubt, and she'd opened the door for Joey. One moment, and she'd made a mess of three lives.

"Don't you dare say 'I told you so,'" she warned Rourke. She wondered if the memories showed on her face.

"It seems I don't need to," he said, though there was no satisfaction in his voice.

She stood there like an idiot. Was she supposed to hug him? Give him a kiss on the cheek? What did he expect? "I didn't know you'd be here," she finally said.

He took her heavier bag and headed for the exit. No hug. Not even a "hey." A smile was too much to hope for. As for that goodbye kiss, she might have imagined it. "I figured you'd need a ride," he told her.

"Thanks, Rourke."

"Don't thank me yet. I came here to intercept you."

"What?"

"To stop you from going off to Camp Kioga."

Their boots crackled over the ice-crusted surface of the parking lot. "Then you wasted a trip," she said. "My mind is made up. For the foreseeable future, that's my new address."

He slung her bags into the back of the Ford Explorer. "It's ten miles from nowhere."

"Which I find extremely appealing, especially after experiencing life in the big city." She climbed in the passenger side.

"You're staying with me," he said, starting the engine.

She laughed. "I just love a man who's not afraid to boss people around."

"I'm serious, Jenny."

She stopped laughing. "Oh, my God. You are."

"Living that far away in the middle of winter is a bad idea."

"So is bossing me around."

"This has nothing to do with any bossing of anyone. There are just too many reasons for you not to live up there."

"Those are your reasons, not mine."

They pulled into the truck bay behind the bakery where her car was parked in a utility shed. Jenny found herself sorting through a confusing array of reactions. She was reluctantly but undeniably happy to see him. And stupidly thrilled to know he was worried about her. And annoyed at the same time.

"I'll tell you what," she said. "I'll call you every night to let you know the ax murderer let me live another day."

"Not good enough."

"It is for me," she said. "Deal with it."

He was silent as he transferred the luggage from his car to hers. Fine, she thought. Let him sulk. It wasn't her job to keep him from worrying about her.

"I can take care of myself," she assured him. "I've done it all my life, and I can do it now. Let's stop in at the bakery. I'll give you a Napoleon."

They entered by way of the back door and were greeted by a cacophony of busy noises, the clang of racks being moved around, the whir and grind of machinery, and the smooth ripples of jazz from the stereo.

Jenny inhaled, and felt the yeasty, fresh atmosphere invade every cell of her body. She was home. Until she'd gone away, she hadn't realized how much this place was a part of her. Whether she liked it or not, this bakery was in her blood and bones. It was knit into her very soul.

"There you are, you city slicker." Laura came out of the office to wrap her in a soft-armed embrace. "The place hasn't been the same without you. But I want you to know, we're getting along fine." She eyed Rourke. "Most of us, anyway."

He scowled at her. "I'm trying to persuade her not to move up to the cabin."

"Why not?" Laura asked. "It's perfect—away from it all, the ideal place to work on her book."

"I heard you were moving to the winter lodge." Daisy Bellamy came whisking through the double door from the shop front. "It's great out there," she said, her face sparkling with animation. "You'll love it. We spent the summer at Camp Kioga last year and it was fantastic."

"Thank you," Jenny said emphatically to both Daisy and Laura. "It's nice to know some people think it's a good idea." She went upstairs to her office to get some files she wanted to work on. Daisy followed her, hovering in the doorway. "I need to tell you something."

"All right."

"In private." Daisy glanced over her shoulder, then stepped into the office.

"Are you all right?"

"Yes." But the girl's face had gone from sparkling to the color of cold oatmeal. Beads of sweat stood out on her forehead and upper lip, and, looking at her, Jenny felt a thrum of worry. "Daisy, have a seat. Do you feel all right?"

Daisy rubbed her hands on the front of her apron. "I get a little nauseous now and then, but I'm not sick. I'm pregnant."

The statement hit Jenny like a blow. Daisy, pregnant. She was just a kid. Of course, there was no reason for this to come as a surprise. Teenage girls had been getting themselves in trouble since the beginning of time. Beautiful, smart girls with their whole futures ahead of them—Jenny's own mother. Her best friend, Nina. Every girl who ever let passion sweep away caution and common sense put herself at risk of an unplanned pregnancy.

Okay, she thought. *Deep breath.* She tried to imagine what Daisy was feeling. This was huge. Daisy was no dummy. She knew it was huge.

Daisy shut the door behind her and sat in a chair across from Jenny. Her chin trembled and she drew in a sharp breath, then faced Jenny squarely. "I don't know where to start," she said.

"How about you start by telling me anything you feel like telling me. I might not have any answers, but I promise I won't judge you or get angry. Nothing like that."

Daisy slumped a little. "Thanks."

It felt strangely gratifying to have her young cousin's confidence. Yet she felt helpless as well. What in the world could she tell this girl, or do for her, that could make a difference?

Daisy was eerily controlled when she began to speak. "It was just before my mom was due to go overseas. Between that and the divorce, I was all messed up. And then they both started ragging on me about college, you know?"

"Sorry. I don't know," Jenny explained. "I grew up a lot differently than you did. Though I suppose you could say I do know what it's like to be pushed into doing something you don't want to. Maybe we have that in common. So you don't want to go to college?"

"Nope. Which, at my school, is like saying I don't want to breathe. Totally unheard of."

Jenny got a clear picture of a very unhappy young woman, simmering away, yearning for a different life. Philip had told her a bit about his younger brother Greg's situation. According to Philip, the divorce was torture for Daisy's parents and that probably tortured the kids, too.

Jenny came around the desk and took her cousin's hands in hers. Every one of the girl's fingernails was chewed to the quick. "Tell me what I can do to help you."

Daisy lifted her gorgeous delft-blue eyes to Jenny. "You're already helping."

Daisy nodded. "It's weird. I go to school, I hang out with my friends, and it feels like I have a normal life. And then, *wham.* I remember I'm pregnant. And that makes me feel like an alien from another planet."

Jenny still remembered how terrified Nina had been, and how, as her pregnancy progressed, she had become…different. There was something about a pregnant girl walking the corridors of a high school that set her apart from the rest of the world, as though she existed in her own private bubble. Was it still like that in high school?

"I can't say I have any experience in this area," she said, "but I do in the area of being an adult. When you're growing up, you can't wait for the day when no one tells you what to do. Once you reach that place, though, there are times when you wish someone *would* tell you what to do."

Daisy let out a glum sigh. "No kidding."

"When I was your age, I felt the same way. I couldn't wait to get out of Avalon when I graduated high school."

"What happened?"

"My grandpa died, which left my grandmother and me all alone with the bakery. And still it would have been okay for me to leave because Gram had Laura to help her, and this whole town full of people who loved her. But then Gram had a stroke. She never told me I had to stay. She would have found a way to cope on her own. But how could I do that? I just couldn't walk away." She paused, pierced by a memory of the plans she'd made, and how everything had fallen apart for her. "I ended up living at home, running the bakery, taking care of my grandmother, and the years just kind of flew by."

"Do you wish you'd done something different?"

Before the trip to New York, she would have instantly said yes. Now she realized the life she'd been living had been the right one after all. Even though it wasn't glamorous or exciting, she belonged here in this small town, running the bakery, surrounded by people who cared about her. "It's a funny thing," she tried to explain to Daisy. "Things have a way of working out, even if they're not what we had in mind. I remember standing in a hospital waiting room, and the doctors were asking me to make this huge decision about my grandmother, and I just felt…paralyzed. I would've given anything to have somebody make the decision for me. But there wasn't anyone except me. I had to make the call and live with the consequences. Which is not such a terrible thing," she hastened to add, and touched Daisy's shoulder. "Whatever you decide, the experience will make you learn and grow in ways you never imagined."

"I hope you're right. Because I've, um…I've decided to have the baby. My parents know, and they're, like, kind of okay with it. I mean, as okay as you'd expect, under the circumstances. No idea if it's right or not, but I just couldn't…destroy a life. My whole family is broken up, but I figure the baby and I—we'll be a little family of two."

"I see. That's…good," Jenny said, though inwardly she cringed. Daisy was so young, and a baby was such a huge responsibility.

"So am I fired?" Daisy asked, tucking her hand into her pocket.

Jenny gave a laugh of disbelief. "You can't be serious. Of course you're not fired. In the first place, I love having you work here and in the second, firing someone due to pregnancy is against the law."

"All right." Daisy stood up, letting out a sigh of relief. "I'd better get back to work. It's crazy, I know. I'm scared one minute and excited the next."

"I don't blame you. I think everyone expecting a baby must feel that way. It'll be all right." She had no idea whether or not that was the truth. She wanted it to be. She knew Daisy did, too. Becoming a mother at a young age was possibly the hardest thing a woman could do. Some rose to the occasion and shone, like Nina. Others, admittedly, failed at it. Jenny's own mother was a prime example.

Daisy opened the door, paused. "How about you? Do you think you want kids one day?"

"I'd better work on having a date."

"Are you and Chief McKnight, like—"

"No," Jenny said swiftly. "Why does everyone keep asking me that?"

"Just curious." Daisy led the way downstairs. There was no one in the café. Zach was showing Rourke something on the computer.

"What are those pictures?" Jenny asked, looking over Rourke's shoulder at the computer monitor.

"Daisy took them," said Zach.

Daisy handed Jenny a coffee mug. "I loaded them onto the computer as a screen saver. I hope you don't mind."

Rourke stepped aside so Jenny could have a closer look. They were shots taken around the bakery, not just snapshots or documentary photos. These were intimate and appealing, and also unexpected—a close-up of Laura's hands shaping a mound of dough with gentle expertise. The face of a bright-eyed toddler as he regarded the trays of shaped cookies in the curved-front display case. A rack of just-baked bread, the loaves lined up with geometric precision.

"These are incredible," Jenny said. "You're really good, Daisy."

Zach gave Daisy a nudge. "Told you."

Daisy cleared her throat. "So I was wondering if you'd let me make some prints to hang in the café."

The idea appealed to Jenny. "You have to promise to sign each print and let me get them professionally framed."

"Well…sure." Daisy looked surprised, while Zach beamed with pride.

"That was nice of you," Rourke said as they left the bakery.

"It's mutually beneficial. She does beautiful work, and the café needs sprucing up." It felt right, bringing more people on board at the bakery, stepping back a little. "When I left, I wasn't totally convinced the bakery would run without me."

"And now?"

"I'm surprised. In a good way." She unlocked her car and brushed the snow off the windows. A group of people across the way caught her eye. She recognized Olivia, laughing as she came out of Zuzu's Petals and— "Oh, God," Jenny murmured.

"What is it?"

"That's Olivia's mother and her grandparents. Olivia warned me that they'd be coming up to help her plan the wedding. Is it too late to hide?"

"I'm pretty sure they've spotted you."

Indeed, Olivia had her arm raised in greeting. Just for a moment, Jenny felt a sickening wave of resentment. There was Olivia, surrounded by her mother and grandparents, beaming as though she'd won the lottery. And she had, of course. She'd been born a Bellamy, still had both parents and both sets of grandparents, and she was planning her wedding to the man of her dreams. She was younger than Jenny. Better educated. Blonder. It was hard not to draw comparisons. Harder still not to resent her sister.

Jenny hoped none of that showed on her face as she and Rourke crossed the street toward Olivia and her family. This would be as awkward for them as it was for her. With her smile frozen in place, she greeted Olivia's mother, Pamela Lightsey, and grandparents, Samuel and Gwen Lightsey. Pamela appeared to be the quintessential Manhattan socialite, a glossy beauty who was polished from head to toe. Diamond stud earrings winked from her earlobes under a luxurious-looking broadtail lamb hat. Despite the cold, every eyelash was in place and she wore a gracious hostess's smile. "How do you do?" she said, but her eyes told a different story. Her eyes said, "So you're my ex-husband's love child."

Gwen and Samuel were a prosperous-looking couple in their seventies, silver-haired, utterly poised—or so Jenny thought at first. There was something flinty in Gwen's gaze, a chilly disapproval Jenny understood completely. Thirty years ago, the Lightseys had a perfect future mapped out for their daughter. Pamela was to marry the son of their best friends, and they would all be one big happy family. Except that Philip had met Mariska Majesky. The affair had lasted only one summer, and he had married Pamela after all, but clearly it wasn't a happy union. Jenny sensed that the Lightseys blamed Mariska. If he'd never met her, perhaps he would have been content with Pamela forever.

The Lightseys greeted Rourke warmly, mentioning their acquaintance with his father, the senator. Jenny and Olivia shared a look, and Olivia mouthed, "I'm sorry."

Jenny offered a conciliatory smile. "How are the wedding plans coming along?" she asked.

"Just fine. And I wanted to ask you something," Olivia said. "I would love for you to be a bridesmaid."

Pamela stiffened as though someone had shoved an icicle down her back, and Jenny realized this was the first Olivia's mother had heard of the plan. Pamela pressed her mouth into a thin line of disapproval, and nearly shook with the effort to stay silent.

Although Jenny was tempted to accept immediately, she reminded herself that it was Olivia's day, and she deserved better than to suffer her mother's unhappiness. "Olivia, I'm flattered," she said. "But—"

"No buts. I only have one sister. I'd be honored if you'd be a part of the wedding party."

"Can I think about it?" she asked. "I'll let you know, all right?"

Samuel Lightsey was studying her. "You look so much like your mother," he said. "It's uncanny."

Gwen tucked her hand into the crook of his arm. Jenny suspected she was holding him in a vise grip. She smiled politely at Samuel. "I didn't realize you had met my mother in person."

Samuel cleared his throat. "I misspoke. Perhaps I saw her in passing, a long time ago."

Rourke refused to allow Jenny to drive to Camp Kioga unless he plowed and sanded the road, and she was glad enough for his help. He also insisted that she take Rufus, the eldest of his dogs, a malamute mix he'd found in an abandoned apartment. Rufus had thick fur and oddly pale blue eyes, and he had a watchful way about him. He rode in the backseat, imbuing the car with his doggy aroma as he looked eagerly out the window. The sharp vee of the plow blades cut a swath through the pristine snow on the road, and salted gravel rained down from the bed of the truck. Jenny followed slowly, keeping back far enough to stay out of range of the pinging gravel. The tree branches on both sides of the road were weighted by snow, creating a landscape so beautiful that she didn't mind driving along at a crawl, admiring the scenery.

"'I misspoke,'" she murmured, talking to the dog as she drove. "Well, I think the old codger's lying." She tried to figure out why. The answer was probably lost in the distant past.

She was distracted by a white rabbit that leaped out from the roadside and crossed in front of her. Rufus lunged at the window, smearing it with slobber. She slowed to let the rabbit pass and watched it scamper into the woods, until the white of its fur melded with the snow and faded from sight. Rufus settled back, whining with disappointment.

She drove more carefully the rest of the way. Rourke used the plow to clear a big rectangle of space in the parking area outside the compound. Then they went to inspect the premises, and the dog bounded joyfully through the drifts.

"This is a bad idea," he said, not for the first time.

"Enough already." She ran through knee-deep snow as light as air, kicking up a cloud of flurries. "Don't be a wet blanket," she said, taking out the key Jane had given her. "Come and check it out with me."

They stepped under the archway at the entrance, wading through the drifts of snow. The entire compound resembled a winter wonderland. The building known as the winter lodge was the oldest structure at the camp. It had been built for the camp's founders, the Gordon family, who emigrated from Scotland in the 1920s. Jenny stood looking at the solid timber building. She wondered if Rourke was thinking about the other time they'd come here together. Maybe he didn't even remember. "Home, sweet home," she said.

"Looks like something out of a Stephen King novel."

So much for him having romantic associations of the place. "Oh, hush. It's perfect. If I can't finish my book here, then I don't deserve to call myself a writer." Excitedly, she opened the door.

The place had been refurbished the previous summer and now it was spectacular, its river-rock fireplace rising two stories to the vaulted timber ceiling. Near the kitchen and dining area was a red enameled wood-burning stove. At one end under the eaves was a sleeping loft accessed by a ladder. The bedroom had the old-fashioned luxury of a bygone era, with an adjoining bath and a rustic slant-top writing desk at the window overlooking the lake.

Rourke ignited the hot-water heater and made fires in both the woodstove and fireplace. Jenny came out of the bedroom, beaming.

"I'm starting to like being a Bellamy," she said.

"I still think you're crazy."

"Are you kidding? People pay a fortune for places like this up on Lake George or Saranac Lake. I wish you could be happy for me."

"I don't like the idea of leaving you here in the middle of nowhere."

"In case you haven't noticed, this 'nowhere' is a short drive from town. It's got electricity and phone service, so it's not like I've been set adrift on an ice floe." She had an urge to touch his forehead, to smooth away the scowl from his brow, but she resisted. "I need this, Rourke. This time away with myself—it's something I probably should have done long ago. And it's perfectly safe. Remember, my grandfather used to come up here ice fishing every winter. I might even try it myself."

"I swear to God, if you go out on that ice, I'll take you back to town in handcuffs."

She laughed to cover an unexpected visceral reaction to the idea of him handcuffing her. "News flash, Rourke. I'm a grown-up and you're not in charge of me."

"Maybe not, but guess what? I'm the chief of police and this place is in my jurisdiction. So don't be surprised if I decide to patrol—"

"You wouldn't."

"Watch me."

"You're nuts."

"What's nuts is you staying here. Dammit, Jenny. Why are you being so stubborn about this?"

"It's not me being stubborn," she said. "It's a declaration of independence. I've lost everything, Rourke. And the only thing that makes it bearable is that I have a chance to start over from scratch."

"This isn't starting over. It's hiding."

"Screw you, Rourke."

"We tried that," he snapped. "It didn't work."

"That's it," she said, about to lose it. "You're out of here. You'd better leave, or I'll—"

He tugged on his gloves, one at a time. "You'll what? Call the police?"

Food for Thought

by Jenny Majesky

Comfort Food

There is almost always food involved in the happiest moments of our lives. Maybe not the big fireworks moments—a marriage proposal, the birth of a baby—but the quiet times, like when you're a kid, and you bring home a good report card. Someone almost always gives you a cookie.

And then there are the not-so-happy times. That's when comfort food means the most. As a girl, my grandmother had scarlet fever and, tucked in bed, she could smell the scent of cinnamon from her mother's baking and forever after, the scent of cinnamon was the scent of love.

Comfort food is also important when you get together with your girlfriends to sit around and talk. It's not possible to do that without food, if you ask me. My grandmother always baked with great joy, and she knew that food can be comforting because of the associations we make between the food and the people around us, or the emotions the tastes and smells evoke. Spiced with nostalgia, scented with love, a taste of true comfort food is like getting a hug from someone special.

POLISH APPLE STRUDEL

    3-4 tart apples, peeled, cored and sliced thin
    1 piecrust
    2 tablespoons butter

1 (5-ounce) jar walnuts in syrup
1/2 teaspoon cinnamon
1/2 teaspoon allspice
1/2 teaspoon ground cardamom
3 tablespoons brown sugar
3 tablespoons honey
1 tablespoon cornstarch
1/4 cup plain breadcrumbs

Preheat oven to 375°F. Sauté apples in butter over gentle heat until they soften. Add walnuts, spices, brown sugar and honey. Then add cornstarch and stir to dissolve. Cook until the mixture thickens.

Roll the dough into a rectangular shape and place on a piece of parchment on a large baking sheet. Spoon apple mixture down the middle of the rectangle, bring the edges up and pinch to close. Score the dough with a few slashes along the top. Sprinkle breadcrumbs over the top.

Bake for about 30 minutes, until golden brown. Let stand for 10 minutes or more. Serve plain or with a dollop of sweetened sour cream.

Twenty-Five

~~~~~~~~~~

1998

Dear Mom,

I'm still engaged to Joey. I know you'd probably say I'm too young, if you even cared, but we decided on a long engagement because he doesn't want to leave me alone on some army base, far from home. Marrying Joey makes sense once he gets out of the service. Gram's not doing so hot and she needs me to stay close. And all Joey wants is to settle down in Avalon and make a life here. Gram is just crazy about him. She keeps telling me what a wonderful guy he is and what a great husband he'll be. When he came back on leave last year, we picked out wedding bands at Palmquist's, and they were on layaway forever. I just brought them home and I feel a very strange giddiness—nerves, maybe? Because the wedding bands make the future seem so real.

We're not rushing into anything, though. The rings will wait. Everything will wait. Joey's been deployed, and since he's a ranger, he can't even say where and what he's doing because it's a top-secret mission. He had forty-eight hours to say goodbye to me. Rourke and I saw him off at the train. Rourke's a police of-ficer now, did I tell you that? He got his degree in law enforce-

ment and is working in Avalon. I think his family is horrified by
it all, since he's the only son of Senator Drayton McKnight and
is supposed to "do better" than being a small-town cop, but that's
another story. I'm supposed to be writing about Joey. My fiancé.
Fiancé. It looks so official in writing. At the station, Joey promised
he'd come back in one piece. It was all I could do not to cry, but
Joey was all smiles. He's so devoted to the rangers. One of his battalion buddies told him that if he's conscious when the medevac
carries him out, it means he didn't try hard enough. They laugh a
lot. Maybe that's how they deal with the danger.

He had a bit of news for me—he's asked Rourke to be his best
man, and of course Rourke said he would. And then Joey asked
Rourke to take care of me while he's gone. Those were his exact
words: "Take care of her, man. I know that's old-fashioned, but
I'm not shitting you. Look out for her."

Rourke said he would, as if he even had a choice.

Why do guys always feel like they need to look out for women?
He*llo*, it's almost the new millennium and I've been running a
business on my own since I was seventeen. I think I can look after
myself. It's sweet of Joey to worry, though. Sweet, and maybe a
little smothering.

And then he kissed me so long and hard that I started feeling
self-conscious. Don't get me wrong—I wanted that kiss. He's a
soldier, and he was going away again. I wanted to imprint him on
me, somehow, but instead, all I could think about was that we
were standing in a crowd of people, sucking face like there's no
tomorrow. I wish I could have just let the kiss sweep me away
and make me forget the whole world, but my mind kept wander-
ing to the spectators around us. Then Joey had to get on the
train— "See you around, sweetheart," he said as though he was
just going to the next town instead of halfway around the world.
And then he was gone.

As I watched the train pull out of the station, I didn't look at
Rourke. I couldn't. I was afraid of what I'd see in his eyes.

Have you ever had that feeling, Mom? That if you look at

something, then you'll be forced to acknowledge it, and everything will change?

So Joey's overseas, doing things I can barely imagine, and life goes along. I run the bakery, I take care of Gram. I don't see much of Rourke these days. He dates a lot of different girls and he works hard. He calls now and then to ask about Gram and the bakery. Honoring his promise, I suppose, to "look out for me."

And why in God's name am I questioning any of this? Joey adores me. I adore him. After we're married, he wants to live at Gram's for as long as she needs us. He has a great dad. I love Bruno like a father. Each time we meet, Bruno folds me into his thick, strong arms. He smells of hair oil and peppermint gum, and he told me Joey had a heart like a lion.

And Joey has enough certainty for both of us. He knows, beyond a shadow of a doubt, that I'm it for him, and I always have been. Joey claims that even when we were kids, he just knew.

I wish I could say the same. But guess what? I *still* don't know.

Every year, I tell myself, I finally don't need you, Mom. Finally, I've outgrown my needing you. And then I find myself wishing you were around, because I have so many questions. How do you know you're doing the right thing? Is there any way to tell, or do you just have to go for it, hope for the best, and pray it wasn't a giant mistake?

What good does it do to want something I can never, ever have? And here's the thing. Maybe I'm wrong, but I don't think so—I get the idea Rourke feels the same way. And he's just as scared as I am.

President Clinton was being interviewed on NPR about U.S. intervention in the Kosovo war, and Rourke wanted to listen, because he suspected that was where Joey might have been deployed. Instead of listening to the radio, he turned his attention to Naomi, his girlfriend. Well, she wasn't his girlfriend anymore as of ten minutes ago. Once again, things hadn't worked out.

"You're a complete bastard." Naomi yanked a T-shirt on over

her head, covering her best assets. Her head popped out, and she glared at him. "A complete and total bastard."

He wondered why he bothered. He kept going into these relationships thinking—hoping, praying—that this would be it, that she was the one he was looking for. And then, inevitably, things deteriorated. Wanting it to work out wasn't enough.

Feeling weary, he peeled back the covers and got up and found a pair of shorts. Getting dumped was undignified enough. He might as well get dressed. "I never wanted to hurt you," he said, nearly choking on the words. He'd said them too many times before, to too many women.

Clinton was explaining how the nation was now out of debt, the budget balanced, the economy stable and it was time to turn our vision outward, to peacekeeping in the larger world.

"You don't even see me," she said. "You don't even know who I am."

God. She was right. He didn't know who she was. He only knew who she *wasn't*.

"I'm sorry," he said. And that was true. He was sorry for her. Sorry for himself. And sorry he kept looking for something he'd already found but couldn't have.

She left without another word, a beautiful woman, now damaged by him. He hated himself for doing that, for inflicting wounds she didn't deserve. By the time she was on the road, headed back to the city, he'd nearly forgotten how they'd met. Was it at a summer concert at Woodstock, or at a bar down in Kingston? Maybe she was one of the women his mother had set him up with. Although his father had never forgiven him for becoming a cop and moving to a tiny river town, his mother kept trying to bring him back into the fold, introducing him to polished, educated young women as though they were offerings.

He ought to swear off women altogether. But that was impossible. Women were…like air. Necessary to survive.

He could do better. He would do better. It was just a matter of focus and discipline. These were things he considered himself good at. They were traits that had been drilled into him, and he practiced them every day on the job. It ought to be a simple matter to extend that to his personal life. Why did he even need a personal life, anyway? He should stick with what he was good at—police work. Crime investigation and crisis intervention, public safety, tactical awareness, bringing offenders to justice were all he'd ever wanted to do. That's the ticket, he thought. Focus on the job.

Each day as he dressed for the morning briefing, he felt a sense of irony as he put on his protective vest, his carbon-fiber holster and ASP. His own father had sponsored the state regulation requiring body armor for peace officers. Now that Rourke was a grown man, Drayton McKnight was suddenly interested in protecting his son.

Rourke held steady to his vow, focusing on what he was good at. He worked overtime for the good citizens of Avalon—and for the bad ones, too. Sometimes his calls were absurd—a citizen complained that his neighbor's black Lab kept fouling his yard. The next day, the dog's owner reported that someone had spray painted a Day-Glo orange obscenity on the side of his dog. Other times, they were heartbreaking—a high-school girl overdosed after being sexually assaulted. An elderly citizen had been scammed out of her life savings. He treated each call as a serious matter, from a complaint about a loud party to a domestic disturbance. His job was not exactly an adventure, but this was the right place for him. Sometimes he thought he was crazy to make his life here, a spectator to Jenny and Joey's love affair, but he felt a deep sense of connection to Avalon. This was where, as a boy, he'd discovered what freedom was.

He used his personal time to study—negotiation, administration, community relations. He adopted dogs that had been impounded or abandoned and devoted his free time to training them. Every night at the end of his shift, he checked his e-mail. Joey was an excellent correspondent, and with e-mail, communication was instantaneous. Rourke sometimes learned breaking news before it broke. Despite the screening process, Joey offered a vivid picture of his life in an undisclosed location, which seemed to consist of physical discomfort and boredom interspersed with the pure adrenalin rush of life-or-death action. Joey ended nearly each note with a reference to Jenny: "Keep an eye on my girl." "Eat a kolache for me." "Tell her I'll be home before she knows it."

Lately, his battalion seemed to be on the move, and Joey's correspondence was more sporadic. He was going on night ops now, often transported with his battalion in a specially configured Chinook helo. He had a stomach bug but concealed it because he didn't want to miss out on the action, which sounded typical of Joey.

Rourke was in the backyard one night, letting the dogs out for one last run, when he heard the phone ring. Although it was well past ten, he stayed up late with them to make up for his long hours on the job. He gave the soggy tennis ball one final lob and sprinted to the kitchen, wiping his hand on his jeans and then searching for the handset. Too late. By the time he found it wedged between the sofa cushions, the voice mail had kicked on. Muttering with impatience, he listened to the message.

"It's me," she said, and didn't have to explain who "me" was. Ordinarily, she would offer a cheerful greeting, but tonight there was something in her voice. Something that froze Rourke in his tracks. "Please," she continued. "I need you to come over. Please."

He forgot he was a public safety officer as he drove to her place, running stop signs and speeding as though pursued by demons. He surged into the driveway, got out of the car and took the porch steps three at a time.

Jenny was waiting for him at the door. He knew before she even said a word. One look at her face, and he knew. *Joey.*

She was drinking champagne—the bottle of Cristal she'd been saving for Joey's homecoming, and it was nearly gone. She shook her head, mute, and then seemed to melt against him, pressing her cheek to his chest. He set aside her glass and held her. She didn't cry, didn't make a sound, but she was shaking from head to toe.

"Tell me," he whispered, stirring the cinnamon-scented hair by her ear. "You can tell me."

"Not yet," she said. "Just…let's stay like this for a minute."

Any inkling of hope he had of being wrong died in that moment. Under ordinary circumstances, he and Jenny tried to avoid physical contact. It was an unspoken agreement between them, enacted the moment she got engaged to Joey. She and Rourke were too volatile together and always had been. When he was around her, the surface of his skin seemed to heat and the world shrank to the number of square inches beneath her feet. And yet she was forbidden territory.

Tonight's circumstances were far from ordinary, though, and this embrace, open and raw, was the only place on earth he wanted to be right now. They breathed as one. Touched with pain-filled tenderness, they tried to escape into each other so they didn't have to move on to the next moment, to the moment when they would have to face what had happened.

Eventually, she pulled back. "There's more champagne," she said, gesturing toward the kitchen.

Rourke felt as if he was on fire as he went to the pantry, found another bottle and popped the cork. It seemed like a lousy thing to do, inappropriately celebratory, but he did it anyway. He knew this particular bottle came from the case his parents had sent to Joey to congratulate him on his engagement. A Krug Blanc de Blanc, one of only a few thousand bottles produced. Rourke drank the champagne at room temperature straight out of the bottle. Lowering it, he looked across the room at Jenny. Snow White, he thought. She was so pale, her hair and eyes so dark. And haunted now, with a sadness so deep he could feel it in his chest.

"Your grandmother…?" Rourke asked.

"She's already asleep. She was sound asleep when Bruno called. She doesn't know anything about this yet, and I might as well let her have one more night before telling her." Jenny glanced at the hallway leading to her grandmother's room. "Let's go upstairs to talk. I don't want to wake Gram."

Rourke felt as though he was made of wood as he followed her. When Jenny's grandmother got sick, she couldn't negotiate stairs anymore, so Jenny had turned a downstairs room into a bedroom for Helen. She'd transformed the upstairs into a private haven where she could spend her time writing and waiting for Joey. After they were married, they planned to live here. After they were married… With a shaking hand, Rourke took a long drink of champagne.

When Jenny finally started to talk, her voice sounded soft and slurred with disbelief. She recited the news as though she'd been saying it over and over in her head, memorizing the horror— *There was a mishap with a transport helicopter, no survivors from Joey's Ranger battalion.*

Rourke felt no shock, just a bleak and terrible sense of destiny. As she told him the few details she knew, they finished the bottle of Krug and opened another. "He and sixteen others were in a Chinook helicopter somewhere in Kosovo. It went down in a ravine, and there were no survivors. The names won't be released officially for several days but Bruno heard right away. He got a call by satellite phone from someone in the battalion," she said in a broken voice. "It's not official, there hasn't been a formal casualty report yet. But…no survivors."

Icy pain howled through Rourke. Joey. His best friend. His blood brother. The best guy in the world. For a few moments, Rourke couldn't breathe.

Jenny looked up at him, her face reflecting his agony.

Rourke hated it that she had been alone when the call came in. "Joey's dad—"

"He's with his sisters in New York. I guess I'll—we'll—see him at the…oh, my God. Will there be a funeral? A memorial?"

"I don't know. Who knows about these things?" He kept seeing images of Joey, a goofy, big-eared kid who had grown into the kind of man everybody liked. They had shared all the important moments of their lives, from lost teeth to lost kittens, sports victories and defeats, graduation and of course, summer camp. Rourke felt as if a limb had just been lopped off.

And yet, pushing through the empty whistle of grief inside him was something else. Something…guilt and sadness, tenderness and rage.

He studied Jenny's face for a long time. Found a Kleenex and dried her face. Then he leaned closer and held her in a way he never had before, not even when he wanted to, not even when she'd practically begged him to. His arms encircled her as though sheltering her from a bomb attack. He held her so that he felt the entire length of her body against his, could even feel her heartbeat, and still it wasn't close enough. He touched her in a way he'd thought about a thousand times, tracing his thumb along the line of her jaw, tilting her face up to his, and he wanted to kiss her, to drown in her and forget.

Somehow, the way they both loved Joey became tangled up with the way they felt about each other, and they were kissing, and it was crazy but they were kissing and moving toward the bedroom, desperate to escape the truth but trapped there, together, with the darkness closing around them. Their clothes made a trail down the hall to her room and by the time they reached the bed, there was nothing between them, nothing at all. She tasted of champagne and tears, and she wound her arms around his neck and kept kissing him and wouldn't let go. It was crazy, she was crazy, they were both crazy, but she wouldn't let go.

She kept hold of him, but pulled back so her mouth was just a whisper away. "He told you to take care of me," she said. "How are you going to do that, Rourke?"

The phone rang, piercing knife-sharp through Jenny's alcohol-fogged sleep. She stirred, moaning as she tried to hide from the noise, but it kept flaying at her. Her head felt like a rock, impossible to lift. Finally, mercifully, the shrill ringing stopped and across the room, the answering machine clicked on and she could hear the sound of her own voice picking up. She stretched and encountered a warm, naked body under the covers. Strong arms slid around her and tucked her close, and a sleepy sigh gusted against her neck. God, oh, God. Rourke. She had slept with Rourke. Joey was dead and she'd had drunken, mind-blowing sex with Rourke.

She was going to burn in hell.

The caller started speaking into the machine, and it sounded uncannily like Joey. Which meant she was probably still drunk, or dreaming, because Joey was dead, lost in a helicopter crash. Like a sleepwalker, she went stark naked to the dresser where the small black box of the answering machine was still recording a shockingly familiar voice. "…all a mistake," he was saying. "My name was on the manifest, but I wasn't on that chopper…"

Jenny laughed aloud, the tears streaming down her face as she snatched up the phone and said, "Joey."

There was a long-distance delay, and then he said, "Babe, I'm so glad you picked up. I know it's five in the morning there, but I had to let you know I'm okay. I just got off the phone with my dad. There was a big mix-up at the last minute. I wasn't on that transport…"

She couldn't speak. She could barely breathe, and she was shaking with relief as Joey explained something about a manifest made out by a staff sergeant and handed off to someone else to be recorded. While boarding the chopper, Joey was injured and sent to the infirmary. "Like an idiot, I didn't have my goggles on and something flew into my eye. They're sending me to Germany for surgery."

"Jen?" Rourke called from the bed. "Who's on the phone?"

She whirled around to shush him, but it was too late. "What's Rourke doing there at this hour?" Joey asked, his voice changing, sharpening.

And Jenny knew, in that instant, that Joey had probably been aware for a long time of this thing between her and Rourke. "I asked him to come over the second I heard," she said. "He's your best friend. Who else would I call, Joey?"

He didn't answer. Instead, he said, "I'm being discharged. The Rangers don't have much use for a one-eyed soldier. I'm coming home."

She was standing there, still naked and warm from Rourke's touch, holding the phone when he crossed the bedroom toward her, his hair tousled, his eyes confused. And even now, when she looked at him, Jenny felt a surge of pure helpless lust, mingling with the shame.

And she realized then that she wasn't going to burn in hell after all. She was already there.

Food for Thought

by Jenny Majesky

On Fire

People like to set things on fire. Admit it, when you see a flaming dessert, you're impressed. There's something mesmerizing about the way the flames run like a river and then go out, leaving behind a delicious, unmistakable essence.

There's a primal attraction to burning things. According to a Polish proverb, fire is never a gentle master. Henry James claims that what is needed is "unrestrained passion, fire for fire." Which is a little scary, if you ask me, but that just makes this all the more delicious.

BURNING LOVE

8 slices bread
3 cups heavy cream
1 whole egg
3 egg yolks
1-1/2 cups sugar
1/2 teaspoon nutmeg
1/2 teaspoon cinnamon
1/4 cup rum
1/2 cup raisins or currants, steeped for 15 minutes in
a cup of very hot water (reserve liquid)

Preheat the oven to 350°F. Dice bread into cubes. Whisk together cream, whole egg, egg yolks, 1/2 cup sugar, nutmeg, cinnamon, and 1 tablespoon of rum. Combine bread cubes and cream mixture.

Drain raisins and reserve the liquid. Add raisins to bread mixture. Spoon mixture into soufflé cups. Place cups in a baking pan filled with hot water 1/2 inch deep. Bake until a knife inserted in center of custards comes out clean, about 30 minutes.

Just before serving, combine reserved liquid and remaining sugar in a small saucepan and bring to a simmer, whisking constantly, over high heat. When sugar turns amber, carefully whisk another 1/2 cup of hot water. Return to a simmer and cook until mixture becomes the consistency of syrup. Stir in remaining rum and return to heat for 15 seconds. Remove saucepan from heat and touch a match to sauce. Pour flaming caramel over puddings and serve.

Twenty-Six

Daisy was surprised and even somewhat pleased by the way her family reacted to her news. Almost everyone took it in stride. There was no shock and horror. More like sympathy and understanding. Oh, her brother Max thought the whole thing was gross and told her she was an idiot, but at his age—eleven—he pretty much thought all girls were idiots. And he did admit the prospect of becoming an uncle was cool.

On the day she had chosen to tell her friends, she awoke to the blinding white beauty of a snow day. Even before she checked the school district's Web site for closure information, she knew. Snow day. What greater gift could there be? There was something so magical about a snow day—unplanned, an entire day when everything would simply stop, suspended until the roads were cleared. No school. No work. All obligations and appointments canceled, all deadlines extended. Nothing to do except laze around. Instead of squirming through civics, she could sleep in and eat breakfast while watching *Dialing for Dollars*. Instead of scrambling for an excuse about her undone physics assignment, she could finish it up at her leisure.

She was just about to burrow back under the covers when her cell phone rang. She glanced at the screen and then flipped it open. "What are you doing up? It's a snow day."

"Exactly," Sonnet said, her voice musical with excitement. "Dress warmly, but wear layers. We might be working up a sweat where we're going."

Daisy couldn't help smiling. Sonnet always had some kind of adventure up her sleeve. "What's up?" she asked.

"Bring your camera," Sonnet said. "Meet us at the bakery in half an hour. We're going snowshoeing. Zach's bringing all the gear."

It must be a sign, Daisy thought, closing her phone and pulling on insulated underwear. A snow day, and an invitation out of the blue. Maybe today was the day she was supposed to tell them. As she brushed her teeth, she turned sideways and studied her silhouette in the mirror. Her body had been taken over by an alien life force. She vacillated between bouts of nausea and insatiable cravings. Her boobs were tender and getting too big for her bra. Yet her stomach still looked flat and her jeans still fit. She tried to picture herself with a giant belly, but couldn't imagine it, even now. Still, it was time to tell Sonnet and Zach. Today.

They took Zach's Jeep up the road to Meerskill Falls. It was plowed now, because Jenny was living up at the lodge. They wouldn't disturb her though, as the hiking trail led to the head of the falls. The cascade tumbled hundreds of feet down the cave-studded granite cliffs and emptied into a deep pool, quite far from the winter lodge.

Daisy got out of the car and turned her face to the sky. Then she checked to make sure her camera had plenty of power and a big memory disk. There was something about the quality of light in winter that she found both pleasing and challenging to photograph. She loved the contrasting depths, the stark images against the endless white snow, and she'd learned to adjust her light meter and filters to create beautiful pictures even when the light was dull and flat. That wasn't the case today. The sun had emerged, carving dramatic shadows and textures in the landscape. She took a picture of a birch grove, the slender branches like long strokes of ink against the field of snow. The way the morning light fell over them made the trees glow.

The trail was covered by a season's worth of untouched snow, and it wasn't long before they had to put their snowshoes on. Zach had three pairs of high-tech shoes that weighed next to nothing and practically floated them over the snow. It was a funny thing about Zach. His dad, who was way older than most dads, seemed to spend money like there was no tomorrow—although God forbid he should ever leave anything in the tip jar at the bakery. Yet, Mr. Alger had a habit of buying the best, most expensive of everything including cars and clothes and even snowshoes. He was kind of schizoid because then he would lecture Zach about not pulling enough hours at the bakery. Crazy. People ragged on teenagers for acting crazy, but maybe that was only half the story. Maybe they ought to look at the parents for a change.

She tried to picture her kid as a teenager, but the image wouldn't form. She simply could not fathom the idea that her body could create a life-sized human, let alone one that sassed its mom and got in trouble at school. Still, she vowed she would be a different kind of mom. She'd be best friends with her kid. They'd listen to the same kind of music and she wouldn't yell about grades and getting into the right school. All that belonged to some far-off someday, though. At the moment, she needed to worry about breaking the news to her friends.

One thing about snowshoeing, she discovered. It was hard work. Halfway up the trail, she stripped off her parka and tied it around her waist. Then off came her muffler and hat, which she stowed in her backpack. She might have attributed this to a hormone surge, which her pregnancy books talked about, but then she noticed that Zach and Sonnet were trudging along, too, bathed in sweat.

When they reached a footbridge spanning the waterfall at midpoint, she called for a water break. "I have to get some pictures, too," she added. Last summer, the waterfall had been a raging torrent bursting from its hidden source high above and then hurling itself onto the tumbled rocks far below. Winter had frozen the cascade into blue-green ice that striped the hillside like tall, delicate pillars. Icicles bearded the fringes of the cataract. In the middle, a tall column of ice plunged like a dagger into the frozen pool at the base.

Daisy found amazing angles to photograph. She lay flat on her back to frame the bridge, an old concrete structure with two tall arches spanning the deep chasm below.

"There are rumors that it's called Suicide Bridge," Sonnet said. "I've heard two tragic lovers jumped off it and killed themselves."

"Yeah, and you can hear their ghosts wailing on windy nights," Zach added.

Sonnet sniffed defensively. "This is Washington Irving territory. Ghost stories come with the landscape."

Daisy took a picture of her friend, whose expression was both annoyed and cute.

As though she felt the attention, Sonnet turned to her. "Hey, what would you say to taking my senior photo? You know, for the yearbook?"

Daisy was surprised and flattered. "Sure, why not?"

"I'd pay you, of course," Sonnet offered.

Sonnet and her mom had to pinch every penny, saving for college. "I wouldn't charge you anything," she said, experimentally framing Sonnet in her viewfinder.

"I would insist on it." Sonnet's sense of fairness rose up. "Dale Shirley charges, like, three hundred dollars. I'd have to save up for weeks to afford him."

Shirley was a busy local photographer whose work adorned the Chamber of Commerce brochures, the annual Christmas calendar they gave away at City Hall and of course, the Avalon High School yearbook. Daisy thought it sounded like a dream job, getting paid to take pictures. "He can charge because he's got all these credentials and his own studio and stuff," she said.

"Nah," Zach said, "it's because he's been around forever. I don't want to use him, either, but my dad will probably make me."

Zach's dad was all concerned with looking good for his run for mayor.

"Not if I take a better shot," Daisy said, and snapped a candid picture of Zach as he contemplated his father. Zach was totally made for the snow, the way a wolf was. His blond hair, smooth clear skin and strangely light blue eyes made him look wild and unearthly.

Sonnet peered over her shoulder, reviewing the shot. "Crazy," she said. "You're like the Aryan nation poster boy."

He tossed a handful of snow at her. It burst into a cloud as it hit her shoulder. "Shut up," he said.

"You shut up."

Daisy turned the camera on them both. Sonnet was a willing subject, mimicking a model's poses. She braced her hands behind her and tilted back her head. Her riotously curly hair escaped the knitted hat, and Daisy had captured the moment, knowing instantly that it was a good shot. Sonnet was not high-school pretty, and she hated her looks, but that was nuts, Daisy knew. Sonnet was gorgeous in ways beyond the grasp of high school boys. She had creamy café au lait skin and long tumbles of tight, inky curls. Her wide mouth and tilted, almond shaped eyes gave her an air of mystery—until she smiled, and then she was as open and friendly as a puppy.

Sonnet let Daisy take as many shots as she wanted. Patient and helpful, she was a good sport about it. Another thing about her— sportsmanship. She had a great attitude about everything. And the funny thing was, of all the kids Daisy knew, Sonnet Romano had the most strikes against her, the most reasons to cop an attitude or fail in school or be a slacker. She was born to an unwed teenage mother, she was biracial, she and her mom barely made ends meet.

Yet despite having the deck stacked against her, Sonnet was a straight-A student who was a year ahead in school. She was a national merit scholar, a talented musician and a kindergarten tutor. She had been accepted by early decision to college, and was awaiting news of a financial package. She was, as far as Daisy could tell, everyone's dream kid, the sort of trophy child parents could brag about, patting themselves on the back as they took credit for how good she was.

Sonnet was the kind of daughter Daisy's mom wished she had. Instead, Daisy's mom got a daughter who didn't give a shit about school or college, who partied herself into oblivion and got pregnant by a boy she didn't even like.

"Enough already," Zach said as Daisy took another series of shots. "You're going to break the camera."

Daisy took a picture of his taunting face.

"See those ledges up there?" Sonnet pointed to the overhanging cliffs. "My uncles told me they're ice caves." Sonnet had, like, six uncles, who resembled the cast of the Sopranos. "Caves in the hillside that are lined with ice. I read about them in the library archives for a history project last year. Some of the cliffs in the area have these caves with ice so thick it never melts, even in summer. It's one reason they named the town Avalon."

Daisy tilted her head to one side. "Okay, you lost me."

"From the legend of King Arthur," Zach said. "Merlin's Crystal Cave. Avalon was the place the High King went after he was mortally wounded in his last battle."

"I must have missed the memo," Daisy said. "I don't know why you guys put up with me. I'm a dunce." Which was ironic, she thought. She had attended the most competitive, most exclusive school in Manhattan. These two kids went to a run-of-the-mill public school. Yet they both seemed so much smarter than her.

"You're not a dunce," Sonnet said.

"You have no idea," Daisy said, bracing herself. It was time. She had to get it over with. Right here, right now. "I need to tell you guys something," she said in a rush, letting the words escape before she could chicken out.

They must have sensed the urgency in her tone, because they both gave her their full attention. She hesitated, the way she'd done when she'd told her dad, trying to memorize the way they were looking at her now. She was about to change their perception for good.

"It's, um, it's kind of a big deal." She carefully lowered her camera, felt the weight of it tugging at the back of her neck. "I'm going to have a baby. It's due in the summer."

The words fell into a silence so complete, it was like a vacuum had sucked them out of the air. Daisy looked at them, her only friends in this town, and held her breath. She refused to breathe until they spoke, reassuring her that they wouldn't stop being her friend. For a moment, they just stared at her. Then a red flush crept into Zach's face and he looked supremely uncomfortable, the way Max had when she'd told him. Sonnet's eyebrows went up, and then down. "Hey, that is a big deal."

Daisy nodded. "It's not the smartest thing I've ever done, but it's done. I was going to, you know, terminate it, but at the last minute I couldn't. So here I am."

Zach seemed to find something endlessly fascinating in the hollow of a tree by the bridge. He clearly didn't want to participate in this conversation.

Finally Sonnet spoke up, sounding a little flustered. "Wow. I mean, wow. That's unexpected."

"No shit," Daisy said.

"Is this why you left your old school?" Sonnet asked.

Daisy shook her head. "I didn't know. I mean, I wasn't sure."

"Is the baby's father going to help you out?" A peculiar tension threaded itself through Sonnet's voice. Daisy knew that Sonnet's relationship with her father was a difficult one, fraught with secrecy due to his position in the Pentagon.

"I haven't told him. I haven't even decided whether or not I will. He won't be happy, I can tell you that."

"He should have thought of that when he—when the two of you—"

"True," Daisy agreed. "We both should have thought of that."

Sonnet put a mittened hand on Daisy's shoulder. "You'll be all right," she said.

Daisy smiled at her. "That's the plan. So anyway," she said brightly, "I got through the ordeal of telling my parents, and…we'll deal." She had to believe that, had to believe having a baby was not like falling into an abyss.

The three of them were silent for a while, and Daisy felt a measure of relief. That wasn't so hard. She figured there would be a period of adjustment, and then they'd go back to the way things were. For a while, at least. After the baby came, she had no idea what would become of their friendship. Zach hadn't said a word, but she could tell he was embarrassed. His cheeks and ears were red—and not just from the cold—and he averted his eyes. Sonnet seemed to sense the need to move on. She shaded her eyes and studied the cliffs. "My uncles say you really have to look in order to find the caves. And you have to watch for avalanches."

"My dad told me it's a complete waste of time," Zach added. "He said it's not even worth the trip."

"Since when do you listen to your dad?" Sonnet asked.

Daisy regarded the hanging cliffs, their silhouettes carving mysterious shapes on the untouched snow. "Let's go check it out," she suggested.

"Are you serious?" Zach looked apprehensive.

"She's right." Sonnet got up and tapped her snowshoes together. "Look at that blue sky. We should at least go to the top of the mountain, right?"

"Agreed." Zach stood. "No point in getting this close and then not going all the way." He shrugged into his day pack and led the way up the trail.

"We're like the first pioneers," Daisy said. "The first to find the mountaintop."

"I doubt that," Zach said.

"Me, too," Sonnet agreed. "My uncle Sal told me they found Indian artifacts in some of the caves, and stuff from pioneers, too. Before refrigeration, the caves were used for food storage."

"Nature's deep freeze," Zach said. "Seems like a long hike to get there."

The path became steeper, the snow forming deep-rimmed bowls around the bases of the trees. Daisy felt a little breathless and wondered if that was just her, or the pregnancy. Her doctor had said she could and should keep up with her usual activities, although she shouldn't do any extreme sports. Was this extreme, hiking up a mountain? No. Rockclimbing, like she'd done last summer with Julian Gastineaux, a.k.a. the most amazing boy on the planet, was extreme because it involved scary harnesses and sheer rock faces and risky Spiderman maneuvers. Compared to that, hiking was almost, literally, a walk in the park.

Sonnet reached the summit first, turned and waved at them. "Okay, so we're not first." She indicated a decidedly man-made structure—a fake totem pole with a plaque that said, "Meerskill Mountain. Elevation 4016 feet."

Sets of initials and words, dating back to 1976, had been gouged into the totem pole. A whole history of area kids, rendered meaningless by the passage of time.

"Look," Sonnet pointed out. "'Matt was here.' Maybe that's your dad—Matthew Alger."

Zach shrugged. "Could've been. He used to work at the camp when he was in college."

"My dad, too," Daisy said. "It was a family tradition for all the Bellamys, until the camp closed ten years ago." Daisy was glad Olivia had moved up from the city last summer. Daisy had spent last summer at the camp with her dad and brother, helping to get the place ready for her grandparents' fiftieth anniversary celebration. Her mom hadn't come; she'd only dropped by the camp to deliver divorce papers and to pay her respects at the Bellamys' anniversary. Daisy wondered if the four of them had stuck together in the wilderness, would they have figured out a way to stay together for good?

One good thing had happened last summer—they'd met Jenny. Uncle Phil's illegitimate daughter.

Illegitimate. Daisy stuffed her hands in her pockets and angled them across her lower belly like a shield. She hated that word, illegitimate. Like the baby had done something wrong.

Sonnet snowshoed to the edge of the hill where the snow was

thick and deep. "This is where the avalanche came down. Let's find those caves before it gets dark."

They each had a set of ski poles, which they used to sink into the snow to make sure there was solid ground before they stepped. Zach found a granite wall rising up, its face striated and gouged by indentations.

"I'm going to check them out," Sonnet said, reaching down to unfasten her snowshoes.

"No way," Zach said. "You're not climbing this rock."

"Watch me."

She was good, Daisy recognized, watching Sonnet. Having done a little rock-climbing in the past, she recognized a good technique when she saw it. However, Sonnet had zero safety gear.

"Hey, don't climb any higher than you're willing to fall," she cautioned.

"Just fall on your ass," Zach said. "That way, you've got a big cushion."

"Ha ha," Sonnet said, breath puffing from her in a cloud.

"A gi-normous cushion."

Daisy elbowed him. Then she took some pictures of Sonnet's progress.

Sonnet came to a shadowy spot in the rock face. "Well," she said, "it's a cave, but there's no ice in it." To illustrate, she dropped a handful of stone and dust which littered the snow like a stain. She found a couple more from her perch on a rock ledge, but they were just hollows and indentations in the rock. Each one was empty, except there was a bird's nest in one of them.

"You might find some bats," Zach called to her.

"Some what?"

"Bats."

"Sure," she said. "Good one, moron."

"Swear to God, this is a bat habitat," Zach insisted. "They hibernate in the caves. If you disturb one, it could bite you and then you'd get rabies."

"I'm so scared." Sonnet was on a deep ledge about fifteen feet above them, exploring the series of indentations in the rock. "Hello," she said. "What's this?"

Daisy aimed the camera. Maybe Sonnet had found something.

"This might be an ice cave," Sonnet said, standing on tip toe. "I can't quite see." She jumped up a little.

"Hey, take it easy," Zach said, looking genuinely worried.

"Why, Zachary." Sonnet put on a phony Scarlett O'Hara accent. "I didn't know you cared."

"I just don't want to have to carry your fat ass down the mountain."

"Ha," she said, reaching into the cave again. "I'll have you to know I—"

Her words dissolved into a yell. By sheer reflex, Daisy pressed the shutter of her camera. At the same instant, something—a bat? A bird? An angry demon from another realm?—burst from the cave on a whir of wings and rose to the sky.

Sonnet fell, seeming to float backward, almost suspended in a mist of flying snow. A half a second later, she landed, hitting the soft drifts and sinking out of sight. Her scream disappeared along with the rest of her.

"Sonnet!" Zach yelled her name with hoarse desperation. His speed, given the fact that he was wearing snowshoes, was amazing. He all but flew to the spot where she had landed, calling for her.

Daisy came nearly as quickly, her camera bouncing forgotten against her chest.

Zach was on his knees, reaching down into the snowy well into which Sonnet had fallen. "Say something," he yelled. "Please, Sonnet, I'm begging—"

"I love hearing a moron beg," came an annoyed, slightly muffled voice.

Daisy felt sick with relief as she took off her snowshoes and joined Zach in digging Sonnet out. They were idiots, all of them. They had no business up here in the middle of nowhere, in the middle of winter, messing around where no one could find them if they got in trouble. When it came to doing stupid things, Daisy was the champ, but even she could tell this was a bad idea.

"Thank God for all this snow," Sonnet was saying as Zach grabbed both her hands and tugged her forward. Her eyes were bright, her cheeks glowing. "It was my soft place to fall." She swam through the soft, powdery snow. "Thanks, you guys," she said.

"Let's go back," Zach said. "I'm freezing. Here, I'll help you with your snowshoes."

"Hold on," Sonnet said. "Hand me one of those ski poles."

"What is it?" Zach asked, passing her one.

"I think I found something."

"Probably the mother of that hibernating thing you woke up," Zach said.

"No, look." She pushed at the snow, and instead of running into the side of the rock face, the end of the pole kept going.

"Another cave," Sonnet said.

"Big deal," Zach said. "It's probably—"

"Check it out." The snow collapsed and Daisy found herself looking at an opening in the rock face, this one big enough for all of them to fit inside if they went on their knees.

"Now this is a cave." Zach switched on his flashlight and shone it around. Once they knelt to squeeze in, there was enough headroom to stand.

All right, so it wasn't as impressive as the one Sonnet had described. There was no glittering blue crystal lining the walls, like Merlin's cave. It was hard to distinguish the ice from the rock because it was coated with a fine layer of dust. Beneath their knees, the floor was uneven and covered with grainy dirt like the kind left behind in the snow banks after a long winter. She took a few pictures. As the flash swept through the space, it illuminated places that looked as though they had lain undisturbed in darkness forever. "Maybe we're the first people ever to come here," she suggested.

"Yeah, except for whoever left that gum wrapper behind." Zach shone the flashlight beam on it. "Juicy Fruit," he said.

"You guys." Daisy was reviewing her pictures on the camera. "Check this out." She turned the small screen toward them.

"Not your best work," Sonnet said.

"No, look at the back of the cave." It showed up clearly in the photo. What appeared to be a random pile of rubble was actually a stack of rocks in different shapes and sizes.

Sonnet grabbed the flashlight. "So how crazy is that?"

"Look at the rocks," Daisy said. When someone built a wall, she knew, it was for a purpose, either keeping something in or keeping something out.

She held the light while Zach and Sonnet pulled some of the rocks away. "It was probably some bored kids from Camp Kioga," Sonnet said.

"How bored would I need to be to put a stack of rocks inside an ice cave?"

Daisy grabbed the light and peered over the top of the rock pile. An eddy of cold air—colder even than the air of the outer cave—wafted over her face. It reminded her of the walk-in freezer at the bakery—a freezing blast with a faint aroma of something that didn't belong. A mustiness.

"Give me a boost," she said to Zach. "I think I see something."

He laced his gloved hands together. She stepped in and immediately conked her head on the ceiling of the cave.

"Hey," she yelled, blinking away stars of pain. She aimed the flashlight beam and gasped. Here, the walls of the cave were definitely rimed with ice, the crystals winking in the beam of light. And there was something on the floor of the cave, another pile of rocks, or maybe— It wasn't, thought Daisy. It couldn't be. But...

"You all right?" Zach asked. "You're shaking."

She looked down at him. "You have to see this."

"What is it?"

She didn't want to say. She wanted so badly to be wrong. Moving carefully, she stepped down and motioned for Zach to check it out.

"Hey, are you all right?" Sonnet asked her. "You're white as a sheet. You look as if you've seen a ghost."

"I think I just did," Zach said.

Daisy could tell from his voice that she hadn't been mistaken. "Help me up again, will you?" she asked. "I need to take some pictures."

Twenty-Seven

Rourke got up early and went for a run on the trail by the river, with the dogs loping along with him. There was a gym shared by the fire station and PD, but he preferred getting out in the air and pushing himself until his lungs screamed from the cold. Then he showered and dressed for the day, straightened his house and fed the animals.

Having had Jenny there, even for a brief time, drove home a truth he'd been avoiding for many years. He lived a lonely, emotionally sterile life and he longed for something more. There. It was out, something he didn't want to admit but couldn't escape. Before this latest thing with Jenny, he'd convinced himself to be content with his pets and his one-night stands; now he couldn't pretend any longer. There were things he wanted that he probably didn't deserve, and he wasn't sure what to do about it.

He'd spent a long time—his whole career, really—studying the baser aspects of humanity. Police work opened people's lives to him, but by its very nature the job offered glimpses of people at their worst. Here in this small town, the chief of police didn't sit in a glass-enclosed office issuing orders. More often than not, he found himself out in the field, where inevitably he came up against the seamy side of life. Avalon had corruption and violence, not like a big city, but the elements were there. Even though this was a small town, it was still a place where men got drunk and beat their wives and hit their kids, where punks cooked up crystal meth in their grandmothers' basements, where schoolgirls shoplifted and football players dared each other to dangle from the train-trestle bridge and spray paint Knights Rule in bright orange on the water tower. There was plenty of drama to keep Rourke busy—but all that drama, all the things he saw on the job, tended to make him jaded. It made him wonder why people bothered to give their hearts to one another, because most of the time, they ended up breaking them.

Now that Jenny was back, though, he understood.

Just as she'd promised, she phoned him every day to check in. And just as he'd anticipated, it wasn't enough. He didn't know if she was calling him out of a sense of duty, or if it was simply to keep him from carrying out his threat to show up every day to make sure she was all right.

He paged through several pink slips with messages on his desk. Things were slow because it was a snow day. Department offices were manned by a reduced staff. One of his father's assistants had called to invite him to the senator's annual Presidents' Day luncheon—euphemism for $500-a-plate fund-raiser. This was followed by a message from his mother, dutifully reiterating the invitation. Rourke saw his parents only on rare occasions; the wounds of childhood had never completely healed. He crumpled both messages and slam-dunked them into the circular file. There were also messages from two women—Mindy and Sierra—both of whom he'd dated a while back.

No—not dated. Each woman he'd encountered in a bar, hooked up with them over the course of a weekend and then put them on a train back to the city. Technically, that was probably a date. He didn't recall giving either woman his phone number, but the persistent ones always managed to track him down. He added the pink slips to the circular file. He didn't do second dates.

And—this was where he got really pathetic—ever since Jenny had broken open his heart, he didn't even do first dates. He was as celibate as a monk these days, a painful state of being. But not as painful as meaningless sex. He used to imagine that it satisfied him, but these days, he couldn't even pretend anymore.

Just ask her out, he told himself.

He'd already tried that, and she'd said no.

Ask her again.

That was damn humiliating. Did he care about that? Was he willing to face rejection again?

Before he answered his own question, he picked up the phone. She answered by the third ring. "Hello," she said in a warble of good cheer.

"It's me," he said, turning his back so the people in the outer office couldn't see his face through the glass. He liked to think he had a poker face, but when it came to Jenny, he wasn't so sure. Then he held his breath, wondering if it was presumptuous to assume she knew who "me" was.

"Oh…hi, Rourke."

Okay, so it wasn't presumptuous. Yet her voice changed from its eager chirp to a note of caution. "Sorry to rain on your parade," he said.

She laughed. "I'm expecting a call from Mr. Greer. My agent. God, can you believe I have a literary agent? Or will, if I can get this book together."

"Sure, I can believe it."

"Really? You're not just saying that?"

"I don't know what the big deal is. You're going to write a great book and it'll be a bestseller. You told me so when you were, what, eleven years old?"

"And you still believe that?" Her voice softened. "Oh, Rourke."

Her *oh, Rourke* made him physically unfit for mixed company. He sat down behind his desk and swiveled his chair toward the wall. "Listen, I was just wondering…" Damn, why was this so hard? *Would you like to have dinner at the Apple Tree Inn?* One stupid little question.

"Wondering what?" she prompted.

"If, uh, everything's okay up there."

"Sure," she said. "Everything's perfect. I can't imagine a better day to work on my project."

His heart managed to skip a beat and sink at the same time. She seemed genuinely happy to be away from him. It must've been torture for her staying at his place. "It's a snow day," he told her. "I wanted to make sure you've got everything you need."

"Every day is a snow day up here," she said. "That's what's so great about this place." She sighed into the phone, and her voice turned wistful. "I'm alone with myself, and I find myself remembering things about the past…"

About us? he wondered, but didn't ask.

There was a knock at the door, and Rourke swiveled around in his chair. Nina Romano came in without waiting for an invitation. He took one look at her face—taut, edged by panic—and said to Jenny, "I need to go. I'll call you back."

Thank you, Nina, he thought. He'd managed to get off the phone before making a total idiot of himself.

She spared him only a quick glance. "Jenny?" she inquired, nodding toward the phone.

Damn, was he that obvious? "What's up?" he asked, ignoring her question.

"I know where the money's going. It's being stolen by Matthew Alger."

It took Rourke for a moment to catch up with her thinking. "The city finances," he said.

She nodded and slapped a printed spreadsheet on the desk. "He was pretty clever about it, making transfers from special and restricted funds into the general fund, and then helping himself. Oh, and he took cash from traffic citations and then indicated in records that the tickets had been dismissed as community service. And he didn't even have authority to do that." Nina was sputtering now. "The bastard. I can't wait to—"

"Don't say anything to Alger yet."

"Too late." Nina stood aside and motioned Matthew Alger into the office. She pinned him with a fiery glare. "So Rourke tells me I shouldn't have said anything to you," she snapped. "I'm sure he's right, but I have to confess, I don't have any experience dealing with city officials who steal. You're the first."

"I don't know what the hell you're talking about."

Classic, thought Rourke. This was something he heard every day on the job and most of the time it was bullshit. Alger was lying. It was there in the flick and shift of his eyes, in the posture of one hand covering the other.

"So are you going to arrest him?" Nina demanded.

God save him from people who tried to "help" him with his job. "We'll call the state auditor," Rourke said, scribbling a note. "Right away."

Nina grabbed the spreadsheet. "But what about—"

His buzzer sounded. He craned his neck to see the front desk. "Yeah?"

"Three kids to see you, Chief," said his assistant.

Rourke looked at Alger. "We're done here for the moment." He shifted his attention to the intercom. "Send them in." A visit from three kids was not unusual. Thanks to his youth group, a lot of local kids considered him approachable, a problem solver.

He got up and opened the door. To his surprise, in walked Zach Alger, Sonnet Romano and Daisy Bellamy. They were dressed for outdoors, backpacks clanking with snowshoes, their cheeks stained red from the cold. Alger was clearly taken by surprise, too. He glared at Zach. "You in some kind of trouble?" he asked.

Rourke could see Nina biting her tongue. He knew she wouldn't accuse Alger in front of his kid—for the kid's sake.

"No, sir," Zach said, managing to make the "sir" sound like an insult. An uncomfortable silence stretched the moment out. Finally, Matthew Alger stepped toward the door. "I'll be in my office."

"Bye, Mr. Alger," Sonnet said, all politeness.

She nudged Zach, and he said, "See you, Dad."

The three of them watched him go. Rourke checked out his visitors, a habit with him. One quick perusal could tell him if a kid had been fighting, or was the victim of an assault, if he was on something or in shock. Rourke even knew, without any high-tech device, when a kid was lying. At the moment, the only message he was getting from these three involved disquiet and…fear, probably. Daisy Bellamy, whom he barely knew, looked particularly pale and troubled. She wore a camera on a strap around her neck, and seemed to be cradling it unconsciously with her hand.

"Been out hiking, I see," he said, hoping to prod them into talking to him.

"We have," Sonnet said, stepping forward.

"You don't look too happy about that. I thought you guys loved snow days."

"We went snowshoeing today," Daisy said.

"On the trail above Meerskill Falls," Zach added.

"We had permission," Sonnet said. "It's on Camp Kioga property and Daisy's dad said it would be okay."

The hike up to Meerskill Falls and beyond was not exactly well marked, but by traveling in a group of three, they had probably been safe enough. Around here, kids got in trouble the same as they did anywhere. There were just more scenic places to do it.

"We wanted to check out the ice caves," Daisy said. There was an odd tremor in her voice as she turned on her digital camera and angled the preview screen toward him. "We found one, too. Actually, Sonnet found it. I took a bunch of shots."

Strange that these kids weren't all talking at once. Kids usually couldn't wait to blurt things out. Rourke studied the thumbnail photo, his skepticism firmly in place. People brought a lot of things to police stations, items they mistook—in all innocence or ignorance—for other things. A bit of antler shed in the woods was mistaken for human bone. A tuft of animal fur stuck in the bark of a tree was deemed the hair of a missing child. Buried treasure turned out to be fool's gold. In ninety-nine percent of cases, the discovery had a perfectly logical—and non-criminal—explanation.

Not this time, though. This time, there could be no mistaking what he was looking at.

"You took these today?" he said.

The kids nodded in unison.

"Did you touch anything?"

Sonnet shook her head. "I don't think so."

"I'm going to need the memory card out of this camera," he said. "Is that all right, Daisy?"

"Sure." She slipped it out of the camera, her eyes large and frightened.

"You did the right thing, you guys," he said, and reached for the intercom to buzz his assistant.

Twenty-Eight

＊＊＊＊＊＊＊＊

Jenny was trying to re-create a scene she barely remembered. Like she'd told Rourke on the phone, it was a perfect day for working on her project. She'd awakened to a light-drenched world of new-fallen snow and had duly called everyone she promised to call each day—Nina, Laura, Olivia and Rourke. She called them because she knew that if she didn't they would call her.

She set the scene perfectly for a day of work. She made a fire in the potbellied wood-burning stove and set the iron teakettle on top to boil. She parted the curtains to view the lake out the window, a vast unbroken expanse of white, with the tiny snow-clad island in the middle. She fixed a pot of white snowbud tea and dressed in jeans and a cloud-soft cashmere sweater. She settled on the overstuffed sofa in front of the fire, booted up her laptop computer and…

Nothing.

It was awful. Here she was in the ideal situation, alone with her thoughts and memories, and she couldn't seem to write. The words wouldn't come or when she forced them out, they sounded trite, like the text of a greeting card or radio ad.

What was the matter with her?

She didn't even feel like the same person who had whipped out her newspaper column just hours before deadline, the words flying from her fingers as she captured a scene with the instant clarity of a snapshot, followed by a recipe to illustrate her point. Often she had no time to spare when she dashed off her column with a feeling of confidence and satisfaction.

And now she had all the time in the world, yet she was dithering. At first, she used the excuse that all her grandmother's precious handwritten recipes had been lost in the fire. Without them to pore over, how could she bring the past to life?

Just an excuse, she admitted. Especially after the *Troubadour* had covered the fire and Nina had issued a call for photos and memorabilia from anyone who might have such a thing. To Jenny's astonishment, she returned from New York to discover that Nina had collected a box of various items—a photograph here, a page from a book there, an ancient rate sheet from the bakery, a set of high-school yearbooks from Jenny's years, and from Mariska's as well—in the 1970s. Most of the items also came with a brief heartfelt note—*so sorry for your loss*—and a few came with monetary donations, which she promptly turned over to Gram's church. All this from the people of a town Jenny had longed to leave, that she considered constricting and provincial. Maybe Rourke was right after all. She was in the place she belonged.

Still, Martin Greer had set her a task that was completely different from anything she'd ever done before. It wasn't enough to offer recipes and vignettes. She needed to examine the workings of the family bakery on a deeper level. He wanted detail and emotion the column didn't require. He wanted pathos—her mother's abandonment, her father's absence and dramatic reappearance. And although Mr. Greer had only seen Joey mentioned in passing, he had sniffed out the tragedy there. Jenny wasn't sure she could find the words to write about that.

Frustrated, she got up and paced the floor, her thumbs hooked into the back pockets of her jeans. She snapped on the radio. Only one station came in clearly up here, and the music selections were old and tired, but sometimes the murmur of background noise was preferable to silence. She paced some more, paced through "My

Sharona," and wasn't even tempted to dance. The song was followed by an amateurish-sounding ad spot—"Palmquist—your family jeweler since 1975," the announcement concluded.

In 1975, her mother had been an attractive teenager, and after school worked at the jewelry store as counter help. She was ambitious, Gram and Grandpa had told Jenny, taking on the counter job in addition to the bakery in the morning. Even Jane Bellamy remembered that about her—always trying to get ahead.

Jenny flipped open one of the donated yearbooks to a shot of her mother. There was a bright recklessness to Mariska that, according to Laura, drew people to her. Jenny didn't have that quality. Maybe if her mother had stuck around, she would have learned it.

But did she want to be like Mariska? Did she want to be so enamored of adventure that she'd eventually leave her home behind for good?

"I hope you're happy, wherever you are," she said to the girl in the photo.

She became aware of a hot, metallic smell and realized the water had boiled away in the iron kettle on the wood-burning stove. She put on an oven mitt and carried the kettle to the sink to refill it, the loud hiss startling Rufus from his nap on the hearth rug. "Sorry, boy," she said.

The reek of dry iron and hot steam teased at her, awakening a distant glimmer of memory. Something came to attention inside her, and she shut her eyes, picturing a scene from the past in minute detail. The kitchen smelled of iron and steam, and a familiar song played on the radio—"867-5309/Jenny."

She rejoined the past, her imagination stepping into the scene she'd been struggling to describe. It was winter, and she was very small, sitting at the round Formica table with a cup of hot chocolate. The cup was in the shape of an elephant's head, its two ears forming the handles.

Her mother stood at the stove, swaying to the music. Every time "Jenny, Jenny" came from the radio, Momma would turn and sing along, pointing to Jenny and making her giggle.

"What you making?" Jenny asked, eyeing the pan on the stove.

"A fortune," Momma said with a laugh.

"What's that?"

"You'll find out when you're older."

"Can I help?" Jenny slipped down from her chair and crossed the room, her Winnie-the-Pooh slippers scuffing on the linoleum.

"No," Momma said in a voice that said she really meant it. "It's hot. Don't touch. These are sinkers for fishing."

Jenny stood back and watched. The windows were open, Momma said to get rid of the fumes. She poured dark liquid from the pan into a tray. Then she danced all the way to the end of the song. She was so pretty and happy. "I think I'll go out and celebrate."

"No, Momma," Jenny protested. "You always go away."

"And I always come back. Now, let's wait until these cool. Then we can put them in Grandpa's tackle box. Be careful you don't lose a single one."

A popping sound came from the woodstove and Jenny opened her eyes, blinking at the harsh light on the snow outside. That was probably her clearest memory of her mother, and she realized the scene had repeated itself more than once. Yet there was something missing, something she didn't get. Despite all her big dreams and ambitions about getting rich and seeing the world, Mariska still went fishing with her father in winter when they had to make a hole in the ice.

Jenny wondered what had become of the homemade sinkers, if they were still around somewhere and if they looked the same as they did in her memory. Maybe they were still in the tackle box, undisturbed by time. Putting on her jacket, gloves and boots, Jenny headed out to the shed where the salvage from the fire was stored. It was still snowing, and she had to lift her legs high through the drifts. Rufus bounded along with her, plowing a swath through the snow. A snow emergency had been declared for both today and tomorrow, perhaps longer. Only essential vehicles were supposed to be out.

She had to dig a trench with her hands in front of the rolling wooden door of the shed. Once inside, she sorted through the stacked boxes until she found the one that contained her grandfather's fishing gear, which had been salvaged from under a sink in the utility room. She brought it over to the door where the light streamed in, diffused by the thick falling snow. She set the box down and opened it, the action raising hinged trays filled with the expected rusty fishhooks and melted objects that might have once been plastic bobbers and lures. A few misshapen weights had survived but most had melted, spread over the bottom of the box and rehardened. A handful of sharp-edged pebbles lay strewn in the bottom of the box. Tugging a mitten off with her teeth, she picked up one of the pebbles. Except it wasn't a pebble. It was too round and symmetrical. Jenny frowned. Rubbed it on her jeans. Took off her glove and dug at it with her thumbnail. Found a fillet knife and scraped the soft alloy away.

Her gasp sounded loud and desperate in the snow-cushioned silence. She shut the box and hurried as fast as she could to the lodge. This was crazy, she thought. Completely crazy. She had to be wrong, she just had to be. Except a little kernel of knowledge inside her knew the truth.

Jenny hurried back to the lodge. She let the dog in and took off her parka and boots. Then she sat at the table and cleaned some of the stones as best she could, trying to imagine what on earth had been her mother's purpose, praying there was some innocent explanation. But as the seconds ticked by, she felt only suspicion. She tried to figure out a way not to sound demented when she told Rourke what she'd found. Her hand shook as she dialed his number at work. His assistant said he was unavailable except in case of emergency.

"It's not an emergency," Jenny said. "Not like that, anyway. Please ask him to call me when he gets a chance." She hung up and then dialed Nina, who wasn't available either. On a snow day, Jenny reminded herself, public servants were busy keeping people safe. She tried the bakery. Earlier, Laura had said she'd probably open late and close early.

Laura herself picked up. "Sky River Bakery."

"It's Jenny. Is everything all right?"

"Sure," Laura replied with a smile in her voice. "We're busy, in fact. Only Mariel Gale and I made it in, and we're swamped because so many places are closed. How about you?"

"I'm getting plenty of snow but I'm fine. Listen, is Rourke around?"

"Haven't seen him."

"Nina?"

"Not her, either. What do you need, hon?"

Jenny swallowed hard, struggled to keep her voice matter-of-fact. "I was going through some of the things salvaged from the fire and I found something my, um…I think it's something my mother did, a long time ago. Laura, I don't quite know how to say this. I think I found a fortune in diamonds in my grandfather's old tackle box." She paused. "Tell me that's not as crazy as it sounds."

There was a silence so long that Jenny feared the line had gone dead. Then she heard faint sounds from the bakery—the jangle of the bell over the door, the beep of the register, a murmur of voices. "Laura? Did you hear what I said?"

"I heard."

She knew something. Jenny could hear it in her voice.

"You have to tell me," she said. "Was my mother stealing from the jewelry store where she worked?"

"No, doll. She never stole from Palmquist's." A pause. "The diamonds—they were the price she demanded to keep you a secret."

Food for Thought
by Jenny Majesky

Why Bowl?

This is a spicy cookie with almonds, and is traditionally molded into giant 12-inch shapes using carved antique molds of the saints. At home, a flat pan will do. This is a richer variation, filled with almond paste.

My grandmother never worried about dieting. People of her generation tended not to, while nowadays we're fanatics about our intake of carbs, calories, transfats… Maybe we should reconsider our grandmothers' philosophies. Gram simply never overate. She believed that if something was good enough, then you didn't need to eat a lot of it in order to feel satisfied.

However, the fact is, her baked goods tend to be loaded with refined carbohydrates, which are directly converted into fat. To burn off the calories requires 30-47 minutes of running, 40-60 minutes of cycling, 85-120 minutes of walking or 90-135 minutes of bowling.

SPICE OF LIFE

    1-1/2 cups flour
    1-1/2 teaspoons baking powder
    2/3 cup butter or margarine
    3/4 cup plus 2 tablespoons sugar
    1 tablespoon ground cinnamon
    1/2 teaspoon ground cloves

1/2 teaspoon freshly grated nutmeg
a pinch of cayenne pepper
1 tablespoon milk
1 teaspoon lemon zest
1 (7-ounce) package almond paste
1 egg, beaten
4 tablespoons sliced almonds and a sprinkle of coarse
  sugar

Preheat oven to 350°F. Combine flour and baking powder. Cut butter into flour mixture. Add sugar, spices, milk and lemon zest. Roll out dough on floured surface into a rectangle 1/4-inch thick. Cut in half. Place half on heavy sheet of aluminum foil, folding the edges of foil up around dough to make a shallow, fitted pan. Brush the top of this layer with beaten egg.

Roll out almond paste to fit on top of dough and lay it on top of this. Cover with remaining half of dough, pressing down lightly. Brush top with beaten egg. Scatter almond slices over the top, pressing them lightly into dough. Bake for 40 minutes, or until done. Let cool, then cut into bars.

Twenty-Nine

~~~~~~~~~~~~~~~~~~~~

1983

"We have an agreement," Mariska said to Laura. "That's all you need to know."

Laura stood in astonishment, gaping at her friend. They were in the cavelike vault of the bakery freezer. Laura had shown up at three forty-five in the morning as usual to open. She normally had an hour before anyone else arrived, but this morning Mariska had startled her by showing up. Instead of getting to work, however, she had brought Laura to the walk-in freezer. There, Mariska had shown her a small box lined with black velvet. Peering at the contents, Laura was pretty sure she was hallucinating. Mariska assured her that these were one-carat round diamonds, investment grade, which meant they were colorless and internally flawless. They had been given to her, she explained, by Mr. and Mrs. Lightsey, of Lightsey Gold & Gem in New York City. They had an "agreement."

"I don't understand," Laura said. "Who are they? And why did they give you the diamonds?"

"I told you…" Mariska closed the box and pressed it to her chest.

"Right, the agreement," Laura said. "What I meant was, why? Who are these people?"

Mariska slipped the box into a zippered belt around her waist. "I need to move these. I thought keeping them in here would be safe, but after yesterday's power outage, I was getting nervous."

"Nervous about what?"

"I kept feeling like someone was watching me."

"Who?"

"Just…someone. I thought of a better hiding place. I need to tell someone, though, in case, well, you know."

"In case what?"

"Something happens to me. It won't, I swear. It's just a precaution. Anyway, you're the only one I can trust."

Laura was unnerved by the ominous tone. "If you trust me, then you'll tell me the whole story."

They went into the bakery, where everything was gleaming, waiting to start another day. Laura eyed her friend. Mariska was more beautiful than ever, her constant travels having imbued her with a special sense of style, as if she had stepped from the pages of a Paris fashion spread. She wore a silk scarf and carried a soft leather bag with casual ease, and even at this hour, she seemed possessed of a peculiar restless energy. She adored traveling the world, and found life in sleepy Avalon, New York, almost unbearable. Although she adored her daughter—everybody adored Jenny—she couldn't seem to settle down. And now this, thought Laura. Just when she thought Mariska couldn't have any more secrets, there was this.

As Laura busied herself with a honey-wheat mixture, Mariska finally began to talk. "Mr. and Mrs. Lightsey are the parents of Pamela Lightsey, the girl Philip Bellamy married," she said.

Now Laura remembered. The Lightseys were summer people, friends of the Bellamys.

"They were desperate for Philip to marry Pamela, and they knew he wouldn't do it so long as I was around," Mariska continued. "I knew the moment I told Philip I was pregnant, it would be over for him and Pamela. The thing is, the Lightseys knew that, too. They said if I'd break up with Philip—and make him believe it—they'd make it worth my while. They're in the diamond trade, so…" She patted the belt containing the diamonds.

That night, at Mariska's insistence, Laura and Mariska went out, stopping at Scooter's, a popular hang-out on the river road. The two women sat at a bar-height table sipping drinks and catching the eye of several guys. Well, Mariska did, anyway. Next to her, Laura felt as plain as white bread.

Some local guys parked themselves at the next table—Terry Davis, who worked up at Camp Kioga year round, Jimmy Romano, a teacher at the high school, and Matthew Alger, who worked for the city. When it came to flirting, Mariska was an expert, but Laura was content to simply sit back and watch. It was an art, the process of lighting up when a guy looked at you, holding his attention with your eyes and your body language. Although it required intense concentration, it had to appear completely natural and spontaneous.

Before long, Mariska was whispering and giggling with Matthew, who looked as though he was about to eat her up. Laura excused herself and went to the ladies' room. Within a few minutes, Mariska joined her. "What's the matter with you?" she asked.

Laura could see that she was drunk. "I keep thinking about the things you told me today…what you did…"

"It had to be done, okay? The bakery wasn't doing so hot that summer, in case you forgot."

"I remember."

"It was a way to save it."

"Philip would have helped you," Laura said. "If you'd told him about the baby and married him, the Bellamys would have stepped in."

Mariska stared at her. "And how would that make me look? Like an idiot who got pregnant and married a guy in order to use his money. You know me, Laura. I would never do that."

Ah, yes, her pride. "So it's better to be a single mother and take a bribe than to marry the man you love?"

"I was eighteen years old. I had no idea about love and marriage. Sometimes I think I still don't. But I've always understood the value of money."

A flushing sound came from one of the stalls. Laura's blood chilled. Good Lord, someone had heard their conversation. A dark-haired woman came out and washed her hands at a sink. One of the Romanos, Laura observed. Angela, maybe, she couldn't keep them all straight.

When she left, Laura looked wildly at Mariska. "Do you think she knows what we were talking about?"

"It doesn't matter. I took care of everything today. The only one who saw was Jenny, and she's too little to know what's going on."

"Isn't what you did illegal?"

"Look, I had something the Lightseys wanted," she said in exasperation. "And you didn't see me buying new cars and clothes, stuff like that. I didn't want to arouse anybody's suspicion." When she needed money, she explained, she would take one or two stones at a time to a diamond exchange on Forty-seventh Street in New York, or sometimes to the one in Toronto or even in Europe somewhere.

"So why are you telling me this today? Why now?" Laura asked. She had always been somewhat in awe of Mariska—of her looks, her nerve, her self-confidence. Now she felt something else besides awe—shock and disapproval.

"I might need to go away for a while," Mariska said. "Longer than usual."

Food for Thought
by Jenny Majesky

A Colorful Cordial

My grandparents had very few treasures because they brought so little with them when they emigrated from Poland. The treasures they had were precious, and one that stands out in my memory is a set of crystal cordial glasses. My grandfather went to Brooklyn one year and bought a set imported from Poland. They had the color and cut of jewels—ruby, sapphire, emerald, amethyst—and they were only used on special occasions. A birth, a death, a holiday. Krupnik is a hot honey-and-spice cordial that brings warmth to any occasion.

KRUPNIK

1 cup honey
1/2 cup water
1 crumbled bay leaf
1 teaspoon pure vanilla extract
1 teaspoon grated lemon peel
a pinch of nutmeg
10 whole cloves
2 pinches of cinnamon
3 cups 100-proof vodka

In a pot, combine everything except vodka. Bring to boil, reduce heat and simmer, covered, for about 10 minutes. Strain, discarding spices. Add vodka and heat gently but do not boil. Serve immediately, preferably in crystal cordial glasses.

Thirty

G iving people bad news came with the job, Rourke reminded himself as he trudged through hip-deep snow to the lodge at Camp Kioga. It had always been that way. In training, he had studied the optimum methods of delivering the news and providing support. On the job, he had been called on to arrive on strangers' doorsteps, to tell unsuspecting people that the unthinkable had happened— an accident, a death, an arrest or some other incident that would forever change the lives involved. Those moments haunted him for years afterward.

Due to the snowfall, the road to the camp wasn't even accessible with a snowplow. He'd used a snowmobile with deep-snow tracks, and had then been forced to hike the final leg by snowshoe. One of his deputies had pointed out that he could contact Jenny by phone, but there was no way Rourke would do that. He needed to tell her this in person.

It was dusk by the time he reached the lodge, and the snow was coming down harder than ever. He focused on the golden glimmers of light in the windows, the friendly puff of smoke coming from the chimney. He pictured Jenny inside, maybe sitting at her computer or fixing something to eat, listening to music, thinking or dreaming. And with that image came a piercing surge of tenderness, and the knowledge that had been with him for at least half his life. One summer long ago, he'd fallen in love with Jenny. He'd spent years trying to fall out of love with her. Now he was forced to acknowledge that he'd never succeeded. The notion brought him no joy. Somewhere in the world, there were people who were good at love, who found it bright and easy, something to give meaning to their lives. Rourke was not one of them.

He stopped in front of the lodge and took off the snowshoes. The front stairs were layered with snow and a fringe of icicles hung from the eaves. As he passed beneath them, a big section fell, stabbing silently into the snow. He called Jenny's name and then knocked at the door. Rufus sounded the alarm, baying and hurling himself at the door.

Good dog, thought Rourke. He liked the mutt's protective instincts.

The door opened and Rufus lunged, then instantly dissolved into a puddle of affection when he recognized Rourke. Jenny stood back, wearing an expression Rourke found hard to read. She was anything but happy to see him, and she looked…was that guilt on her face? What did she have to feel guilty about? She was wearing jeans and a sweater, and her hair was in a ponytail. She stood with her arms folded protectively in front of her.

"Rourke," she said. "I wasn't expecting you."

Clearly. "I need to talk to you. I, uh, wanted to say this in person."

She frowned and her gaze shifted, much like… He couldn't shake the notion that she was acting like someone brought to the booking desk at the station.

He stepped inside and shut the door. With Rufus prancing around him in welcome, he took off his boots and parka. It felt good to peel off a few layers. Snowshoeing was hot work. "Can we have a seat?" he asked her.

"Um, sure." She gestured at the sofa.

Rourke decided to be quick about it. She seemed distracted and mystified, and holding out was just cruel. "A body was found in the ice caves above the falls," he said without preamble.

She looked utterly confused. "A body."

"Yes."

"A human body."

He nodded. Though he wanted to touch her, he kept his fists clenched. "Sonnet, Zach and Daisy were up there snowshoeing. There's been no positive ID of…" He started to say "the remains" but let his voice trail off. "A recovery team will go up as soon as the weather clears. I think you need to know, to be prepared for the news." All right, he thought. Get it over with. "The deceased is almost certainly your mother."

He watched the words sink in like a slow burn, the initial confusion deepening to comprehension and then pain. She didn't say anything, didn't move except to press her hands flat on her knees and study them intently.

"I compared the, um, clothing to the description in the original missing persons report," he explained. He had reread the archived report, though that hadn't been necessary. He'd gone over it so many times over the years that he'd memorized it, and the moment he'd seen Daisy's photos, he had known. "It's pretty conclusive." He paused, hating the fact that he was hurting her. "I'm sorry."

She sat very still for a few minutes, seeming to go away somewhere. She swallowed, tucked a stray lock of hair behind her ear. Then she took a deep, unsteady breath. "I used to keep a journal, when I was young," she said in a faint voice. "I started every entry 'Dear Mom.' It was my way of making her real to me. Even when I hadn't heard from her in ten, fifteen, twenty years, she was always real to me, the person I told everything to, always there, whenever I needed her."

"Jen, I don't know what to say. Except that we'll figure out what happened to her. I swear I won't let it rest."

She was eerily calm, though he suspected there was a lot going on inside her. Then she cleared her throat, and her gaze shifted, and once again, he had the impression that she was acting guilty.

"Um, about that," she said. "My mother had a secret…I just

found out." She got up and went over to the table. Beside her laptop was a rusty tackle box, charred on the outside, something salvaged from the fire. She handed him a teacup that appeared to
contain a handful of tiny stones. "I think these are diamonds," she
said. "In fact, after calling Laura, I'm sure. And I think whatever
happened to my mother stems from this."

Rourke took one of the stones in the palm of his hand while
she explained that they had been hidden inside fishing sinkers, the
homemade sort.

A chill slipped over him as he considered the possibilities. Mariska was in possession of a hidden fortune, and she had somehow put herself in danger. "We'll have to verify what this is," he
said. But that chill told him Jenny was correct.

She stood by the table, looking small and lost. "I was so angry
at my mother," she said at last. "I blamed her for leaving me and
never coming back. I...don't know what to feel now." She folded
her arms under her breasts as though to hold herself together.

Here was the thing. Rourke knew for sure he was a son of a
bitch, because what he was feeling was a sting of pure lust for this
woman. It was nothing new, but here he was, in the wake of
tragedy, wanting to take her to bed. He'd done it before, when they
thought Joey had died. And here he was again, reporting another
tragedy and still wanting her. Rourke was the Grim Reaper with
a hard-on.

"Why are you looking at me like that?" Jenny asked.

"You don't want to know."

Food for Thought

by Jenny Majesky

Come Spring

In Poland, the Thursday before Lent is known as *Tlusty czwartek* (Fat Thursday). When the day arrives, we know springtime is just around the corner. It's traditional to enjoy Mazurki, which are thin cakes. Each grandmother passes the recipe down to her daughter and so on, down through the generations. The family gathers and shares the Mazurki, and passionate arguments ensue as people choose their favorites. This one nearly always wins the competition.

MAZUREK

1/2 cup pure, unsalted butter
4 ounces baking chocolate, melted
1 cup sugar
3 eggs
1 teaspoon vanilla
1/4 teaspoon salt
2 tablespoons milk
2 cups flour
icing made from 1 cup powdered sugar and
    1-3 tablespoons of milk
chopped walnuts or pecans for garnish

Preheat oven to 350°F. Cream butter; add melted chocolate and sugar and mix well. Stir in eggs, one at a time. Stir in vanilla, salt and milk. Gradually add flour and mix well. Spread in greased 15 x 10 x 1-inch pan and bake for about 20 minutes. Drizzle with icing and sprinkle with chopped nuts. Cut into squares and serve.

Thirty-One

1998

Rourke's Saturday-night watch had just started when a call came in—personal. He picked up at the duty sergeant's desk and stood looking out the window at the bleak, stormy weather. "Officer McKnight here."

"It's me, bro," said a welcome voice. "Home at last."

"Joey." Rourke shut his eyes and thought, Thank God. Joey was finally back. After the mishap that had resulted in a mistaken report of his death, Joey had been sent to Landstuhl Regional Medical Center in Germany. There, he'd undergone several procedures to save his eye, but nothing had worked. He'd been transferred to Walter Reed and finally honorably discharged.

"Yep, that's me," he said. "Otherwise known as 'Lucky.'"

Rourke sensed the bitter irony behind his words. Joey had lost much that night. His brothers-in-arms, whom he'd loved with unabashed ferocity, as well as his right eye. Not unexpectedly, the incident had changed him irrevocably, and a new hard wariness became apparent in his sparse e-mail messages and phone calls.

"Where are you?" Rourke asked.

"I'm in Kingston, at the station. Next train's not for an hour. I need a lift to Avalon. Planning to surprise the little woman, you know? She's big on surprises."

Rourke's mouth went dry. What had happened between him and Jenny that night had been a huge mistake. Mutual grief had stripped away all their defenses, but that was no excuse. And the hell of it was, he'd do it all over again if he had the chance, even though guilt ate at him every time he thought about it.

Until that night, he hadn't known sex could be so powerful, a possession of sorts. And he hadn't known how important that was, or how devastating when it was taken away. He had surrendered willingly, though. The second Joey had called the morning after and they realized their mistake, a sick guilt had frozen Rourke and Jenny, and they'd avoided each other ever since. Neither was sure whether or not Joey had figured out what had happened, but a terrible suspicion haunted them. They'd betrayed him in the worst possible way.

"So whaddya say?" Joey prodded.

"You been drinking, Joey?" he asked.

"Hell, I'm a soldier. A veteran. A one-eyed veteran. Of course I've been drinking. How about you swing down this way and give me a lift?"

A thirty-mile drive involved a little more than "swinging down." Rourke glanced around the station. "I'm on duty. I'll have to check with the sergeant—"

"Aw, c'mon," Joey said. "You're out in a patrol car anyway. You can just cruise down this way."

"Hang on a minute and I'll ask."

"Since when does the great Rourke McKnight ask for permission, anyway?" Joey's tone turned belligerent. "Usually you just help yourself." He paused, then added, "Know what? I don't need a ride after all. Never mind."

"Joe—"

"I'll see you later," he said, and then he was gone.

Rourke scowled at the phone receiver as he hung up. The exchange left him unsettled. He entertained a brief impulse to drop by Jenny's house to give her a heads-up, but decided against it. Joey wanted to surprise her, and there was no way Rourke was going to ruin that. Okay, he thought. He'd see about getting away to find Joey and bring him home.

Within seconds, however, a call came in and he was ordered to do a knock-and-talk at the Round Table Arms apartments. A neighbor had complained of loud noises from a family fight, a depressingly common occurrence. However, when he checked the dispatch and saw that it was the Taylor household, he shifted into gear. Grady Taylor was a mean son of a bitch when he drank, and there were kids in the house. Rourke hated guys who beat their wives and kids, hated them with a fury that made him far more dangerous than any drunk swinging his fists.

He sped through the driving rain, the cruiser fishtailing on the wet, oily pavement. He reported to dispatch and headed up a flight of iron-frame stairs. Sure enough, the argument was still going on—a man's gruff voice and a teenage boy's whiny, belligerent tones. He rapped on the door with his nightstick. The door jerked open.

"Is there a problem, Officer?" Grady Taylor didn't look the part of a violent man. He was overweight, but his business suit fit well, his tie undone and casually draped around his shoulders. He didn't fool Rourke, though. Rourke spotted the violence in his glittering eyes and in the way his hair was slightly mussed and the raw spots on the knuckles of his right hand.

"I guess I need to be asking you that," Rourke said, looking past Taylor. In the background stood a lanky teenage boy in hip-hop garb—oversize sweatshirt, sagging pants, chains draped from his pockets. The kid was wiping his mouth with the back of his hand. When he saw Rourke checking him out, he turned away as though ashamed.

"No problem here, Officer," Taylor said amicably. "My boy and I were just having a little disagreement. Teenagers, you know…"

Shit. Did he actually expect Rourke to nod in agreement? *Yeah, teenagers.* "Looks like the disagreement was with your fist," he said.

"It's none of your damn business," Taylor spat. "Jesus, what are you, twelve years old? You got no idea what it takes to raise a kid, to keep him safe—"

"He's not safe here," Rourke said, then motioned to the boy. "Tell you what. You come with me, and we'll take a little ride, give you both a chance to cool off."

The kid didn't need any more encouragement than that. He grabbed a big coat and walked toward the door, stuffing his hands in the sleeves.

"Don't you dare set foot outside this house." Taylor's voice lashed like a bullwhip. "I swear to God, I'll—"

"You'll what?" In a blaze of white-hot fury, Rourke brought the nightstick up and across the big man's throat, pinning him back against the door. "You'll what, you lousy son of a bitch?"

Taylor's eyes snapped with rage and his fists came up. Rourke felt himself pushed to the very edge of his control. He pressed harder, the nightstick against the guy's throat. Just try me, you fat fuck, he thought. Just push me a little harder….

Taylor's face turned dark red as he struggled for breath.

"Dad," said the kid. "Hey, Dad."

The voice cut through Rourke's fury and he stepped back, releasing the pressure. Damn, he'd almost… Taylor sagged against the door frame. Rourke turned to the kid, who seemed to have forgotten his bleeding lip. A bright ribbon of blood trickled down his chin and he shook with fright—not at his father, but at Rourke.

"Let's go," Rourke said to him. "I'll give you a lift to a friend or relative's house, okay? It'll be all right."

The kid was quiet as they went outside into the battering rain and got into the cruiser. Rourke reported in, then handed the kid a wad of Kleenex for his mouth. He kept glancing up at the apartment, a worried expression on his face. Kids were incredibly loyal to their monster fathers. The boy offered the address of a friend, said he could stay there for the night. Then he rode in sullen silence.

He's scared of me, Rourke thought.

After dropping the boy off, he'd meant to go pick up Joey, but just as he was pulling away, the radio monitor sounded. Late-model Mustang versus freight train, at the railroad crossing outside of town, just a few blocks from Rourke's location. Emergency vehicles en route.

Rourke had a premonition before he reached the scene. He felt it like a ball of ice in his gut. Somehow he knew even before he saw the hectic, unnatural glare of emergency lights, the mangled car, the smoke and sparks flying into the night air as rescue workers extracted the victim. Even before he fought his way through the tangle of EMTs and equipment and looked at the victim, into eyes that were glazed with confusion, beyond pain. Joey was being strapped to a narrow backboard, his face chalk white.

Rourke's heart sank like a rock. *Joey.* He was in such a hurry, he'd borrowed or rented a car and raced home to Jenny. Rourke was a fool for thinking Joey would wait for the train. That was the stupid thing. He should have known and, job or not, should have dropped everything and driven to pick up his friend.

"Joey," he said, stepping in beside two frantic EMTs. "Hey, buddy, it's me. Can you hear me?"

Joey's eyes fluttered. There was blood everywhere, more blood than Rourke had ever seen, dark as an oil slick, mingling with the rain.

"You know him?" one of the EMTs asked. The look on the guy's face told Rourke to brace himself for the worst.

"Yeah," Rourke said, reaching for…there was no place to touch. There were tubes and blood everywhere. "Damn, Joey, look at you."

His mouth twitched. "Rourke. Man, I…sorry."

"Hey, don't worry." Rourke spoke over the swarming EMTs. He felt sick, but somehow managed to smile. "Don't be sorry," he said. "You're doing good, Joe. These guys are going to help you."

There was some ineffable quality to Joey's smile, a glow, almost; clearly Joey knew he wasn't doing good at all.

"Tell her…" His eyes rolled back.

"Joey—"

He focused again. Moved his mouth but no sound came out. His eyes rolled back again.

"She knows, buddy. I swear, I…" Something changed. A shudder went through Joey. "Dammit," Rourke yelled. "Do something. Can't you fucking do something?"

Jenny was startled by a knock at the door a little before 9:00 p.m. Gram had just settled in front of the TV, and Jenny was wearing her soft but ugly pajamas. She grabbed a sweater, feeling a bit sheepish. It was only nine o'clock at night and here she was in her pajamas, like an old maid. Other people her age went down to the Whistle Stop Tavern for drinks on a night like this, or they were tucking in their kids. She suspected she was the only one in Avalon who was in her pj's, sipping a mug of chamomile tea and getting ready to watch a rerun of *Buffy the Vampire Slayer* with her grandmother.

Hugging the sweater around her, she opened the door. There stood Rourke, his cap tucked under his arm, standing with shoulders squared and face forward in a formal military stance. Her heart stumbled.

"Rourke?"

He stepped inside, and she saw something she had never seen before—he was about to break down. His face was drawn and pale, his eyes red-rimmed. His hands were shaking. He was shaking all over. "It's Joey," he said.

"Joey? But he's in Washington, D.C. At Walter Reed. I was going to visit him next weekend—"

"He was discharged." Rourke cleared his throat. "He was on his way back to see you and there was an accident."

Her mind leaped to a place of hope—this was another false alarm. It had happened once and could happen again. Somebody had passed on wrong information. If she could just shut her eyes and believe that, everything would be all right. But her eyes, traitors to hope, stayed open and saw the truth spattered in blood on

Rourke's uniform, even on his skin, under his fingernails. He'd clearly made an attempt to clean up; she could see the comb furrows, smell the fresh soap, but it didn't matter. This time, Joey was gone.

She started to sink, her knees suddenly liquid. Rourke grabbed her arms, propping her up. He was talking to her, and he looked like a different person, someone who had been damaged almost as badly as Joey. She could see his lips moving as he explained what had happened. She could even hear his words: Joey had jumped on the first train to New York and then out of the city, the express to Kingston. The ink was still wet on his discharge papers. At Kingston, he'd rented a car to drive the rest of the way to Avalon. He wanted to surprise her.

Surprise.

Food for Thought

by Jenny Majesky

Mourning Meal

Whenever a cherished friend passed away, the family would call my grandmother because she was a genius at putting together a menu for a crowd on short notice. The centerpiece of the meal was, of course, the funeral hot dish—a savory mixture baked in a roasting pan that resembled a small bathtub. Here is a version for a smaller crowd. It doesn't cure sadness, but it's said to comfort an aching heart.

AMERICAN LEGION FUNERAL HOT DISH

  1 pound ground beef
  1/2 onion, chopped
  1 cup frozen sliced carrots
  1 cup frozen cauliflower
  1 cup frozen chopped broccoli
  1 can cream of mushroom soup
  1 can cream of chicken soup
  3-4 stalks celery, chopped
  2 tablespoons soy sauce
  1/2 teaspoon white pepper
  1 12-ounce bag chow mein noodles

Preheat oven to 325°F. Fry hamburger and onion in large cast-iron pan, breaking hamburger up into small pieces. Drain and place in large baking pan. Mix vegetables, soups, celery, soy sauce and pepper, then combine with meat in pan. Fold in 2/3 of chow mein noodles (8 ounces), cover and bake for about an hour. Sprinkle remaining chow mein noodles on top. Put cover back on and bake another 15 minutes.

Thirty-Two

The wind had stopped and the snow drifted straight down in big flakes, wrapping the lodge in a cushion of silence. Jenny pulled the cuffs of her sweater down over her hands to warm them. "I do want to know, Rourke," she said. "I do want to know what you're thinking."

He shook his head. "Not important. Are you all right, Jen?"

She nodded. "Is it strange that I'm not crying hysterically?"

"No. She was gone for a long time."

"I feel…relieved in a way. At least I know. When you first told me about her, it was like something cold and tight unraveled. Now I know why—it's because I don't have to be angry anymore. I spent years being angry at her, thinking she simply didn't love me enough to come back. When in reality she was trying to save the family business, and she was desperately unhappy but doing the best she could, and something terrible happened to her. I should have loved her all along instead of being angry and resentful. It makes me wish…" She didn't quite know how to finish the thought. "It makes me wish I'd spent my emotions differently."

"Or not at all," he muttered.

And that, of course, was the way Rourke saw a situation like this. Don't get involved and you won't get hurt. She shifted uncomfortably as he kept staring at her with haunted eyes. She felt a squeeze of regret because she understood him all too well; he looked as lonely as she felt. After Joey was killed, they could have—should have—turned to each other for comfort. Instead, they turned their backs on each other. They'd both been so damaged by the past—afraid to love, afraid to lose themselves, to be hurt, to entrust their hearts to another's keeping. "It's because of Joey, isn't it?" she whispered. "That's why you never let yourself get close to anyone."

"That's why I never let myself get close to *you*."

"Rourke, that makes no sense—"

"He knew about us."

"Did he tell you so?"

"No. He knew, though."

"And that's what you've lived with all these years."

"It's not the sort of thing you forget. He loved us and we betrayed him and he knew, and the second he died, we were frozen there, with no chance to… We can never fix it." Something in his face reminded her of the boy she'd once known—anger and vulnerability and a stark yearning that had touched her heart. Even then, he'd been both damaged and overprotective. It came through now in his refusal to forgive himself for something he couldn't change.

"I don't know about you," she said, "but I talk to Joey all the time. I'm not going to torture myself over whether or not he knew about us. I refuse to do that, and I wish you would, too."

"It's not a choice for me," he said. "I could have prevented his accident the night he died. I could have dropped everything, driven down and given him a lift."

"God, Rourke, will you listen to yourself? You can't save the world. It's not your job."

"Oh, sorry, I thought it went with being a cop."

The ideal role for him. Save people and then walk away. Not this time, she decided. This time, she wouldn't let him. "You do the best you can," she said. "We all do, and yes, sometimes it's not good enough but that's the way things go. You say we shouldn't be together, we've never been good together, and I say you're wrong."

"Bullshit. It should have been you and Joey. You and he were perfect together. It was the way things should have been."

She glared at him. "That's something *you* decided. You didn't even give me a vote. For your information, Joey and I weren't 'perfect.' Nobody is. I loved him, but never in the way I loved you." The admission rushed from her before she could stop it. She took a deep breath, mortified yet curiously relieved. Finally, she'd told him the truth, and so far, the world hadn't come to an end.

His reaction was less than encouraging. He swore and glared at her, got up and went to the window, standing with his back to her. Darkness gathered over the lake, and outside there was not a single glimmer of light. "Bad idea," he commented at last. "You didn't want to be with me. I got word my best friend died and all I could think about was the fact that now I could fuck you."

She knew he was being deliberately crude. His temper had never fazed her. "That's not what you were thinking and you know it. That's a story you've been telling yourself to make sure you spend your life feeling guilty about what happened. What you really felt, what we both felt, was the loss of someone we loved with all our hearts. Someone we loved so much that we didn't let ourselves love each other because of him. The problem is that you and I *are* good together, and we tied ourselves in knots trying to ignore that. And every time we pretended, every time we denied our feelings, we made things worse. Are you seeing a pattern here?"

Rourke turned from the window to face Jenny. Her words took hold of his heart, squeezing until he couldn't stand it anymore. Crossing the room in two strides, he put his arms around her and pulled her close, and she fit perfectly in his arms. Her soft, flowery smell enveloped him and in the midst of what was probably one of the worst moments of her life, he felt a terrible surge of affection for her.

When she tilted her face up to his, he kissed her delicately, the taste of her impossibly warm and sweet. She kissed him back with an ardor he'd dreamed about for years, and they didn't speak anymore but strained together, pressing close until Rourke nearly shuddered with need, but at the same time, he had to wonder if this was a replay of the other time, when they thought they'd lost Joey. With an effort he pulled back and asked her with his eyes. She said nothing but took his hand and led him into the bedroom, where a light burned low beside the bed. And there, finally, he showed her his heart in the only way he knew how.

The snow came down in slanting sheets, piling against the side of the lodge until it nearly reached the windowsill. In the middle of the night, Jenny lay on her side next to Rourke, watching him.

This night had been so long in coming. When they finally let themselves go, it had been an explosion of emotion and it was better than dreams and left her feeling a contentment so deep it made her eyes tear up. The intimacy they'd shared was like nothing she'd ever experienced before, and the piercing sweetness of it caught her unawares. Her feelings for him eclipsed the pain and grief that had surrounded and insulated her.

A weak glimmer of light struggled through the gray dawn. She'd lost count of the number of times they'd made love, learning the landscape of each other's bodies in a slow series of discoveries. At some point he had phoned the station to tell someone they were all right; they'd return after the storm had passed.

And for some reason, as she lay listening to his breathing and the beating of her own heart, the tears wouldn't stop. His eyes fluttered open and he touched her cheek with his thumb. "I'm sorry," he said.

"You don't understand," she said, trying to sift through the emotions spilling out of her. "That's not…I'm not sad. Just…relieved, in a way. Not just about my mother, but…about us." All right, she thought. Might as well go for broke. "I've wanted this for so long. Didn't you know?"

He offered a half smile, his expression soft in the dim light from the stove in the other room. "That's why I tried so damn hard to stay away. What we did—what happened with Joey—how could we ever be happy together after that?"

"How? Like this." She gently touched his face, the faint beard stubble and the wave of blond hair on his brow. She kissed the crescent-shaped scar on his cheekbone. "Remember the day this happened?"

"The day we met. I got in a fight over you." He studied her for a long time, but it didn't make her self-conscious. She liked having him look at her, because when he did, he couldn't hide the lust and affection in his eyes.

"I never needed you to protect me. I didn't then, and I don't now. I just need you…" *To love me.* She couldn't quite bring herself to say it.

"Okay," he said, as though she'd spoken it aloud.

There was a world of meaning in that one word, and she laughed and moved into his arms as he laid her back on the bed. "It's going to be another snow day," he said.

"Perfect," she answered.

Much later in the morning, the wood for the stove ran low and Rourke went out to get more. There were several cords stacked next to the main lodge a couple of hundred yards away. He put on his boots and snowshoes and a pair of work gloves and a Mackinac jacket. "I'll be right back," he said.

She squinted out at the landscape, a wilderness of white mounds and the endless flat expanse of the lake. The woods and other buildings were shadowy blurs. "Don't get lost," she warned him.

He laughed and kissed her. "After last night? Are you kidding?"

She shut the door behind him and leaned against it. Dragging an old toboggan behind him, he headed out, Rufus bounding at his side. She watched until his figure faded and gradually disappeared. She felt a happiness so intense, it stole her breath. *Finally.* She knew loving him for the rest of her life wasn't necessarily going to be easy, but it was exactly what she wanted. And that made all the difference. Her discontent and restlessness had never been caused by her ties to the bakery and to Avalon. Everything made sense now that she was with Rourke.

She shivered and went to check the stove. The last log had burned to embers and it was getting cold in here. She went to the bedroom to put on a few more layers—some thick socks and a pair of sweatpants, a sweater and her warm slippers. She paused to glance in the mirror. Her hair was wildly mussed, her lips mysteriously full and…was that a stubble burn along her jawline? Even in her disheveled state, she had never looked more supremely happy than she was in this moment. Smiling, she picked up Rourke's shirt. The smell of it made her dizzy with wanting him again. On impulse she pulled the soft cotton shirt over her head. She touched his other things—the wool gabardine of his jacket, the leather of his sidearm, now securely snapped into its holster.

The wind picked up, howling with an almost-human voice across the lake and through the trees. Jenny wished Rourke would hurry. He'd been gone maybe fifteen minutes, and she already missed him.

Happiness was such a simple thing, Rourke thought, leaning into the wind as he dragged the toboggan to the woodshed. Why hadn't he figured it out until now? It consisted merely of knowing where you belong in the world, and whom you belong with. The irony was, he'd known it from the first moment he'd seen her, a kid in pigtails and unlaced sneakers. But knowing it and achieving it turned out to be two different things.

Achieving it meant facing up to some hard truths, like the fact that he could never change the past, and serving a self-imposed penance did nothing but feed his own bitter disappointment. He finally got it. The way to come to terms with Joey's death wasn't to run from happiness but to run toward it. He used to avoid Jenny because he didn't think he deserved Joey's happy ending. After last night, he realized there was a different way to see it. Being happy with Jenny wouldn't change what had happened, but at least it was a way to face a future that was suddenly bright with possibility. He needed to marry her. The thought was simply there, fully formed; it wasn't a matter for debate. It was the simple truth he'd been hiding from himself for too long. He wondered if she'd think it was sudden, or if she would understand. He didn't want to scare her, though.

The old wood was stacked under the eaves of a utility shed a hundred yards from the lodge. The huge rounds were knit together with cobwebs and had not been split. Great, he thought. He hoped there was a maul or ax in the shed.

Rufus wanted to play. The snow made him frisky and he leaped and bounded, barking an invitation. Rourke laughed and chased him around for a while, working up a sweat despite the weather.

Later, he found a maul and got to work on the wood. He wasn't sure how much they would need, but if it turned out he and Jenny were snowed in forever, it would be fine with him.

Rufus barked again, though this time it wasn't the playful bark; Rourke knew the difference. He set aside the maul and went to find the dog. The big malamute was plunging toward the camp entrance, or so it seemed. The visibility was next to nothing, thanks to the snow.

Rourke squinted and shielded his eyes. Someone was coming. His first thought was Connor or Greg, maybe to check on things. But why would either of them come up through the biggest snow of the year?

The visitor was a dark blur, moving fast, almost seeming to skim across the snow. An experienced snowshoer. Rufus was still barking furiously, probably freaked out by the guy's movements on the snowshoes.

Rourke waved his arms to get his attention. "Hey," he yelled. "Over here."

The visitor paused, and Rourke could make out his oversize

hunting jacket. There was a sound, nearly swallowed by the wind, but unmistakable to Rourke—gunshot. The dog emitted a yelp, ragged with pain, and exploded off into the woods.

And Rourke felt a fiery sting in his chest. He told his feet to move, but they wouldn't obey. The snow was icy soft when he landed, facedown.

I'm an idiot, he thought.

Jenny heard a popping sound—once, twice—and tilted her head to the side. The winter woods were full of unexpected noises—the crack of ice-coated branches, the thud of snow as they hit the roof, the scurry of deer foraging among the trees.

She went to the window and looked out but saw only the vast field of whiteness. She turned on the electric range and set the kettle on to boil for tea. Without the heat from the stove, the room was getting cold, fast.

At last, she heard Rourke outside, feet stomping on the porch. She ran to the door, opened it. "Thank God, you're—"

But it wasn't Rourke. It was someone in a ski mask, holding a gun on her. She had a fleeting, hysterical urge to laugh. A gun? She wasn't seeing this. Then the stranger broke into action, pushing her inside and shoving the door shut. Her mind froze. She couldn't even think. She blurted out, "What's going on? Where on earth did you come from?"

The intruder didn't reply but seemed to be scanning the room. She didn't allow herself to look around, to check for a stray article of clothing or something that would indicate she had not spent the night alone. Rourke was wearing the borrowed jacket. His clothes, including his gun, were in the other room.

The stranger spoke at last. "Have a seat," he said, indicating a wooden ladder-back chair. From a loop on his dark pants hung a set of handcuffs. Good God, she thought. Was he a cop? She thought about the calls she'd made after discovering the diamonds—Laura, Rourke's deputy, Olivia, Nina. What was she thinking? You didn't babble about discovering a fortune in diamonds. Somehow, the information had fallen into the wrong hands.

She sat down instantly, her gaze glued to the black-gloved hand, the gun pointing at her. At the same time, she thought of Rourke and the sounds she'd heard a few minutes ago. Something had happened. And where was the dog? She looked at the gun again and a curl of dread tightened inside her. If he were able, Rourke would be here right now, she thought. She was about to start begging the stranger but suspected histrionics would make no impression. Deep in her gut, she knew what he wanted.

"Let's make this quick," she suggested, her voice surprisingly steady as he advanced on her with the cuffs. She jumped up, startling him into thrusting the gun in her face. Jenny amazed herself by staying focused. As though nothing had happened, she went to the kitchen counter, showing him the saucer with the diamonds. They rattled as her hand shook. "This is what you came for, isn't it? Maybe my mother was willing to die for these. I'm not."

"Set that down," the intruder said.

The voice was vaguely familiar but she couldn't place it. She put the saucer on the counter and stepped back. Her assailant removed one glove, picked up one of the stones. It didn't look like much. "Everything I found is there," she said, feeling each second crawl by with a painful tug on her heart. Rourke, she thought. Where was Rourke?

Before she was even aware of it, she glanced at the bedroom door and only realized her mistake when the man spoke. "He can't help you now."

So he knew. He'd seen Rourke. "Where is he?" she demanded. "What—"

"Sit down." The intruder repeated his order.

As she moved toward the chair, Jenny felt something turn cold and solid inside her. This man wanted the diamonds. Maybe he was the one who had killed her mother for them. Maybe he was the one who had stolen her childhood, the source of all the agonizing unanswered questions about Mariska. Jenny felt herself turning into a different person, someone who was harder and angrier and yes, stronger than the gunman. All her life she had done the right thing, lived safe, doing as she was told. The intruder figured she would obey his every command. He had miscalculated. How could she be afraid now? Rourke had taught her that the best defense of all was to fight. To fight and never give up.

Instead of sitting down, she drew herself into a crouch and then lunged at the intruder, her knee hitting him square in the crotch in a maneuver Rourke had shown her.

He doubled over and she heard the breath leave him. The next target would be the eyes, but he fell back, out of range, though the ski mask remained in her fists. His face was white with agony, nearly as white as his pale blond hair.

"Matthew," she said. At first, it didn't make any sense at all. And then it made perfect sense. He'd heard about her discovery and had come for the diamonds. Like a numbskull, she'd told Laura and then left messages all over town, trying to reach Nina and Rourke. She remembered her visit to Zach's house, too, and the boy's sad admission about his father's gambling woes. She had made the decision then not to tell Rourke, but now she knew she should have done exactly that. Rourke would have found a solution before it came to this. Still, she couldn't have known—no one could have known—Matthew would make such a desperate move.

He was breathing hard, still pale with pain, yet his arm was steady as he leveled the gun at her. For a moment, she simply stared at the cold black eye, frozen by terror. "Take the diamonds and go," she said, desperate to go looking for Rourke. "They aren't important. Please, just go."

"I can't do that. Not now."

She'd seen his face. He wouldn't let her go. "I know, Matthew," she said. "I know." She needed to divert his attention, maybe slow him down. "But…tell me what happened to my mother. I've wondered all my life."

"She fell from Meerskill Bridge." His voice was chillingly matter-of-fact.

Jenny had an image of her mother falling, her limbs fluttering in the wind, the crushing impact of the rocks and boulders at the base of the falls. "Did you push her?" she demanded, feeling a sick hatred for him.

"I said she fell." The gun wavered the slightest bit.

Good, she thought. He's agitated. Maybe his concentration would break.

"She liked to go out, Mariska did, and she liked to party. She let the cat out of the bag about the diamonds one night, years ago. One thing led to another, and we went to the bridge. She was tipsy and she fell, and since I was the only one present, I got scared people would think I'd done something to her."

It must have made him insane to lose her before he'd forced her to give up the diamonds, Jenny thought. She pretended not to be watching the gun. "So you…you took her up to the cave."

"It was an accident," he insisted.

She took a deep breath, catching the scent of the shirt she was wearing. Rourke's scent. "All right," she said. "Whatever." Then, in a gesture of surrender, she brought both hands out and up, offering herself to him.

The moment he reached for the handcuffs, she brought both fists up and swung outward, hitting his jaw so hard that she felt her hand bruise. Maybe she even broke a bone. Then she raced for the bedroom, knowing she had only seconds. He lurched after her just as she released the safety on Rourke's gun and swung toward him.

See it, then shoot it, Rourke had told her. There was a split-second window of opportunity. She held a gun on him. This was her chance. She could shoot him right now. She saw Matthew's hand come up, saw his weapon pointed at her. She squeezed the trigger. He howled and staggered back. His gun was gone. She had no idea where it was and could only hope he didn't, either.

She saw a glimmer of Zach's face then, so like his father's, his desperation to love and protect his dad shining from his eyes.

"You bastard," she said to Matthew, and tried to see where his gun had fallen. She couldn't find it. "Move," she said. "We're going to find Rourke."

He hesitated, his eyes narrowing speculatively. He held his hand inside his parka. Was he bleeding, or still holding the gun? No, if that was the case, he'd have used it by now.

"Don't make me do it, Matthew," she whispered. "I don't want to, but I swear to God I will."

His hand came up, and he leveled the gun at her face. "So will I," he said. "And then you'll lose your chance to find out where Rourke is."

She knew she was being played, knew he was probably lying about Rourke, but even the slimmest of chances was better than none at all. Her hand shook as she lowered the gun, then dropped it to the floor with a thud. As he bent to pick it up, she fled to the kitchen. There was only one thing Matthew wanted. The diamonds. She scooped them up and kept running for the door. A blast of cold hit her as she sped outside, already scanning the area for Rourke but unable to locate him or the dog.

Shouting at her, Alger burst out onto the porch. A shot rang out and a sob tore from Jenny as she ran, her progress nightmarishly slow through the drifts of snow. She made it to the dock, turning abruptly, her fist held out over the snow-covered surface of the lake. "Don't come any closer," she called to him. "You don't want me to drop these. If I do, you'll never find them."

He stopped where he was, the gun still pointed at her. "Hand them over," he ordered.

Good, she thought. This was what he wanted. "Tell me where I can find Rourke."

It had stopped snowing and weak rays of sun colored the sky, imbuing the landscape with magical light. The wind had calmed to nothing. Where was Rourke? Off in the distance, a shadow flickered, and she was seized by a terrible sense of hope. She forced herself to keep staring at Alger, refusing to give away her thoughts with a searching glance. The shadow seemed to recede and then return.

Rourke? Or maybe the dog?

Matthew came at her and she knew he wouldn't stop. But she also knew he wouldn't shoot her so long as she held the diamonds in her hand. She saw a blur of movement behind him. He lunged, and at the same moment, she flung the stones. They scattered in a wide arc and disappeared, sinking into the snow-topped surface of the lake.

Thirty-Three

~~~~~~~

The second Jenny stepped into the brightly lit lobby of the hospital, she felt a squeeze of pressure around her lungs. Three times before she'd come here—for her grandfather, for Gram and to the basement morgue for Joey—and left with her heart in pieces. Plunging her hand into her pocket, she took out the bottle of pills and headed for a watercooler.

Wait a second, she told herself. The worst is over. Matthew Alger was in custody and Rourke had been airlifted to the hospital. Rufus was at the vet's. Two police officers had brought her back to town, and another two had taken Alger away. The snowstorm had subsided and the town was digging out. She had nothing to panic about. Well, except the fact that Rourke had undergone emergency surgery. The thought made her nearly double over, reminding her of the terrible risk of loving someone, loving him so much that losing him would destroy her.

It was a reality she couldn't escape. Rourke McKnight owned her whole heart, and even the prospect of losing him couldn't change it. And something else—it didn't even make her want to change the way she felt. How different this was from the old Jenny, the one who had been so guarded with her feelings. There were not too many good things to say about having a gun pointed at you, but that might be one of them.

The officer escorting her—a nephew of Nina's—seemed to notice her hesitation, and he stood to one side, waiting. She shut her eyes briefly, took a deep breath, then left the pills in the bottle and kept walking.

As they exited the elevator, she saw what appeared to be at least half the police department crammed into the waiting room. They stood around drinking coffee and talking in low voices, though everyone fell silent when they noticed her.

No, she thought, her heart congealing with cold. Don't you dare get quiet on me. "Which room?" she demanded. "Where is he?"

"ICU," someone said, indicating a glassed-in suite of rooms. "Just out of surgery. But it's family only—"

"What are you going to do?" she demanded, heading for the glass door. "Arrest me?"

They didn't have to. The door had a magnetic lock controlled by the duty nurse, and all Jenny could do was stand outside like everyone else, waiting in a state of abject dread. Through the double-paned glass, she could see busy hospital personnel and a bed surrounded by so much equipment it was almost impossible to see Rourke.

One of Rourke's deputies approached her. "He came through like a champ. He's stable. They'll let us know the minute we can see him."

Jenny nodded, feeling her throat swell as exhaustion seeped through her. All the terror of the previous hours had taken its toll. She didn't know what time it was, only that it was dark now. She couldn't recall the last time she'd eaten or slept. Her hand ached and was swelling, even though someone had given her an ice pack to put on it. She swayed against the window, staggering a little.

"Hey, take it easy," said a soft voice, and a gentle arm slid around her shoulders.

It was Olivia, a parka thrown on, her blond hair in a messy ponytail. Beside her was Philip Bellamy. Jenny recalled that he had come up earlier in the week. "We just heard," Olivia said.

Philip paused, cleared his throat. "Daisy told us about…Mariska."

Jenny found she couldn't speak, so she nodded. She was overwhelmed—by the danger she'd survived, by worry about Rourke and the shock of learning the truth about her mother. Yet now she realized she wouldn't have to face these things alone. Her sister and father flanked her with a solidarity she hadn't expected.

Olivia handed her a cup of strong tea.

"Thank you," Jenny said, finding her voice at last. "I'm glad you're here. It's been…this has been unbelievable."

"I know." Philip patted her on the shoulder. Unlike the other times, it didn't feel awkward but comforting. He said, "I'm so sorry to hear about what happened to your mother. So very sorry."

Jenny sipped her tea. She kept looking over at the nursing station. "Thank you. I…it wasn't exactly a shock. I mean, for her to be gone so long, with no word, eventually, the conclusion that she was dead was inevitable. Still, without concrete proof, I could always imagine she was out there somewhere."

"I thought so, as well," Philip said, and his voice sounded rough with emotion, reminding Jenny that he had once loved Mariska, too. He raked a hand through his hair. "I just don't get it, any of it."

Olivia and Jenny exchanged a look. "It had nothing to do with you, Dad."

"She…my mother saw an opportunity," Jenny said. "I can't defend what she did, but under the circumstances, I think I understand. She made a deal with Mr. and Mrs. Lightsey, and I suppose she never saw how complicated it could get, or that it might hurt someone besides herself."

"Grandmother and Grandfather Lightsey should have known better," Olivia said. "They took advantage of a girl when she was young and scared and pregnant—"

Philip held up a hand to stop her. "When you're a parent, you'll do anything to make sure your child gets everything you want her to have. I'm sure they truly believed Pamela and I would find happiness together, and that Mariska would be taken care of by the fortune they gave her."

Ultimately, the Lightseys had discovered one of the oldest truths in the world—that some things could not be bought with money. They had managed to make Mariska go away; their daughter had married Philip, just the way they'd planned. But it had been a difficult, unhappy marriage. Ultimately, no one had gotten exactly what they wanted.

"What about the diamonds?" Olivia asked. "I was just curious."

Jenny studied the pattern on the tiled floor. "Um, I doubt we'll ever see a single one of them." She explained about her confrontation with Matthew Alger, and the way she'd flung them out onto the lake moments before Rourke had staggered up behind him and disarmed him. "I'm sorry," she said.

"Don't be," Olivia insisted. "It's for the best. I suppose, technically, they belonged to Lightsey Gold & Gem, but it wouldn't seem right to give them back. And anyway, the diamonds aren't important. What's important is that you're all right."

Jenny took another sip of her tea, only to find that she'd drunk it all.

"I'll get you a refill." Philip took her cup and headed for the elevator.

"He's just glad to have something to do," Olivia explained. "Not so good at waiting around."

"Is anybody?" Jenny felt nauseous. Her hand throbbed but she ignored it.

Nina burst through the door, spotted Jenny and rushed over to her, hugging her tight. "I can't believe this is happening," she said. "You're okay?"

"Yes. And Rourke will be all right." Jenny had to believe it. "Nobody's been allowed to see him yet."

"I feel horrible," Nina said. "Even responsible, in a way. Matthew was stealing the city blind, and I never caught on. That was why he was so desperate for the money. He needed to replace what he'd stolen before the auditor figured out what he was up to."

"None of that is your fault," Jenny said.

"I know, but I still feel terrible. I feel terrible for Zach, too."

"Are you Miss Majesky?" A nurse came over and addressed Olivia.

Olivia shook her head. "That's my sister, Jenny."

Jenny tried to read the woman's expression but couldn't. No, she thought, please no.

"I'm Jenny Majesky," she said. "What's the matter?"

"He's asking to see you," the nurse said. "Actually, he's not asking. More like demanding."

Jenny swayed against her father, who steadied her. Both he and Olivia walked her to the door of the ICU. She went alone through the door, and the nurse took her to a hand-washing station and helped her don thin paper scrubs.

She didn't know the stranger in the bed, surrounded by rails and tubes and equipment. Bags of medicine hung by the bed, and his chest bore a web of wires affixed with stickers. His face looked as if it were cast in colorless wax. Then he blinked and she felt his gaze on her. His eyes were still bluer than blue, and his lips were moving.

"You'll need to come close," said the nurse. "He just had a tube removed from his throat, and he can only whisper."

Jenny hurried to the side of the bed. Smile for him, she told herself. Don't let him see how worried you are. "Hey," she said, studying his face. The crescent-shaped scar on his cheekbone, a souvenir of that long-ago summer, stood out starkly against his pale skin. She reached over the rail and tried to take his hand, but there were things clipped to his fingers and tubes running everywhere. Finally she settled on touching his shoulder, feeling the reassuring warmth of him through the palm of her hand. "I'm glad you're okay. And you have a lot of people waiting outside who'll be glad, too."

"Rufus?" he asked.

"An officer took him to the vet. He's going to be all right." She hoped she wasn't lying. A bullet had grazed his flank and the vet had assured her he'd heal.

"And you?"

She took a deep breath. She was ready to risk it all with him—more than ready. And the ultimate risk was to open herself up completely and quit worrying about the consequences. All right, she thought. Go for it. "I love you, and I'm not leaving you, ever. You'd better get used to me."

His eyes narrowed, but she couldn't tell what he was thinking. One of the machines made a rhythmic sucking sound, which echoed loudly in the room. "So here's the thing." He paused, coughed a little, and the rest came out in a whisper. "I was going to ask you to marry me. I was thinking maybe in the fall or next winter. But I changed my mind."

Jenny braced herself. The trouble was, she couldn't keep that wall in place, the one she'd erected to protect herself from her feelings for Rourke. That didn't work anymore. She felt everything for him and it wasn't as if she could pop a Xanax and get over it.

He was trying to smile. She could see that. "I changed my mind," he said again. "I don't want to get married next fall or winter. I want to get married *now*."

"Now?" she whispered.

"Well, as soon as I'm out of here. I said I'd tell you someday how I wanted to end up. I'm telling you now."

Now? Did she dream of being a bride, surrounding herself with friends and family, planning a special day she would never forget? Maybe, but there was a much more powerful dream, and it wasn't about a single day but about the rest of her life. *Yes.* Her emotions dissolved into a feeling so powerful that it tinged everything in a gauzy haze. Even here in this strange, antiseptic place, with machines pumping and beeping, the world had never looked more beautiful to her.

"I wish I could beg you on my knees," Rourke said, "but I guess I've got to do it flat on my back. I've loved you for more than half my life, Jenny Majesky. I want you to marry me and be my wife."

She gazed down into his face. He was a complicated, difficult man. She'd been hurt by him many times, but that was because he'd worked so hard to stay away from her. Everything was different now.

"I have a feeling you're not a big fan of diamonds," he said. "That's convenient, because I don't have a ring. I'll get you one if you want, though. Anything. Rubies and pearls. A giant sapphire, whatever. Just say you'll marry me. And for God's sake, stop crying."

"I'm not crying." She was, though. She couldn't help herself. "I'm saying yes, Rourke, forever, yes."

Food for Thought

by Jenny Majesky

Everyday Celebrations

The perfect ending to every meal has nothing to do with dessert and coffee, and everything to do with the company you keep. Even so, any celebration can be made more enjoyable by food. At the Sky River Bakery, we create cakes for every occasion, and our customers are always bringing us more ideas. Not just weddings, birthdays and anniversaries, but first communions, graduations, retirements, funeral wakes, births and national holidays. My grandmother, Helen Majesky, created this one for Mr. Gordon Dunbar's hundredth birthday, but it's appropriate for any happy occasion, if you ask me.

CELEBRATION CAKE

    2 cups flour
    4 teaspoons baking powder
    1/2 teaspoon salt
    2 sticks pure unsalted butter, melted
    2 cups brown sugar
    4 eggs
    1/2 cup bourbon whiskey
    1/4 cup water
    1 (6-ounce) package chocolate chips
    1 cup chopped pecans
    Hot Buttered Whiskey Glaze

Preheat oven to 325°F. Grease and flour a 13 x 9 x 2-inch baking pan. Combine flour, baking powder and salt. Melt butter and add it to flour, along with brown sugar, eggs, whiskey and water. Pour batter into prepared pan. Sprinkle with chocolate chips and pecans. Bake 50-55 minutes or until center of cake is firm and edges begin to pull away from sides of pan. Cool about 15 minutes, then drizzle with glaze.

HOT BUTTERED WHISKEY GLAZE

Melt 1/4 cup butter. Whisk in 2 cups confectioner's sugar, 1/3 cup bourbon whiskey, 1 teaspoon vanilla and blend well.

Epilogue

Two years later

"Hold it right there," Rourke said, tugging Jenny to a halt on the sidewalk. "I just need to look at this for a while."

Rufus, whom she held on a leash, obediently halted and sat back on his haunches. Jenny turned to check out the display in the window of the Camelot Bookstore. The local shop had devoted an entire window display to her first food memoir and recipe collection, *Food for Thought: Kitchen Wisdom from a Family Bakery*, by Jenny Majesky McKnight, with photographs by Daisy Bellamy. The beautiful, oversize volume looked as warm and rich as her grandmother's pies. It had been published a week earlier, and Jenny was floating with happiness.

"It's a book," she said, grinning and shaking her head. "I still can't believe it's a book."

The day it was published, there had been a party at the Sky River Bakery. They'd had to have special traffic control because of the crowd. Jenny wasn't sure if people came for the whiskey cake or for an autographed book, but they came in droves.

"Let's go in and buy a copy," said Rourke.

"I have a whole box of them at home."

"Like that's going to stop me." He held the door and they went inside together, bringing the dog along. It was library-quiet in the bookstore, and the clerk behind the counter didn't recognize Jenny, wrapped up in a wool hat and muffler against the February cold and fat as a kolache with her pregnancy. Rourke paid for the book and grinned at the clerk.

"It's by my favorite author."

Jenny practically fled out the door. "I don't think I'll ever get used to this."

The street was deserted; people were staying in out of the cold. He slipped the book from the bag and opened it to the first page. *Dedication: In loving memory of my grandparents, Helen and Leopold Majesky.* "Somewhere," he said, "I have a feeling they're incredibly proud of you right now."

She nodded, but without warning, tears threatened, perhaps due to pregnancy hormones, but maybe because it was impossible to think of her grandparents without thinking of her mother. There had been an autopsy on Mariska's remains. Her injuries were consistent with a fall from a great height—from Meerskill Bridge. Alger hadn't lied about that. She'd fallen, but he was so afraid he'd be accused of killing her that—after realizing she didn't have the diamonds with her—he'd hidden the body. He was serving time now, and Zach had gone to college. Enough, she thought. Let them rest—Mariska and Joey and her grandparents.

"Hey." Rourke put the book away and drew her close. "The book is beautiful." He ran his hand over her rounded belly. "You're beautiful, and I love you." He had an uncanny knack for catching her mood. This came as no surprise; he always had.

She caught their reflection in the glass of the shop window, two survivors, soon to be a family, and what she felt, in the middle of winter, was a kind of warmth the cold could never touch.

Dear Reader:

Thank you for reading this story, and for coming along on the journey of Jenny and Rourke. Some of you might have caught the reference to the family who stayed at the winter lodge in the fall. This family's story can be found in my novella, *"Homecoming Season,"* in the collection *More Than Words 3*.

The next book in "The Lakeshore Chronicles" is *DOCKSIDE*, an exuberant celebration of love and life as friends and family gather once again at Camp Kioga on Willow Lake.

This time, the purpose of the gathering is life's most joyous occasion—a wedding. And not just any wedding, of course. This one will have an unexpected guest or two who are guaranteed to entertain you…and maybe even steal your heart.

Happy reading,
Susan Wiggs
www.susanwiggs.com